THIS WAY
MADNESS
LIES

THIS WAY
MADNESS
LIES

THOMAS WILLIAM SIMPSON

WARNER BOOKS

A Time Warner Company

Warner Books, Inc., 666 Fifth Avenue, New York, NY 10103

 A Time Warner Company

Printed in the United States of America
First printing: January 1992
10 9 8 7 6 5 4 3 2 1

Library of Congress Cataloging-in-Publication Data

Simpson, Thomas W. (Thomas William), 1957-
    This way madness lies : the story of an American family /
Thomas W. Simpson.
        p.   cm.
    ISBN 0-446-51612-0
    I. Title.
PS3569.I5176T47   1992
813' .54—dc20   90-50522
                                                              CIP

Book design by Giorgetta Bell McRee

For my mother and father,
and for Lorelei, who provided method to the madness

The Past

Edmund Winslow m. Anne Murrow 1597

|

Giles Winslow b. 1599; m. Edith Van Cleef 1621

|

Edmund Winslow b. 1625; m. Molly Richford 1647

|

Freeman Winslow b. 1649; m. Eleanor Lane 1677

|

Henry Lane Winslow b. 1680; m. Rebecca Bailey 1708

|

Robert Bailey "Jawbone" Winslow b. 1713; m. Anna Carlson 1744

|

Henry Lane Winslow II and Robert "Mad Dog" Winslow, Jr. b. 1746
Robert "Mad Dog" Winslow, Jr. m. Katherine Fox 1782

|

Henry Lane Winslow III b. 1790; m. Lorelei Constantine 1811

|

William Giles Winslow b. 1815; m. Emily Schaffer 1839

|

Barton Henry "Gentleman Bart" Winslow b. 1840;
m. Dorothy Hayes 1861

|

John "Crazy Legs" Winslow b. 1863; m. Caroline Dayton 1888

|

Charles Winslow b. 1892; m. Martha "Shady" Matthews 1916

|

Henry Winslow b. 1917; d. 1969
William Bailey Richford "Wild Bill" Winslow b. 1920
Robert Winslow b. 1922; d. 1944
Helen Edith Winslow b. 1926; d. 1952

The Present

William Bailey Richford "Wild Bill" Winslow m. Virginia Muller
1945
|
Virginia "Ginny" Winslow b. 1946
Helen Richford Winslow b. 1947; d. 1952
Mary Winslow b. 1949
Henry and Robert Winslow b. 1950; Robert Winslow d. 1969
Edward "Little Eddie" Winslow b. 1954
Joseph Winslow b. 1958
Barton James Winslow b. 1959
Emily Anne Winslow b. 1961

The Future

Virginia "Ginny" Winslow m. Aaron Cohen 1974
|
Madeline Cohen b. 1975
Adam Cohen b. 1977

Henry as Bobby Winslow m. Irene Biddford 1979
|
Katherine "Katie" Winslow b. 1981
Constance Winslow b. 1985

Edward "Little Eddie" Winslow m. Christine Grady 1976; divorced
1984
|
William Bailey Winslow b. 1976
Edward Winslow, Jr. b. 1978
Henry Winslow b. 1979
(All three boys adopted by Todd Sullivan in 1986)

Emily Anne Winslow m. Frankie Santoro 1985; divorced 1988
|
Rosa Santoro b. 1986

Lear (on the heath in a storm before a hovel): When the mind is free the body is delicate. The tempest in my mind does from my senses take all feeling else save what beats there. Filial ingratitude, is it not as this mouth should tear this hand for lifting food to it? But I will punish home. No, I will weep no more. In such a night to shut me out! Pour on, I will endure. In a night such as this! O Regan, Goneril, your old kind father, whose frank heart gave all—Oh, that way madness lies! Let me shun that. No more of that, no more of that!

from **Shakespeare's *King Lear***

Father calls me William, sister calls me Will; Mother calls me Willy, but the fellars call me Bill!

Eugene Field

Monday, June 18, 1990 . . .

Chapter One

Before we get started I just wanted to let you know I plan to stay out of this mess as much as possible. My job here is to tell a story, not settle old family squabbles. At times I will undoubtedly be tempted to inject a few of my own personal attitudes and assumptions about these characters. Hopefully, I will rarely give in to these temptations. An occasional display of mischief, however, remains inevitable.

Life, so they tell me, is short and I know people these days have many things they need and like to do. They don't want some fool writer slowing them down with a story overloaded with a lot of excess baggage. So I'll do my best to keep the ball rolling, keep these characters moving in the right direction, keep the dialogue crisp and the descriptions flowing smoothly. I pledge to run off at the mouth only when absolutely necessary. But bear with me, for as you will see, it is a long way from there to here; a long way from the beginning of a man's life to its earthly end; a long, long way from the rise of a family's New World sojourn to its reluctant but self-inflicted fall. If indeed a fall is in the making.

This story covers several hundred years of New World history, and a touch of Old World history as well, but we are interested mainly with the latter half of the twentieth century, our present age, the year 1990. More specifically, we will focus on the third week of June; that week when the daylight lasts so long in the northern hemisphere, and the nights are so sweet and short; too sweet and too short, one might think, for so much deception, so much conniving, so much treachery.

There will be murder, cold-blooded murder, more than one even, if the historical accounts I have read prove true. These accounts read iffy on who exactly committed these murders, so I suppose guilt will flow from my pen, from my imagination, unless, reader, I decide to let you *be the judge and jury. Such a decision may upset many people, however, since most readers expect the writer to provide, if not exactly the ending they desire, at least an ending. But all of that is a long way off, and I, quite frankly, don't feel like thinking about it just yet. I have a lot of other things on my mind just now: characters and conflicts, plots and subplots, points of view and those blasted points of attack when I must bring the action to a crescendo, slam you over the head to wake you up, to keep you reading.*

You see, I want you to enjoy the hours you spend inside these covers. I want to give you your money's worth. Books ain't cheap and time is money. A novel, even one based so tightly on fact, should entertain and stimulate as well as exasperate and confound. I want you to look forward to turning off your TV, climbing into bed, and opening to that new chapter where you left off last night. I want you to want more. . . .

Look there: an old man. An old man falling! Not that old a man. Not too many sleepless nights past seventy. Three score and ten just a few short months ago. Seventy but still working fifty or sixty hours a week fifty weeks a year. Seventy but still masturbating, still enjoying the company of much younger women; one very special woman in particular. Seventy but still playing tennis in summer and squash in winter. Still fly-fishing in the spring and hunting ducks with his old Browning semiautomatic shotgun in the cool days of autumn. Still doing most of the things he has always done. Not really too old yet for anything, he'll tell you, except maybe camping out, sleeping on the hard ground, fixing his breakfast over an open fire in a greasy pan. He'd caught his fill of those exercises during the war and during those solo hikes up in the mountains of Maine. No, not too old; still a son of a bitch of a fighter with some ass left to kick, but nevertheless in a trough of trouble now. Halfway down that long, steep, narrow flight of back stairs and still falling, somersaulting, the back of his head twice thumping against the hard oak treads he refused many times over the years to cover with carpet so they would be less lethal in the event of an accident such as this. He told his first wife carpet was a waste of money. He told his second wife if she put down carpet he'd rip it up with his bare hands. So now still falling and knowing already that pain will be part of the near future, pain and probably a long stint in bed, in convalescence. "Goddammit to hell!" He fights against the fall, but momentum has its way with him. He hears the brittle bone in his left ankle snap, like a dry twig, he thinks, and then he feels something slip in his left shoulder. But old Wild Bill Winslow is out cold in that dark hallway at the bottom of the stairs before he can see the busted ankle and the dislocated shoulder all crooked and twisted and jammed up behind his back.

In bedrooms, bathrooms, bistros, and fire towers from California to England, the wife and the sons and the daughters of old Wild Bill shudder almost imperceptibly as their Provider tumbles down those back stairs. But not one of them recognizes the sign, except, perhaps, Mary, the lovely and prophetic Mary, who sits all alone in a clean and quiet pub just off Piccadilly waiting for the rainy afternoon to pass so she can stroll over to Westminster Abbey and hear the innocent sing the Evensong. At the moment she shudders she sees the Wild One falling, but she has seen her father falling many times before. Almost daily for forty-one years she has seen him falling in her dreams and in her visions. So she sips her pint of cool bitters and thinks nothing more about it.

The others simply shrug the shudder off as something purely physical, something they cannot control. From Bar Harbor to Bel Air, from Aspen to the Adirondacks, they shrug off that shudder like packhorses shooing away flies with their tails. These Winslows have no time and no mind to concern themselves with the reasons behind some sudden and inexplicable shudder. They have far more important considerations on their minds. They are out there in the world spreading Manifest Destiny, covering every inch of the earth's surface with their Winslow presence, with their Winslow greenbacks, with their wicked Winslow smiles. Even had they recognized the sign they would not have worried about an old man falling, especially an old man who, in their twisted and troubled minds anyway, deserved to fall.

And so, no one found Wild Bill for several hours. And who finally did find the Wild One? But, of course, young Evangeline. The sweet and beautiful Evangeline. She had seen Billy's Benz up in the driveway when she went out for her morning run. And she had seen it there when she returned some forty minutes later. Her watch read nearly eight o'clock by then, an almost ungodly hour for Billy Boy to have not yet left for the office. But still she went into the cottage, rousted her two young sons, then pulled off her shorts, shirt, and Nikes, and stepped into the shower. After toweling dry her slim, sensual twenty-nine-year-old body, she fed her boys, who were now on their first day of summer holiday. Between pouring their juice and buttering their toast and filling their bowls with homemade granola, the lovely Evangeline glanced out the window which looked out across the tennis court and the swimming pool to the driveway where the big Benz continued to sit motionless and without a driver. Nearly eight forty-five. During the four years on the estate she had only once seen the car still in the driveway at such a late hour. And that was the winter before last when a twenty-four-hour bug had knocked the Wild One off his feet for almost sixteen hours. But what, she wondered, could it be this time? She washed up the dishes, gave the boys a list of chores, pulled on her work boots, and still the Benz was in the drive. *Okay,* she told herself, *I better go up there and take a look, he might be in trouble.*

She knocked softly on the back door. After all, with a family as large as his, she never knew who might answer, who might be at home. She had to be on her guard at all times. He had told her as much. But no one came. She rang the bell, knocked harder. Still nothing. She banged on the door, rattled the glass. Only silence emanated from the enormous house. So finally she went back down to the cottage, found the key he had given her years before, and returned to the back door. Dreading what she might find, she stepped inside, into the back foyer behind the kitchen. She called his name. "Mr. Winslow? Hello, Mr. Winslow? Good morning. It's Evangeline." Nothing. Not a sound. Nothing but silence. As quiet as the cathedral on the day of mourning for a dead and popular sovereign. So then, standing there in that vast kitchen, surrounded by all those windows and all that stainless steel, she whispered, "Hello, Billy? Billy Boy, are you there? Are you all right, Billy Boy?"

She waited for a reply but received none. So she crossed into the dining room with its crystal chandelier and magnificent mahogany table big enough to seat twelve and still not impinge upon the flailing elbows of its dozen hungry diners. She moved with caution, fearing both what she might find and who might find her. Into the front hallway and two steps down into the sunken living room filled with antiques from the early eighteenth century when the New World Winslows had first encountered affluence. One of the pieces, that solid cherry chest on chest, Wild Bill had once told her, had been in the family off and on for two hundred and fifty years. Two hundred and fifty years! Evangeline had a difficult time dealing with anything that happened before the early seventies.

She went through the living room, past the door to the study, and slowly down the long hallway which led to the back stairs. Midmorning but still the hallway harbored darkness. She could not remember where the light switch was. Her fingers feeling along the walls, she crept forward. Finally her hand found the switch, but at the exact same instant her left foot found the side of the Wild One's head. Evangeline jumped, screamed, and very nearly fled. But faith prevailed. She regrouped, relocated the switch, and brought some overhead light to bear upon the situation. And there below her he lay: the Wild One, Wild Bill, Billy Boy, William Bailey Richford Winslow.

Evangeline saw his left shoulder all twisted up like a corkscrew. She felt the two golfball-sized bumps on the back of his head. She feared if he was not dead already he would be soon. She rearranged his shoulder as best she could, then held his head in her arms and started to cry. The crying slowed when the big, thick neck moved first to the left and then to the right. And her tears stopped completely when, for just an instant, his wild blue eyes opened wide, looked into her own, smiled, and then fell closed.

Evangeline wept but this time tears of joy. She thanked the Lord for his attention and then she called the cops and the first-aid squad. Within an hour the Wild One, still unconscious but nevertheless on the road to recovery, had himself a big private room on the fourth floor at Morristown Memorial Hospital in Morristown, New Jersey.

Chapter Two

———————————————————•———————————————————

New Jersey? some folks out there might be mumbling. Am I about to read an entire novel about New Jersey? The armpit of the nation? Land of a Thousand Smells (mostly foul)? That great suburban wasteland pinched between the Big Apple and the City of Brotherly Love? That vast corridor of concrete running from stem to stern, from the strip malls of Mahwah to the neon glitz of Atlantic City? That state which boasts such cultural civic centers as Newark, Camden, and Bayonne? Land of chemical factories, oil refineries, and toxic-waste dumps? Crossroads of the Revolution, third to ratify the Constitution, early and eager voice in support of the Emancipation Proclamation? Yes, I reply, to all of these questions, yes yes yes! An entire novel about the tiny Garden State; a state, by the way, which still deserves that cognomen, which still produces some of the world's finest fruits and veggies: tantalizing tomatoes, luscious apples, delicious blueberries, succulent corn on the cob. New Jersey deserves its own epic saga. New Jersey is America. The state defines America more clearly and more honestly than Texas, California, and New York put together. Politically, economically, socially, culturally—New Jersey offers a sort of historical divining rod into the heart of the American Experience. And besides, this is where the Winslows live. And have lived since 1624. That's right, 1624. A dozen generations before the birth of Wild Bill Winslow, the first Winslow ventured across the stormy Atlantic in an old and rickety wooden sailing ship. A dozen generations, and all of them born, and most of them raised, right here between the Hudson and the Delaware. So read on, and try, if you can, to see beyond your misconceptions and low estimations of this pint-sized province. Pretend you know nothing. Let your imagination roll.

* * *

Word of Wild Bill's fall spread rapidly across the planet with the aid of Ma Bell and the ease of Touch-tone service. Sweet Evangeline, after doing all she could to make the Wild One's dreary hospital room feel more like home, dialed up the second Mrs. William Bailey Winslow at the family's summer bungalow on Frenchman Bay in the fashionable section of Bar Harbor on the rugged and rocky coast of Maine.

"Yesss?" answered Bettina Winslow, after the fifth or sixth ring. Bettina Winslow had been Bettina Von Culin until she married Wild Bill Winslow. He was fifty-eight when they married. She was just thirty-two, a mere babe, but recently divorced, no children. That was in the very late summer of 1978, a time of year that had for many decades sent the libido and the moods of the Wild One reeling.

Wild Bill's first wife had died in the fall of 1975 when a drunk in a Rolls-Royce Silver Shadow drove up onto the sidewalk outside of their Fifth Avenue apartment across from the Metropolitan Museum of Art and ran her over.

Virginia and Bill Winslow had just come from the St. James Theatre on Forty-fourth Street where they had seen the Royal Shakespeare Company give an admirable performance of *King Lear*. Wild Bill loved Shakespeare. And as he always did after a show, he pretty much insisted they walk back to their apartment along Central Park. The fact that the walk covered forty blocks and took most of an hour did not deter him. After a show, especially after Shakespeare, he needed to walk. All the way up Fifth Avenue the Wild One babbled on about the plight of Lear. "He sealed his own fate, the fool. Anyone with kids knows they can't be trusted. And that goes double for the ones who assure you they can. Did Shakespeare have kids? I doubt if anyone with kids would have written that play. But I love the damn thing anyway. Great stuff! God, how that Limey could tickle the language! . . . What do you say we stop for a beer, Ginny old girl? Maybe you'd like to go dancing, shake a leg before hitting the hay?"

Virginia smiled but declined, as he knew she would. Just as he knew not to push it. The midnight walk was enough for one night. "Yeah, you're right," he said, "I think one tragedy is plenty for this weekend. No use me creating another one out there on the dance floor."

But moments later tragedy did indeed strike again. Halfway

between Eightieth and Eighty-first, just a few short steps from the entrance to their building, they heard a woman scream. They turned. The Rolls closed in, moving fast, totally out of control. Virginia froze. The Wild One could see she was not about to move. He tried desperately, instinctively, to save his wife of thirty years, but the shiny chrome bumper of that big Silver Shadow brushed him unemotionally aside. And a moment later that famous front grille slammed into the elegant figure of Virginia Winslow, crushing her chest, killing her instantly, leaving not a single breath in her tall, slender body.

Wild Bill Winslow, Willy to his wife, may not have been the world's most wonderful husband, certainly not the most sensitive, but he loved his wife and during their thirty years together he had almost always treated her with kindness and respect. He thought of her as the Finest Woman in the World. Virginia, he knew, had not married him for his money, believing at the time of their wedding that he was just another penniless Marine Corps captain recently returned from a three-year military hitch in the South Pacific where he had single-handedly saved the Western world from those imperialist Oriental warmongers.

In 1945 Wild Bill Winslow didn't give a damn about money. He was a twenty-five-year-old war hero with a chest full of medals and a hankerin' for love. The guy had survived Guadalcanal, Iwo Jima, Okinawa. His right thigh had been ripped open by a Jap bullet. The palm of his left hand had been pierced by a Jap bayonet. His eyes had very nearly been blown right out of his skull when a Jap hand grenade exploded inside his foxhole. He had survived malaria, dysentery, and some South Pacific strain of the clap which he thought for a while would cause his pecker to fall off. No, Wild Bill Winslow didn't arrive stateside thinking about money. Money would wait. The family had money, plenty of money. Or so he thought. What the Wild One wanted was a cold beer and a hot bath and a clean woman. The Wild One wanted love. He wanted a pretty woman to love him and caress him and worship him and make him a whole battalion of babies. He wanted his own private army to keep the peace. Wild Bill had seen enough of war.

Virginia Muller fulfilled his requirements perfectly. She stood tall and slim and pretty in her crisp white nurse's uniform when the Wild One walked into the doctor's office on Fifth Avenue across the street from St. Patrick's Cathedral. He was there to have his eyes examined by a real doctor, not some half-crazed field medic with a bag full of wet bandages and a syringe dripping with morphine and maybe someone else's blood.

Wild Bill smiled at the pretty young lady. Virginia couldn't help herself; she smiled right back. And who could blame her? Captain William Bailey Winslow, USMC, cut quite a figure in his Marine Corps blues. He stood straight and tall with his wide shoulders back and all those medals gleaming on his chest. He filled that room with his presence, with his fine white teeth and his brilliant blue eyes. In September of 1945, in the U.S.A., a man wearing the uniform of a United States Marine was a bona-fide hero, bigger than life, someone to be respected and admired, exulted even, sort of a Deity of Democracy.

Virginia stood quietly outside the examining room door while the doctor examined Wild Bill's eyes. She tried not to listen when Mr. Winslow told the doctor the dirty joke about Emperor Hirohito's fling with General Tojo at a sleazy Tokyo sushi bar. But she could not help but hear his great booming laugh. He laughed long and loud and without inhibition. He found his own jokes much funnier than the doctor did.

Finally the doctor, a short grim man who had not taken part in the war, said something about tiny fragments in the right eye which could cause infection and should be removed.

"So go ahead, Doc. Just gimme a bullet to bite on," roared Wild Bill, Virginia hanging on every word, "and cut loose those dirty Jap fragments. I don't want nuthin' made in Japan pollutin' my body. Those bastards are history anyway. Far as I'm concerned we should've dropped one of them A-bombs on every Jap village from the East China Sea to the Bering Strait. That'd've paid 'em back for Pearl."

The doctor thought this over, nodded reluctantly, then said something about scheduling an operation on the Wild One's eye. Virginia, fearful the examining room door would open while she stood there eavesdropping, was just about to return to her desk when she heard Mr. Winslow ask, "Nice dish you got out there welcoming the invalids, Doc. She married?"

Two weeks later she was. She married Captain William Bailey Richford Winslow at Manhattan city hall on October 10, 1945. Her best friend, Nancy Schaffer, was her maid of honor. Her father, Joseph Muller of Brooklyn, an iron worker at the Naval Shipyard, gave her away. Bill Winslow had a black patch over his right eye and a glistening sword hanging off his left hip. His best man was Captain Ernest Turnbull, fellow survivor of the South Pacific campaign. A dozen first and second lieutenants backed up their commanding officer. They hooted and hollered during the entire service. Virginia wore white and Wild Bill wore his finest Marine Corps blues.

The couple honeymooned at a dreary seaside hotel somewhere between Southampton and Montauk. They were the only guests that week. Every day it rained. The food was bad and the service even worse. The newlyweds could not have cared less. The Nazis had been destroyed, the Japs had been bombed into oblivion. The war was over. Everything from here on out would be a party, a roll in the hay. Or so they, like millions of other folks across America, wanted to believe.

Wild Bill found a liquor store with some potable champagne. Virginia found a market with fresh Long Island melons and several excellent kinds of cheese. They ate the melons and the cheese and sipped the champagne and took long walks on the bleak, deserted beach with the wind blowing and the rain falling. They did their best to get to know one another both physically and emotionally. Of course they told a great many lies which led them to believe they agreed on virtually everything. As the years went by, however, they would come to realize they agreed on virtually nothing; especially sex, politics, and how to raise children.

The Wild One told his new bride he wanted to take her to his home in New Jersey to meet his family: his mother and father and sister and two brothers. Virginia asked him endless questions about his family but he kept telling her she would have to wait and see for herself.

As soon as the newlyweds returned from their honeymoon they set out for the Garden State. On the lower west side of Manhattan they caught the ferry across the Hudson. Virginia admitted she had only ever been to Jersey once, to the boardwalk at Asbury Park back before the war.

They took the old Delaware Lackawanna & Western line out of Hoboken station bound for points west. The train stopped in Newark (already showing signs of urban and industrial decay), Orange, Maplewood, Millburn, Short Hills, and Summit. In Summit they had to change trains for the Gladstone Branch. A porter helped them with their bags. He was polite and friendly and twice saluted the Marine Corps captain.

Then west on a rickety old train with pull-down windows and polished floors. Almost immediately the train broke clear into clean, low, rolling hills scattered with oaks and maples and elms bursting with autumn color. Wild Bill held Virginia's hand as the slow train rumbled through New Providence and Berkeley Heights and Millington. The towns were small with little more than the train station and a post office and a general store, maybe a diner and a filling station. And beyond the town limits mostly farms and trees and open land.

Then farther west through Basking Ridge and Bernardsville. The hills grew higher and more remote, the farms bigger and less accessible. Virginia looked out the open window. She kept saying how beautiful it all was, how she had never known New Jersey looked like this, so much lush countryside so close to New York City.

"My grandfather brought his family out here nearly sixty years ago," said the Wild One. "I don't think things look too much different now from how they looked then."

Virginia nodded and closed the window. The October afternoon had grown cool and breezy. She shivered but she did not know if it was the weather or this trip into the unknown.

"Since then," added the Wild One, "this countryside hasn't really changed all that much. I guess we've got a few more families, a few more homes, but not many."

Forty years later Wild Bill's grandchildren would not be able to say the same. Change crouched right around the next bend in the tracks. The Garden State was poised to become Bedroom Alley, an endless frontier of suburban bi-levels and pillared colonials. And Wild Bill Winslow would have plenty to do with these changes. He just didn't know it yet. His own future was as mysterious to him as a dog's knowledge of the cosmos.

At three o'clock on that fine autumn afternoon with the sky high and blue and the air crisp and perfectly clean, Wild Bill Winslow welcomed his new bride to Far Hills for the first time. The train slowed, hissed, and ground to a halt. Wild Bill stepped off, took a deep breath, and held his wife's hand. "This, pretty lady," he said, "is Far Hills, the town the Winslows call home.

And have for three generations." He bowed and added, "Hopefully, we'll make it four. If you love it, we stay. But if you hate it, or even dislike it in any way, we go. The choice will be yours."

Of course, these were empty words, spoken sincerely but no more meaningful than most verbal declarations we humans sometimes make when the mood strikes us. You see, neither of the newlyweds knew it that day, but the Wild One's fling in the South Pacific was more or less the end of his physical ramblings. He was a member of the Winslow line who, when given a choice, remained close to home, fought his battles on familiar turf, struggled to keep the family protected and united. Regardless of what the Wild One told his wife that day, he wasn't going anywhere. But there was another branch of the family which leaned toward disruption, rebellion, destruction of the status quo. It had been this way, as we shall see, for generations. Everyone has a role. Had Wild Bill understood his role that autumn afternoon in 1945, the future would have been much simpler, much easier to manage. But he, like most if not all of us, ventured forth daily into darkness.

He helped Virginia off the train and into the back seat of the waiting cab, the town's only cab, an old Checker owned and operated by Jimmie Maxwell, a local yokel who also ran the post office and had a chimney sweep service.

In 1945 maybe three hundred people lived in Far Hills. Most of those lived outside of town on working farms or country estates. The town itself, really nothing but a row of buildings on the north side of Route 202 about half a mile from Bedminster, had a lumberyard and a car dealership (American Motors), plus the obligatory train station, post office, and general store where you could buy everything from canned soup to barbed wire.

"Head for the hills, Jimmie," commanded Wild Bill, "I'm goin' home."

Jimmie swung the big cab out onto Route 202. The newlyweds sat side by side in the white Checker's enormous back seat. Wild Bill stretched out his long legs, cupped his hands behind his head, and let loose a big smile. "We're almost home, Mrs. Winslow, almost home. Been a long time comin'."

Half a mile outside of town they turned off 202 and headed up into the hills. In those days the road was very narrow (barely wide enough for two cars to pass) and in many places it had never been paved. Loose gravel shot out from under the tires of the speeding Checker. Tall trees lined both sides of the road. Virginia said it looked like a tunnel, a tunnel of leaves. The leaves dropped off the trees onto the road. Virginia turned and looked out the back window at the falling leaves. She felt excited but sad, and a little afraid. *So far from Brooklyn,* she thought, *so far from home, so far from Father.* Then the Checker broke free of the trees where the land leveled out. They drove for almost a mile along a ridge with a long vista looking west and north. They could see farms and fences and treetops. Then back into another tunnel of leaves and the road wound higher through a series of steep switchbacks.

"You really live up here?" Virginia asked, more than once, her feelings strewn between awe and fear and expectation.

Wild Bill just grinned and nodded. "I used to sprint up and down these switchbacks in the summer to get myself in shape for the upcoming football season. Man, that seems like centuries ago."

Then they were out of the switchbacks and riding along a higher ridge near the crest of the hill. "Next driveway on the left, Jimmie," Wild Bill said, "in case you'd forgotten."

Jimmie nodded, then swung the Checker into a wide drive guarded by two massive stone pillars adorned on top by a pair of bigger-than-life bronze birds: a bald eagle, its wings spread ready to fly, and a turkey vulture, its head ugly and proud and defiant. The driveway ran flat and straight for the distance of nearly three football fields. Red maples, at least a hundred of them, each one sixty to seventy feet high, stood sentinel along both sides of the drive. The trees blazed scarlet in the late afternoon sun.

The maples gave way as the drive opened up in a wide sweeping circle before it reached the front of the house. But Virginia did not at first see the house. She saw the large fieldstone pool in the middle of the drive and the enormous marble statue which was actually a fountain in the middle of the pool. It was a life-size replica of Lady Godiva perched naked upon her white stallion. When operable, fresh water flowed from the good lady's prominent nipples, but this day the fountain issued forth not a trickle of water and the water in the pool lay stagnant and dirty and littered with leaves. The leaves lay everywhere: on the drive and in the azalea beds and all across the wide expanse of lawns.

Wild Bill Winslow stepped out of the Checker. The sky had

clouded over. The sun had disappeared. A cold gust of wind swept across the driveway. The Wild One shuddered, then recovered and took a long, slow look around. He had been waiting for this moment a long time; this moment when he would return home from the war, whole and healthy, a hero. But something was not right. Something felt strange. An eerie silence hung in the autumn air. *Maybe*, he thought, *I should've called, let them know we were coming.* But he had wanted it to be a surprise, a grand surprise, the sudden and quite unexpected arrival of the middle son after a nearly three-and-a-half-year absence, and with his brand-new bride in tow. He had been out of touch entirely for more than three months, since before the battle on Okinawa. He had not written or received a letter since sometime back in early July.

He listened again to the silence, and then thought, *To hell with it, it must just be the long ride from the city.* He helped his wife out of the cab. He removed the bags from the trunk. He paid Jimmie the fare, threw in a substantial tip, thanked the young man many more times than necessary. Then he watched Jimmie climb back into the cab, swing that big Checker through the circle, and head back down the long drive. He sighed. All this while Virginia stood a few feet away staring first at that naked woman on horseback and then at the front of the enormous house, her mouth hanging wide open. She kept telling herself to relax, to just take it in, to keep her questions to herself. There would be plenty of time later for answers, and maybe a good cry.

The fountain and the house had both been designed and built by Wild Bill's grandfather, John "Crazy Legs" Winslow. The house was made of local stone and timber in the Tudor style. Crazy Legs had modeled his house after an old English manor built by a Winslow ancestor back during the brief reign of Queen Mary. The main difference between the house built in England and the house built in America was the ruler used by the architect. Crazy Legs had insisted that everything in his house be exactly twice the size as its counterpart in the old English manor house. For months the architect balked at this insistence, until one day Crazy Legs set him straight. "When you work for Crazy Legs Winslow," said the twenty-seven-year-old self-made millionaire, "you do what Crazy Legs says. And when Crazy Legs says twice as big, he means twice as big. That means the rooms, the walls, the windows, the doorways, the stairways, the ceilings—everything. Now if you can't sit there on your fat little ass and multiply by two, I'll find me a pencil pusher who can." That conversation took place in the summer of 1890. In the spring of 1893 the enormous house was finally finished. And except for a few compromises determined by architectural limitations, Crazy Legs got the house he wanted.

Virginia did not see that first day the paint peeling and the stones that needed repointing and the loose slate shingles on the roof. She saw only the immensity of the three-story house with its massive front doors and its vast center hall and its two identical wings spreading out on either side, easily as far from one end to the other as a city block in the old Brownsville section of Brooklyn where she had spent the first twenty-three years of her life. Before her stood a palace. She could hardly believe her eyes. She had imagined her husband's boyhood home in rural Jersey as a modest woodframe farmhouse, possibly without plumbing or central heating.

"So, kid," Wild Bill asked, his momentary duel with doubt now behind him, "how do you like it?"

All Virginia could do was smile. She was too intimidated to speak. So Wild Bill swept her up into his arms, carried her up the half dozen marble steps of the semicircular portico, and threw open those thick oak doors. He stepped across the threshold into the front foyer.

"Mother," he yelled, "Mother! Your son has finally found his way home! Perhaps not your eldest, surely not your wisest, but easily the handsomest of your war-weary trio has returned from his battles with those Oriental dragons who did dare strike a blow at the beloved homeland of the Winslows!"

Virginia giggled and told him to put her down, but he held her so easily and so securely that she thought she could have stayed there in his arms forever.

"Mother! Father! Young Willy has arrived!"

Little sister Helen, just nineteen at the time, responded to the Wild One's rowdy arrival. She appeared high above the newly-weds on the second-floor landing. She leaned over the dark mahogany banister, her finger pressed to her lips. "Shhh," she insisted, "be quiet. Father's sleeping."

"What?" boomed the Wild One. "At this hour in the afternoon? Come, little sister, you must be joking?"

*   *   *

But alas, there weren't too many jokes that autumn afternoon. It seems Wild Bill's younger brother Robert had been killed a year and a half earlier during the Allied invasion of Italy at Anzio. Shot dead in the chest by an Axis bullet, probably one fired from the carbine of some half-starved, half-crazed son of Mussolini. And his older brother Henry had been severely wounded almost three years earlier during the desert campaigns between the Allies and Field Marshal Rommel. A fragment from an artillery shell had opened up a pretty fair sized hole in the right side of his head.

Helen told the newlyweds she went to visit Henry at the new Veterans Administration Hospital over in Lyons every Sunday. "I stand there and talk to him," said the pale, pretty young woman, her eyes wet with tears, "but he has no idea who I am or what I want." She did not look at them when she spoke. She hung her head at a crooked angle and stared at the marble floor.

The bad news continued to flow from Helen's mouth right there in the middle of the front hall. It seems Charles Winslow, Wild Bill's father, had taken his oldest son's head wounds very badly. "Papa," Helen said, "has spent the last two and a half years shuffling from room to room, pacing from one end of the house to the other. He works little, says less, and drinks gin from morning till night." Martha Winslow, Wild Bill's mother, had handled her oldest boy's injuries without too much distress, but news of young Robert's death had pushed her over the edge. "Mama," Helen said, "began to deteriorate the same day the telegram arrived from the War Department."

"What do you mean, Helen, deteriorate?" asked the Wild One. "Where's mother?"

"She's in the hospital," Helen answered. "When we didn't hear from you, William, not a word, not a single word, and with casualties on Okinawa so incredibly high . . . well, I think both of them just assumed you were dead, and that they had lost all three of their sons. Mother had a breakdown, oh, it must be six or eight weeks ago now. You should have called, William. You should have called or at least sent a telegram. You should have let us know you were all right." All this with her eyes fixed firmly on the floor.

"So it's my fault," demanded the Wild One, his voice rising, his tears held at bay by anger, "it's my fault Bobby's dead, Henry's a vegetable, and mother is in the hospital? It's all my fault?"

Young Helen, thin as paper and white as a ghost, stood perfectly still. For a moment she said nothing, then suddenly her head snapped up and her eyes met her brother's eyes. "I never said it was your fault, William. I never said anything like that."

Wild Bill, his suspicions outside confirmed, did not know if he wanted to scream or cry or punch the walnut-paneled walls. He stood there in his best Marine Corps blues feeling more afraid and more vulnerable than he had in years, since that first day he had been under Jap attack back in '42 on that crummy little coral island of Vella La Vella. "Why the hell didn't anyone tell me, Helen? Why didn't someone let me know?"

Helen needed most of a minute to respond. Her eyes drifted back to the patterns in the marble floor. "They—we—decided it would be better if you didn't know. You were so far away. We felt—"

"*You* decided? What does that mean, *you* decided? Christ, Helen, what about me? Don't I get a say in whether or not I find out those greaseball wops killed my brother or that those slimeball Nazis blew my other brother's head—"

"Don't, Will," interrupted Virginia, "don't make it any worse than it already is."

Wild Bill caught his breath, rubbed his temples. He thought the pain and the misery had ended the morning his plane lifted off the runway on Okinawa. But he could see clearly now that it hadn't. He hugged his little sister. She felt lighter than a bag of air. She did not bother to hug him back.

Wild Bill carried his and Virginia's bags up to his old bedroom on the third floor. He tore off his uniform, the buttons popping, and threw it in a heap into a dusty corner. He lay down on the soft bed, where, for over an hour, he cried into Virginia's breast while she gently held his head and stroked his hair with the long, slender fingers of her right hand.

"Welcome home, soldier," the Wild One's voice kept mumbling, over and over and over, "welcome home."

Chapter Three

———————————————•———————————————

"Hello? Mrs. Winslow?"

"Yesss."

"Hello, Mrs. Winslow. I'm sorry to bother you. This is Evangeline."

"Evangeline?"

"Yes, Evangeline."

"Oh, yes, Evangeline. I didn't recognize your voice. What is it, dear?"

"It's your husband."

"Yes?" Bettina Winslow had only arrived at the house in Bar Harbor a few days earlier and was still busy preparing for the summer season. She did not expect to hear a word from or about her husband until the last week in July when he arrived for his annual one-week visit. The Wild One loathed Bar Harbor, its summer people anyway, those stuffy urbanites from Boston and New York with their beloved bankrolls and their trust funds who believed, absolutely, that they were at least a little better than everyone else because they had money. He hated them and they knew he hated them so they hated him in return. He hated his wife also, who was just like them, and she didn't like him much either. The only reason he spent a week there in July was to remind himself what a bunch of swine the rich were and to find out who was bedding his pale, anorexic wife, as well as because he still loved to sail and the sailing on Frenchman Bay and on Blue Hill Bay was some of the most beautiful and exciting sailing in the world.

"He's in the hospital, Mrs. Winslow."

"What? The hospital? Is he all right?" *If he dies I'll be rich,* was her first thought, but she suppressed it like a monk suppresses the desire to touch his genitals. "What happened?"

"He fell down the stairs," answered Evangeline. "He has a broken ankle and I think maybe a shoulder separation. Plus a couple of pretty nasty bumps on his head. Right now he's unconscious, but the doctor assures me he should be—"

"Unconscious!"

"Yes, but he—"

"He fell down the stairs! Fell down what stairs?" *That clumsy old man,* his wife thought, *he was probably half-snookered on bourbon.*

"The back stairs."

Just like the peasant he is and always has been, thought Bettina, *using the back stairs.* "Well, I suppose I should come home."

"Should I call the rest of the family, Mrs. Winslow?"

Bettina thought this one over before answering. She would just as soon leave his kids out of this, but said, "I suppose you should call the little darlings. *If* you can find them."

"I'll do my best, Mrs. Winslow," said Evangeline as she tried to calm the dislike she felt for the woman on the other end of the line.

"That's fine, dear, you do your best. And I'll see you . . . soon. I'll be there, when I can. By the way, you're quite sure he's not about to expire?"

Evangeline frowned and pulled the receiver away from her ear. "Yes, Mrs. Winslow," she answered, "quite sure."

"All right then, dear. Thank you for calling. Good-bye."

The line went dead. Evangline hung up the pay phone. She took a deep breath and returned to the private room at the end of the hall. Billy Boy lay there, breathing evenly, his mouth slightly open, his eyes closed, his injured leg packed in plaster from the tips of his toes to the bone just below his left knee. The leg hung from a rope-and-steel apparatus attached to the back of the bed. A pile of pillows kept the leg steady. A roll and a half of surgical tape had been wrapped around his right shoulder. Several yards of ointment-soaked white gauze covered the bumps on the side of his head. He looked a lot like his great grandfather Gentleman Bart Winslow had looked after he'd been wounded during Pickett's Charge on the third day of fighting at the Battle of Gettysburg. Only Barton died from his wounds whereas it looked like Wild Bill would live to tell his story.

Evangeline kissed him lightly on the lips, then settled down on the wooden chair beside the bed to wait for him to awaken. She got up only once late in the afternoon to call her friend and ask after her boys. She had dropped them off at Peggy Arnold's house on her way to the hospital. Peggy told Evangeline not to worry, the boys were fine and she would look after them until the crisis had passed.

The late spring evening slowly faded outside the hospital room window. Evangeline gazed out the window and thought about what should have been done that day. The roses should have been sprayed and fed, the perennial beds weeded, the day lilies divided, the mums pinched back for good measure. *So many things to do this time of year,* she thought. *But there's plenty of time. It's not even the first day of summer.* Evangeline knew the gardens could take care of themselves, would undoubtedly flourish if simply left alone.

Nurses and doctors came into the room from time to time to check on the patient. "Everything looks good," they reassured Evangeline, "everything looks fine." They tried to get her to go home for a few hours and get some rest but she said she preferred to stay at his side. They must have thought she was his wife, or more likely his daughter, because they did not make her leave, not even long after visiting hours had ended. They only smiled and nodded and went away.

Night finally fell. The hospital grew quiet and still except for a low hum running through the building like a steady stream of electricity. Evangeline listened to the hum and tried not to think about what would happen if Billy Boy died. Of course she knew that even if he survived this fall he would not last forever. He was seventy years old, forty-one years her senior. He would die, long before she was ready to lose him. But she knew and even partly understood the foolishness of thinking of such things and so she returned to the steady hum of the hospital and to the steady rhythm of his breathing.

Sometime just before midnight he stirred for the first time. She had been asleep but awoke just moments before he opened his eyes. The room floated in the filtered light of the parking lot below and the slice of waning moon hanging overhead. She could see his face perfectly. It was the face of a man maybe fifty, not seventy. The only lines on the face were laugh lines running north from the corners of his mouth up across his cheeks. He had never taken care of his face, had abused it with bad soaps and too much sun and never enough sleep and an overindulgence in alcohol, but still the shadow of youth lingered. He, Evangeline thought, was far more handsome than most men half his age. And his eyes, those incredible eyes; they were the eyes of a twenty-year-old: clear blue and curious and wild with wonder. She sometimes wondered how she had ever fallen in love with a man old enough to be her father, a married man as well, a man with seven grown children. But it had happened, and she had rarely, if ever, regretted pursuing her emotional instincts.

The eyes opened. He needed a moment to understand. She smiled down at him and squeezed his hand. He squeezed back, strong and firm and deliberate.

"Well goddammit, Angel," he said, "I think you might be right, I think there might really be a God."

She smiled and kissed him softly on the forehead. "Of course there is, Billy Boy. All you have to do is believe it."

"That sounds like something one of your brethren would say."

"Not just mine. Yours soon also."

"If they'll have me."

"Don't worry, Billy Boy, they'll have you. Although after your accident we may have to miss the Monthly Meeting this Sunday."

Wild Bill thought it over, paused while the pain took a shot at his skull. "Not on your life, kid. I've been waiting almost a year for them to pass judgment on yours truly. I'm not about to miss the moment of truth."

"Sunday is only six days from now. I think we'll have to wait till next month."

"No way. I'll be there Sunday if I have to go in a hearse."

"We'll see. Right now I think you better get some rest."

The Wild One took a deep breath. He felt like someone had stuck his head in a vise and tightened down the screws. "I guess I fell down the stairs, huh?"

Evangeline nodded.

"I guess I should've covered those damn stairs with carpet."

She held her finger to her lips.

The Wild One closed his eyes, but after only a moment they snapped open again. "Okay, Angel, I'll rest, but first there's one thing I want you to do for me."

"What's that, Billy Boy?"

He smiled up at her. "Take off those tight jeans and that—"

"Billy Boy!"

He let loose the best laugh he could muster under the circumstances. It sounded strained and hollow, but a pretty fair bellow nevertheless. "Just kidding, Angel, just kidding. Although I'll bet if you gave me half a chance I could get the old snail to play a tune or two."

"Forget it, Billy Boy. We'll sing when I say it's time to—"

He grabbed her and tried to pull her onto the bed but she pushed herself away. "You're out of your mind."

"Maybe."

"You want to break the other leg?"

"Hey, as long as I don't break my third leg I don't give a damn what happens to the other two."

She shook her head, fought the urge to smile. "Do you really have something you want me to do?"

He nodded, then waited again for the pain to clear. "I want you to call them, call them home. All of them."

"Your children?"

"Right. The kiddies." The Wild One scratched the coarse stubble under his chin. He looked up at the shadows dancing on the ceiling. "Call them. Tell them I'm dying. Tell them I'm dead. Tell them whatever you have to tell them."

"Why don't I just tell them you've had an accident?"

He shook his head. "No, that won't do it. That won't bring—" He wanted to say more but the pain got in the way.

"Okay, Billy Boy," whispered Evangeline. "I'll call them. I'll bring them home." She knew he was asking her to do what he could not do himself.

Wild Bill closed his eyes and took another deep breath. The side of his head continued to pound. He found the two massive bumps with the tips of his fingers. After a moment he added, "Better call the Bitch too."

"Don't call her that, Billy Boy. It sounds terrible. And besides, I already have."

"Did she jump for joy at news of my possible demise?"

"She said she'd be here as soon as she could."

That brought a smile to the Wild One's face. "What do you say we poison her when she gets here? Something slow and agonizing."

"What do you say you stop talking like an ass and get some rest."

"But Angel, I mean it. I'd be doing the world a favor. And just like in the movies, with her out of the way we could get hitched."

"This is not a conversation which will continue for much longer."

The Wild One knew she meant it. He had gone too far. "Sorry," he said, "I was just fooling."

"I hope so."

"Except for the part about getting married."

"That's just your concussion talking, Billy Boy."

"No, Angel, I mean it, I've been thinking. And not just since I took this spill. For a long time now I've been thinking. I have some changes in mind, some things I'd—"

"Forget it, Billy Boy," said Evangeline. "I couldn't marry an old man like you anyway. You're old enough to be my grandfather."

She smiled down at him and held his head in her arms. He kissed her lightly on the hand. And then he was sound asleep, his breathing slow and steady and secure, like the breathing of a tired little boy fast asleep on his mummy's lap.

Chapter Four

Evangeline did as Billy Boy asked. If he hadn't asked she probably would have done it anyway. She wanted to call his kids. She wanted to bring them home.

Evangeline knew some of them. She had known Emily, the youngest, most of her life. None of Billy Boy's kids, however, knew about her relationship with their father. Those who knew anything about it at all thought Evangeline had been hired to tend the gardens and look after the estate.

Evangeline called Ginny, the oldest, first. But before the phone rings out in Bel Air, California, I'd just like to say a few preliminary words about Wild Bill's children. Their interests, ambitions, and conflicts are, as you shall see, wide-ranging, but they are all Winslows, the sons and daughters of Wild Bill and Virginia Winslow. I don't know exactly what this fall their father has taken down the back stairs will do to challenge them, but I do think the fall and the events to transpire over the next few days will undoubtedly change them. Who will step to the fore? Who will be lifted by these events? Who will be lowered? Who will rise? And who will fall? Let's take a look:

Virginia "Ginny" Cohen worried while getting breakfast on the table that her daughter, Madeline, fifteen, was having sexual intercourse with her new eighteen-year-old boyfriend, Stu, the one with the gold earring who drove around in the forty-thousand-dollar Porsche. Ginny also worried that her son, Adam, thirteen, was already smoking marijuana and maybe snorting cocaine. She'd found marijuana seeds in the pockets of his blue jeans and powder residue on the top of his dresser. The powder might have been foot powder; she wasn't sure yet. She planned on having it tested at a private lab over in Glendale. Ginny looked at her children sitting there at the breakfast table slumped over their bowls of frosted flakes and she wondered what had gone wrong.

Virginia "Ginny" Winslow had left for California, for Hollywood, a few months after graduating from high school in 1963. She had starred in several high school plays, including the role of Katherine in *The Taming of the Shrew*. Her father, Wild Bill Winslow, that old lover of the Bard, had praised his daughter for her performances. So when she told him she wanted to act professionally he said it sounded like a great idea. He suggested New York or even London as the best places to gain experience. But Ginny had other ideas. She did not want to do live theater, she wanted to do movies. She imagined herself on the Silver Screen playing opposite such stars as Warren Beatty, Robert Wagner, and Marlon Brando. She dreamed of being Bigger than Life.

But Wild Bill loathed the movies, found them contrived and excessively dull, and of course he told her so. He told her the only real actor was a stage actor, all other actors were frauds, phonies, paid puppets. He told her screen acting was a waste of her time, a waste of her talent, a waste of her life.

She cried. But later she dried her tears and told him he was always trying to run her life; he was always trying to run everybody's life. And then she packed her bag and took a train to the coast.

Several times over the next ten years Ginny returned home to the Compound, to the big house in Far Hills. Usually she was broke and suffering from depression and attacks of anxiety. Dear Old Dad never failed to tell her he'd told her so. But Mom, ever supportive, buoyed her daughter's confidence with some good home cooking and a sympathetic ear. After a couple months Ginny usually felt ready to take on the Hollywood warriors once again. And so off she would go: out the door of the big house in Far Hills and across the plains and over the Rockies to Tinseltown.

In the late '60s she made a whole series of commercials for a Japanese car company. These commercials incensed the Wild One. Every time he saw one on the TV he flew into a rage. Usually he would call her on the phone and remind her that those smiling Japs had not too long ago tried to kill him. He made such an issue of these commercials that Ginny decided not to renew her contract.

She did a dog food commercial and one of the original lite beer commercials, but year after year the Silver Screen eluded her. She went to hundreds of auditions but always something was wrong: too thin, too fat, too tall, too short, hair too long, hair too dark, voice too bold, voice too meek. "I'll change," she lamented more than once, "I'll be whoever you want me to be." But always, without fail, she heard the casting director say, "Thanks, maybe next time," then shout, "Next please! Come on, people, let's move! We haven't got all day."

And so in 1973, her twenties fast drawing to a close, her precious beauty no longer quite so vivid, her once prominent ego crushed by so much failure and rejection, her well-being decimated by a decade on Daddy's dole, Ginny decided the time had come to take the bull by the horns. The bull happened to be Dr. Aaron Cohen, a thirty-three-year-old bachelor and pediatrician with a beautiful house in Bel Air and a list of patients that included the sons and daughters of some of Hollywood's biggest stars.

Aaron was a small, mild-mannered man with horn-rimmed glasses who worked hard and never said anything he was not supposed to say. He could hardly believe his own good fortune when, at a mutual friend's party, Ginny Winslow expressed interest in his practice. They married soon after, on New Year's Day 1974, with the understanding that Ginny would of course continue her career. But by spring she was with child. A second one came along soon after the first. Madeline and Adam stormed into the world and took conrol of Mommy's time, and although Ginny would never allow herself to admit it, she resented those two screaming infants who quickly turned into screaming toddlers and then into drug-taking, sex-engaging teenagers. She resented them but nevertheless loved them, cared for them, needed them.

Ginny blamed her father for her failures. She felt he had never been behind her, not one hundred percent. He had wanted her to take a different path and when she refused, he deserted her, criticized her every move. She blamed him also for the death of her mother. She felt sure he could have, should have, done more to save her. He should have thrown his body in front of that

Silver Shadow. He should have been a better husband, a better father. And she hated him for marrying Bettina Von Culin. All that bitch ever wanted, from the very beginning, Ginny knew, was Wild Bill's money. Although the fact that Bettina was six weeks younger than Ginny might've had something to do with why she found the marriage so repulsive.

But nevertheless, when sweet Evangeline called while the Cohens were finishing their breakfast and told the eldest daughter about her father's flight down the back stairs, Ginny gasped and replied, "Oh my God! Is he okay? Will he be all right?"

Evangeline, the lie like hot peppers upon her lips, said quickly, "He's been drifting in and out of consciousness. I think you'd better come."

Ginny assured her she would be on the first plane east. She knew Aaron would support her decision. She hoped he might even accompany her.

Helen, had she lived, would have been contacted next by Evangeline, but she died a mysterious death in 1952 at the age of five. She went to bed that stormy winter night a strong and precocious child but she never again woke up. During the dark hours she suffocated. No one in the family ever knew exactly why or how it happened. But on the same night, at the other end of the house, in the opposite wing, Helen's namesake died also. Auntie Helen, Wild Bill's little sister, passed away after a long illness which one doctor had called "a nervous disorder," another doctor had labeled "a new and very rare form of leukemia," but which an old and respected family friend had probably correctly diagnosed as "heartache due to tragedies beyond her influence."

Did Auntie Helen hold a pillow over little Helen's face until little Helen could breathe no more? More than one member of the family hinted at this possibility but there has never been any positive proof. The child was found lying on her stomach, her pillow covering her head. The even more peculiar circumstance of the event was that little Helen and her three-and-a-half-year-old sister Mary, with whom she shared a bedroom, had decided, after their mother had kissed them good night and turned off the light, to change places, to switch beds. Why? No one knows. Not even Mary. Probably just because it might be fun. But possibly because the ebb and flow of one's life is beyond one's personal control.

Whatever the reasons, for thirty-eight years Mary has not passed an entire day without wondering, at least briefly, if she had been the one marked for death.

Mary Edith Winslow sat in the center of the nave under the great vaulted ceiling of Westminster Abbey. Her beautiful blue eyes closed, she whispered the words of Psalm 139 along with those sweet, melodious voices of the Abbey's boys choir.

> *O Lord, thou hast searched me, and known me.*
> *Thou knowest my downsitting and mine rising;*
> *Thou understandest my thought afar off.*
> *Thou searchest out my path and my lying down;*
> *And art acquainted with all my ways.*
> *For there is not a word in my tongue,*
> *But, lo, O Lord, thou knowest it altogether!*

The voices reached into every corner of the great hall, filling the space, Mary thought, with perfect harmony, perfect innocence. Why, she wondered, did little boys have to grow up and become old men? Mean, nasty, perverted old men? Why? Why couldn't they just play their boyhood games and learn their lessons and sing God's songs and leave the world alone?

Tourists from every corner of the earth crowded into Westminster Abbey on that fine late spring evening to hear the choir sing the Evensong. They sat or stood quietly, almost reverently, as the young boys worked their way through the psalm. Mary resented the tourists, their chatter, their cameras, their loud shoes. She preferred the Abbey empty; just her and the boys. Some evenings in the dead of winter when the days were short and a frozen mist fell from the dark London sky, she had sat in an almost empty hall. On those gray and gloomy evenings only the very devout and, of course, the solemn vergers came to hear the boys sing. Those were her favorite evenings, the ones she would always remember, the ones when God's voice spoke loudest.

Mary had been in England for almost three years. She had been living in the same small hotel out on Cartwright Gardens in the Bloomsbury section of London ever since her arrival. She paid, usually with her father's money, three hundred pounds a month for the tiny room overflowing now with floor-to-ceiling stacks of books and magazines and photocopied articles about those long-ago times. Mary had come to England originally to find out more about her ancestors who had first come to America in the first half of the seventeenth century. One source had led to another, however, until she found herself digging back into the early years of the Tudor reign and the brutal tyranny of Henry VIII.

Mary made frequent forays into the country, especially east to Great Burstead in Essex where her ancestors had lived before setting out for the New World. She had visited the house upon which her great-grandfather, John "Crazy Legs" Winslow, had based the house in Far Hills. She had knocked on the door and introduced herself to the family, told them about her research into her family's past. Mr. and Mrs. Hopkins and their two teenage children found the thin, pale, pretty girl from New Jersey a tad strange, but nevertheless they invited her into their home, which looked exactly like her home in Far Hills, only smaller.

The Hopkins family had lived in the house only seven years. They knew virtually nothing about its long and complex history. The only Winslows they knew ran a bed and breakfast down in Devon, "a dandy B and B," said Mr. Hopkins, "comfy beds, crispy bacon." He told Mary much of the house had been rebuilt over the years, but that some of the rooms still retained the original stone and timber framing built back in 1577.

Mary recognized immediately the similarities in the two structures. She walked slowly through each room, practically passing through the walls and cupboards like a ghost. Mrs. Hopkins followed for a while but after half an hour she gave up and went back to her kitchen. Mary touched nothing, made barely a sound. But she absorbed everything: the walls, the woodwork, the doors, the air, the floors, the ceilings. She knew well from her research and possibly from her past lives what the house must have looked like four centuries earlier. History repeats itself, she knew, and so too do families. In the dining room she could hear her ancestors arguing about religion; father Edmund Winslow, once a good Catholic but now an even better Anglican, a devoted servant of Elizabeth. And why not? Hadn't she won the important battles, made the economy flourish, given him and his family a standard of living never before known in that corner of England? But his son, Giles, just twenty-one, now there was a man of conviction, a regular rebel. He criticized the Queen and her council on almost every point, especially religion. Yes, Mary could hear him at the supper table pleading his case for the Puritans, for religious freedom, for the right of every man to worship as he pleased, not as pleased that old spinster of a queen. Mary heard it all, every word, and she would have listened all night long had not Mr. Hopkins, in his proper English way, come into the dining room and informed her that the family was about to dine and perhaps the time had come for her to take her leave. . . .

The psalm ended. Mary sat quietly, her hands folded on her lap, but all around her the tourists squirmed. Some wanted a better view, a better seat. Others wanted out, a chance to escape before the next song began. Mary did her best to ignore the melee. She caught a passing thought, something from the day before when she had suddenly shuddered and seen her father falling. And sure enough, at that very moment, Lois Chilton, teenage daughter of the woman who ran the hotel where Mary lived, came quickly across the nave, her neck craning from side to side in a desperate attempt to find the face she sought.

Mary turned, stood, and said quietly, "Here, Lois, I'm here."

Lois smiled, her braces shining. She was a tall, clumsy girl, struggling daily to grow into womanhood. She waved and made a beeline through the rows of folding chairs. "Mary, my God! I never thought I'd find you in this madhouse."

"What is it, Lois? What's happened? Is it my father?"

Lois looked positively frightened. "How did you know? Mum just got the call."

"From whom? From a woman named Bettina?"

"No," said Lois, "her name was Evangeline. Such a pretty name. I wish my name was Evangeline."

"Yes?"

"Yes, right, I'm supposed to tell you Evengeline called because you father's had some kind of accident. He's fallen or something. Mum sent me to get you. You're supposed to call home immediately."

Mary saw one of the vergers eyeing them with contempt. "We'd better go outside."

"It's just started to rain."

"That's all right."

They made their way over to the east aisle and started for the door just as the young voices broke into song. Mary stopped, turned, took Lois by the arm, whispered softly, "Listen, Lois, isn't is beautiful? Isn't it wonderful?"

Lois narrowed her eyes but nodded. "It is, Mary, yes. . . . Shall we find a cab or take the Underground?"

Mary did not bother to call Evangeline. She instead packed a small bag with her essentials, walked down to Russell Square, and caught the Underground out to Heathrow. The only seat available that night was a first-class fare on British Airways Flight 179, arriving at Kennedy International Airport early the next morning. Mary paid for the seat with her father's American Express card, 839.00 one way. She was on her way home.

Chapter Five

———————————————————•———————————————————

After the birth of his third daughter, Mary, in February of 1949, Wild Bill Winslow began to seriously question his wife's ability to produce a male heir. He was not about to divorce her or behead her for this offense but he did on more than one occasion make it a topic of conversation in the privacy of his and Virginia's bedroom. In those days it was not widely known that the father had more to do with a child's gender than the mother. Wild Bill therefore suggested that maybe Virginia ought to do something about her, shall we be nice and say, inadequacy.

Anyway, Virginia, always (at least in those early days) the dutiful wife, went to see her obstetrician. She explained her problem and asked his advice. He smiled, gave her a patronizing examination, and assured her that all she had to do was keep trying. And as an afterthought he gave her a prescription for a brand-new, just-released fertility drug.

Whether or not the drug had anything to do with it I don't know, but ten months after she popped the first pill Virginia gave birth to twins, a pair of fat and screaming laddies who pushed and shoved to the last to see who would get top billing. Henry made it first. His father named him Henry in honor of the boy's shell-shocked uncle still living over at the Veterans Hospital in Lyons. Seven minutes later his little brother stuck his head out and squinted up into the bright lights. Robert, they christened him, in honor of his uncle who had died at Anzio.

The boys looked exactly the same in every way right down to the tiny birthmarks on their butts.

Even their mother had a difficult time telling them apart. But as they grew into adolescence their personalities emerged. Henry was loud and boisterous and adventurous, just like his father. Bobby on the other hand preferred solitude. He loved to read and walk in the woods and listen to music. And while Henry was outside playing football, Bobby was usually inside practicing the violin. Henry was the apple of his father's eye and Bobby the apple of his mother's.

In 1969 events concerning the nineteen-year-old brothers get a little complicated, but I think if we set the record straight now it will shed some light on the Big Picture and make it easier for all of us to understand some of the conflicts we will be dealing with later. In his senior year of high school Henry Winslow was the captain of both the football team and the basketball team. He also ran the hundred-yard dash and threw the javelin on the track team. But his grades weren't the greatest. In fact, they were god-awful; a C-minus average, and only that high because the football coach was Henry's history teacher and he gave Henry an A even though the boy had earned a D. But when it came time to apply for college Wild Bill stepped in and took control. He made a few calls, wrote a few letters, and soon his boy had been accepted to Lehigh University out in Bethlehem, Pennsylvania. Lehigh was Wild Bill's alma mater and for twenty years he had been one of the school's most generous alumni. The Admissions Board, after careful consideration, saw great potential in young Winslow.

Bobby, an excellent student, had little trouble gaining acceptance to Princeton University. He graduated number one in his high school class, edited the school literary magazine, and played first violin in the school's orchestra. Princeton welcomed him with open arms.

Both boys did well their first semesters at college. Henry played free safety for the varsity football team and Bobby discovered both physics and the antiwar movement. College campuses across the country were heating up pretty good in those days, what with Tricky Dick Nixon recently getting elected and the war in Vietnam escalating and pictures of dead American soldiers appearing nightly on the evening news. By spring demonstrations against the war were as common on campus as Frisbees, faded blue jeans, and marijuana cigarettes.

Henry Winslow didn't really give a damn about the war, hadn't really given it much thought. But he instinctively didn't like the idea of protesting the war. It was like burning the flag or spitting on the steps of the U.S. Capitol: you just didn't do it. Well, one sunny spring afternoon up there in the hills above Bethlehem in late April of '69 all hell broke loose. It seems a conflict arose between a group of Lehigh students staging a protest against the war and another group of students staging a rally in support of the war. Henry marched with the war supporters, not because he had any deep-rooted feelings about it, but because all the others guys from the team were out there and he didn't want to look like a pansy.

So the way the story goes, violence soon broke out and Henry Winslow punched one guy in the face and broke his nose and then threw an associate professor of English off a first-floor balcony, breaking the guy's leg in three places. For these offenses Henry, as you might expect, was banished from the Lehigh campus forever. So what did he do in order to redeem himself in his totally pissed off father's eyes? He went out and enlisted in the United States Marine Corps, another Wild Bill alma mater. His mother cried. His father knocked him down, called him a dumb horse's ass. But the next day off Henry marched for basic down in the swamps of Parris Island, South Carolina.

Henry took a lot of abuse down at Parris Island, more than his fair share. No one knew exactly why. It just happens that way sometimes. The drill instructors picked him out that first day and ran him ragged. They tore him up so bad both physically and mentally that after four weeks of basic, Henry "Macho Man" Winslow actually got down on his hands and knees and begged for mercy. That of course was not a smart thing to do. It only made matters worse. Once those DI's drew blood they turned into a pack of wolves. They swarmed on Henry after his breakdown, focused all of their psychotic energy on him twenty-four hours a day. In the middle of the night they would slip into his barracks and wake him up and taunt him with the oily barrel of an M-16. "You goin' to 'Nam, pussy. You goin' to the jungle. You goin' to play ball with the gooks, Mr. Macho Football Man. You goin' off to die for your country, boy."

And sure enough, when orders came through at the end of basic, Henry Winslow was assigned to I-Corps, First Infantry, Da Nang, South Vietnam. Not too many rich white kids earned that kind of special frontline duty, but Henry had performed so poorly on his written exams that radio repair school or truck maintenance school was out of the question. So when his immediate superiors recommended him for the infantry, the sick puppies on the third floor concurred. They decided to drop this guy Winslow right in the middle of the shit. Not only did he deserve it, but he'd be an excellent example for all those bleeding-heart shitbag liberals who kept screaming about how only poor niggers were getting killed in the rice paddies.

Henry went home for a few days before he had to go fight the war. He looked terrible: black circles under his eyes, not a single hair on his head, his scalp pink and peeling, his entire face rigid with fear and fatigue. His first night home, up in their bedroom on the third floor, he told his twin brother about the horrors of boot camp, about being beaten and humiliated. He told Bobby he did not think he could take it anymore, he had to find a way out. He said he'd even been thinking seriously about deserting to Canada. "I'm scared, Bob," he confessed, "scared shitless."

Bobby listened with compassion in his eyes but delight in his heart. He had never seen his brother grovel. It made him feel good to watch his brother suffer. He only wished Wild Bill were there to hear this talk of weakness and desertion. And then, when Henry had spilled his guts empty, opened himself up entirely, brother Bobby had a brilliant idea. He got up off his bed, went into the bathroom, and locked the door. When he returned to the bedroom half an hour later he had completely shaved his head. Not a hair remained. "I'll go, Henry," he said calmly. "I'll take your place. I'll go to 'Nam."

And so he did.

The brothers had a few details to work out, but two days later when the family gathered on the front lawn to wave good-bye to their soldier son and brother Henry, they were in reality waving good-bye to their quiet son and brother Bobby. Henry, playing for the first time in his life the role of Bobby, explained to the others that he had shaved his head in order to protest his brother's flight to Vietnam. The family accepted this, although Virginia knew right from the first something was amiss. But the day after Bobby, as Henry, left for 'Nam, Henry, as Bobby, left for summer session at Princeton, so Virginia set her suspicions temporarily aside. She had several other youngsters demanding her attention.

Bobby, as Henry, landed in Da Nang where he spent several days trying to figure out how to load and clean his M-16. Long before he had mastered the weapon his squad received orders to move north to Hue. The squad got caught in a firefight their first night out. Bobby tried not to panic. He tried to act like a soldier. He wanted to act like a soldier. He wanted to prove to himself that he was more of a man than his macho brother Henry. All of his academic, literary, and musical success had done nothing to dim his desire to be a man, the kind of man who would make his father proud. The fighting grew close. Vietcong swarmed through the night screaming and shouting obscenities in broken English. Suddenly Bobby found himself shouting back, rushing forward, firing his M-16 wildly into the darkness. "I'm the wild one, you ugly slanty-eyed motherfuckers, the wild one!" The next thing he knew a bullet ripped into his shoulder. And then another one blew open his groin. He fell facedown into the mud. He had a few minutes to think about home. He thought about the time he was on stage playing the violin at the school recital when he glanced out at the audience and saw *his old man out there sleeping, snoring like a fucking pig. Then a stray bullet shattered his skull and Bobby, playing the role of Henry, was dead, stone dead.*

The ironic part of Bobby's death is that twelve thousand miles away at the Veterans Administration Hospital in Lyons, New Jersey, Bobby's Uncle Henry had finally decided to call it quits. He'd hung in there without a past and without really any hope for the future for twenty-five years. Twenty-five years roaming through those sterile hallways that smelled of urine and death and disinfectant. Twenty-five years listening to strangers scream in the middle of the night. Twenty-five years without dreams, with nothing but nightmares and clocks to pass the time. Twenty-five years of living hell because some psychopath in Germany wanted to rule the world. . . . So at the age of fifty-one, at the precise moment that a third 'Cong bullet ripped open his nephew's skull, Uncle Henry Winslow flipped his own switch by grabbing onto the high voltage generator in the bowels of the hospital's commissary; thus ending, supposedly, the lives of both Henry Winslows.

Forty-year-old Henry Winslow shuddered in response to his father's collision with the back steps. Now in his twenty-first year of acting out the role of his brother Bobby, Henry stood watch in the fire tower on the summit of Snowy Mountain in the central Adirondacks. And he stood there still all those many hours later as his father's friend and lover tried in vain to reach him by telephone.

Henry, as Bobby, was doing double duty for a sick ranger, an old friend who had been snake bit while fishing for bass on Lewey Lake. His buddy would survive the viper's venom, but not too soon for Henry. He had been up in the tower for almost thirty-six hours and the chore of keeping his blue eyes open had become almost impossible. But keep them open he did, with pots full of steaming coffee, frequent check-ins with the boys over at Tower Central, and occasional trips outside onto the narrow ledge where the combination of height and wind blew all thoughts of sleep from his mind. Henry had to stay awake. It had been the driest spring in thirty years. Not a drop had fallen in May or June and none was forecast for the early weeks of summer. And the heat: unbearable. Already the mercury had climbed into the high nineties, an unpleasantness usually reserved for the dog days of August. Yes, Henry had to stay awake. He had to do his duty. The mountains were dry, the forest a tinderbox. So far they had been lucky: nothing but a few scattered fires and each of those easily contained because of early spotting and immediate action on the part of local fire fighters. Relief, Henry knew, would come. Eventually someone would come to take his place. He had to stay awake. *I have to stay awake.*

Meanwhile, behind the scenes, far below the fire tower, a small group of friends and neighbors worked together to get word to Bobby Winslow that his father had taken a fall and might, at that very moment, be dying.

Henry, as Bobby, lived out in the boondocks with his wife and two daughters on the northwest shore of Blue Mountain Lake in pretty much the geographic center of the Adirondack State Park. The cabin where they lived had electricity and running water but no telephone or TV set. The family's address was simply Box 9, Blue Mountain Lake, New York, 12812. Probably only twenty people in the whole world knew exactly where the Winslows lived. None of those people were members of Henry Winslow's New Jersey family however. They knew Bobby lived near Blue Mountain Lake but no one in the family had ever seen his cabin or been invited to spend a weekend.

As might be expected, Henry had a few problems after he died in Vietnam. Actually the problems started even before he died. They began when he went down to Princeton for summer session and people kept coming up to him and saying, "Hey, Bob, nice haircut. Get you head caught in a lawn mower?" Henry would look at these people and not have the slightest idea who they were. He had to restrain himself from busting them in the jaw. Then physics class started and things really turned strange. Henry did not have the first clue what the formulas on the blackboard meant. But right away he knew his brother knew because the professor kept calling on him to explain their complexities to the rest of the class. Henry feigned a sore throat that first day, complete laryngitis the second day, and the third day he simply stayed away; went over to the gym and shot some hoops. On the fourth day of class news of his death arrived so he was excused to go home and be with his family. He never returned.

Back in Far Hills the Winslow family was in deep mourning over the death of the two Henrys. Henry considered breaking the news to his parents and siblings but decided the shock would be too much of a burden for them to bear. He decided to wait until a more opportune time. He played his role of Bobby well, denouncing war in general and especially that terrible, unjust war in southeast Asia. His body was sent home for burial, and during the services at the Bernardsville Presbyterian Church, he told a gathering of family and friends, "Henry was my brother, my alter ego. I will miss him. We were as one."

That night, as he slept fitfully in the bed where his brother had once slept, his mother slipped quietly into the room. She stood at the end of the bed and studied the naked body of her son. After a moment, her voice low, she asked, "Henry? Henry, are you awake?"

The young man came around slowly. His eyes finally opened, he sat up on his elbows. "Mom," he asked sleepily, "what is it? What's the matter?"

"Nothing, Henry," she said, "I just wanted to make sure you were all right."

"Sure, Mom, I'm—" But he didn't finish. He didn't say another word.

After a few moments Virginia turned and left the room. She took their secret to her early grave six years later.

Bobby's death completely altered the direction of Henry's life. He acted strange in every conceivable way, but because he could blame the strangeness on his brother's death no one in the family uttered a word.

"Identical twins are a different breed," Virginia told her other children when they broached the subject in their older brother's absence. "They behave in ways normal people simply cannot understand."

And so Henry became Bobby, and it did not matter that the new Bobby acted not a lick like the old Bobby. The change became part of the cycle of night and day. Not even Wild Bill, still mourning the death of his favorite son, caused a commotion. He barely noticed when Bobby quit Princeton and enrolled in the forestry school at Paul Smiths College in the Adirondacks. No one said a word as the seasons passed and Bobby never ventured home for a visit. Years slipped away and the only contact he made was the occasional telephone call on Christmas or on someone's birthday. Obviously the guy must've been suffering with his

*terrible secret. Why he didn't just come forward with the truth is one of
those imponderables: difficult to know or understand.*

Evangeline, frustrated by her inability to contact Bobby, finally
called the Blue Mountain Lake post office. "Oh sure, I know
Bobby Winslow," said Aggie Merlin, the woman who sorted the
mail. "Know his wife Irene a sight better but I know Bobby some
too. A wonderful girl that Irene. Big as a house right now.
Pregnant with their third, don't you know? Anyway, Bobby, he's
like a monk, likes to spend most of his time alone. Now I don't
mean that bad, understand, I just mean that true. By the way,
who are you?"

Evangeline explained about Bobby's father. Aggie understood
perfectly. "Oh I remember well when my papa passed on. Saddest
day of my life it was."

"So do you think you can get word to Bobby to call home?"

"Course I will, honey, just as soon as we get off the line."

News like this was a big event in Blue Mountain Lake. Big
enough for Aggie to close down the post office. She hung out a
sign (*Back Later, Just Relax*) in the window and walked over to
her brother-in-law's tackle shop along the lakefront. Aggie told
Power Merlin about Bobby Winslow's father dying at that very
moment down in New Jersey. Pretty soon everybody in town
knew. Power sent his son Power junior by speedboat over to the
Winslows' cabin on the north side of the lake. While Power
junior was gone Earl Bigby stopped by the tackle shop for some
freshwater prawns and maybe some jawboning, heard the news
about Bobby's papa, and told Power he thought Winslow was on
duty up at the Snowy Mountain fire tower. So Power told Aggie to
look after the store while he and Earl rode over to Snowy in Earl's
Jeep. While they were gone Power junior got back with Bobby's,
really Henry's, wife Irene and their two girls Katie and Constance.
Irene, a tiny woman with auburn hair and a swollen belly and a
backbone of pure steel, thought it would be much faster if she
called Fire Tower Central and had them contact Bobby by radio.
Aggie thought that sounded like a right good idea so that's exactly
what Irene did. Fire Tower Central responded immediately by
contacting their tower on the summit of Snowy Mountain. The
dispatcher tried and tried but he couldn't raise anyone on the
radio. This news was reported back to Irene, who thanked the

dispatcher and asked him to please keep trying. He assured her he would. By this time most of the residents of Blue Mountain Lake had gathered at Merlin's Tackle Shop so they could stay close to the action.

Earl and Power drove the Jeep as high up on Snowy's western fire road as possible. When they could go no farther they got out and started walking. It took them half an hour to reach the base of the tower. They shouted into the wind but received no response. So they started climbing. By the time they had climbed the three hundred and fourteen tower steps both of them were huffing and puffing and barely able to draw a breath. And what did Earl find when he finally pushed open the trapdoor and stuck his bald head up into the tower? He found Henry Winslow, who he thought was Bobby Winslow, sprawled out on the steel floor snoring like an old hound dog and a voice screaming through the radio, "Come in Snowy One! Snowy One, do you read! This is Fire Tower Central. Snowy One! Hey Bobby! Are you up there Bobby? Are you okay? Are you all right?"

Henry, as Bobby, was just fine. The poor guy just needed some shut-eye is all. Earl and Power got him up, poured him some coffee, and told him what they knew. Then, with Earl manning the tower, Henry, as Bobby, and Power headed back for town in Earl's Jeep.

Henry, as Bobby, listened to Aggie's report, and then, like his sister Mary, he decided not to call home but to just head straight for Jersey. So he kissed Irene and Katie and Constance good-bye while all the townsfolk looked on. He patted his wife's swollen belly and told her to take good care of his son. She assured him she would. He told her he would call just as soon as he had news. And then he climbed into his beat-up old 1964 Ford F-100 pickup and headed south for the first time since 1975 when he had made the same drive in the same truck to attend his mother's funeral. As he drove off all of Blue Mountain waved farewell and wished him Godspeed.

Chapter Six

———————————————•———————————————

Evangeline let the telephone ring at least thirty times. Edward Winslow, sixth child and third son of Wild Bill and Virginia Winslow, lay on his back on the bedroom floor staring up at the ceiling and pretending as hard as he could not to hear the ringing. The more the phone rang the more he pretended not to hear it. He had no intention of answering it. Edward had not answered a telephone for six years, not since that night his ex-wife had called to tell him Children's Services was sending a policeman and a social worker over to the house to get the kids. He had not answered a door in six years either; not since those two cops and that social worker had come to the door and handed him the court order instructing him to release his three sons into their custody. No phones and no doors; and not really much of anything else either for six long, painful, agonizing years.

Edward Winslow's situation demands details. I want you to begin to understand some of the reasons for his long and psychologically destructive estrangement from his family. His breach from the Winslow compound, unlike brother Henry's, is not easily summarized or neatly categorized.

Edward "Little Eddie" Winslow made his debut on one of the hottest July afternoons ever recorded. The temperature outside was well over a hundred degrees Fahrenheit. His dear mother later claimed it was not much cooler in the delivery room. Not only did Little Eddie insist on being removed by cesarean section, but he also came out feet first, Virginia's only breech birth in nine deliveries. She swore the boy had cried even in the womb.

Edward was born in 1954, more than four years after his next oldest siblings, Henry and Bobby. Almost another four years would pass before the next Winslow was born, Edward's younger brother Joseph. So Little Eddie grew up isolated and alone in that large family; in many ways all by himself, like a lonely island between mainlands, "like the calm at the eye of the storm," his mother used to say, even though from the very beginning she had seen a terrible storm brewing in Edward's deep blue eyes.

He learned to walk and talk months earlier than his older brothers and sisters. All through infancy and puberty and adolescence Edward performed at accelerated levels. Both physically and mentally he did things quicker and with less strain that other kids. Reading came early and easy. So did bicycle riding and arithmetic and hitting a baseball and catching a football. The boy possessed all the best qualities of his twin brothers. He had Henry's prowess on the playing field and Robert's flair for academics. Almost everyone agreed Edward would do great things.

The one person who seemed not to notice this exceptional lad, however, was the boy's papa, the Wild One. Two imposing obstacles stood between Little Eddie and his father. One was Wild Bill's work. During the late '50s and early '60s, when Edward so desperately needed his father's praise and encouragement, the Wild One was too busy getting rich, spreading suburbia across the Garden State. The guy worked six days a week, sixteen hours a day. He had, after all, half a dozen kids to feed, and no doubt more on the way. When he did take the time to notice his kiddies, his attention usually went straight to Little Eddie's other obstacle: his older brother Henry. Henry was tearing up the high school gridiron at the time and Wild Bill had dreams of his boy playing in the National Football League. That had been one of his own ambitions but war and marriage and family had forced him to abandon the idea. So like many a father before and after, he placed his hopes in his boy. Many was the night around the Winslow dinner table that Wild Bill and Henry would dominate the discussion with whether or not Henry would play free safety or flanker for the New York Football Giants. Henry had the instincts, the speed, and they all thought the courage, to play either position.

Edward did everything in his power to gain his father's attention and admiration. He dominated every athletic team he played on in grammar school and in junior high school. Year after year he brought home perfect report cards, an A in almost every subject. But perfect report cards rarely received more than a "Job well done" and maybe a five-dollar bill from the Wild One. He had seen plenty of those already from Mary and Robert.

Virginia of course knew the boy needed his father. She knew that for all his youthful skills and natural talents he was nevertheless emotionally fragile. He needed pampering. Virginia told her husband as much many times in the privacy of their bedroom. But Wild Bill just shrugged off her warnings with a laugh, insisting the boy could make his way without his old man's interference.

Edward's big chance finally came when Henry, actually Bobby, came home dead from southeast Asia. The Wild One went into a state of depression following his oldest son's death but when he pulled himself together he found Edward waiting in the wings. A sophomore in high school that fall, Edward was starting halfback for the varsity football team. He ran for a hundred and seventeen yards his first game. His second game he ran for eighty yards and scored a pair of touchdowns. In his third game he ran around the right side in the final minute for a forty-one-yard touchdown run that capped an 18–13 come-from-behind victory. That's when the Wild One finally started to sit up and take notice. He labeled his son the Great White Hope.

But the Great White Hope played his final football game just a few weeks later on Thanksgiving morning. While running over left tackle he collided with a two-hundred-and-twenty-pound linebacker. He went down and didn't get up. They had to take him off the field on a stretcher. He had neck and back injuries. The doctor told his parents it would be safer if the boy did not play football again.

"Is that an order?" asked Wild Bill. "Or a suggestion?"

"It's a very strong suggestion," replied the doctor. "Another blow could be debilitating."

"Don't worry, Doctor," said Virginia, "we're not going to risk his health for some stupid game."

Edward never played football again. He said he wanted to play but Virginia would not listen. She told both her son and her husband that the subject was not even open to discussion. So Edward turned his attention to baseball. But Wild Bill had little interest in baseball. He found the game slow and dull. He soon stopped calling his son the Great White Hope.

In the fall of 1972 Edward entered Cornell University. His first weeks there he wanted nothing more than to go home to Far Hills. He practically begged his mother on the telephone but she reassured him that soon the homesickness would pass. He did not believe her but he agreed to stay.

Edward did not make friends easily. He spent most of his time alone. He worked hard at his studies and tried to think up new ways to win back his father's favor. Over Christmas vacation he pleaded with his mother not to make him go back. She asked him to try one more semester. He reluctantly agreed.

In the spring he tried out for the baseball team. He made the club and even drank a few beers with the guys. It was enough to keep him going. The following fall he declared premed as his major. He made the decision on his own, without consulting anyone, not even his mother. For years he had heard his father talk about how great it would be if one of the kids went to medical school, if one of them actually became a doctor. "I don't think we've ever had a doctor in this family." So Edward decided he would be the first. He would earn a degree in medicine and forever remain his father's favorite son. That was his plan. And when he informed his parents of his decision, the Wild One immediately celebrated by patting the boy on the back and guaranteeing him financial assistance right through residency. His mother voiced her pleasure as well, but privately she worried that the rigors of studying medicine might send her middle son over the emotional edge.

Right up through the end of his junior year Edward did very well. His grade point average hovered between 3.4 and 3.7, pretty good considering he took only the most difficult courses. He also continued to play baseball in the spring. He even found the time to volunteer several hours a week to a campus organization which raised money for needy students. By almost all acounts Little Eddie was an excellent, well-rounded member of the Cornell undergraduate community.

But then in the middle of September 1975, Edward's relatively thin emotional lifeline began to unravel. On Labor Day he kissed his mother good-bye before setting off for his senior year. She hugged the boy to her breast and asked him not to work too hard, to relax and enjoy his last year of college. He kissed his mother on the cheek and assured her he would try. But less than three weeks later, while studying for an exam in organic chemistry, Edward received word of his mother's death. The news came without warning, as though a perfect stranger had just walked up to him and smashed him over the head with a baseball bat. Just like that his mother was dead. He would never see her again. Not even in her casket. Wild Bill had decided to keep the box closed due to the extensive damage the front bumper of that runaway Rolls had inflicted upon his wife's skull.

Edward went home to Far Hills for the funeral and he stayed home until after the New Year. He probably would have taken the entire year off, and perhaps even longer, had not Wild Bill ordered him back to school, told him the time had come to quit mourning, to carry on with his responsibilities and his commitments. Edward resented this intrusion upon his misery but he kept as silent as a shadow and did exactly as his father demanded.

Ithaca seemed even colder and grayer than usual that winter. Walking up Buffalo Street from his apartment to campus, the winds howling off Cayuga, Edward often felt a sadness which brought tears to his eyes. Sometimes he would sit in his classes or in the library and just suddenly begin to cry. He missed his mother, wondered sometimes how he would ever live without her. Often he would awaken in the middle of the night and find it both unbelievable and unbearable that he could not pick up the phone and hear her voice. He would lie awake for hours, tossing and turning and fighting off fits of fear and panic.

Then one day, at a meeting for the organization to help needy students, Edward met Christine. She had been with the organization almost as long as Edward but he had never noticed her before. Girls had not been a priority during his first three years at the university. He had too many other activities on his schedule to worry about his libido. But Christine had had her eye on him for a long time. She knew he was a premed major, an excellent student, a varsity athlete. She had even seen him play baseball. When he had disappeared in the fall she had inquired about his absence. She knew his mother had died. And now that he was back she felt the time had come to make her move. And move she did. Like wildfire. Christine filled that void left by Virginia's death before Edward could come up for air. Her actions may have been the work of an opportunist, but Edward, she thought, was the man of her dreams.

That summer, just a few days after classes ended, Christine Grady married Edward Winslow at the Roman Catholic Church in Christine's hometown of Newburgh, New York. Wild Bill Winslow did not approve of the marriage. Not only did he feel Edward was too young and only marrying in response to his mother's death, but he also had a deep-rooted, if not totally articulated, aversion to Catholics.

The Wild One slipped into Edward's motel room the night before the wedding and slapped his son around a little just to show his displeasure. "You want to screw up your life, kid," he said, his finger on Edward's chest, "then go ahead and screw it up. I don't give a damn what you do."

Little Eddie used his fist to break the mirror in the bathroom after his father left the room. He punched the glass with all his strength while tears streamed down his cheeks. His knuckles came away bruised and bloodied. The next day his hand was too swollen to accept the gold band his bride offered him during the ceremony.

What Wild Bill did not know because Edward had not told him or anyone else was that he and Christine had decided to marry without delay primarily because Christine was with child. Being a good Roman Catholic she would not even consider an abortion, and so Edward did what he felt he had to do: he married the girl. And why not? He thought he loved her. He trusted her and longed to be in her arms, close to her motherly breast. He needed her strength and her praise and her ability to run the show.

In the fall he went back to Cornell to earn his degree. And in winter Christine gave birth to their first son. They named him William, in the hope of winning the lad's grandfather's favor. The Wild One did indeed express some interest. After all, little William Bailey Winslow was the first male heir of his generation.

The following fall Edward entered the Cornell University Medical School in Manhattan. With Wild Bill paying their way but refusing to allow them to live in his Fifth Avenue apartment, the young family settled into three small rooms on Seventy-sixth Street, a block and a half from the East River. Edward performed admirably as a first-year medical student but almost daily he felt the old pangs of adolescence. He needed, maybe more than ever, his father's approval. His decision to become a doctor had been made with his father in mind, and yet the Wild One hardly seemed to notice. All Wild Bill wanted to know was how much money to send and where to send it. Beyond that he displayed little interest in his son's ambitions.

That summer Christine gave birth to their second son. They named him Edward, Jr.

Edward senior's second year of medical school proved far more difficult. The work became more complex, more demanding. And he seemed to have less time to do the work, less time to prepare for his examinations. Christine did her best to keep the boys quiet in their tiny apartment, but many evenings it was past midnight before Edward could concentrate on his studies. Some nights the noise and the pressure and the work load brought Edward nearly to the point of rage. He would sit at his desk in a corner of the bedroom, his head in his hands, the blood pumping against his temples, and more than anything he wanted to scream, smash his fist through the wall, rip his medical books into confetti. But he did none of these things; he just sat there and took it, waited it out, forced himself to persevere.

Late that summer their third son was born. They named the infant Henry after his dead uncle who was not really dead but living remotely up in the Adirondacks.

Crisis came that fall, right around Halloween. The pressure finally overwhelmed him. Edward blew his cork one afternoon while practicing a surgical procedure on his cadaver. While attempting to perform a tracheotomy, the scalpel slipped and Edward cut his dead patient's throat. Soon after the errant cut Little Eddie suffered a nervous breakdown and had to be hospitalized. For the next two months he uttered not a word and spent as much as eighteen hours a day sleeping. The doctors kept insisting Edward would be fine. "The young man," they said, "needs rest and relaxation. He has been under too much strain, too much stress."

Wild Bill did not understand any of this. He went to visit Edward at the hospital and told the boy to get the hell out of bed and back to work. "What's all this crap about a breakdown?" he asked. "Winslows don't break down, boy. Winslows tough it out, grin and bear it, bite the bullet and get back in the fray. Look at you lyin' there on your butt like some goddamn woman. It's disgusting."

To make matters worse, the Wild One had recently married Bettina Von Culin. With this frisky new babe in his life he had no time to waste on kids who thought they were sick. He went to visit Edward only twice during the boy's two months in the hospital. The first time he called Edward a woman, and on his second visit he tried to bribe the boy with money. "Get your butt out of here by the end of the week and I'll give you ten grand cash. Ten grand to get yourself back in school, back on the job. You've got three kids out there depending on you. You've got to beat back these demons, Eddie me boy. Club these bastards to death or they'll hold you by the balls for the rest of your life."

Edward said not a word to his father. He wanted to tell the old bastard to fuck off but he could not bring himself to say it. Soon after the Wild One departed, however, Edward made the decision to drop out of medical school and do something else with his life. He thought about it for the next several days and then decided to move his family back up to Ithaca, earn a master's degree in biology, and then, perhaps, teach or do research.

Little Eddie did not know it then, and in fact would never know it, but his dead mother had helped him make this decision. Virginia had been keeping an eye on him ever since her funeral. She knew her middle son needed special attention. Deceased, she could not actually offer her support directly to the boy, but through sheer force of will she could occasionally turn his thoughts in one direction or another. Some of you may consider this total nonsense, but if so ask yourself this question: what, really, is inspiration? A difficult word, not easily defined. But we've all experienced it at one time or another; those mystery thoughts, those magical moments, those realizations from nowhere. Maybe you think inspiration is Divine, and perhaps it is. But I, like Mary and more and more like Wild Bill, believe the dead are Divine, that a family has a soul, and that that soul lives on forever.

When Wild Bill learned of Little Eddie's decision he went nuts. He called Edward every obscene and derogatory name that came to mind. For over an hour he verbally castrated the boy. But in the end he agreed to finance the move. He also agreed to pay Edward's tuition plus all of the family's living expenses while the boy worked toward his master's degree.

Christine was probably even more unhappy than her father-in-law with Edward's decision to drop out of medical school. He had not even consulted her before making the decision. He had just done it. Edward becoming a doctor had been the main motivation in their lives almost from the day they'd met. Now he was suddenly calling it quits. Christine felt cheated, used. She had given him three sons in three years. She had made sacrifices, put on hold her own aspirations. But she had done so willingly because the sound of Dr. and Mrs. Winslow pleased her, because she imagined a pleasant and affluent life-style as the doctor's wife. But now, suddenly, Edward was talking about becoming a teacher. *A goddamn biology teacher,* she thought, *not even a professor, just a stupid high school biology teacher. Jesus, son of Mary.* Nevertheless, Christine went along with the move back to Ithaca. She did not really know what else to do. She set up housekeeping in a small rented house in Cayuga Heights, a mile north of the Cornell campus, and waited to see what would happen next.

In June of 1982 Edward completed his master's degree in biology. That fall he taught his first class at Cortland High School, some twenty miles north of Ithaca. Wild Bill had been supporting the family for six years by this time, sending them biweekly checks for rent, food, and other essentials. Edward had long been troubled by this financial dependence so when he wrote to his father in the middle of September, he imagined the letter as his own personal emancipation proclamation. He thanked the Wild One for his financial support, but then added it would no longer be necessary, he could now manage on his own.

By Christmas, Christine realized they simply did not have enough money to pay the rent, make the car payments, buy food and clothing, and just make ends meet. She asked Edward to write to his father to see if he might once again come through with a little cash. Edward absolutely refused. He would not write to his father. No way. He insisted that thousands of other families made do on a teacher's salary; he saw no reason why they couldn't do it also.

As the New Year rolled along money became more and more a source of conflict. Several times a week all that winter Christine and Edward argued over money. They argued at the breakfast table and at the dinner table. They argued in bed at night and in the bathroom in the morning. "The kids need new shoes," Christine would insist. "There's nothing wrong with their damn shoes," Edward would reply. "Your father's a millionaire," Christine would say. "I don't give a damn if he's a billionaire," Edward would counter, "I ain't asking him for one red nickel." And if the two weren't arguing about money, Little Eddie was probably holed up in his tiny study off the living room reading books on existentialism and patricide.

By Easter Christine had reached the end of her emotional rope. She felt her life slipping away, as though she no longer had control. Her degree from Cornell in political science seemed like an accomplishment from some distant lifetime. Some mornings she could hardly get out of bed. She felt tired and anxious even after a good night's sleep. She could no longer find the energy to argue with Edward. Had she possessed the courage she probably would have left him, packed up the kids and just driven off, at least for a few days, long enough for Edward to reevaluate the situation. But instead she did nothing, and so moved irreversibly toward her own nervous breakdown.

For a while she told herself it was just a virus but after several weeks she had to face the truth. She was depressed. She had to fight off an almost constant desire to cry, to just lie down on the floor and weep. She finally snapped on a warm and muggy Saturday afternoon in early May. She had been out shopping for food. As usual there had not been enough money in the checking account to cover all the things she needed. Edward was home baby-sitting. But by the time she arrived home the kids had ripped apart the living room. The two younger ones, both of them soaking wet, howled on the floor while their older brother smashed a lamp shade to smithereens with his plastic wiffle ball bat. Father Edward sat back in his tiny study oblivious to the noise and the destruction. He was engrossed in a book about a tribe of Indians in the Amazon who killed their parents when the old people became useless and infirm.

Christine needed three months in the hospital to recover. She needed drugs to keep her calm, and more drugs to help her sleep. Edward went to see her several times a week. During the first month he treated her with kindness and understanding. Once he even apologized for not being a better husband. But little by little his tone changed. He began to resent the fact that his kids had gone to live with their grandmother in Newburgh during his wife's illness. He began to accuse his wife of being lazy, of being an inferior mother and wife. And then along about her tenth week in the hospital, Edward showed up, told her she was a fake, wasn't really sick at all, just wanted a vacation from him and the kids, and then he stormed out. He drove to Newburgh, collected his boys, and took them home. Christine's mother, uncertain of her son-in-law's mental health, did not want to hand over the children but legally she had no choice. Edward was, after all, their father.

Now the precise sequence of events becomes a bit hazy at this point but we do know most of the facts even if we do not know their exact order. You see, Edward had lost his cool, blown a fuse. He got back to Ithaca with those three kids and he more or less barricaded the family in their tiny house. He closed the drapes, locked the doors, and told the boys, who didn't know what was going on, that they were under siege. Under siege from what? asked the oldest. Under siege from the bad guys, answered the father. And so for the next several weeks they only left the apartment to fuel the car and buy supplies. They always went out at night under cover of darkness.

They did go out during daylight one morning a few days prior to Christine's release from the hospital. Edward drove to the hospital, and while the kids waited in the car, he went up and told his wife not to bother coming home, they could manage fine without her. Well, that was the beginning of the end for Edward. During the next two weeks he had Christine and Christine's family and then his own family all pounding on his front door. They wanted to know what was going on, why was he acting like some kind of weird, demented person? Edward just shoved the couch in front of the door and told them all to go away. They went away all right, but of course Christine called in the authorities. She hired a lawyer and within a few days the lawyer had gotten a judge to issue a court order demanding that Mr. Edward Winslow release his three sons into the custody of Tompkins County.

That's when Christine called Edward on the telephone and told him the cops were on their way. Edward called her a traitor and pulled the phone off the wall. When the cops arrived he opened the door but refused to let them enter. The woman from Children's Services explained about the court order. Edward told her to tell the judge to go fuck himself. The cops told Edward to stay cool. Edward told the cops to go fuck themselves too and then he slammed the door in the woman's face. Well, the cops got pissed off, broke the door down, and rushed into the house like a couple of SS storm troopers on a Jew hunt. Little Eddie battled them like a knight defending his castle and his kinfolk, but in the end, of course, he was defeated, dragged away in handcuffs. His boys and his dead mother watched the battle from behind the sofa. All of them were helpless. The middle son's psychosis had won the day. The cops threw Little Eddie into the Tompkins County Jail for striking an officer and resisting arrest.

"Yes? Hello?"

"Hello? Is this Samantha?"

"Yes it is. Who's this?"

"My name is Evangeline. I work for Mr. Winslow . . . Edward's father."

"Yes?"

"I've been calling all day, trying to get hold of Edward."

"Yes, well, I just got home from the office and Edward does not answer the telephone."

"I see."

"Did you need something?" Samantha asked the question with a measured amount of shortness. Samantha Tuttle had been Edward's psychologist for three years, until she'd become his second wife.

"Yes, well, I really need to speak to Edward." Evangeline had heard about Samantha and her Rasputinlike influence over the middle son. She felt immediately intimidated. "It's very important."

"May I ask what you need to speak to him about?"

"His father's had an accident."

"A serious accident?" Samantha asked without missing a beat.

"I'm afraid so," answered Evangeline, her desire not to tell too big a lie shadowing her every utterance.

"Is he alive?"

"Maybe I'd better speak to Edward."

"Maybe you'd better speak to me first. Edward, you see, isn't particularly well."

"Okay, fine," said Evangeline, not wanting trouble. "I'll tell you and you can tell Edward."

"Yes, I think that would be best."

And so Evangeline explained once again about the Wild One's fall down the back stairs and the broken ankle and the separated shoulder and the two big bumps on the back of the head, exaggerating all of it just a little so that she would not have to exaggerate any of it too much.

"Do they think he'll live?" asked Samantha.

Evangeline hestiated. *Of course he'll live, you fool,* she thought, *but I'm not supposed to tell you that.* "It's very hard to say. He was unconscious for several hours and may still be. I think it would be best if Edward came to see him."

"You do, huh?"

Evangeline balked, but only for a moment. "Yes," she said firmly, "I do. And as soon as possible."

Samantha needed a moment to recover. "Well, that's fine for you to say but perhaps you do not know or understand the situation. Edward and his father have not said more than a dozen words to one another for almost six years."

Evangeline knew all about the situaion, at least from Billy Boy's point of view. She also knew how to be tough and direct when circumstances demanded it. "Be that as it may," she said, "Edward's father has been injured, and rather severely. What matters now is the fact that Edward is his son. The past can wait." And then, before Samantha could reply, Evangeline added, "Wouldn't you agree?"

Samantha hesitated, then said curtly, "I will tell Edward what you've told me."

"Thank you," said Evangeline. Enough said. Anything more would only be ugly and unnecessary. She said good-bye and hung up quickly.

Chapter Seven

When the telephone rang in Joseph Winslow's Aspen condo, young Winslow had just convinced his latest love to do the deed while in the saddle of his custom-made mountain bike. They were both naked and high on coke and neither of them could stop giggling. Joseph did not know exactly how he would get the job done once he had the young lady in the saddle, but such a problem would never for a moment stop him from trying. "I'll worry about getting it in," he liked to say, "once I've got it up."

Joseph Muller Winslow, thirty-two, was named after his grandfather, Virginia's father, who had died in the fall of '58 just a few days before little Joseph was born. Joey was a quiet baby, the most trouble-free of Virginia's nine infants. He always waited patiently for the breast and if his mother was preoccupied with other duties he would just lie still, usually with a smile on his face and a glint in his sky-blue eyes.

Joey had eyes like his father, fabulous eyes, wild eyes, eyes that made people stop and stare, especially the young ladies. His eyes were not dark and gloomy like Edward's but perfectly clear, almost luminescent. And even before the boy knew the full power of his eyes, he had learned to use them to get what he wanted.

In a family of tall, handsome men with strong backs and broad shoulders and fine, chiseled features, Joseph Muller Winslow was the tallest, broadest, finest-looking male the family had produced in several generations. He looked very much like his great-great-grandfather, Colonel Barton Henry Winslow, who had fought to preserve the Union and who had died a valiant death on the third day of July 1863 at the bloody battle of Gettysburg. Gentleman Bart, as his troops had called him, liked the furious sound of battle. He was a fighter, a skilled horseman who always led his troops into the fray, his sword held high and gleaming. His descendant, however, was not a fighter. Great-great-grandson Joseph had never really fought for anything in his entire life. He believed in almost nothing beyond his own personal right to have a good time.

At the tender age of fifteen Joey Winslow lost his virginity to the mother of his best friend. Her name was Mrs. Anderson, and although she seemed quite old to Joey at the time she was actually only thirty-three. She seduced the young Winslow boy one afternoon when he had come over to the house looking for her son. They gathered in her bedroom several times after that first time, and probably their sexual liaison would have continued had not Mr. Anderson been transferred to Chicago. Joey never forgot Mrs. Anderson, her intensity, or her totally uninhibited style of lovemaking.

A Freudian psychiatrist might suggest that Joey's unrelenting desire to constantly seek fresh, firm female bodies might be an unconscious attempt to resurrect his romance with Mrs. Anderson. Proponents of Carl Jung, on the other hand, might relate his obsession to his mother's tragic end. Joey would undoubtedly say he just liked to fuck. But of course our actions and our motivations have complexities we never fully understand. Joey was only seventeen when his mama died, a senior in high school, a time of incredible vulnerability and insecurity. He, like every seventeen-year-old male, did his best to stymie these emotions. He kept his feelings bottled up inside, released them only as pure elixirs of masculine energy. Sure, he got laid a lot, but he couldn't even bring himself to shed a tear the day they lowered his mother into her grave in the family cemetery on the hill behind the big house in Far Hills.

Every generation of Winslows for as long as anyone can remember has had its substance abuser. For several hundred years this meant the family drunk, that staggering kinsman who preferred the company of alcohol to the company of God, friends, and even money. But this present generation had found booze a bedmate: dope. Booze and dope, dope and booze; Joey, more than any of his siblings, brought the two together. He started some serious drinking while still in grade school. He used to slip into Wild Bill's liquor closet with an empty quart bottle of Pepsi Cola and fill it up with bourbon, scotch, gin, vodka, whatever he could find. Then he'd take it out into the barn where he and his grade-school buddies would suck it dry, giggle, and play grab-ass for an hour or two, and then throw-up. In high school Joey liked to smoke grass with his beer and his whiskey. From there he graduated to acid, speed, and that lovely drug known as angel dust. Smoke some angel dust and within a couple minutes you felt all at once like God, the devil, and Mick Jagger. Dust sent more than one of Joey's drug buddies to the loony bin. But nothing seemed to bother Joey. He could drink, smoke, sniff, and snort virtually any combination of booze and dope and still get up in the morning feeling stable and even relatively sane. Between the ages of eighteen and twenty-eight Joey experimented with virtually every illegal recreational drug known to Western man. In the end he liked beer, bourbon, grass, and coke the best; and many was the night he introduced all four of these delicacies into his body at the same time.

Joey went to college, several of them in fact. He matriculated at four different universities from Boston to San Francisco, but he never stayed at any one institution for more than a single semester. He usually passed his courses but rarely with distinction. The only people who might remember Joey Winslow from his college days were the loose and lovely young lasses who caught his fancy and the drug dealers who knew he always carried a pocketful of cash.

In the fall of 1986, a drug buddy of Joey's in San Francisco told Joey he was heading for Colorado to pass the winter. Joey decided to go along. He had nothing better to do. By Christmas he had discovered Aspen. It had everything he wanted: an endless supply of booze, drugs, parties, and loose women. It also had some pretty good skiing, which Joey stumbled upon more or less as an afterthought.

Joey spent two years in Aspen learning the ropes, figuring out who was who and what was what. He tended bar, sold dope, even held a regular job in a ski shop for a couple months. He slept in many different beds with many different women. Twice he contracted the Aspen clap, a locally transmitted sexual disease which the doctors treated with extremely potent injections of penicillin and vitamin B-12.

Joey took some lessons and turned himself into a pretty fair skier. By the end of his second winter in Apen he looked like a pro gliding down the mountain in his pale blue ski suit and his Wayfarer sunglasses. He worked hard on his skiing because a skier who looked good on the slopes brought in the good-looking ladies later, après ski, and all winter long, from Christmas till Easter, the beautiful ladies just kept streaming into Aspen by bus, plane, and limousine. Sometimes to Joey the town seemed like nothing but a giant whorehouse.

But after two years on the bedroom lam Joey decided he wanted more from his Aspen experience. He was sick of sleeping on couches and getting thrown out of condos at five o'clock in the morning because some rich bitch expected her husband at any minute from Houston or Buenos Aires. Besides, Joey was sick and tired of tending bar, of pouring shots and beers for stockbrokers and TV anchormen. He had also recently been warned by one of the local cops that if he kept dealing coke he might find himself busted. So what did Joey do? He called his old man, the Wild One, of course.

"Hey Dad," he said, "I have this really good opportunity to buy a ski shop here in town. It's a small shop but it's right near the new gondola and in the summer they sell mountain bikes. I think with a little fresh capital the thing could really go."

So Wild Bill flew out to Aspen to take a look. The store was about the size of a large closet and the accounting books were a mess, but in the end the Wild One decided to take a chance. He figured he had to do something. Otherwise he feared his boy Joey would be a drunk and a bum and a gigolo for the rest of his life. The deal went like this: Wild Bill would put up the cash and Joey would run the shop. They'd be partners. Twice a year Wild Bill would fly out, check over the books, and as long as everything looked clean and on the level, he would maintain a financial interest.

Joey signed on without a moment's hesitation. He renamed the ski shop Winslow's West, and almost from day one he made money. He made money mainly because just by luck he found a young lady with brains and beauty to manage the place. She was smart, honest, and hardworking; a farm girl from somewhere in the Midwest who had left the plains several years earlier to seek her fortune in the mountains. She took her work seriously and never stole a nickel. Joey, not the brightest guy in the world, was smart enough to see he had a winner in Sara Tonner, so he refrained from bedding his manager. Instead he treated Ms. Tonner with professional respect. She was free to hire and fire, to order and sell, to decorate and advertise, exactly as she pleased. Joey simply left her alone.

He bought himself a cozy condo near the slopes, a big-screen color TV, and a five-thousand-dollar stereo with CD player, Bose

speakers, power amps, preamps, and graphic equalizer. He impressed
the women with his taste for classical music, a taste acquired from
his mother at a very tender age. With Wild Bill's money pouring
in to finance the shop, Joey wallowed in the good life. He always
had plenty of booze, generous amounts of grass, and a deep bag of
coke. In Aspen that meant friends, lots and lots of friends; friends
who would immediately desert you if the gravy train ran out of
steam, but friends nevertheless.

"But what about the phone, Joey?" she giggled.

"Let the machine fuck the phone, honey," he said, "while I
fuck you."

Joey had the young lady whose name he could not remember
up on the seat of his mountain bike, but the possibility of penetration looked pretty slim. Simply not enough room, and not nearly
enough stability. And the cocaine was beginning to make him
testy, almost nasty. And the telephone. *Why,* he wondered, *didn't
the damn machine answer the damn telephone? That's why I bought
the goddamn machine in the first place.* Then, finally, it did. He
heard his own voice answer softly, "Hey, what's happening? I'm
working right now but if you leave a message I'll get back to you
real soon." Beeeeep!

And then a soft, sweet voice, "Yes, hello, Joseph, this is
Evangeline, Evangeline Pennington. I'm calling because your
father has had an accident. It looks pretty serious. He's in the
hospital. Please call me as soon as possible at 201-234-67—."

Joey left the young lady perched up on the mountain bike and
crossed to the telephone before Evangline finished giving the
number. He cut off the machine and lifted the receiver. "Evangeline,
hi. This is Joey. I just walked in the door this second. What's
going on? What's happened? Is Wild Bill okay?"

So once again Evangeline had to do her duty, ride that fine line
between honesty and deception. She explained once more about
the fall and was just about to tell him the urgency of the situation
when he interrupted.

"Say no more, Evangeline, not another word. The Winslows
are a family of scoundrels, no doubt about that, but I at least
know when duty calls. When the old man goes down, I'm there,
no questions asked. Consider me as good as on the next plane
east." Joey paused, and then, after a few seconds, "And Evangeline?"

"Yes?"

"Thanks for calling. I'll be looking for you. I'll see you in Far Hills."

The Chevy cargo van stood stranded along the hot and deserted stretch of Georgia highway running east into the Okefenokee Swamp. Steam hissed out of the engine compartment. Barton Winslow, thirty, youngest of Wild Bill and Virginia's sons, stood in front of the large van and wondered what to do. His knowledge of engines included where to put the gas and possibly, if he looked long and hard enough, the location of the oil dipstick. But he was afraid to lift the hood for fear the whole van might, at any moment, explode.

Straight back down the highway he could see the sun beginning to set, and the heat still shimmering off the black asphalt. Barton tried to stay calm, not his strongest characteristic. He scared easily and had learned to live with the sudden shivers of fear which ran unexpectedly through his body several times every day.

Barton tried to remember why, hours earlier, he had made the decision to leave the interstate south of Savannah and head for the Okefenokee. It had something to do with the new sculpture taking form in the back of his mind but he could no longer recall the exact nature of the project. The project no longer mattered to him. He just wanted to be safe and secure at the house on Captiva Island.

Here's a story to put in Barton's character pool. We'll be referring back to this from time to time because it's one of those moments we novelists find so illuminating. It goes like this: When Barton was four years old, his sister Mary, exactly ten years to the day older, went into the boy's bedroom in the very early morning and told him she had just had a very important dream. The dream started a long time ago, before the Revolutionary War, on the banks of the Hudson River in the town of what would later be called Hoboken. A young man, an ancestor named Freeman Winslow, stood at the water's edge, hammer and chisel in his hand. Before him lay a large piece of dried driftwood. The young man had started to carve the driftwood into the figure of a two-headed serpent. But before he could finish, the dream jumped ahead three hundred years and there stood another young man, very similar in appearance, standing in front of a different body of water but with the same hammer and chisel in his hand. Mary told Barton the second young man in her dream was him. She told him the dream was evidence that he was destined to become a great sculptor. Young Barton listened and nodded his head up and down as though a four-year-old could actually comprehend such philosophical nonsense. But he did understand. He must have, because over the years, even during the difficult times following his mother's death, he worked diligently to fulfill his sister's prophesy. He started with Play-Doh and never looked back. More important, he never questioned the validity of Mary's dream or her interpretaiton of it.

After Barton graduated from high school he enrolled at the New York School of Design in Manhattan. He made this move with the firm ambition of becoming an accomplished sculptor. Right from the beginning he showed promise, but more as a graphic artist than as a carver or a stonecutter. He could draw quickly and accurately. More than one of his instructors told him he would do well on Madison Avenue, in the world of advertising. But Barton rejected this expression of his artistic talent. No way did he intend to waste his skills selling soap and cigarettes and cereal. He, like many an artist before him, had more esoteric ambitions in mind. He also had Mary's dream. So after two years at the School of Design, Barton quit and set off to become the finest sculptor of his generation.

His decision to quit school did not sit well with his father. Wild Bill did not like the idea of art school in the first place, but quitting was even worse; the Wild One hated a quitter. Still, after a speech or two on the subject of quitting Wild Bill backed off. He had never understood his youngest son. He had always found the boy detached, strange, almost spooky. Barton had no interest in athletics and so far as Wild Bill knew the boy had never been in a scrap. Had Barton come along earlier in the Winslow line, the Wild One would no doubt have made things much tougher on the boy.

"He's very sensitive, Will," Virginia would tell her husband in bed at night, "but he's so little trouble. Just let him be."

"But he'd so goddamn weird."

"Not weird, Will, just different."

Wild Bill and Virginia did not know about the dream. No one knew about the dream except Mary and Barton. Mary told Barton never to mention the dream out loud. It might, she said, damage the dream's credibility. Barton assured her he would tell no one. This seemingly innocent secret, however, had an alienating effect on young Winslow. It kept the boy remote, distant, removed from the bosom of the family.

His own dreams recurred over and over, almost nightly. There were two. The first concerned the night his mother died. But in his version that Rolls-Royce Silver Shadow ran over and killed everyone in the family except him. His other dream had Virginia still alive and well. In this dream the entire family sat around the dinner table chatting amiably, everyone smiling and getting along and laughing at all the right times. Barton knew this dinner scene had rarely if ever taken place. He knew there had mostly been insults and arguing before, during, and after dinner. And he knew following his mother's death there had been no dinners together at all. His mother's death, he knew, had been the family's death. Barton longed to bring the family back to life, to cast off the alienation he had felt since early adolescence, but he had no idea how to bring about this resurrection. And as long as he held on to Mary's dream and kept that dream a secret he was powerless to reunite the family.

In the winter Barton lived in his father's house on Frenchman Bay in Bar Harbor. The town was virtually deserted in the cold months except for fishermen and drunks and artists and writers. Barton spent most of his time alone, out on the heated porch overlooking the bay. But he rarely looked out at the water. He worked long hours on his sculptures. His main diversion was music, which he listened to from morning till night. Bach, Mozart, Handel, and Vivaldi were his favorites; just as they had been his mother's favorites.

In the summer, as soon as his stepmother Bettina arrived, Barton packed his Chevy van and headed south for his father's beachfront house on Captiva Island on the west coast of Florida. There also he spent most of his time alone, out on the screened-in porch overlooking the Gulf of Mexico and working more long, hard hours on his sculptures. And there too he had his music; mostly classical, but occasionally some rhythm and blues. Maybe it had something to do with the hot, humid weather and the old Negro gentleman who took care of the gardens.

The day Bettina arrived back on Captiva, usually in the middle of October, Barton packed up his Chevy van once again and headed north for Bar Harbor. This east coast, Maine–Florida connection had been the young man's routine for eight years, a routine he often considered changing but never did.

His sculpting, however, had gone through many changes. Barton had worked with clay, cardboard, concrete, plastics, plywood, hardwoods, aluminum, and steel. Sometimes he felt as though each medium was a whole new direction. Over the years there had been many more moments of despair than elation, many more feelings of failure than satisfaction. But still he persisted, partly out of artistic conviction, partly because he feared change, but mostly because he had this misconstrued notion about destiny.

For two years now he had been working with wallboard (Sheetrock) on plywood. His theme was the deception of symbols. The work he had almost completed, the work which took up most of the space in the back of the van, was a huge, representational view of modern America. He had taken an eight foot by four foot piece of standard Sheetrock and cut it out into the geographical shape of the continental United States. This he had nailed to a three-quarter-inch-thick piece of eight foot by four foot plywood. The plywood he placed in a special stand out on the enclosed porch overlooking Frenchman Bay. For hours and days and even weeks he contemplated the shape of the Sheetrock. Slowly, without pushing or pulling, he allowed his feelings about the shape, and about what the shape represented, to flow to the surface. He prevented nothing, subdued nothing. All around him were cans of acrylic paint; dozens of cans, dozens of different colors. And as many brushes of various widths and designs. For many days he did not even bother to uncover the paints. But finally, late one afternoon, the urge came. Without really knowing why, he dipped a tiny pinhead paintbrush into a can of blood red and touched it gently to the Sheetrock. He did this with his eyes closed, and when he opened his eyes a moment later he saw the red dot covered the approximate location of the estate where he had been raised in Far Hills, New Jersey. For more than an hour he stared at the red dot. Then he began to laugh and to cry all at once. Barton wrapped a bandanna around his eyes so that he could not see and then he proceeded to dip the pinhead paintbrush into the can of blood red. He touched the Sheetrock randomly but the red dots appeared in very specific locations. One landed on the coast of Maine, another on the west coast of Florida. Then one on the exact location where his mother had been struck down by that runaway Rolls, and another on the banks of the Hudson where his ancestor Freeman had whittled his carving of the two-headed serpent. In the days and nights to follow, with Bach's *Brandenburg Concertos* echoing through the house, more colors began to flow from Barton's pinhead brush. Slowly the white background began to disappear.

Had Bettina not arrived in Bar Harbor for another two days, Barton felt certain he would have finished what he called his painted sculpture. But Bettina had parties to give and parties to attend, so Barton packed up his gear and drove away in his Chevy cargo van. On his way south he thought about stopping off in Far Hills to visit the Wild One (occasionally he did this) but for reasons he did not fully understand, he allowed the New Jersey Turnpike exit for home to slip by noticed but unused. Had he used that exit Barton would have been home when Wild Bill fell down the back stairs.

Barton waited over an hour with his broken-down van. In that hour not a single car went by in either direction. He considered walking but could not decide whether to press on or go back. He knew he had driven at least three or four miles after turning off Highway 441 back in Edith. He didn't feel like walking fifty feet, much less three miles, not in that heat, not in that country where he knew no one and feared practically everything.

Barton did not know it but while he stood there in the shade of the cargo van vacillating, the telephone at the beach house on Captiva kept ringing and ringing. Evangeline did not really know when Barton would arrive on Captiva but she had learned from Bettina that he had left Bar Harbor four days earlier. Plenty of time, in her mind, to drive down the coast. Of course Evangeline had no way of knowing Barton had spent an eventful day in Washington D.C. with an old friend or that his cargo van had a blown air hose in rural south Georgia. All she knew was that Billy Boy had asked her to contact the children, round up the kiddies, and that was exactly what she intended to do.

The telephone stopped ringing. Barton heard a car coming. *Thank God,* he thought, *finally.* He saw the last rays of the late afternoon sun glance off the two aluminum canoes stacked on top of the full-sized Ford Bronco. One of those sudden shudders of fear raced through Barton's body. He had no idea why. The Bronco drew close, slowed, stopped. Four men stepped out. They had on dungarees and soiled T-shirts. None of them had shaved in several days. They had been in the swamp "canoein' and campin' and rasslin' gators." They felt mean and ornery.

"Trouble, boy?" the driver drawled.

Barton nodded. "Overheated, I guess." Another shudder of fear.

The four southern gentlemen stared hard at Barton and then at his New Jersey license plate. Two of them began to circle the van.

The driver scratched his beard. "I got me a bad feelin' your grandpappy killed my grandpappy at Shiloh, boy." The southern drawl seemed to drag on for hours. "Now what you plan to do to make amends, Yankee?"

Barton swallowed hard. He was not prepared for this. He did not know what to do or what to say. "My great-great-granddaddy was killed at Gettysburg," he mumbled.

The four southern gentlemen laughed. Barton did not like the sound of their laughter.

"You think we oughta make that James Dickey 'Deliverance' bullshit come true, boys?" the driver asked his pals. "Make this here Yank squeal like a pig?"

This brought a belly laugh from all of them. All but Barton. He visibly began to tremble.

"Don't shake so bad, boy. We ain't gonna butt fuck you. We ain't queers. And even if we was we wouldn't rassle you. We know most a you Yanks got that there syndrome makes you scrawny and sickly. All we want's yer money and anything else valuable you got in the back of that there fancy-ass van."

Barton missed most of this discourse. He was too busy getting ready to run. And run he did, straight back down the middle of the highway, straight into the setting sun. Two of the southern gentlemen took off after him while the other two stayed behind to ransack the van. They took his stereo and his two hundred mostly classical cassettes. They took his clothes and his paintbrushes and most of his paints. They took his knives and his razor blades and his hammers and his chisels and his framed poster of Vincent Van Gogh's bedroom. They took almost everything except the Sheetrock on plywood which rested upright in the back of the van in a special frame Barton had built to transport the work to Florida. The two southern gentlemen did not touch the sculpture. They did not even like to look at it. It scared them somehow. It made them want to get the job done and get the hell out of there.

Back out on the highway Barton fought like a caged cougar. He had no idea he could fight with such tenacity. But the thought of being gang raped by those four southern madmen did something to his psyche. He would not be violated. For years Barton had been struggling with his sexuality, trying to understand his physical desires. His homosexuality had surfaced but only rarely, most recently up in D.C. the day before yesterday, and always with a great deal of pain and guilt. He wanted to be sexually unbound, to come free of doubt and perversion, *but my God*, he thought, *not like this! Jesus, this is a nightmare, a horrible and vicious nightmare!*

They needed force to subdue him, excessive force. One of the southern gentlemen held him from behind while the other one drove his knee solidly into Barton's groin. He then slammed his fists repeatedly into Barton's chest and abdomen. Before the beating ebbed Barton had a ruptured testicle, a sprained wrist, cuts and bruises from head to foot, and a set of ribs that felt like they'd been stampeded by a herd of wild boars. Barton passed out from the pain and while he was out the four southern gentlemen tied him up, stuffed a rag in his mouth, and tossed him into the back of the van along with that strange piece of plywood with the weird vibrations emanating from it. Then they climbed back into their Ford Bronco and drove off forever into the sunset.

The little girl picked up the telephone. "Hullo?" Her voice sounded soft and sweet.

"Hello," said Evangeline, "is this Rosa?"

"Yes." Rosa stroked the back of the big Persian cat while she spoke.

"This is Evangeline, Rosa."

"Hi, I'm playing with Shakespeare." Rosa liked to suck her thumb while she stroked the cat but her mother had forbidden any more thumb sucking as of last Sunday, her fourth birthday.

"How are you, Rosa?"

"I'm okay." The cat stood, stretched, arched its back, and moved slowly away across the thick carpet. Rosa watched him go, her big blue eyes instantly sad at his sudden, unannounced departure. She watched him settle in the spot of late afternoon sunlight streaming through the big picture window overlooking Central Park. As soon as she could hang up the telephone Rosa knew she would head straight for the sunny spot.

"Is your mother home?"

Rosa had been told to say mommy was in the bath if anyone called but it seemed okay to tell Aunt Evangeline the truth. "She had to go to the store for cat food. There was no more food for Shakespeare."

"But she'll be right back?"

"Yes."

"Okay, Rosa. Would you tell her I called? And tell her I'll call back in a little while."

"Okay, I will. Bye." Rosa hung up the telephone and headed directly for the sunny spot. She curled up next to the cat and waited for Mommy.

Mommy was Emily, Virginia and Wild Bill's youngest child, their fourth daughter, third surviving. Emily Anne was twenty-nine, a full fifteen years younger than her sister Ginny, the sister she had worshipped and emulated as a kid.

Emily and Rosa lived in Wild Bill's Fifth Avenue apartment. They had lived there for almost two years, since the day Emily walked out on her husband. She walked out on Frankie Santoro because he had a violent temper and had more than once beaten her up. He also liked to sleep with young, pretty, aspiring actresses like Emily who were trying to break into the business by doing commercials. Frankie Santoro made TV commercials. He was big in TV commercials, very big, and only thirty-five years old. But Emily, by the time she left him, thought Frankie was a creep, a louse, a scuzbag. And besides, she wanted to act, not sell underarm spray and hair gel and douche. Emily had decided to become an actress because Ginny was an actress, but as she grew older she decided her sister had made enough commercials for one generation of Winslows. She wanted to perform Shakespeare, live, onstage, and not just because such an ambition put her in good favor with Wild Bill.

For the first twenty-four years of her life Emily did absolutely nothing wrong; at least nothing her parents knew about or cared to notice. She did exactly as she was told and rarely, if ever, did she cause any trouble. Wild Bill and Virginia gave her everything she wanted, everything money could buy. If she wanted a pony, Papa bought her a Thoroughbred. If she wanted to take ballet lessons, Mama hired the finest instructor available. She would have brought Nureyev to Far Hills had Rudolf been willing to ride the train.

Too bad little Emily did not receive the two things she needed most: love and affection. Virginia did her best to provide these nourishing emotions but by the ninth child her reserves had run pretty low. The last thing she wanted on the eve of her fortieth birthday was another demanding infant. Virginia had other things on her mind besides children. She wanted to go to concerts and plays and museums. She wanted to travel and spend some time alone, all by herself. Mothering had lost some of its charm. And Wild Bill, well, he gave the girl whatever she wanted, more or less bought her the inventory of F.A.O. Schwarz. But the Wild One had little time to play with his daughter, to take her places like the zoo and the circus, to tuck her in bed at night. He was always out making deals, buying land, busting his butt in his never-ending quest for more money, more wealth, more control. And so poor little Emily grew up believing love was just another commodity, something that could be bought and sold.

Emily was only fourteen when her mother died. Her mother went into the city for the weekend and never came back. Emily survived this terrible turn of events by pretending with all her youth and all her imagination that it had never happened, by acting as though her mother had not died because she had not ever lived. And also by giving up her virginity not long after her fifteenth birthday to the first boy who ever told her he loved her.

Emily took solace in sex. Sex gave her both pain and pleasure. Sex was an escape from the torment of adolescence. She enjoyed the control she had over the young men who sought her sweet spot. The actual event of insertion more often than not bored her but the scenes leading up to the deed never failed to arouse her, to make her feel powerful and superior. She liked to make those little boys trying to act like men suffer and beg. She treated them like so many marionettes dangling from the ends of her manipulative strings. But in the end, after all the little boys had run home to their mommies, it was Emily who suffered. She no longer had a mommy. She had her big sister Ginny who tried to take Virginia's place, but with only minimal success. Not only did she live three thousand miles away, but Ginny's instincts as a mother were not particularly well defined.

Emily went to NYU for a year but dropped out to take acting classes full time. "Another actor in the family," grumbled Wild Bill, "Jesus H. Christ." But Emily thought she could be a great actress because most of her life had been an act, an untruth, a deception, scene after scene of make-believe, a fairyland where fantasies came true as long as she smiled and did what all the other actors wanted her to do. Also she had a tremendous ego.

Too bad New York was rampant with beautiful young ladies with tremendous egos and made-up lives. The competition was intense. And Emily, for all her positive star qualities, lacked perhaps the most important one: ambition; back-stabbing, gut-twisting, mind-boggling ambition. Having been brought up rich and pampered she could never fill the role of the starving young artist. She hadn't even earned her Actor's Equity card yet but already the girl lived on Fifth Avenue, drove a restored '57 Jag XK-140, and took holidays to Vail and the south of France. Emily did not have to become a star to earn these privileges. The Wild One provided them for her. So while the competition went to a dozen auditions a week, read for any part no matter how silly or demeaning, Emily maybe made an appearance, maybe not, depending upon the play, the character, the theater, the playwright, how her voice felt, how her eyes felt, how Rosa felt, even how the damn cat felt. Emily wanted to be a star, more than anything she wanted her name up on that marquee; she just wanted to do it without too much pain, without too much strain.

She was beautiful in a superficial, Silver Screen kind of way. And she had the skills, the talent. She knew how to move, emote, deliver a line. Maybe she wasn't Bette Davis or Meryl Streep, but given the right part the girl could do the job. She performed admirably as the manipulative and revengeful bitch in a couple of afternoon soaps. But these roles lasted only a few weeks before her character was run out of town by the show's women of virtue. She also did some Off Off Broadway, like out on Long Island and over in Pennsylvania. She had the chance to play one of the three sisters in Beth Henley's *Crimes of the Heart* at a playhouse in New Jersey not too far from her Far Hills home, but for reasons she never quite understood she declined the part.

In the summer of 1985, at an audition for yet another new Neil Simon play, Emily caught the eye of Frankie Santoro. Frankie frequented auditions in the hopes of finding fresh faces for his TV commercials. He spotted Emily immediately. She did not get the part in the Neil Simon play but she did get the part of the spunky young mother in Frankie's new fabric-softener-that-stops-static-cling commercial. And six months later, mainly because Frankie was an Italian Roman Catholic and Emily absolutely could not cope with yet another abortion, the two married. The couple settled into Frankie's spacious apartment on the Brooklyn side of the Williamsburg Bridge and five months later little Rosa pushed her way into the world.

Emily's marriage to Frankie Santoro ended, at least in the eyes of Wild Bill, her twenty-four-year run of never doing anything wrong. It would not be too harsh to say that the marriage infuriated the Wild One. Not only did he loathe the Italians and dislike those Catholics, but he took one look at Frankie Santoro and saw a thug, a stupid, loudmouthed, low-class thug. And he wasn't too far from right. He told his daughter she was making a horrible mistake, but of course she chose not to listen. She thought Frankie was wonderful, a real charmer. After all, he wanted to use her in his new dog food ad, and he had plans, big plans, for a full-length romantic comedy set in Buffalo and starring, of course, his lovely young Emily.

But then Frankie had a string of unsuccessful ads. Business turned bad. Frankie blamed Emily. He hit her for the first time one night when she could not get Rosa to stop crying. Frankie hit her again a week later because the telephone bill was so high, mostly calls to her big sister Ginny out in Bel Air. A month later he beat her up pretty bad after he came home drunk and found her lying on the living room floor drinking wine and watching a videotape of her new commercial. A few weeks after that he bloodied her lip, blackened her eye, and bruised her arm because she told him father had been right, he was a low-class, disgusting wop whose family never should have been allowed to leave the island of Sicily. He responded by calling her a spoiled WASP bitch with a stinking pussy and a foul mouth. Then he put his hands to work while his wife screamed and his daughter looked on in horror.

The next morning Emily and Rosa left Brooklyn forever. A court order was obtained, through the work of Wild Bill's powerful Manhattan attorney, barring Frankie Santoro from seeing his daughter or harassing his wife. He tried for a while to have the order rescinded but after a few months, the two females firmly entrenched in the Wild One's Fifth Avenue apartment, Frankie said, "Fuck it," and he split for the coast.

This time Emily picked up the phone. "Hello?"

"Hi, Emily. It's Evangeline."

"Hi, Rosa said you called. Listen to this. I think I got a part.

Shakespeare in the Park. They're doing *King Lear*. I auditioned for Cordelia. They like me. I think I got it."

Evangeline waited patiently for Emily to finish, then replied, "That's great, Emily. You must be pleased."

"Pleased? Are you kidding? Cordelia! Wait'll W. B. hears. He'll freak out. It's the biggest part I've ever had. This part could take me places. It could be the one."

Evangeline hesitated, then said, "I'm calling, Emily, because your father has had an accident." Once again Evangeline explained about the fall and the injuries.

"Is he critical?" asked Emily nervously. "I mean, like, could he die?"

Evangeline thought she heard fear in Emily's voice. She could not bring herself to tell even a tiny lie. "No," she answered, "the doctors seem to think he'll be fine. But he's pretty banged up. He was asking for you. He wanted me to call you."

The anxiety ran out of Emily's voice. "You mean he was able to talk?"

"Yes...briefly. I think he would like you to come home though, to come and see him."

Emily looked out the window, out across the park. It was almost time for the evening performance to begin. "Yes," she said, finally, "of course I'll be out to see him. Rosa and I will come tomorrow. In the afternoon. We'll take the train." In the morning she had to see the casting director about the role of Cordelia in *King Lear*. "Do you think that will suit him, Evangeline? Do you think tomorrow afternoon will be soon enough?"

Evangeline held her tongue. *No need to be sarcastic,* she told herself. "Yes," she said pleasantly, "I think so. I think tomorrow afternoon will be just fine. I'll tell him you're coming." And then she quietly replaced the receiver, happy that chore was finally over.

Chapter Eight

———————————————•———————————————

While his lady love battled the present, Wild Bill drifted into the past. He drifted back to that generation of Winslows who lived in Great Burstead, Essex, in the east of England at the start of the seventeenth century. He witnessed the growing rift between Edmund Winslow and his twenty-one-year-old son, Giles. Their rift began as a simple disagreement over religious freedom. But within a few years their discord had grown into a chasm three thousand miles wide. The Wild One watched this chasm grow while asleep in his hospital bed. He watched it grow in a long and vivid dream, but in the middle of the night when he awoke that dream remembered hung there in his mind like a confirmation. He knew what he had to do. And with his girls and boys hopefully heading home, he hoped to do it soon. In the shadows on the ceiling he saw the faces of his seven surviving children. He closed and rubbed his eyes. Moments later he drifted into light sleep and again traveled back to the Old World in an unconscious search for solutions.

On the same day in 1616 that King James I had four young ladies burned at the stake for allegedly practicing witchcraft against the monarchy, Giles Winslow fled Great Burstead with the authorities hot at his heels. The king's paranoia of Puritans was as intense as his paranoia of witches. James had decided to round up a few young Puritan zealots and make an example of them. No way did he intend to let these religious heretics worship and preach against his decrees. Which is exactly what Giles had been doing. He and several other opponents of Anglicanism (which they thought nothing but bastardized Catholicism) met regularly to give sermons and interpret the new King James Bible in their own way. Giles never admitted this his entire life, not even to himself, but his desire to seek an alternative religious life-style was as much a rebellion against his conformist, middle-class merchant father as it was against the theological status quo of the day.

When word came down from Hampton Court that the crown sought the heads of a few prominent Puritans, the local authorities in Great Burstead, Essex, immediately went on the hunt for young Winslow. He had on more than one occasion stood on top of a wooden crate in the middle of the town square and demanded religious freedom for all Englishmen. The authorities had been itching for a chance to arrest him and either burn him at the stake or let him dangle from the end of a rope.

Giles had friends, however, and before the authorities could round him up he had slipped out the back door of his father's manor house (the same house his direct descendant John "Crazy Legs" Winslow would use as the model for his Far Hills estate) and across a field of flax. Young Winslow left town on the south road, crossed the Thames, and headed for the coast. Within a few days he had booked passage across the Channel and within a week he was safely in Holland, in the town of Leyden, along with several hundred other Puritan exiles.

The Dutch did not exactly welcome the English, but they tolerated them and allowed them to hold their religious services as they pleased. Late in 1619 word reached Leyden that an expedition would soon be leaving for the New World, for America. Many Puritans returned to England in the hope of crossing the Atlantic and starting a new life. Giles Winslow certainly would have been among this group who would one day be immortalized as the Pilgrim Fathers, but young Winslow had something far more important on his mind: love. No way could Giles leave Leyden without his twenty-year-old sweetheart Edith Van Cleef. So the *Speedwell* sailed for Southampton and its historic rendezvous with the *Mayflower* whilst Giles groveled at his lady's feet. Religious convictions be damned. Giles wanted to bed Edith.

She was a great beauty of sound mind and sturdy character, Edith Van Cleef Winslow, female progenitor of all New World Winslows. She married Giles, finally, in 1621, after a long and faithful courtship. And then in 1624, not really out of a search for religious freedom but simply for the exuberance of personal adventure, the Winslows and their two young sons set sail on the *Nieu Nederlandt* along with thirty other mostly Dutch families

who would become the first Dutch settlers in America. Some of
the families disembarked at New Amsterdam, others up the Hudson
at Fort Orange. Giles and Edith sought an even more primitive
destination so they stayed aboard until the last. Finally, in the late
summer of '24 the *Nieu Nederlandt* anchored off a small island in
the Delaware River some twenty miles north of present-day Philadelphia. There the Winslows, along with two other families and
several single men, went ashore and began immediately to build
what they hoped would be a permanent settlement.

For several seasons the settlement prospered. Relations with the
local Indians proved amiable, those first winters were not too
harsh, and there were more births than deaths. Four more
Winslows joined the family, including Edmund John Winslow, the
very first Winslow born in the New World. Giles and Edith
named the boy Edmund in memory of his distant grandfather.
(*Giles, you see, like many an expatriate before and after him, rarely
passed a day without thinking about home.*)

Sometime in the late fall of 1628 (*we have no way of knowing the
exact date*) tragedy struck the settlement at Burlington Island. No
one knows for certain who was responsible (*some have suggested
local Indians, some have claimed the Spanish, others have pointed a
finger at English privateers*), but on that chilly autumn morning
twenty-eight of the thirty-four settlers were brutally murdered.
Only one adult male survived. He was across the island hunting
turkey. Edith Winslow and her middle son Edmund survived along
with Millicent Voorhees and her two daughters because they had
gone off early in the morning on a search for wild berries and acorns
to add to their Sunday dinner. When they returned in the late
afternoon the dead bodies lay everywhere. Their small cluster of
huts had been set afire. The entire settlement had been ransacked.

Edith found Giles at the edge of the wood, behind what had
only hours earlier been their home. His body was burned and
butchered. So were the small bodies of her five other children.
They lay in a charred heap, not far from their father. They were
burned almost beyond recognition. Only their mother could have
identified them. They were the first of many Winslows to die
violent deaths in the New World.

The Wild One came wide awake when Edith discovered her
children. He let out a soft scream. His heart pounded against his
chest. His breath came in quick, frantic gasps. He saw Evangeline

sleeping in the chair beside the bed. The sight of her soothed him. He lay back, calmed his breathing. He tried hard to imagine the terrible pain Edith must have endured. And little Edmund as well. *Although actually the Wild One knew the boy as Edward, not Edmund. Somewhere along the generational line the name had been passed incorrectly. And if names can go astray then so too can facts and figures. Wild Bill's own middle son would have been named Edmund, not Edward, had he known the true identity of his ancestor. All nine of his children were named for deceased family members. And as Mary would discover during her investigations, sometimes much more than just names were handed down.* But whatever the name, the Wild One lay there in his hospital bed and felt the pain his ancestors must have felt. It must have been unbelievable, unbearable. Then he saw his own wife lying dead on the cold sidewalk. He saw his baby girl lying dead in her bed, little Helen, just five years old. He saw his eldest son, Henry, blown to pieces by those dirty gooks. He saw his older brother, Henry, fried to death by the electrical generator in the bowels of the V.A. Hospital . . . Wild Bill had seen his share of death, had endured his share of pain and misery. He closed his eyes and thanked the Lord for the survival of Edith and little Edward (Edmund). Had they died, the Wild One knew, the Winslow line in the New World would never have gotten off the ground. But they lived, they made it through, they beat the odds. "Goddamn right," said Wild Bill softly to the night, "Goddamn right." Not only were the Winslows among the earliest European settlers in the New World, but they were also one of the very first families to settle in what would later be called New Jersey. The Wild One took great pride in this fact. A pride he felt his own offspring did not share.

Wild Bill roamed through that vast, voiceless house waiting for dawn on that cold October morning in 1945. Even in those familiar surroundings, the corridors of his youth, he felt lost. He felt cheated. He felt confused. Death, he knew, had come a-calling. His little brother was dead, his big brother no better than dead, shell-shocked beyond repair. His mother broken down, his father falling fast from too much tragedy and too much booze. And his little sister Helen pale and eerie as a ghost. Wild Bill didn't feel wild that morning; he felt meek and troubled and scared. Upstairs his new wife slept peacefully but he gained little comfort from that. She was still more of a stranger than a part of the family.

He wandered silently through the rooms where there had been so many parties during his youth. His parents had loved parties. They threw parties all the time, parties with dozens of guests, hundreds of guests even, guests who would arrive at dusk and often not leave until the following dawn. They drank and danced and sang and argued and drank some more. The Wild One remembered well. He and his brothers would race through the house causing mischief, playing tricks on the sotted guests, hiding from their dull, dim-witted nanny who tried, but inevitably failed, to keep the triumvirate in tow. The boys loved especially to go out into the great front lawn and play in the fancy cars which had brought the guests from as far away as New York City and Philadelphia. Many of the cars had their own drivers who by early evening were usually sound asleep behind the wheel. The Wild One and his brothers would climb up into the towering red maples lining the drive. They carried sacks filled with chestnuts. Once safely hidden up in the high branches they began their bombardment of the fancy cars. They hurled their arsenal onto the roofs and bonnets until they succeeded at waking the drivers and bringing them out into the open, out into the darkness. Then the boys grew quiet, the Wild One insisting they make not a sound, until the drivers, after a lengthy discussion, returned to their posts.

Wild Bill smiled at the memory but it checked the reality of the present for only a moment. He knew he could remember the good times from now until doomsday but good times past couldn't do a lick to change the troubles and misfortunes that had recently battered the family.

He had much to do but no idea where to begin or how to proceed. This vague notion that his youth had suddenly slipped away hung over him like a heavy wool shroud. The rooms, he realized as the first light of the new day began to penetrate the darkness, looked dusty and unused. The windows all needed washing and the furniture looked as though it had not been dusted or polished since news of Pearl Harbor had reached the mainland.

Depressed, almost despondent, the Wild One finally found the courage to venture upstairs to the south wing, to the master bedroom. He climbed the wide front staircase, the palm of his hand riding the smooth mahogany banister. He walked slowly down the center hallway, through the study with its floor-to-ceiling bookcases, through the sitting room where he had sat many times on the lap of his grandfather, Crazy Legs Winslow, and finally up to the two massive Burmese teak doors leading to the bedroom. He hesitated, then knocked softly. No answer, not a sound. He knocked again, louder this time. Still nothing.

Then suddenly, from behind, "What do you want?"

The Wild One turned and saw his sister Helen standing there in a flannel nightgown, her arms wrapped tightly around her frail chest.

"I want to see him."

"Now? At six-thirty in the morning?" She spoke to him as though she had no idea who he was, as though he might well be a stranger. She moved forward as if intending to block his way.

"Go back to bed, Helen," said the Wild One. "Sleep for a week. You look like a ghost."

She stopped, bowed her head. "I don't need you to insult me, William. I don't need you to tell me what I should and shouldn't do." She spoke very softly but firmly.

"I know," said her big brother. "I know and I'm sorry." Wild Bill put his arms around his little sister and held her close. She felt like nothing but skin and bones, a nineteen-year-old sack of flesh and marrow.

"It's been so difficult around here," she whispered, "so terrible." And then she started to cry.

He ran his fingers through her hair. It felt thin and greasy. *Christ*, he thought, *what the hell has happened here? This was a good-looking young lady when I left in '42. Spunky, never lost for a laugh; the life of the party.* He wanted to make Helen smile, grill her some pancakes, dress her up in a pretty summer party dress, take her out on the town. But she broke away from his embrace, dried her tears on her sleeve, stepped back, and said, "Don't stay long, I don't want you to tire him." And then she disappeared into the shadows.

Wild Bill sighed, then quietly pushed open the doors and stepped into the bedroom. All he could see at first was darkness. Long, heavy drapes covered the windows. "Dad," he said, "it's me, Willy. Your boy, Willy, Dad. I'm home. I'm home from the war, Dad. I'm back. A hero returns." He said the last in a whisper.

Charles Winslow did not stir, did not make a sound. His son

assumed he must still be asleep. Wild Bill decided to open the drapes, let in the morning light, maybe even open a few windows, the air smelled dank and dusty, like death.

The master bedroom was the most magnificent room in the house, the pièce de résistance of Crazy Legs Winslow's vision of wealth and opulence. Crazy Legs had modeled the room after the bridge of a great oceangoing luxury liner. The wall where one entered was perfectly straight and true, but the rest of the room swung in an endless arc, a great half-moon with twelve-foot ceilings, teak floors and enough windows to see most of New Jersey on a clear day. With the drapes open one could look east, south and west across rolling hills and hay fields and stands of tall evergreens, white oaks, black ash, and red maples. Glass doors opened out onto a wraparound porch protecting the entire bedroom. Wild Bill had spent many mornings of his youth playing in that room, running around out on that porch, climbing up onto the roof.

"Hey, Dad," he said while drawing open the first drape, "remember the time I climbed over the railing out on the porch and fell over the ledge?" He had the drapes open and could see the first glow of a new day just rising over the treetops to the east. His father did not respond, either to his story or to the morning light. "I fell right into that pile of manure the gardener was getting ready to spread under the azaleas and the rhododendrons. I didn't get hurt, not even a bruise, but I smelled something awful for the next couple days. Mom made me sleep out in the room over the garage."

Still Charles Winslow did not respond. He lay there silent and unmoving in that massive, handmade cherry bed, protected at each corner by a carved pair of bald eagles and a carved pair of turkey vultures. The birds perched atop the corner posts eight feet above the floor. The same sculptor who had chiseled the birds at the end of the drive had carved the birds for the bed. Crazy Legs had demanded eagles and vultures, no other birds would do. For Crazy Legs the eagles represented majesty and success; the turkey vultures represented the economic battle he had waged to achieve that success.

Wild Bill paused to look at the birds, then he went about the business of opening the room to the new day. One by one he drew open the drapes. He pushed open the windows but only a few inches for he could feel the October chill in the air and see the

gray frost covering the grass and the fallen leaves. He did not
want the old man catching cold. Helen would give him all kinds
of hell for that. Another story from his youth came to mind but
this one involved his dead brother Robert so he decided not to
tell it. If the old man was awake it would only upset him. So
instead he just slowly worked his way around the room, not once
even glancing back at the bed. He feared what he might find
there between the sheets. But then all the drapes were pulled
away, all the windows and doors open a crack, and the Wild One
had nothing more to do. He knew what had to be done however.
First he glanced around the room. The same thick Persian rug
covered the floor. The same cherry dressing mirror stood beside
the door. The same leather chair and ottoman sat next to the
bed. The same paintings hung on the available wall space, including the priceless painting of the Maine coast by Winslow Homer
which Crazy Legs had bought from the artist in 1899. The room
was exactly as Wild Bill remembered it, including the position of
that massive cherry bed. It occupied the middle of the room and
faced south so that its sleepers could rise with the sun and
immediately feel the power of conquering a new day. Crazy Legs
had positioned the bed there on purpose for he was a man who
saw every dawn as the beginning of a fresh adventure. He enjoyed
waking up and shaking his fist at the world beyond the windows
and shouting, "Here comes Crazy Legs Winslow, you lazy sons of
bitches, so get out of my way or I'll mow you down!" His wife
would tell him not to use such foul language but he would just
laugh his haughty laugh and say it again the next morning. Crazy
Legs had one very special rule he lived by: he never did anything
anyone ever told him to do; he did exactly as he pleased.

Wild Bill remembered the way his grandfather began to moan
and groan and twitch that afternoon in 1923. The Wild One was
only three years old at the time but he remembered it as though it
had happened just last week. He bounced on his grandfather's
knee while they rocked back and forth in that old rocker repaired
by Crazy Legs's father before the Colonel went off to fight the
Rebs. Little Willy Winslow kept laughing and screaming and
demanding to be bounced higher and higher. "Shit, boy, you're a
regular wild one," Crazy Legs said, "a wild one if ever there was
one. You're going to be hell to hold back, boy, hell to hold down.
I can see that by the glint in your eye."

"Yeah," said little Willy, bouncing and bucking like a bronco, "that's me, the wild one, I'm the wild one."

"Old Wild Willy," said his grandfather. And then Crazy Legs went stone rigid and the Wild One fell off the rocker onto the floor and started to cry, and Crazy Legs started to moan and twitch, kind of gently at first like maybe he had a crick in his neck or something, but then he really started to bounce around, out of control, his eyes rolling around in his head, saliva dribbling out of his mouth, and then he was out of the rocker, on the floor with Willy, and the Wild One was crying both from falling and from the strange antics of his grandfather, and then, then his mother came running, and his father, and his brother, and, and, he couldn't remember exactly but the next thing he knew he was in his little bed down the hall and his mother was telling him Crazy Legs was dead, dead, dead... Only he wasn't dead, no way, not yet; the old man had another whole life to go...

Wild Bill woke up, his breathing short and heavy. Sweat ran down his face. He did not know at first where he was. The room looked strange. It felt cold and smelled like death. But then he saw her sitting there sleeping with her head against the wall, his sweet Angel, Evangeline. "Everything's okay," he told himself, saying it very softly but hoping she would wake up and comfort him with her kind words and tender lips. But Evangeline did not stir so he closed his eyes and finished remembering that morning he went to see his father back in the fall of '45.

Charles Winslow, just fifty-three at the time, lay there in that giant cherry bed without responding, without uttering a sound, without making a move. Slowly Wild Bill crossed the room. He approached the bed. He thought about sitting on the edge of the bed but decided against it. That would be too close, too intimate, too risky. He hadn't been within ten feet of his father in probably twenty years. Old Charles lay on his back right in the middle of the bed. Only his head and arms stuck out from under a great heap of bedclothes. The arms were bent at the elbows, his hands perfectly folded across his chest. The face looked pale but peaceful. *Christ*, thought the Wild One, *the old son of a bitch looks beyond pale, he looks dead. . . .*

And sure enough, the old boozer was dead, dead as a doornail, dead as a fly caught in a spider's web. He'd been dead near a week by the time Wild Bill finally laid eyes on him. He died from too much booze and too much sorrow. He died after having lost or spent nearly every nickel of the many millions he had inherited that day in 1923 when his papa, John "Crazy Legs" Winslow, recovered from his stroke, kissed his grandchildren good-bye, and announced, "I'm sick to the bone of being a rich, selfish cocksucker. I'm going off to be somebody else. See you all sometime." Charles died by throwing a piece of rope (not just any rope but an authentic piece of one-inch heavy-duty sisal hemp imported from the Yucatan and spun at the Winslow Cordage Factory in Hoboken, New Jersey) up over the stringer beam in the master bedroom, tying the rope around his neck, pulling out the slack, standing on the end of the bed, and jumping off until he swung there above the floor long enough to suck the life out of his body. Now the Wild One had to get close, he had no choice. He threw off that heap of bedclothes, suppressed a desire to scream, and then he saw, very clearly, the raw red rope burns seared into his papa's neck.

The Wild One, as you might easily imagine, took off down the hallway in search of his little sister. He found her in her bedroom staring at an old photograph of her dead brother, Robert. Helen told him that yes, their father had been dead for almost a week. She'd cut him down and taken him to the finest undertaker in Bernardsville who had fixed him up as good as new. She had then brought him home after informing all interested parties that her father's funeral would have to wait until after the arrival of the dead man's sons. More than the funeral, however, was the fact that Helen did not want to be all alone in that great house on top of the hill. She wanted her papa, dead or alive, in the house, down the hall, close by. And so she put him to bed, tucked him in, and drew the drapes so he would not have to face another dawn.

Well, Wild Bill listened to this tale of woe and then more or less flipped out. The young man's homecoming had not been that sweet and this corpse posing as his father felt like salt being pressed into an open wound. He ranted and raved at his little sister Helen but she had many days earlier lost her grip on reality so his anger did little to relieve the situation. Virginia finally calmed him down, tucked him into bed, stroked his pulsating temples until he drifted into an anxious slumber … Before too many more days passed they had Charles safely in the ground where he belonged.

Tuesday, June 19, 1990...

Chapter Nine

———————————————— • ————————————————

Henry, as Bobby, was the first of the Winslow children to arrive at the big house in Far Hills. He drove all night in his '64 Ford pickup. The F-100 had a top speed of between forty and forty-five miles per hour, on a downhill grade, so Henry didn't make very good time, not even on the New York Thruway. It took him several hours and several cups of coffee just to coax the pickup over the hills leading out of the Adirondack Park. He hit Glens Falls just after dusk and started south. Even with the sun down Henry could feel the heat. It poured through the open windows. The heat made him want to sleep. After his long stint in the fire tower up on Snowy Mountain he knew he needed sleep. No way could he make it all the way to Jersey without at least a little shut-eye. So he pulled off at a rest area somewhere south of Saratoga Springs, north of Albany. He parked the pickup in an out-of-the-way corner in the shadows away from the bright parking lot lights and instantly fell asleep.

Now Henry had no way of knowing, but a few weeks earlier in almost the exact spot where the pickup was parked, a guy and his girlfriend had been murdered in cold blood, bludgeoned to death with the flat end of an ax and then shot several times with a twelve-gauge shotgun. These murders, like the murders of the settlers on Burlington Island back in 1628, remained a mystery. The newspapers said something about drugs being the motive but the cops felt some late-night rest-area loony was responsible for the killings. The New World may have grown older but it was still remarkably lawless.

These murders were why, when they saw the picks and axes in the bed of Henry's pickup and the shotgun hanging in the rack across the rear window, those two New York State troopers approached cautiously, their revolvers drawn. Henry, as Bobby, sat there with his head resting against the stock of his grandfather's old Remington twelve-gauge, snoring fitfully, and dreaming of the days when he and Bobby would play hide-and-seek in the attic of the big house on the hill. He had himself well hidden in his grandfather's First World War army trunk when all of a sudden, out of nowhere, these two bruisers pulled him out of his truck, threw him up against the hood, forced his legs apart, roughed him up, and ordered him to keep quiet or they would kick the crap out of him. They held the picks and the axes and the shotgun in front of his face and demanded to know who he planned to chop up and then blow away before the night was over.

"What the fuck are you assholes talking about?" Henry Winslow demanded. "I'm a fire fighter, you ugly shitbags," he shouted, forgetting even after all those years that he was supposed to be Bobby, meek, mild-mannered Bobby Winslow, "so get outta my face or I'll fuck both of you up so bad you won't be able to shit or drink water for a week."

"You're a fire fighter?"

"That's right, shitbag, a fire fighter, up in the Adirondacks. Forest fires."

The cops didn't much like being called ugly shitbags but Henry did have on the uniform of a New York State forest ranger. Then they found his fire-fighting helmet and fire-fighting vest behind the seat of the pickup, so they calmed down, checked him out, and ordered him on his way. They told him rest areas were for resting, not sleeping the night away. So Henry flashed those troopers the bird and climbed back in behind the wheel of his F-100. He started the engine and headed south, after almost eight minutes of sleep.

All night long, at every rest area and thruway exit, Henry stopped for coffee and a long piss. He kept the radio turned up full blast even though all he got was static since the antenna had been busted off in a drunken brawl at some Saranac Lake saloon ten or twelve years earlier. Still, he listened to the static. Anything to help him stay awake. He kept both windows rolled all the way down and every few seconds, between sips of java, he stuck his head out the window and screamed into the wind.

Last winter Henry had turned forty. He had not seen his father or any of his brothers or sisters for fifteen years. All the way home he wondered if this would be a good time to tell them the truth, tell them what had happened all those years ago when he and Bobby had changed identities. He wanted to tell them, for more than twenty years he had wanted to tell them. Every single day of his life Henry thought about telling them, just standing tall and making the announcement. But for reasons he had never fully understood he hadn't been able to do it. He couldn't bring himself to say, "Yeah, Dad, I just wanted to tell you, I'm Henry. Bobby died in 'Nam back in sixty-nine, not me." No, he couldn't do it. No way. *But maybe,* he thought, *maybe I can, maybe it's not too late. As long as the old man's still livin'. Long as that son of a bitch hasn't gone and died and left me to forever deal with this monkey on my back.* "Live, you old bastard," he screamed into the wind, "live at least another day!"

He drove over the border and into New Jersey about 4:30 A.M., bouncing up and down on that tattered seat, pounding his fists against the metal roof, and shouting out random, often erroneous lyrics from old rock-and-roll songs of the '60s, songs by groups like Buffalo Springfield, Jefferson Airplane, Hot Tuna, The Psychedelic Furs, and The Band. Henry sang as loud as he could, at the top of his lungs.

At least a gallon of coffee swam through his system. He belched and farted and slapped himself on the side of the face. And somehow he kept going, kept moving, driving south, heading for home, for Far Hills. He drove west on Interstate 80, then south on I-287. The Garden State began to shimmer and glow in the early morning light. Henry started to giggle uncontrollably. He thought the giggles came from too much caffeine and not enough sleep, but actually it was the long-awaited journey home and the close proximity of his boyhood exploits which caused his chuckles and cackles. He felt nervous, excited, almost giddy with fear and expectation.

Then off the interstate and south on Route 202. He passed through the center of Bernardsville. At just after six A.M. the town was quiet, practically deserted. It looked pretty much how he remembered it from when he was a kid. The shoe store where his mother took him to buy his shoes and sneakers was still there. The movie theater where he and Bobby and Ginny and Mary had spent many Saturday afternoons looked the same, maybe a new marquee and new movie posters in the windows. The train station was the same, and next door the feed and grain store where they had gone to buy food for their menagerie of family pets: the dogs and cats and horses and birds.

Then beyond Bernardsville and west toward Far Hills. A mile before town Henry turned north and started up into the hills. He no longer had to follow the steep switchbacks which had brought his old man home from the war forty-five years earlier. That road still existed but a new road had been built in the late '50s. It cut through a low pass in the hills, then joined the road that ran along the ridge.

Just as Henry reached the ridge the sun peeked over the horizon to the east. He smiled without knowing it as he drove slowly down the deserted road to his family's driveway. The twin pillars stood guard, the eagle and the turkey vulture gleamed in the early morning light. Henry knew about the birds, why Crazy Legs had put them there at the estate's entrance. As a kid the birds had made him feel special, superior. He enjoyed showing them off to his friends. But now the birds made him feel small and inferior. They reminded him just how little he had accomplished.

All the way down the drive Henry could see how perfectly manicured everything looked: the red maples, the lawn, the shrubs, the flower beds. He felt torn between anger and envy. A part of him had hoped the place would look ragged, worn down, neglected, in need of repair. Deep down inside he had dreamed of returning in the role of savior; the role his father had played all those years ago.

A big Mercedes sat out in front of the house between the statue of Lady Godiva and the front door. No water issued from Ms. Godiva's nipples but the water in the pool was sparkling clear. Henry took a long look at the fountain and the big Benz. The scene looked to him like an advertisement for some expensive brandy. He knew the Mercedes must belong to Wild Bill. His old man had driven a Benz long before the German road car became a status symbol for affluent suburbanites. Henry thought about parking his old Ford F-100 right behind the big Benz but for some reason he changed his mind. He instead swung the pickup off to the right and followed the driveway around the side of the house. He parked the pickup next to the garage, right under the tall American sycamore Crazy Legs had planted on New Year's Day 1900 to welcome in the new century. The tree, just a sapling then, now towered over the garage. Henry had often climbed the tree as a youth. He had no fear of heights, would climb higher than anyone else. The tree was higher than the house, much higher, with a splendid view of the valley from the top. Henry had never spent much time looking at the view. He just liked to climb to the top to prove he could do what no one else had the guts to do.

Henry stepped out of the pickup, let the creaky door hang open. *Jesus,* he thought, *the place looks like a park: everything so quiet and clean and orderly, like some kind of botanical garden.* Of course he knew nothing about Evangeline, about her green thumb, about her magical abilities to make things grow.

He started to knock on the back door then changed his mind. *Shit,* he told himself, *I grew up here, this is my house, I don't need to knock.* He turned the knob but the door was locked. The side door and the front door were locked also. He rang the bell but no one answered, no one came. The big house was empty, not a soul inside.

Henry stood there and wondered what it would be like to live in the big house again. All those rooms, all that space. *What would Irene think of this place? The kids,* he knew, *would love it.* He told himself it had been a great place to grow up, even though that had not always been the reality. Life under Wild Bill's roof had been unpredictable at best. *The Marine Corps and all that bullshit. The guy ran the place like boot camp.*

Henry's cabin in the woods had just two rooms and a sleeping loft. *Still* he wondered, *what more does a man really need?* But at the same time he asked the question he thought about the master bedroom, about him and Irene occupying that huge solid cherry bed with the eagles and the vultures hovering overhead. *I mean Christ, it is mine, all of it, or it should be one day. I'm the rightful heir. I'm the oldest male of my generation.*

After a few minutes Henry wandered back to the pickup. He decided he needed a little rest, a couple hours of shut-eye. It would undoubtedly be a long day filled with reunions and visits to the hospital. So he slipped off his boots and socks and stretched out on the seat of the old Ford. Within a few minutes, the sun rising fast, Henry was sound asleep.

Mary sat in the wide, comfortable first-class seat of the British Airways 747. There, somewhere, forty-one thousand feet over the North Atlantic, smiling flight attendants buzzed around her wanting to indulge her every whim, but Mary kept her eyes closed so they would not ask again what they might do or how they might help. She had been wined and dined and given a warm towel to clean her hands and face. She had been offered coffee and cognac. Or perhaps she would like to retire upstairs to the first-class lounge for a glass of Tía Maria and some tantalizing conversation. "No," she told them, "I'm fine, I think I'll stay right here and try to get some sleep." So they brought her a blanket and a pillow and a pair of velvet eyeshades.

Mary was glad when they finally left her alone. She had no desire to make conversation. She rarely made conversation with strangers unless she felt they could tell her something she did not already know. Besides, tonight Mary had other things on her mind. She had the past, for one, and of course the future. She knew her father was not dead but she sensed his need to tell her something, to tell all the children something, to share with them some important kernel of wisdom. In a sudden and unwavering impulse Mary saw her siblings traveling, converging from all directions by all means of transport, to that hilltop in New Jersey. Some would be delayed, others would fight against this convergence, but in the end, before long, they would all be there, brothers and sisters alike. Even the dead would be represented. There would be aggression, possibly violence. Drastic change would come to several lives. Mary did not yet know the nature of these changes but she had long ago learned that change was more a consequence of the past than the future, usually a past over which those souls living in the present had little or no control.

Consider, for instance, the life of ancestor Edmund Winslow, son of Giles and Edith Winslow. Mary knew his name was Edmund and not Edward. She had often used his life to demonstrate her theory on wayward expansion; i.e., the ability of a family to expand beyond its own capability to understand that expansion; i.e., expansion as determined by fate rather than free will.

Ancestor Edmund sat down in the occupied seat next to Mary and held her hand for an hour or more while the jumbo jet fought its way through some mysterious turbulence.

After the unsettled weather abated he said, "If anyone knows how our inability to control the past and the present affects the future, it's yours truly. I mean, I just went out one day to collect some berries and some acorns with my Mum, and when we got back my father and all my brothers and sisters were dead."

Mary looked at ancestor Edmund, nodded, then rested her head upon his shoulder. She knew how that single, isolated event had changed and shaped Edmund's life, and thereafter the lives of all Winslows to follow. She knew he and his mother Edith and the other survivors of the Burlington Island massacre had made their way across the unexplored wilderness of what would later become central New Jersey, the counties of Burlington, Somerset, and Middlesex. Mary had often observed one adult male, two frightened widows, and three small children wade across rivers, battle wild animals, hide from Indians, forage for food, and sleep out in the cold under the stars during the early days of a new year, the year 1629. She had watched the small, homeless band reach the banks of the Hudson in early February, all of them half-starved and half-frozen. A barge floated them across the river to New Amsterdam where they spent the remainder of that terrible winter regaining their health and trying to put behind them the senseless slaughter of their loved ones.

In time, ancestor Edmund grew into a large, powerful man. He worked on the west side of the Hudson on a huge Dutch plantation in the middle of what would one day become downtown Hoboken. Edmund did not know at the time that his direct descendant, John "Crazy Legs" Winslow, would one day own a vast factory for the manufacture of rope on that very turf. Or that another descendant, William "Wild Bill" Winslow, would construct a vast condominium complex on the same ground where Edmund had raised corn and potatoes. Edmund was a man of few words (Dutch, not English) who drank ale only one night, usually Saturday, per week, attended church whenever a preacher was available, and who took care of his dear old mama Edith until she died of pneumonia at the fairly ripe old age of sixty-six.

In 1647, the year Peter Stuyvesant arrived from Holland to become the new governor of the New Netherlands, ancestor Edmund married Mrs. Molly Richford, a widowed Englishwoman who had recently arrived from New England. Molly was a proper Puritan, much more so than Giles Winslow had ever been. She married Edmund because she needed a strong, honest, and decent man to protect her and provide for her. In 1649 Molly gave

Edmund a son whom they named Freeman in the spirit of the New World, the new frontier. Young Freeman entered the world silent, his blue eyes blazing. Molly said the lad came out smiling; the midwife said it was gas. Whatever it was he was a happy baby. No one ever heard Freeman cry. Except once. He cried that night in '55 at the exact moment when his father, miles away, took an arrow in the throat while fighting the Indians near what we now call Jersey City. Some say the Indians started the war, others blame it on Stuyvesant, on his arrogance and his racist outlook, but regardless of who shot the first arrow, Molly Winslow was a widow for the second time and Young Freeman Winslow was a boy in a wild land without a father.

Mary watched the arrow pierce ancestor Edmund's throat. She sat up startled in her seat and gave out a little gasp. "Oh, don't you worry yourself about that, little lady," said Edmund. "After almost three hundred and fifty years I'm pretty well used to it. It doesn't even hurt anymore."

Mary glanced at the hole in Edward's throat, then up at the flight attendant who hovered over her. "Is everything all right, ma'am? Can I get you anything?"

"Yes . . . No," said Mary. "I was just dreaming."

The 747 touched down at Kennedy International Airport at just about the same time Henry, as Bobby, fell asleep on the bench seat of his Ford pickup. Mary passed quickly through customs since she had not checked a bag or made a declaration of purchase. She walked out into the smoky New York morning, gasped at the explosion of heat and humidity, and stepped into a yellow cab. She told the driver she wanted to go to Far Hills, New Jersey.

"Neva hearda it," said the cabbie.

"That's all right," said Mary, "I'll show you how to go."

"Hundred clams to Newark Intanational. I'll take ya that fa."

"Fine," said Mary. "Newark will be fine."

So off they went. On the way to Newark Mary told the cabbie she had rushed home from London because her father had been in an accident and lay dying. She hoped she would get to him in time. The cabbie, as tough and cynical a New York cabbie as ever lived, came within a tear duct of shedding a tear. More than once he glanced in his rearview mirror at the small, frail, pale woman in the back seat. More than once he had to suppress a desire to weep.

"So," he asked as they sped along the New Jersey Turnpike, "how much furtha ta des Fa Hills?"

"Not far, maybe half an hour." She knew it was more like an hour but she figured it would do the cabbie good to smell the fresh air and see the green hills of her hometown.

Sentiment aside, he told her it would be two hundred bucks cash for the trip. "Okay," she said, without even thinking about the twenty or thirty British pounds and few pence in her pocketbook, "no problem." Then she told him to get off at Exit 14 and head west on Interstate 78.

Fifty-three minutes later, the cabbie really starting to moan and groan, they started into the hills. The sun hung high in the sky now, the heat and humidity surrounding, squeezing that motorized, air-conditioned box of sheet metal. "How da hell am I gonna find my way outta dis place, lady? This is like dem damn Catskills or somethin'. For Chrissakes." He had half an hour ago stopped caring about her dying father.

"Oh," she said, "don't worry, you'll find your way. Everyone always finds their way out. It's finding your way back that's difficult."

He shook his head and mumbled a few choice obscenities. They finally reached the ridge. Mary pointed out the driveway. The cabbie swung the cab between the bald eagle and the turkey vulture. "What da hell's that?" he asked, pointing.

"The birds," answered Mary, "they're like the fleshpots of Egypt."

"Say wha'?"

Mary said no more. Moments later they pulled up behind the Mercedes-Benz 560SEL. "So," he asked, "who da hell lives here? J.D. Rockafella?"

"No," said Mary, "Wild Bill Winslow."

"Neva hearda 'im."

Then came the part about the money. Mary had no American money at all, not a nickel. The cabbie was not real interested in pounds sterling. He kept calling the pounds worthless Limey crap, Monopoly money. Mary said she would send him the money and he said, "Fuck dat, lady, I ain't leavin' till I get my dough." There was of course no *one inside to foot the bill but finally Mary wandered around back and found Henry, as Bobby, sleeping in his old Ford pickup. The last time she had seen him was through a mist of tears at their mother's funeral. Nevertheless, she was not in the least surprised to find him there sleeping, looking like the long-lost relative he was.*

"Bobby," she said, shaking him gently, "wake up. I need to borrow some money." She wanted to get rid of the cabbie as quickly as possible, then she would greet her younger brother in the proper fashion.

Henry, as Bobby, slowly came around, caught the gist of the situation, and managed, after rummaging through the glove box and under the seat, to come up with a grand total of forty-four dollars and twenty-nine cents. The cabbie was not exactly pleased. "You fat pigs wit all da grease is all da same: cheap."

Mary smiled and took the cabbie into the garage, a long stone-and-wood structure with bays for six cars. She told him to take whatever he wanted in payment for the ride from Kennedy. The cabbie looked around. He figured the offer did not include the '57 Jaguar XK-140 or the '69 Mercedes-Benz 250 sports coupe or the brand-new Range Rover four-wheel-drive utility vehicle. So he chose instead a couple of handmade Orvis fly rods hanging on the back wall. "I'll take dees fishin' poles."

Mary had no idea the rods were worth over three hundred dollars a piece. "Fine."

The cabbie placed the rods in the back seat and spit on the hot asphalt. It evaporated instantly. A moment later he settled in behind the wheel of his cab and drove away.

Henry, as Bobby, watched the entire transaction from the rusty tailgate of his '64 Ford pickup. "I'd guess the loss of those rods will not make Wild Bill a happy man."

Mary smiled and crossed to her brother. "He hasn't used those things in twenty years."

"I don't know about that," said Henry, as Bobby, "but I guarantee you he knows they're there. In fact, I'll wager you the price of a cab ride to Kennedy Airport that he notices they're gone within twenty-four hours of his return from the hospital."

"Have you seen him yet?"

Henry shook his head. "Nope."

"Talked to him?"

"Nope."

"Then how do you know he'll ever get out of the hospital?"

"That ornery old son of a bitch?" said Henry, as Bobby, "you couldn't take him out of the game with"—and he pointed to the shotgun hanging in the back window of the pickup—"with both barrels of that old Remington."

Mary looked at the gun. "Jesus, Bobby, you're a regular redneck driving around in that pickup with your rifle in the window."

Henry did not like the association. "I'm no redneck. And that's a shotgun, not a rifle."

Mary smiled and slapped who she thought was her brother Bobby lightly across the face. She then gave him a quick hug and a peck on the cheek. "So," she said, "the two of us have made it. Are we the first?"

"Far as I know. No one's around. The house is locked up tighter than a bank vault."

"Well, it won't be long before the others start to arrive."

"You think so?"

"I know so."

"And how do you know?"

It was like when they were little again.

"I just do is all."

"Yeah but how?"

"Magic, little brother, magic."

Henry thought about it. He took a long look around. "Well, I'll tell you, I came as soon as I got word. But for a long time, for years, I wondered if I would ever see this place again."

"You were a fool to waste your time wondering that, Bobby Winslow," said his sister, "a silly fool."

Chapter Ten

———————————————————•———————————————————

The only flight Ginny could get out of L.A. that Tuesday morning made a stop in Denver. But she bought a ticket anyway because having become an eternal pessimist after so many years of failure she feared the worst, and the worst in this case was Wild Bill dying and her not being there. The idea of leaving behind her two teenage children to have sex and smoke dope had caused her to reconsider making the trip at all, but in the end she knew she had no choice. Maybe the Wild One had screwed up her life, maybe he hadn't been supportive of her career, maybe he had called Aaron "that little kike with a stethoscope" the night before their wedding, but he was still her father and if he was going to die she was going to be at his side.

Ginny leafed through the pages of the *Better Homes and Gardens* she had stuffed into her overnight bag just before leaving the house in Bel Air. She read not a word, not even the captions, barely noticed the fine color photographs adorning most of every page. *Maybe, she thought, I should've brought the kids along, Madeline anyway. Keep her away from that greaser Stu, the rich kid with the fast car and the gold earring. My God, she'll probably be pregnant by the time I get back.*

Ginny had no idea how long she would be in New Jersey. It would of course depend upon the Wild One's condition but hopefully it would not be too long, not more than a few days. Early next week she had an audition for a brand-new toothpaste commercial. Her agent thought she had an excellent chance to get the part. It was a new toothpaste formulated especially for adults with cigarette-stained teeth. Ginny did not smoke cigarettes, never had, and she had the straightest, whitest teeth money could buy. She felt certain the toothpaste company would want her teeth selling their product.

Sitting there at Stapleton International Airport waiting for the Denver passengers to board, Ginny had all these things (kids, career, husband, and father) on her mind when her younger brother Joseph walked right past her seat and down the aisle of the DC-10. Joseph had just flown over the mountains from Aspen and had made his connecting flight to Newark with only minutes to spare. But he did not look harried or rushed. Joseph never looked harried or rushed. "I only go fast," he liked to say, "when I'm sliding down a double diamond or on top of a woman who needs a few more R.P.M.s to crank her engines." Joseph had sauntered over from the Aspen Air gate. He knew the plane wouldn't leave without him.

He cruised down the aisle of the DC-10, slow and easy, smiling and checking out the faces of his fellow passengers. A few faces smiled back, most just looked away. Joseph looked right at his sister but his view was obscured by the *Better Homes and Gardens*. All he saw was the permed blond hair. He would have closed in for a closer look if that traveling salesman with the black sample case hadn't kept pushing him from behind. Joseph glanced over his shoulder, mumbled a, "Hey dude, be cool," then proceeded to his seat. Ginny, sensing conflict, peered over the top of her magazine but little brother Joseph had already slipped beyond view.

They rode that jumbo DC-10 all the way to Newark with only the vaguest sensation that someone they knew might be aboard the aircraft. Their paths almost crossed outside the lavatories when Ginny went into one bathroom to brush her hair just as Joseph came out of another bathroom after having just snorted two fine lines of cocaine.

Ginny left the airplane first and headed straight for the baggage claim area. Joseph had not checked a bag but he felt the need for a quick gin and tonic before hailing a taxi for points west. So sister waited impatiently for her Samsonite pullman to come around the carousel while brother downed a Gilbey's and tried to hit on a young woman exec bound for Dallas, Texas, to peddle a whole new line of computer software. When her flight was called she finished her drink and said, "Maybe some other time, some other place."

Joseph smiled but said nothing.

Brother and sister left Terminal B and walked out into the midafternoon heat and humidity at exactly the same moment but from different exits. They stepped into two different yellow cabs and said, "Far Hills, please," at exactly the same time. The cabs pulled away from the curb and headed west, the one carrying Ginny never more than a quarter of a mile in front of the cab carrying Joseph.

Ginny could not see the cab following so close behind. She had no idea it was there. Brother Joseph could see the cab ahead but he thought nothing of it, not even after they had left the interstate and headed up into the hills. He was too busy listening to the cabbie verbally castrate the New York Yankees and their neurotic owner. Had Joseph possessed even the slightest morsel of deductive reasoning, he might have realized a family member rode in the cab up ahead, especially after both taxis pulled onto the final ridge, the one just a nose behind the other. But no, not Joseph. His brain worked in simple ways. Although perhaps his failure to make a connection with the other cab was an unconscious reaction to his lifelong feud with his older sister. Ginny was twelve years older than Joseph. She had always referred to him as little Dorian Gray when they still lived in the big house together. It seemed like every time she saw him he was staring at himself in the mirror. He in return called her the Wicked Witch of the West, a reference to that loving lady from the suburbs of Oz. Joseph viewed his sister as coming from a whole different generation, one to which he could not relate. The two had never formed a really close familial bond. And so only after the two taxis had pulled between the bald eagle and the turkey vulture did Joseph venture, "Jesus, that must be someone I know."

Brother and sister could avoid one another not a second longer. The two cabs pulled up in front of the house, right behind the big Mercedes. Brother and sister stepped out of their cabs and, *Ho, ho, ho, can you believe this? All the way from Newark. Ho, ho, ho! All the way from Denver. Both of us on the same flight. Ho, ho, ho! And we didn't even see each other. Ho, ho, ho, think of the money we could've saved if we'd shared a taxi. Ho, ho, ho!*

Neither of them had a key to the house so they stood there outside the front door long after the two taxis had driven off. They discussed their course of action. Finally they left their bags and wandered around back. There they found Mary steadying a long extension ladder. And atop the ladder, all the way up on the third story, they saw their brother Henry, who they both thought was their brother Bobby.

Henry, as Bobby, tried to open a third-story window, but it, like all the others, was locked. Slowly he climbed down and the four siblings said their hellos. They were able to ignore the fact that they had not all been together in more than a decade by concentrating instead on how, exactly, they could get into the house, their house, the house where they had all once lived side by side, close together as a family. Mary told Ginny and Joseph that she and Bobby had tried all the doors and windows, including the ones leading to the basement. All were locked. The house, she said, was like Fort Knox. Joseph suggested breaking a window but none of the others thought that was too good an idea. When he asked why not they just shook their heads and said not a word.

"Evangeline," said Mary, "should be home soon. She will surely have a key."

"I hope so," said Joseph, "because this is stupid. I mean we're locked out of our own house. If Evangeline doesn't have a key I'm going to drive Bobby's pickup right through the front door."

The others laughed but all of them silently hoped that someone, anyone, would arrive, and soon, with a key.

"Well," said Ginny, "I just hope Bettina doesn't pull in and find us standing here like a bunch of idiots. I can just see the smirk on her face when she realizes we can't get into our own house. The bitch."

Henry wondered about these women, Evangeline and Bettina. "Bettina?" he asked, "who's Bettina?"

His brother and sisters looked at him strangely.

"Who's Bettina?" replied Ginny. "Bettina is Daddy's new wife. If you can call twelve years new."

"Oh right," said Henry, "Bettina . . . I knew that." And then, after a long and uneasy pause, "I guess I'd just forgotten her name."

Emily and Rosa took a taxi from the Fifth Avenue apartment to the PATH station at Thirty-third Street, entering across from Macy's. Emily carried a small suede suitcase with a change of clothes for her and Rosa. Rosa had on the smallest dress made by Laura Ashley and a brand-new pair of tiny Reebok tennis sneakers. Emily had on the same outfit she had worn earlier in the afternoon to see the director of *King Lear*: a short cotton skirt and tight silk blouse. "Call me Cordelia," she kept telling Rosa. "Call Mommy Cordelia."

Emily and Rosa rode the PATH train under the Hudson River to the station at Hoboken. There they boarded a New Jersey Transit train bound for Summit and Gladstone. All the way west Rosa looked out the grimy window while her mother tried to concentrate on Cordelia's lines from *King Lear*. A thick gray haze of humidity and pollution hung over the industrial sprawl between Hoboken and Newark, a haze Rosa found perfectly normal. She had no idea how beautiful and serene those meadowlands along the Hackensack River had been three hundred and fifty years before when her ancestor, Edmund Winslow, had lived and worked there. She thought smoldering swamplands and dirty, rundown factories with broken windows and giant smokestacks spewing black soot into the air was the way the land had always looked. No one had ever told her different. And unless she had the opportunity to one day ride the rails with her grandfather, the Wild One, probably no one ever would.

Emily knew how the land had once looked, and how it had been ruined over the centuries, especially the twentieth century. She knew because as a kid her father had occasionally taken her to New York on the train. All the way in and all the way out he would tell her how the land had looked when he was a boy and how it had looked a dozen generations before when their family had first come to the New World. The Wild One would describe in vivid detail the incredible wilderness the original New World Winslows had found and settled. He told her about the Indians and the great herds of deer. He told her the soil was so sweet you could eat it, and the water in the Passaic River so clean you could drink it. Emily listened to each and every word her father said during those trips on the train; she hung on every word as though listening to the word of God. But long ago, years ago, she had forgotten. The Wild One's omnipotence had waned with time and experience. Now, when her friends in New York made jokes about the Garden State, Emily laughed right along with them. She kept to herself the fact that she had been born and raised there and that her family had lived there since the 1620s.

Mommy and daughter passed through Summit and Berkeley Heights and Millington. Rosa grew tired of looking out the window and fell asleep against her mother's shoulder. Emily studied the Shakespeare intently but every few seconds she paused to doubt whether she would ever be able to remember all the complex language. *Maybe I should just call up the director and tell him I can't take the part. But no, I have to take the part. It could be my big break. Not that I even have the part yet; not for sure anyway. But he said it looked good for me, real good. He wants an unknown for Cordelia, a fresh face. And that's me, that's definitely me.* And besides, she couldn't wait to see the look on her father's face when she told him she had been cast in *King Lear*, cast as Cordelia, the good daughter.

Just after four o'clock the train pulled into Far Hills station. Emily and Rosa gathered their belongings and stepped off the air-conditioned car. The long late-spring afternoon had grown even warmer and more humid while they had been on the train. The sun hung high overhead beneath a cloudless, slate blue sky. There was no breeze, just the heat and the air wet with moisture.

Emily tried several times to call the big house on the hill. Her brothers and sisters could hear the telephone ringing but they could not get inside to answer it. Actually it had been ringing on and off all day. Emily was not the only one trying to reach the Winslow residence. Nurses at the small hospital outside of Waycross, Georgia, had been trying all day to reach Mr. William Bailey Winslow to inform him that his son Barton had been injured in an aggravated assault but was in stable condition.

Emily finally gave up on the telephone and decided to take a taxi. But a taxi in Far Hills proved a rare commodity, so by four-thirty Emily and little Rosa were walking north along Route 202. Occasionally Mommy, when she found the nerve and liked the looks of the car, would turn around and stick out her thumb. She knew the risk in that short skirt and tight blouse, but the last thing she wanted to do was walk five miles, most of it uphill, in high heels and silk, when it was five thousand degrees out. Emily hated to walk, avoided walking like she avoided Brooklyn. She called a cab, even boarded a bus or a subway before she resorted to walking.

She looked over her shoulder and saw one of those nifty VW Cabriolets with its convertible roof pulled back. It looked like a pretty safe bet so she turned around and stuck out her thumb. The shiny white car screeched to a halt. Emily saw a young guy, maybe nineteen or twenty, with a supershort punk haircut and a pair of mirrored sunglasses. He looked like someone she could handle, someone still trying to find his cool. "Hey," she said, "we're on our way home. Just a few miles up the road from here. Mind giving us a lift? It's awful hot."

The young driver nodded slowly. "Yeah," he said finally, "yeah, yeah, yeah. Get in."

The response caused Emily to hesitate but Rosa had already opened the door and climbed into the back seat. She had no fear of strangers, of rape, of physical violence. She had no fear of anything yet, especially when Mommy was close by.

Emily put the suitcase in the back seat next to Rosa, then stepped into the convertible and closed the door. The driver just stared straight ahead, didn't make a move or say a word.

"We turn off to the left up here," said Emily. "Half a mile or so."

"Right," mumbled the driver as he slammed the car into first and peeled out, leaving two strips of black rubber on the hot asphalt.

Emily sighed but felt happy to sit down. Thirty seconds later she heard herself say, "Here's our turn, right here. Right here on the left."

Before she had even finished he had roared past the turn.

"You missed it," she said.

"I know a better way."

"What do you mean, you know a better way? You don't even know where we live."

"I know where you live."

"Like hell you do."

The driver did not respond. Instead he turned slowly toward Emily, pushed his shiny, mirrored sunglasses down on his nose, and gave her a wicked little smile. His eyes burned red, as though he'd been up for a week smoking reefer and snorting speed and drinking whiskey.

"Stop the car," demanded Emily. "Now!" She wavered between fear and anger, struggled to suppress the fear. "Stop this car, goddammit!"

The driver smirked, slipped his sunglasses back into place, and pushed the engine into fourth. The car shot forward. Emily held tight, then turned around to make sure Rosa was okay. The little girl sat on her knees, facing backward, her long dark hair blowing wildly in the wind. Emily grabbed her, jerked her around, and

found a big smile. She ordered Rosa to put her legs down and face
forward and sit still.

"Okay, Mommy."

Then the music started. Earsplitting rock and roll. Heavy metal.
Emily had heard the song before, somewhere, but she could not
remember the name of the band. *The Meat Men* or *The Burning
Red Eyes*. Something pleasant like that. "Where are we going?"
she screamed into the driver's ear. "Where are you taking us?"

The driver winced and turned the music even louder. Emily was
about to grab the wheel when he slowed, downshifted into third,
and made a sharp left-hand turn. Less than a minute later they
were on the old road up into the hills, the old road with the steep
switchbacks. And then the convertible was on the switchbacks,
downshifting into second on the hairpin turns, pushing hard into
third on the uphill straights. The music screamed, something
about Jesus being the devil and the devil being the mother of
God. Emily screamed even louder, ordering little Rosa to hold on,
to hold tight. But the driver played the turns perfectly, winding
through each one with both speed and precision. He knew what
he was doing. He had been on those switchbacks before. And
then the little car cleared the switchbacks and crested the ridge.
Emily could see the familiar valley far below. The driver accelerated on the flat, easily exceeding seventy miles per hour before he
applied the brakes and brought the shiny white VW to a sudden
stop right at the end of the drive, right between that bald eagle
and that turkey vulture. "I best not take you all the way in," he
said sweetly, "it might cause trouble."

Emily sighed, pushed open the door, and stepped quickly out.
She lifted Rosa and the suitcase out of the back and backed away
from the car. "You're crazy, you know that," she screamed at the
driver, "fucking crazy!"

While at the same time Rosa waved good-bye and shouted,
"Thank you, Mr. Driver, thank you for the ride."

The driver nodded, smiled, and drove away.

*Emily, I can tell you, did not have a key to the big house either.
Well, she had one but had left it behind at the apartment on Fifth
Avenue. She told her siblings as much as soon as she found them
standing around in the driveway.*

Henry, as Bobby, who had not seen his little sister since she was fourteen, could not take his eyes off her. He more than once wondered what she might look like naked. And Rosa. Henry knew nothing of Rosa. He wanted to pick up the little girl and hold her close but he couldn't quite find the courage.

Mary knew about Rosa but she had never seen the child. She studied Rosa carefully from a distance but did not touch. She wondered what role the little girl would play in the scheme of things to come.

Ginny knew all about Rosa. She had flown east to help when the baby had been born. And she had seen Emily and Rosa last summer when they had come to California to visit. And the year before she had spent a few days with them when she and Madeline and Adam had flown east to have Christmas with the family. Aaron had not made that trip. He preferred to spend his holidays with people who did not think of him as a kike.

Joseph had been on hand for that Christmas also. It was the last time he had seen any of his siblings.

So here stood five of Wild Bill's offspring. They'd made it home. They milled around in the driveway between the house and garage. There wasn't too much touching or hugging or kissing between them. They kept their distance from one another. Ginny did hug Emily, gave her a short but tender motherly embrace.

Then they stood around and speculated on the extent of their father's injuries. They talked about the hot, humid weather. They wondered if Edward might actually make an appearance. Ginny and Emily did most of the talking. Mary and Joseph added tidbits here and there, not too much. Henry, as Bobby, said nothing, not a word. Most of the time he did not even know who or what the others were talking about.

And finally, mercifully, Evangeline drove down the long drive in her Nissan pickup, her two young boys bouncing up and down in the back. She had a key to the big house. She had her very own key to the back door.

Chapter Eleven

•

Martha "Shady" Winslow, Wild Bill's mother, hadn't been strong enough to attend her husband's funeral. She lay in a hospital bed a broken, frightened, and tormented woman. Her body had produced three healthy sons, "the only decent thing you ever did," her father-in-law, Crazy Legs Winslow, told her just a few days before he almost croaked in the sitting room off the master bedroom. Crazy Legs had never much liked his son's wife, thought her sly and manipulative. "Go ahead and marry the bitch, boy," he told his son Charles the day before the wedding in the spring of 1916, "but believe me when I tell you she doesn't love you, she loves your money, which is really my money, which means she really loves me." Young Charles married her anyway and the couple lived right there in the big house up on the hill. The relationship between Shady and Crazy Legs remained cool until Henry, Wild Bill's older brother, was born in 1917. The arrival of a strong, healthy male heir caused Crazy Legs to reevaluate his attitudes.

A year and a half later, during the winter of 1920, Shady gave birth to her second son. Now what I'm about to tell you remains purely a matter of speculation, but simple arithmetic points to the possibility that Charles had nothing whatsoever to do with this second child's conception. This second child, who would be christened William Bailey Richford Winslow and later nicknamed Wild Bill Winslow, was quite possibly conceived while Charles was aboard a steamship bound for Paris, France. Charles had managed to avoid direct involvement in the War to End All Wars. But after the Armistice and before the Treaty of Versailles was signed to set the stage for another world war, Charles was sent to France as a translator for the American negotiating team. While the politicians poured over Wilson's Fourteen Points of Peace, a whole other conflict was brewing back home at the Winslow Compound.

Pinpointing the exact moment of Wild Bill's conception is difficult, if not impossible, but the normal gestation period for a human fetus has remained fairly constant over the centuries at between two hundred and sixty and two hundred and ninety days. This numeric reality, coupled with evidence that Shady engaged in physical relations (albeit not necessarily with her fullest consent) with her father-in-law not long after the bon voyage party in early May of 1919, creates the possibility that Wild Billy Winslow was actually the son of John "Crazy Legs" Winslow, his purported grandfather; thus making Charles not his father but his brother.

Wild Bill lay in his hospital bed not long after dawn remembering his mother lying there in her hospital bed. In three years she had aged thirty. When he had left for the war she had seemed so young and vivacious. Sure, she drank too much, both she and Charles had always been far too fond of the bottle, especially the bottle containing the clear hard stuff, but three years shouldn't do that to people, not three short years. Wild Bill had sat there beside her bed and told her about her husband Charles, about how they had buried him in the ground earlier that day, but she did not appear to comprehend exactly what had happened. At first she seemed absolutely delighted to have the Wild One home from the war, happy her middle son had survived, but later, less than half an hour later, she completely forgot who he was. She kept telling him, "Those dirty Japanese and those terrible Nazis have killed my boys, killed all of them dead."

He tried to assure his mother that only one of her boys was dead. Henry, her oldest, was still alive, and so was her middle boy, Wild Bill. The Wild One was still alive and well. But Shady did not believe him. She called him a liar, a deceiver, the son of the devil. She cursed at him and ordered him out of her room. She screamed until the nurses came and asked him to please leave and come back later.

So Wild Bill left one hospital and went to another. He drove to the V.A. Hospital in Lyons where his older brother had been for the past two and half years. Henry no longer even looked the same. He looked old and gaunt and afraid. He had fear in his eyes. His face screamed with horror. His mouth hung open. Drool dribbled down his chin. His eyes stared straight ahead without blinking or seeing anything. He had no idea who the Wild One was, not the slightest clue. Wild Bill tried to find something, some event from the past, some remote incident of joy or victory which might tickle Henry's memory, push through the dead haze, but nothing he tried worked. His brother's expression never changed. "It's like talking to a dead man," he told the doctor.

"No," said the doctor, a tall and solemn man with wire-frame glasses and diverted eyes, "not really like a dead man at all. With a dead man there is no hope."

"Are you telling me there's hope?"

The doctor closed his eyes for just a moment. "There is always hope, son."

"What are you, some kind of goddamn priest?" asked the Wild One. "Don't bullshit me. There's no freaking hope here." Wild Bill left the hospital feeling angry but wiping tears from the corners of his eyes.

Back at the big house in Far Hills he had a visitor. Virginia told him the man was waiting in the library, had been waiting for over an hour. She also told him she had something important to tell him but that it could wait until after the man had left.

The man's name was Cornelius Wyatt, Charles Winslow's longtime friend and attorney. Cornelius, Wild Bill thought, looked old and haggard. He had been his father's doubles partner, drinking buddy, and lawyer for over thirty-five years. Cornelius's father had been Crazy Legs's lawyer. But his son would not be the Wild One's lawyer because his son had been killed at Midway by a Jap kamikaze pilot.

Cornelius stood when Wild Bill entered the library. In his youth he had stood a hair under six feet two inches tall but now age, anxiety, and a pretty fair stoop had shortened him down to five feet nine. Wild Bill towered over him. "Christ, Uncle Cornelius," said the Wild One as he shook the dry, wilted hand, "you look terrible."

Cornelius managed a smile. And then he welcomed the middle son home from the war. But the effort tired him so he got on with the business which had brought him out to the house in the first place. He quite plainly pointed out the reality of the situation as it existed at the Winslow Compound. Charles was dead. Martha was hospitalized. Their eldest son, Henry, was incapacitated and no longer responsible for his own affairs, much less the affairs of the family. The middle son, William Bailey Richford Winslow, was now in a position of responsibility and would therefore have to bear the brunt of the family's debts.

"Debts!" demanded the Wild One. "What debts?"

"I was afraid you didn't know," said Cornelius, looking more glum than ever. He sat down heavily and opened his briefcase. Over the next thirty or forty minutes he spelled out the dire circumstances of the family's financial situation. Charles had lost Winslow Cordage and most of its holdings. The decline had been going on for years, really since the departure of old Crazy Legs. The Great Depression had accelerated the slide and the war years had exaggerated an already tenuous situation. Part of the problem anyway, Cornelius said in his friend's defense, was beyond Charles's control. And so when Charles fell ill after Henry's head injuries confined him to the V.A. Hospital in Lyons, the competition rushed in and took control of Winslow Cordage. They bought the business for a fraction of its true value. But Charles signed on the dotted line without bothering to consult Cornelius because he no longer gave a damn, and because, for many years, he and Shady had been living high on the hog, taking gambling trips to Cuba, buying sterling silver place settings for twelve, treating money like waste water, and incurring fantastic amounts of debt along the way.

"The bottom line," said Cornelius, "looks like Chapter Eleven. I'll have to recommend filing for bankruptcy, unless of course you can get out there and raise some cash, lots of cash, and quick. To save this place, Willy, my boy, you'll have to get out there and kick some ass."

These last three words sounded to the Wild One like the Cornelius Wyatt he used to know: the brash barrister who liked to kick ass in court, the tennis court terror who had kicked enough ass at the Somerset Hills Country Club to win both the singles and the doubles championships from 1926 to 1934. "Don't worry, Cornelius," said Wild Bill, "I'll kick all the ass I have to kick."

"That's the spirit, kid. But believe me, it won't be easy. You'll never get Winslow Cordage back. That's a done deal." Cornelius paused, drifted off for a moment, then returned. "As you may or may not know, your grandfather, old Crazy Legs, believed in never owing anyone anything. He liked to pay as he went. He owned this land and this house outright; never borrowed a dime to build this castle. So this house and these three hundred and twenty acres are your assets, William. They're what's left of the Winslow fortune. Maybe in today's market the place is worth a quarter of a million bucks. Certainly with the war over men who struck it rich will be looking for real estate like this. I estimate your liabilities at between two hundred and fifty and three hundred thousand dollars. Most of that money is way past due. It includes everything from taxes and heating oil and roof repairs to the rather vain and tasteless indulgences of your mother and father, God rest his soul. You sell this place off and probably you can get yourself out of hock. It may be your only way out."

The Wild One needed only a moment to consider his options. "No way, I ain't selling, Cornelius, not now, not ever. They'll have to come and drag me away before I sell this house. Crazy Legs built this place for the family to live in forever. I'm not going to be the one who loses it. Three years in the South Pacific my thoughts of this place kept me going. Now that I'm back I'm here to stay."

"I like your attitude, son," said the lawyer, "but the war's over. The guns and the grenades are going down in the basement. Real soon reality will set in. Reality is going to come crashing through that front door before you can throw the dead bolt. The war had the debt collectors on hold but they're no doubt regrouping even as we speak. You're just a young fellow, William, a war hero with a pretty new wife. You can make a go of things. There'll be plenty of opportunity for you out there to make your own fortune. But first you have to get out from under this mess. I'm talking to you now not as the family's attorney but as an old family friend. You've had a whole heap of tragedy thrown in your lap since you got back. So take some time, catch your breath. Call me in a day or two. We'll work this thing out. Maybe sell off this big old place. You don't have any kids. You don't need all this room. Goddamn place is like a mausoleum. Hell, Will, if you try and hang on here you might spend the next twenty-five years just trying to break even."

The Wild One nodded but had nothing more to say. He showed Cornelius to the front door after they each had a bourbon on the rocks. He assured the attorney he would be in touch by the end of the week. But Wild Bill already knew what he had to do—*the same goddamn thing Crazy Legs would do: hang tough and beat the bastards back with a stick or anything else handy.*

At dinner Virginia had some better news. First she told him that Helen was up in her room with the door locked and refused to come out. The Wild One just shrugged his shoulders. After visits with his mother and his brother, Helen seemed practically normal. Then Virginia told Wild Bill that she had been to the doctor and he had confirmed her suspicions: she was with child, pregnant with their first. The baby was due the middle of next year, in the early summer of '46.

The Wild One started whooping it up the moment the words came out of Virginia's mouth. He jumped up on his chair and hollered, then jumped up on the table and hollered some more. "Well goddamn," he shouted, "I figured if I stayed awake long enough this day would bring me some good news."

He jumped off the table, grabbed his wife, and gave her a hug that just about sucked all the breath right out of her lungs. He kissed her hard on the mouth and told her a hundred times he loved her. Then he swept her up in his arms and carried her through the dining room and the living room and the library and out onto the back terrace. It was a cool autumn evening. A cold breeze blew out of the north. Darkness was settling fast, but they could still see the valley stretching out below, a few lights twinkling in the distance.

Wild Bill kissed his wife again, hard on the mouth, then set her down. "You haven't told me yet," he asked her, "do you like it? Do you like this place? Do you think you want to stay here? Live here forever, or at least for a while?"

She smiled her beautiful smile. "Are you kidding, Will? I love it. I love this place. It's beautiful, the most beautiful place I've ever been. It's like, like Shangri-la."

"Then you'll stay? You want to stay?" He sounded like a little boy asking his best friend to spend the night.

"Of course I'll stay, Will. What else would I do?"

Chapter Twelve

•

Their names had been William, Edward, and Henry Winslow but now their names were William, Edward, and Henry Sullivan. They had been the sons of Edward and Christine Winslow but now they were the sons of Todd and Christine Sullivan. They lived in Kittery Point, Maine, a mile or so from the Portsmouth Naval Yard, where their father, a naval engineer, worked. Todd Sullivan was a good man; quiet, stable, hardworking. He had grown up in Newburgh, New York, right around the corner from Christine Grady. Even as a kid he had hoped one day to marry her. When her marriage to Edward Winslow went sour Todd got his big chance. And hey, so what if she had three kids? So what if she'd spent a few months in a psychiatric hospital? And so what if the only reason he got her was because a thirty-one-year-old divorcée with three kids was not exactly a great catch? Todd knew with his wandering eye and his beaklike nose and his wire-thin lips that he was not exactly a fantastic catch either. He'd been on dates but not many so when his mother called from Newburgh and told him Christine Grady was available he rushed down from Kittery to let her know he was still single. At first Christine was repulsed by the mere sight of her childhood suitor but in time she saw the reality of her situation. Maybe he's not the best-looking guy in the world, she told herself, but he's sweet and he's kind and he loves me more than anything in the world. He also owns his own house not far from the beach, he makes a nice living, and he gets those excellent government benefits. Christine knew she'd be able to get William those braces he'd been needing for two years. His front teeth were growing every which way but straight. And Edward's flat feet; he constantly needed a new pair of those special shoes. And Henry had those allergies; the boy seemed allergic to just about everything under the sun. So Todd and Christine got hitched, and not *too long after the marriage Todd did his duty and legally adopted the three boys. On Sunday, after church, he took them for walks along the beach and sometimes, in good weather, he took the two older boys out for a sail in his eighteen-foot Hobie Cat. Christine hated sailing and she hated that Hobie Cat especially. She thought it looked like a giant bug skimming across the water. Every time Todd took the boys out sailing Christine feared they would never come back. She assumed until she saw them out in the driveway that they were lost at sea forever.*

The boys were already lost to Edward Winslow. He had not seen them since the night the woman from Children's Services had knocked on his door and handed him that court order. He had not seen them or talked to them or written them a letter. But he had thought about them. He thought about his boys all the time, from the moment he awoke in the morning until the moment he fell asleep at night. Edward believed absolutely in telepathy. He believed his sons knew he thought about them and that sometimes they even knew his precise thoughts. He sent them mental messages all the time. He sent them mental birthday cards and mental Christmas cards and mental get-well cards whenever he felt they were sick. And if he received some vague, telepathic message that Edward junior was having a problem with his multiplication tables he would send a mental message informing his son that $9 \times 11 = 99$, $9 \times 12 = 108$, $9 \times 13 = 117$, etc. He felt certain Edward junior received his help and thanked him for it. In this way, using these mental messages, Edward stayed in touch with his three sons. And one day, he felt certain, he would overcome adversity and be reunited with them. He believed he deserved nothing less. His sons had been stolen from him, ripped right out of his loving arms. Over time he had blamed many people for this injustice. At first he blamed his wife. But because he could not stop loving her he eventually had to shift the blame elsewhere. He tried his mother but blaming her barely got him through a single day. The Tompkins County bureaucracy took it on the chin for a fortnight or two. But the bureaucracy was too vague, too impersonal; Edward did not even know the names of the officers who had subdued him and arrested him. He needed a villain with a name and a face and a past. And so he chose his father, the Wild One. And later he added his siblings as accomplices.

Edward knew all about his ex-wife's marriage to Todd Gerald

Sullivan. He knew they lived in Kittery Point, Maine. He knew
Sullivan worked at the Portsmouth Naval Yard as an engineer. He
knew Sullivan had been educated at both MIT and Harvard and
that he had paid $2,269.74 in property taxes in 1988. He knew
Sullivan had a wandering eye and a fairly regular pew at the Holy
Catholic Church in downtown Portsmouth. Edward knew all this
stuff about Sullivan because he thought he should know as much
as possible about the man who had married his wife and adopted
his kids. He had traveled to Newburgh to see the house where
Sullivan had been raised. He had gone to Boston to see the dorm
where Sullivan had lived while attending Harvard. And the year
before last he had traveled to Kittery with no clear objective in
mind but an almost out-of-control fire burning in his soul. He
told himself all he wanted to do was take a look, observe from a
distance, make sure family life was running smoothly for the
Sullivans, make certain this guy Sullivan wasn't beating his kids
or bringing them up too Catholic. The night Edward decided to
go he told Samantha he was just going out to buy a gallon of
milk.

"We have plenty of milk."

"No, I drank it."

"But it's almost midnight, Edward. Can't it wait till morning?"

"No."

Before she could stop him he was out the door and gone. He
left Ithaca, drove east all night long. Along the way he worked
himself into quite a frenzy, especially during the long haul across
the Mass Pike. He crossed the border between Maine and New
Hampshire just as the sun squinted over the horizon at the mouth
of the Piscataqua River. Minutes later he drove past the entrance to the naval yard. He found a phone booth with a phone
book, looked up Sullivan, Todd. And there it was, 19 Brave Boat
Harbor Road. He found the house in no time, a small white Cape
Cod with yellow shutters and weathered shakes on the roof and a
dozen old lobster traps lying in a heap on the gravel driveway. . . .

*That very first glimpse of the house brought Edward's hate and
resentment to the surface. He exploded. All at once he knew what he
had to do: he had to get into that house and get those kids, his kids. He
had to save them from their mother and this jerkoff Sullivan pretending
to be their father. He sat there in the car at the end of the driveway just*

about ready to jump clear out of his skin. He kept sending mental messages in the hope that the boys would receive them and look out the window. But nothing. Maybe it was too early. Maybe they were still asleep. Maybe the messages were not getting through. And then he did it. He just did it. He could not restrain his desires even one moment longer. He jumped out of his car, marched across the lawn, marched right past that aging Honda Accord, his Accord, the Accord he had picked out and his father had paid for but which the Bitch had taken when she had run out on him, deserted him, left him to his own paranoid devices. Then he marched past those lobster traps and up onto the front stoop. He banged on the front door. Five, eight, ten times he slammed the door with his fist. But no one came. No one made a sound. He tried the latch. The door was locked. He pounded on the door again, all the while remembering that night the cops kicked his ass and stole his children right out from under his nose; the cops his own wife had sent—no! the cops my old man sent, that son of a bitch! And at just that instant when the cops cuffed him, he backed up three steps, turned his shoulder into the door, and rushed forward. But that damn door didn't given an inch. It knocked Edward right on his butt. So Edward marched out beyond the lobster traps to get himself a running start. He threw his body against the door, and this time, sure enough, the latch broke and the door flew open. He was inside then, his eyes wide, his heart slamming against the wall of his chest. This is it, he told himself, I'm finally doing what I should've done a long time ago, six years ago. He told himself to stay calm, stay cool, get the job done right, get in and get out fast. He stopped to listen, heard not a sound, not a single, solitary sound. . . .

Edward could have stood there and listened all day but still that modest Cape Cod would have remained silent. There was no one inside, you see, no one at all. They had all left the day before to spend a long weekend up at Baxter State Park. At the very moment Edward broke down the door, his three boys were busy getting their gear ready for the long hike up Mount Katahdin. They had no idea their dad was coming to rescue them. They hadn't received even one of his mental messages.

Edward looked under all the beds and in all the closets and behind all the doors before finally admitting defeat. The family had escaped. He felt certain someone had warned them of his impending arrival. So after ten or fifteen minutes in the house he went back outside onto the front lawn. The only one out there was the family cat, a silky black feline who walked right up to Edward and rubbed itself against Edward's leg.

Edward tried to kick the cat across the lawn but the cat slipped easily away. The rest of the neighborhood had slept right through Edward's arrival and his attack. After lingering for a few indecisive moments, Little Eddie climbed into his car and drove away, leaving the Sullivans' front door hanging there by one twisted hinge.

"So you think I should go?" Edward asked.

"I think *we* should go," answered Samantha.

"Okay, so you think we should go?"

"Yes," she said, for at least the one hundredth time, "I definitely think we should go."

Edward started to rub his face. Whenever he hit a crossroads he rubbed his face. He always rubbed with his left hand, first the chin and then across the mouth and then up and down both cheeks and finally the corners of both eyes at the same time. "So you really think I should go?"

"Yes," Samantha said patiently, "I do."

It was almost five o'clock, almost time for supper. Edward's brothers and sisters, with the exception of Barton who had not yet learned of Wild Bill's fall, had hours ago made their decisions. They had all decided to heed Evangeline's call. In fact, they had already made the long journey home. They couldn't get into the house, but at least they had arrived.

Edward, however, remained unsettled, undecided. He and Samantha had been discussing the various ramifications of a trip to New Jersey for a full ten hours. When the alarm went off at seven o'clock Edward was already awake, already up and pacing the apartment. Samantha knew it would be a long day. She had been through many such days with Edward. At nine she called her office and told her secretary to cancel all her appointments for the day. She knew Edward would need guidance. She did not want him making a hasty or bullheaded decision. Most of all she did not want him making the wrong decision. So at noon, while Edward ate his lunch, she slipped into the bedroom and called Morristown Memorial Hospital to find out what she could about Wild Bill's condition. All the woman on the telephone would tell her was that the patient was conscious and stable. Samantha knew that could mean a thousand things but it surely meant the old man was still alive.

Samantha had been waiting a long time, years, for the right

moment to advocate a reconciliation between father and son. Sammy was no fool. She knew Wild Bill Winslow was a wealthy man. All her life she had craved wealth. She had originally taken on Edward's case because a colleague had told her it would do wonders for her bank account. During that first year of therapy Edward had needed as many as ten sessions a week, sometimes two and three sessions a day. Her practice was not exactly booming at the time, so a single patient spending as much as eight hundred dollars a week paid the whole month's rent on both her office and her apartment. And there were no insurance forms to deal with either. She just sent a monthly bill to William Bailey Winslow, Far Hills, New Jersey, and a few days later she received a check. Occasionally the Wild One would call her on the phone to get a progress report on Little Eddie, but during that whole first year he only once suggested cutting back on the number of sessions. And when she told him that might not be a good idea, he backed off, didn't push her at all. "If you think you're making progress," he said, "then carry on, keep up the good work."

He seemed a reasonable enough man to Samantha, and genuinely interested in his son's mental health. But she knew a few letters and telephone conversations could be deceiving. His son painted a far different picture. Edward told Samantha his father was racist, sexist, selfish, and arrogant. In Edward's eyes Wild Bill was demanding and critical, never loving or supportive. He treated his kids as pawns, not as individuals. He advocated competition and confrontation, never cooperation or collaboration. Edward also blamed his father for his mother's death and for the loss of his three boys. On these last two points Little Eddie never wavered.

Samantha accepted the judgments of her patient, and later she came to believe the attitudes of her husband, but in reality she knew very little about Wild Bill Winslow. She knew about his money, and although she had married Edward because she sort of loved him and did not want to hit forty and then fifty all alone, she also secretly hoped to one day get a slice of the Wild One's financial pie. For almost three years now she had been waiting for the right opportunity to slip Edward back into the family picture. This little accident seemed like the perfect time to make a move. Not only was Wild Bill down but he had sent his emissary out to call a truce. Samantha figured he must be feeling his age, fearing his mortality; he no doubt wanted and needed to make peace with the family.

Edward kept rubbing his face. Samantha wanted to slap some sense into him but she knew it would cause more harm than good. So she waited while he finished, then she crossed to where he sat on the edge of the couch. Little Eddie never sat back on the couch; he always sat on the edge, right smack on the edge.

Samantha sat beside him and took his hands in her hands. "Your father's had an accident, Edward. We don't know how bad he is but we do know he's been hospitalized. He needs you. We both know he's been a terrible father to you, and an even worse grandfather to your kids, but nevertheless he's an old man now and he needs you. I think this is the time for you to go to him, make him see that you are willing to forgive and forget. I really think it would do both of you a world of good."

Edward glanced at his wife, then away. He had never been real secure with Samantha's motives. But her motivations were of little importance and less consequence; Little Eddie needed his Sammy. He needed her in many of the same ways he had once needed his mother, and later his first wife. He needed Samantha to help him make it through the day. "But I don't know," he said, finally, "I just don't know. I'm not sure I believe he's even had an accident."

"What?"

"It may just be a ploy, a smoke screen."

"A smoke screen? By whom?

"By all of them. Don't you see?

Samantha did not see, but that was nothing new. She often found it difficult to follow his thoughts, especially when they became disconnected and paranoid. "Yes, I think so," she said. And then, exhausted from the lengthy session, "Why don't we have supper and talk more about it later."

Edward rubbed his face, fidgeted on the edge of the couch. "Fine, okay, fine. If that's what you want."

So they had dinner and watched the news. In the early evening they went for a walk up through Collegetown and around the liberal arts quad where Edward had spent very little time as a Cornell student. He spoke only about the weather, so Samantha decided not to mention anything more about going down to New Jersey. She would wait for him to bring it up again. If he could not make up his mind by morning she would tell him she was going to see his father whether he came along or not. She knew he would never stay behind alone. But she did not know he was already making plans and those plans did not include her.

Bettina called the hospital in Morristown not long after Samantha. She received the same report: conscious and stable. The words made her feel both happy and unhappy. Happy because it meant she did not need to rush down to New Jersey and feign despair at her husband's side. But unhappy because it also meant the old S.O.B. would probably live to see another day.

At about the same time Ginny and Joseph climbed out of their opposing taxis at the big house in Far Hills, Bettina began packing her Cadillac Allanté for the trip south. She hated leaving Bar Harbor. She had only just arrived, hadn't even been by the club yet to say hello. All the best parties were early in the season when everyone still had fresh faces and fresh gossip. The idea of missing all those parties not only upset Bettina, it made her detest even more than usual her rotten husband. *But maybe,* she told herself, *I won't need to be away that long. Maybe his fall wasn't as bad as originally thought. But what if it is? What if it's even worse? What if the son of a bitch is incapacitated? What if he has broken bones and can't do anything for himself? Will he expect me to take care of him? I couldn't stand it, not for a single minute. I'll refuse. I'll tell him to hire a nurse.*

She finished packing the car and locking up the house at just about the same time Emily and Rosa stepped out of that VW convertible. She spent a moment trying to find some justification for not driving to New Jersey, but she could find none, so she settled into the plush leather seat and turned the key. The big V-8 roared and off she went.

Wild Bill had bought Bettina that grand house on Frenchman Bay as a wedding present. At the time he was fool enough to think the house was the only way he could have her. Bettina had been summering in Bar Harbor for most of her life. Her parents had owned a house there and so had her first husband, Carl Von Culin. She had left Von Culin the year before she met the Wild One because Carl had made some bad investments and some even worse business transactions and had proceeded to lose most of his millions. Bettina had jumped ship before the seas got too rough.

She then put out the word to her wide circle of friends that she was in the market for a new man; rich, of course, and preferably a bit older, either widowed or permanently divorced, and please, no children under twenty.

Wild Bill Winslow fulfilled most of these criteria, all but the one about no children under twenty. When he and Bettina first met in the summer of '77, two years after Virginia's tragic end, Joseph, Barton, and Emily were all still under twenty years of age. But nevertheless, Bettina decided to compromise. There were simply not that many eligible men around, especially men with the kind of cash Will Winslow had. Besides, Emily was the only one still at home and she seemed like a pretty decent kid. So Bettina let Wild Bill know that marriage was a definite possibility, but of course when he first proposed she did not immediately say yes. She did not want to appear too anxious. That's when the Wild One bought the house on Frenchman Bay and offered it to his potential bride as a wedding gift. A month later, in early September of '78, they were married at the First Presbyterian Church of Bar Harbor with some but certainly not all of Wild Bill's progeny in attendance. Henry, as Bobby, was holed up in the Adirondacks and did not even know about the ceremony. His sister Ginny claimed she had a commercial in production but everyone knew the real reason she wouldn't fly east was because she couldn't face the fact that her father was marrying a woman younger than she was. And Little Eddie, well, he was just too busy falling apart at the psychological seams to make the trip from New York to Maine.

Unlike his new wife, Wild Bill had spent only a few summers in Maine before he bought the cabin near Stonington on Deer Isle in the summer of '57. Old Crazy Legs had for years rented a camp either up on Moosehead Lake or on Boothbay Harbor out on Juniper Point. But when he handed his fortune over to his son Charles and flew the coop for Central America, the family trips to Maine ended. Charles and Shady had little interest in wilderness camping or coastal sailing.

Still, young Wild Bill never forgot his summers in Maine. All through the war he kept close by his memories of fishing with old Crazy Legs in Boothbay Harbor. He assured himself he would one day return to the Maine coast if he survived the fighting, if he lived to see the peace. But for the first nine years after the war

Wild Bill and Virginia had no choice but to summer in Far Hills. There was no extra money for holidays. For nine years the Wild One never took a day's vacation. He rarely worked on Sunday or on major holidays like the Fourth of July or Christmas, but every other day of the year he was out there hustling, doing whatever he had to do to repair the damage, rebuild the walls, patch the leaks, restore the family fortune.

But finally, in August of '54, with four kids all under eight (little Helen had died back in '52) and another one in the oven due in November, Wild Bill decided it was high time the Winslows got out of Jersey for a couple weeks. He rented a cabin sight unseen on Penobscot Bay in the small town of Cape Rosier.

The cabin looked as though it had been built and lived in by French fur trappers sometime before the French and Indian Wars. The roof leaked, the porch sagged, and the only plumbing was out back in the mosquito-infested swamp. The paper-thin mattresses on the beds were so filled with bedbugs that the whole family ended up sleeping on the floor. For the first few days everyone bitched and moaned and talked about going straight home, straight back to Jersey. But Wild Bill told them all to stop their grousing. And then he laid down the law: there would be no turning back, no going home, and absolutely no complaining.

Father Winslow rented a small sailboat and a wooden rowboat. He took the twins, just four years old, fishing, and the two girls sailing. Bobby drove a hook all the way through his thumb but the Wild One snipped off the barbed end, pulled it out, bandaged it up, and told the boy to quit crying, much worse things had happened. Henry sliced his foot open on a broken bottle, Mary got sunburned so bad her ears blistered, and Ginny got knocked clean out of the boat when the boom swung around and slammed her in the head. But the worst moment of the entire trip, at least so far as Virginia and the kids were concerned, came when they were packing the car for the trip home and Wild Bill declared his intention to return the following summer.

It took another three years but in '57 the Wild One put together enough cash to buy the cabin on Deer Isle. It was nothing but a simple woodframe bungalow with a living room and a kitchen downstairs and a big sleeping loft upstairs. The whole family slept up there with only a wool blanket hanging on a piece of clothesline separating the children from the adults. Wild Bill thought the cabin was paradise. That might have been a slight exaggeration, what with the mosquitoes and the black flies and the rotten fish smell at low tide and the frequent spells of cool, damp weather even in the middle of July. But the old boy had a point. It was a wild, remote place in those days, still undiscovered by the carloads of tourists pouring into Vacationland.

Their first year in the cabin Wild Bill bought an old leaky rowboat. The second year he bought a Boston Whaler with a small outboard. And the third year he found a small wooden sloop for sale which had already seen its finest sailing days. But it was all he could afford so he bought 'er, rigged 'er up, and headed for the open sea. More than once he ran that sailboat up on the smooth rocks out on the Eggemoggin Reach, and for the first few years of his sailing career his sloop spent more time at the boat repairman's shop than it did in the water. But Wild Bill didn't give a damn. He kept at it and every so often he would find himself on a perfect tack, slicing through the chop, the hull of the good ship *Helen* heeling out of the water, the mainsail and the jib perfectly taut, filled to overflowing with that clean, crisp, Maine wind. That one good tack was always enough to give the Wild One reason to rig 'er up and venture out again. By the late '60s, with Virginia and sometimes some of the kids crewing, Wild Bill had developed the sailing skills to sail his twenty-four-foot day sailer up and down the coast with the best of the old salts. He would take the *Helen II* across Blue Hill Bay, up around Mount Desert Island, and then into the marina at Bar Harbor for a bite to eat before heading home.

It was during these stopovers in Bar Harbor that Wild Bill and Virginia first met acquaintances of Carl and Bettina Von Culin. The Wild One disliked these people immediately, found their forced accents and their lofty manner phony and repulsive. In his gruff but friendly way he used to mock them right to their faces. They didn't even seem to notice. He used to wonder if maybe they were all mocking each other, if maybe they thought he was really just like them.

Well then why, you might ask, if he was really so different from these people and he found them such a bunch of phony snobs, why then did he go and marry one of them? The answer to that one is not all that complex. You see, Wild Willy Winslow was a widower. He'd lost his wife suddenly and quite unexpectedly. For a couple years the poor bastard didn't know which end was up. He had the mind and the body and the energy of a man half his age but he had nowhere to turn, nowhere to stick it. But then along comes this beautiful young babe, twenty-five years his junior, and she seems genuinely interested in him both physically and emotionally. I mean let's face it: the guy was vulnerable. He was ripe for the picking. Too bad he got picked by such a bitch. Although to be fair, and of course we want to be fair here, Bettina Ellsworth Von Culin Winslow was not all bad. She was, like many of us, a victim of her environment. Born and raised with money, where your bankroll and your position in society were the only two things of consequence, Bettina knew nothing else. She learned to do whatever she had to do to hold on to these two tangibles, because, her mother told her, if either one or both of those slips from your grasp, you're finished, kaput, in the proverbial shit house, the godforsaken poorhouse. Now this is not to suggest Bettina might not have been a bitch even if she'd been born and raised poor in the backwater, blue-collar, white-trash town of say, Kittery Point, but it is about the best defense I can mount for her at this particular time.

Bettina made her way out to Bangor and then south through Augusta on Interstate 95. She passed through Brunswick and Portland and Biddeford. In Kennebunk she decided to start searching for a place to spend the night. No way could she make it all the way to Jersey in one day. She drove another half an hour, passed through Kittery, and over the bridge into New Hampshire. She knew Wild Bill's grandchildren lived over in Kittery Point but she had no intention of stopping to see them. Once, a few years back, she had stopped there with her husband (*what she was doing driving all the way from Far Hills to Bar Harbor with him she could not begin to remember*). They had gotten off the interstate, driven into Kittery Point, and called Christine to see if they might drop by to say hello. After a long pause Christine gave Wild Bill directions to the house on Brave Boat Harbor Road. William, Edward, Jr., and Henry were all out on the front stoop waiting when their grandfather pulled up, but it was obvious after only a few minutes that their mother had prejudiced them against the Winslows. After saying hello to their grandfather and giving him a quick hug, the two older boys, William and Edward, slipped out the back door and over the fence, not to return until the big Benz had driven away.

Back in the car, back on the interstate, Bettina said to Wild Bill, "You may as well admit it, those boys are gone. You lost them. It's as though they were never even part of the family."

The Wild One knew his wife said this only to bait him, to hurt him, to dig her fingernails into his back, but still he could not refrain from turning to her and saying, "I'm not a man to admit mistakes, Bettina, but you are easily the worst one I've ever made."

She found his admission hilarious, laughed right in the Wild One's face.

Now she stopped at the Sheraton Inn outside of Portsmouth. All they had available was a two-bedroom deluxe suite. "That'll be fine," she said.

"It's two hundred and eighty-five dollars a night, ma'am."

"That's fine," she said, "perfect."

"And how long will you be staying, ma'am?"

"Just for the night." Bettina opened her wallet and handed her American Express card, actually Wild Bill's American Express card, to the young man behind the desk.

Chapter Thirteen

———————————————— • ————————————————

That small band of Winslows followed Evangeline across the drive. Joseph followed close behind, almost at her side, as they made their way along the winding brick path to the back door.

"You're still living out in the cottage, right?"

"Yes."

"Nice little spot."

"We think so."

"You and the two kids?"

"Yes. John and Paul."

"Right, John and Paul." Joseph turned around and took a quick look at the boys. "Good-looking kids."

Evangeline smiled. "Thanks, I think so."

"So how's the old man? Did you see him today?"

Evangeline hesitated, but only for a moment. "Yes... briefly. He's doing quite a lot better."

"That's good news. But I knew he'd come around. It'll take more than a fall down the stairs to knock him out of the game... By the way, the place looks great. About the best I've ever seen it."

"Thank you," said Evangeline, "it's nice of you to notice." She inserted the key into the lock and turned the knob.

"But I mean it. The lawn, the gardens. You must really know what you're doing."

"I know some, not much. Nature does most of the work. I just sort of help it along, try not to get in the way." Evangeline pushed open the door and stepped into the kitchen.

Mary and Ginny came next. They lived almost seven thousand

miles apart and although they now stood only three feet from one
another that greater distance had not diminished. Ginny told the
story of how she and Joseph had been on the same plane and
taken different cabs but the story had no visible effect on Mary.
She made no sound or gesture beyond a slight nod of the head.
But inwardly she was dissecting the story, placing it in its proper
context. She felt certain the story had a broader, more significant
meaning. It was not merely a matter of her two siblings missing
one another by chance; not simply one of those things, an
unavoidable coincidence. No, Mary knew the story had much
more to do with denial and alienation and the failure of the
family to provide trust and strength and love.

Emily and Henry, as Bobby, came next up the brick path. Henry
stayed a step or two behind his little sister, partly so he would not
have to make eye contact with her and partly because he couldn't
take his eyes off her behind. It was so smooth and firm in that
short skirt. Incestuous daydreams danced in his head. He did his
best to subdue them.

"God, Bobby, I can't believe how long it's been since I've seen
you."

"Yeah," managed Henry, "too long."

"I'll bet it's been since Mama's funeral, and that . . . that must
be like fifteen years ago."

Henry thought about going back to the truck and driving away.
"Yeah, fifteen years."

"I hope that doesn't mean it's Daddy's turn."

"I hope not too."

They took another few steps and then Henry thought maybe he
should say something so he asked his little sister, "How old are
you now, Emily?"

"Twenty-nine."

"Twenty-nine?"

"That's right, twenty-nine. How 'bout you? You must be closing
in on forty."

"Yup," he answered, "forty. . ." And then Henry, as Bobby,
could not think of anything else to say. His mind went completely
blank. He felt strange, like a foreigner in another country. Every
sound, every movement, every thought seemed exaggerated,
threatening. He felt like he had no control. Time stood perfectly
still. It seemed to take forever to make the short walk up that
brick path to the back door. He had more than enough time to

reevaluate his entire life during that walk. Although in reality, he reevaluated only one specific moment, that moment when he agreed to let Bobby take his place in Vietnam. But that single moment seemed to sum up the whole event. He kept moving forward but Henry felt pretty certain he would have to climb back into his old F-100 and drive back to his cabin in the mountains where time slipped more or less uneventfully away. But then he was on the back stoop and through the back door. And then the telephone rang and Ginny moved to answer it, and for a moment Henry relaxed, slipped into the shadow of the hustle and bustle. He didn't have to say a word. All the guy had to do was stand there, another member of the immediate family.

The kids brought up the rear: little Rosa and Evangeline's two boys, John and Paul, named not for the Disciples of Jesus but for those two rock-and-roll legends from dreary Liverpool. Not that Evangeline wasn't religious; she was a member in good standing of the Society of Friends. But the music of The Beatles had formed an important part of her personality, a fundamental part of her education. So her first, almost seven, she named John, and her second, five just last month, she named Paul.

They were good, curious kids who had so far escaped fast-food burgers, commercial TV, and refined sugar. They wanted to know if Rosa really lived in New York City.

"Yeah," said Rosa nodding, "with my cat, Shakespeare."

"And your mom?" asked Paul.

"Yeah, and my mom. She's an actress. Call her Cordelia, she'll like that."

"Who's Cordelia?" asked John.

"I don't know," answered Rosa.

"Our mom's a gardener," said Paul.

Then they walked through the back door and stood in the kitchen among the adults who were all of a sudden very quiet, so they grew quiet also. Aunt Ginny held the telephone to her ear and her right index finger against her lip. Whenever anyone made the slightest sound she gave them a hard stare. She mostly just listened to the voice on the other end of the line, but occasionally she would say something like "I understand" or "Yes, I see."

As soon as she hung up Emily asked, "Something about Dad?"

Ginny reminded herself she was the oldest. "No, Barton."

"Barton?"

"He's been beaten up by rednecks in Georgia."

"What!"

Ginny told them what she knew, which was not much because the nurse on the telephone had not known much.

"But he's going to be okay?" asked Joseph.

"He has some bumps and bruises and maybe a broken bone or two but the nurse assured me he's doing very well."

"Can we call him, talk to him?"

"The nurse said the doctor gave him some kind of sedative and he's been pretty much sleeping ever since they brought him in late yesterday."

"Maybe," suggested Henry, as Bobby, quietly from the shadows, "someone should fly down there, make sure he's all right."

Some of the others nodded but Ginny, the oldest, disagreed. "The nurse told me to call tomorrow morning. We'll be able to talk with both Barton and the doctor then. Why don't we wait until after that to decide whether or not one of us needs to go down there?"

"Hey, listen," said Joseph, "I don't know about you, but if I'd just had my butt kicked by a bunch of Georgia rednecks I'd sure appreciate some support from the old blood. I'm with Bobby, I think someone ought to get down there tonight."

"We haven't even seen Father yet," said Ginny, her voice rising, "and already you're talking about leaving."

"I'm not talking about leaving," insisted Joseph, "I'm talking about going down to Georgia to give my bro' some moral support."

"Let's not argue," said Ginny.

"I wasn't arguing," said Joseph.

"It sounded like arguing to me," said Ginny.

Joseph tried a laugh. "Maybe it sounded like arguing to you but really, it wasn't. It was frank discussion between two opposing factions."

"Oh, don't be a jackass, Joseph."

Joseph decided not to respond to his sister's taunt. For a moment the kitchen stood perfectly silent. Evangeline took the opportunity to shift gears. "I don't want to get in the middle of anything but traveling makes me ravenous. I'll bet you're all pretty hungry."

"Starving," said Joseph, "I could eat a bear."

"Well, I have to fix something for John and Paul and myself so why don't I just whip up something for everybody."

"We don't want to put you to any trouble," said Ginny.

"Believe me," said Evangeline, "it's no trouble. It'll be my pleasure. I'm just glad you've all come. Your father will be so pleased."

"Did I hear you tell Joseph you'd seen him today?" asked Mary.

"Yes," answered Evangeline. She'd been with Billy Boy ever since she had discovered him lying at the bottom of the stairs. But she did not want them to know that. "I did see him today. I thought someone should look in on him."

"Of course," said Ginny, "we appreciate that. We appreciate everything you've done."

"Thank you." Evangeline blushed but covered it up with a smile. "Now maybe I should get busy with dinner. You will all want to go to the hospital tonight."

"That's right," said Joseph, "that's why we've come. To see the old dog." He walked across the kitchen and into the dining room. "I'm going upstairs to find me a bed. See you all in a little while."

They watched him go.

"So, how was he today?" asked Mary.

Evangeline did not at first realize the question was directed at her. "Oh, I thought he looked very well . . . I mean, considering the fall he took." She had no idea how much or how little to say. She thought it might have been better if she had just unlocked the door and gone down to the cottage. This was too much like an interrogation. She had to worry not only about lying but about saying the wrong thing.

"Who found him anyway?" asked Emily. "I never did hear who found him."

"Actually, I did," answered Evangeline, after a brief pause. She thought about trying to explain but feared telling a lie so she instead said nothing.

"*You* did?" asked Ginny.

"Yes." She knew they wanted to hear more. "I did."

Ginny, ever the persistent and overprotective eldest daughter, probed a bit further. "Tell us what happened, Evangeline. How did you happen to find him?"

Evangeline could not avoid a direct question. She had to say something. "Actually, when I saw your father's car still out in the drive in the middle of the morning I wondered if something might be wrong. Your father's such a hardworking man. He's usually gone by seven o'clock. So I knocked on the back door, just to make sure he was okay. When he didn't answer I went and got the key he'd given me for when he goes away and I'm supposed to check the house. I unlocked the door and called his name but still nothing. So I started looking around, and a few minutes later I found him lying at the foot of the back stairs."

"Jesus," said Emily, "that would've scared the living daylights out of me, finding him lying there like that."

"It scared me plenty," said Evangeline. "At first I thought he was dead, I really did." She tried to keep the emotion out of her voice but her eyes gave her away. Anyone looking into her eyes knew the truth. Fortunately, Ginny had just glanced out the window at the cardinal on the bird feeder. Henry was looking at the floor, not looking at anyone. Emily was looking at Rosa and the two boys. Ah, but Mary; Mary was looking straight into sweet Evangeline's eyes. And right away she saw the connection between this young lass and her father. And for just a moment she wondered if this innocent-looking Evangeline had pushed her father down the back stairs, perhaps in a fit of rage, romantic rage. But another look into those clear and lovely hazel eyes dismissed that possibility as ludicrous.

"Well," said Emily, "thank God you found him."

The others, including Henry, nodded. Henry stood off by himself in the far corner of the large kitchen. Occasionally he stole a glance at Evangeline. He decided against incest with his little sister; Evangeline would do just fine. She reminded Henry of his wife, Irene, in her younger, thinner, preparental days.

"Yes," said Evangeline. And then, before their questions could continue, "I think I best get down to the cottage and see what I can dig up for supper. Why don't we plan on eating in about an hour?" She corralled John and Paul. "Come on, guys, let's go home and wash up." Before anyone could respond she had herself and her two boys through the back door and off the stoop.

Those left in the kitchen passed several long moments without saying a word. Finally Rosa pulled on her mother's skirt and said, "Mommy, I have to go to the bathroom." So Emily and Rosa walked out through the dining room and up the wide front stairway to the second floor.

"I think I'll go up and have a cool shower," said Mary. "London feels like weeks ago." And then she too, after locating her bag, ventured upstairs to her old bedroom, the room she had once shared with her older sister Helen.

That left Ginny and Henry, as Bobby, standing on opposite sides of the kitchen. They must have stood thirty feet from one an other, the kitchen was that big. Ginny stood in front of the floor-to-ceiling bay windows on the south side that looked out across the backyard at the long sweep of lawn and down the gentle slope to the swimming pool. Henry stood opposite his sister, in the shadowy end of the kitchen, among the range and the microwave and the refrigerator. Brother and sister were separated not only by time and by space but by an eighteenth-century drop-leaf table first brought into the family by Crazy Legs Winslow back in 1888. Henry stood beside the refrigerator knowing he should say something but just like earlier with Emily he had no idea what to say. The harder he tried to think of something to say the more difficult the formation of even a single sentence became. He was all set to ask Ginny about her husband when he could not remember the guy's name. All he could remember was the guy was Jewish, not that such a thing mattered to him but it was the only fact that came to mind. He knew she had kids but not how many or of which sex. "So," he asked, as casually as possible, "how're the kids, Gin?"

Ginny looked out the bay windows. She'd been watching Evangeline and John and Paul walk across the backyard. "What?" she asked. "Oh, Bobby, I'm sorry, I didn't realize you were still here. What did you say?"

"Nothing," said Henry, as Bobby, "I was just saying it's awful hot in here."

"It is, isn't it?"

"I think I'll open some windows then go upstairs and find a place to hang my hat."

"Yes," said Ginny, "that sounds like a wonderful idea. I hope the others left me my old room. I always like to sleep in my old bedroom when I come to visit."

Ginny said the last as she passed through the doorway into the dining room. Henry stood there then all alone. The sudden solitude made him feel both happy and sad; happy because he did not have to worry about making conversation but sad because he had lived with enough solitude. He didn't really need any more, ever. If he could just stand there for the next twenty or thirty years listening to his brothers and sisters chat and argue and make decisions, he felt sure he could be a contented man.

Henry sighed a massive sigh, a sigh which seemed to originate way down around his ankles. He swung open the refrigerator door. Not much in there but milk and orange juice and a couple blocks of moldy cheese. But down on the bottom shelf, pushed all the way to the rear, Henry found a can of beer, an ice-cold can of Budweiser beer. He popped the top and poured the contents down his dry throat in one long gulp. A little of the beer dribbled down his chin. He wiped it off on his sleeve, crushed the can, tossed the can in the sink, and headed upstairs. Along the way he hoped he would have to share a room with one of his siblings.

By the time he reached the top of the stairs Henry knew the only sibling who might accept him as a roommate was Joseph. Surely none of his sisters would have him. They barely knew him. In fact, they didn't know him at all. They thought he was Bobby. Joseph didn't know him either but at least Joseph was a man. Henry was only eight years older than Joseph but when Henry, as Bobby, left home at the age of nineteen, Joseph was just eleven. The two brothers had never really had the opportunity to get to know one another.

Oh well, thought Henry as he approached the room where Joseph and Barton had slept as kids, *maybe I can change all that.* Henry knocked on the door and turned the knob. He figured it was okay for a brother to knock and go right on in. But he found the door locked.

Joseph, you see, was lying on his bed, naked, and thinking seriously about masturbating. He had locked the door just in case he decided to do the deed. Depending upon the number of times he got laid each week, Joseph beat off an average of once a day. The young man assumed every healthy, high-spirited male did the same. If asked, he would readily admit to this brief, daily indulgence. Still, he didn't like getting caught in the act. "Yeah, who is it?"

Henry hesitated, thought about heading for the hills, or at least down the hall. "Uhh, it's me, Bobby."

Joseph released his member but did not move off the bed. "Bob! What's up, guy?"

"Well... nothing really. I guess I was just looking for someplace to take off my boots. Are there still twin beds in that room?"

"Yeah, sure Bob, but I mean... so what? There's like fifty bedrooms in this dump."

"Right, yeah, I know, but, well, I just thought that—"

"Hey listen, bro', I'm sure the old room on the third floor is still up there waiting for you. The last time I looked the door still had your and Henry's names scratched into the wood where you guys carved them with your Swiss Army knives."

Henry remembered. They had done that one rainy day probably thirty years ago, scratched their names into the front of the door as a proclamation of ownership. "Right," he said, dejected, "I guess I'll just mosey on up there and see how things look."

"Excellent idea, Bob," said Joseph. "And hey, I'll see you downstairs later on, huh?" And with that he tried to mentally arouse himself with thoughts of that luscious young blonde he had recently mounted on his custom-made mountain bike.

Henry turned away feeling low and rejected. On his way down the hall he passed Rosa coming out of the bedroom. She was naked and smiling and dripping wet. "Hi Uncle Bobby, I just had a cool bath, with soap bubbles and everything."

Henry smiled back at his niece. He wanted to pick up the little girl and squeeze her and tell her he loved her but then Rosa added, "Mommy's still in the tub. She always stays in longer than me."

Sexual thoughts of his little sister lying in the bathtub soaping her thighs made him feel like a pervert so Henry decided against touching his niece. He instead patted her lightly on the head and kept on walking. He went down to the end of the hall and up the narrow stairway to the third floor.

Sister Ginny sat on the edge of the double bed where she had slept as a teenager. She had lost her virginity on that bed to Scottie Johnston at the innocent age of fifteen; Madeline's age. It had seemed like such a vulgar act. She'd hated it, hated him, thought at the time she would never do it again, not with him, not with anyone. He had been so rough, so awkward. He kissed her so hard her teeth cut into her lip. And even though she kept saying no no no, he kept shouting yes yes yes, insisting they dip ever closer to penetration. But poor Ginny was so nervous and dry, not a drop of moisture anywhere. Scottie found his terrible way in anyway, although once arrived he didn't stay long. For five or six seconds he twitched and squirmed and moaned and then he just lay on top of her like an old dead cow. All Ginny felt was pain and guilt and this warm fluid running out of her and down her thigh. Then she heard the Wild One and her mother coming up the stairs. They were supposed to be at a party at the Blackwells'.

"My God!" She pushed Scottie Johnston off the bed onto the floor. "Get out! They're coming!"

"What? Who's coming?"

Ginny had the time to think the young man looked very stupid lying there on the floor with that blank expression on his face and his penis stuck to the inside of his thigh. But then she was off the bed and pushing him toward the window. She gathered up his Levi's and flannel shirt. She told him to go out the window, down the old drain pipe, onto the porch roof, and down the trellis. *He listened,* Ginny remembered, *thank God, that stupid jackass listened.*

By the time her parents knocked softly on her bedroom door and stepped across the threshold Scottie Johnston was off, away, and Ginny was safely in bed under the covers.

"Hello, dear," said her mother. "What's the matter? Why are you in bed so early? Don't you feel well?"

Ginny felt terrible. She hurt all over. She wanted to cry. She wanted to tell her mother everything, the whole wretched story. And she might well have spilled the beans had the Wild One not been standing there in the doorway like the Grand Inquisitor. He had a look on his face like he knew exactly what had been going on in that bedroom. Ginny hated him almost as much as she hated Scottie Johnston.

"No," she finally managed to answer without sobbing, "I'm okay. I just sort of had a stomachache. But I feel better now. I think I just need to go to sleep."

Ginny tried not to think about that night twenty-eight years ago but she could not move her thoughts along until she had rehashed every moment of that dreadful evening. And no sooner had she purged it, finally, from her mind than thoughts of her own daughter, Madeline, came storming to the fore. She saw Madeline lying naked on the living room floor with that creep Stu. She saw Stu pushing and pulling and probing, and Madeline giggling, demanding more. The sight nearly took Mama's breath away.

Immediately Ginny called the house in Bel Air and let the telephone ring twenty, thirty, forty times. No one answered. She thought about letting the phone ring until someone did answer, but that, she realized, might take all night. Reluctantly she placed the receiver back in its cradle. But visions of Madeline straddling

Stu on the living room sofa convinced her that she had dialed the wrong number. She tried again. Twenty, thirty, forty more times she let the bell sound, but no one on the other end completed the connection. No one completed the connection because no one was home. Husband Aaron was at the office removing a wood splinter from a Hollywood starlet's baby's butt. Madeline was out on Sunset Strip cruising with Stu in Stu's 911 Targa. And son Adam was over at his buddy's house smoking poorly rolled reefers, eating Chee-tos, and watching reruns of "Hogan's Heroes."

Finally Ginny hung up the phone, opened her suitcase, and carefully put away her clothes. Her underwear and socks she refolded and put in the bureau. Her dresses and blouses she hung carefully in the closet. She pushed aside the curtain and opened the window. As the oldest child, Ginny had been able to choose whichever room she wanted. She liked this room best because it had the best view; at least she thought it had the best view. It was located directly over the kitchen. A wide window seat made an excellent place to sit and look out. She could see the whole backyard from those windows: the swimming pool and the tennis court and the cottage and beyond the cottage the old hay barn. Ginny could no longer see the cottage very well however because the white pines on the far side of the tennis court had grown much taller and bushier since she had first occupied the bedroom.

Had Ginny been able to see into the cottage she would have seen Evangeline cutting up vegetables for a salad, steaming rice, sautéing onions and mushrooms in butter and red wine. She would have seen John and Paul washing their faces and changing their clothes and asking Mom if Uncle Will was going to be okay and when was he coming home from the hospital? She would have heard Evangeline telling her boys not to worry, Uncle Will was going to be just fine and no doubt he would be home by the end of the week. No, Ginny could not see or hear anything going on in the cottage but that did not stop her from wondering and worrying and drawing all kinds of fantastic conclusions. She was determined to find out more about Evangeline, about the young lady's *relationship* with Wild Bill. But at the moment she had more pressing business. She went back to the bed, sat down, and dialed once again the number of the house in Bel Air.

Mary too thought briefly about Evangeline. She thought Evangeline was the most beautiful name she had ever heard. She tried to find an Evangeline in the family's past but there was not, so far as she knew, a single one. This Evangeline would be the family's first. *And what*, Mary wondered, *could that mean? Could it mean the beginning of a new chapter, a fresh start?* The family's history had repeated itself so often that she had good reason to doubt the existence of a virgin soul but that did not preclude the possibility of change. Change, Mary knew, could come anytime, anywhere, in any form. She also knew the family had been languishing, fading, dispersing not only geographically but emotionally and spiritually as well. Some fresh force was needed to bring the New World Winslows back into line. *Perhaps*, thought Mary, *that force was Evangeline.*

Mary occupied the room across the hall from her older sister. It was the same room where Helen had died thirty-eight years earlier. The windows in Mary's room looked out across the wide expanse of front lawn. She could see the fountain and Lady Godiva on horseback and all those red maples lining the long drive. Mary had sat on the window seat beneath those windows and watched history unfold ever since she had been old enough to sit up. She had been sitting on the window seat that chilly afternoon in November of 1963, the same afternoon the President was shot, when she saw the driveway turn into the Hudson River and her ancestor Freeman Winslow standing at the water's edge in what would one day be called Hoboken. Freeman held a hammer and chisel in his hand. He was twenty-five years old. His mother Molly had recently died after a long bout with smallpox. Freeman was a Puritan preacher, but a poor one both financially and spiritually. Mother Molly had driven the boy to the pulpit, more or less told him from a very early age that he would be God's servant in the New World. Freeman did as his mama ordered but the young man had only limited faith and even more limited oratory skills. His Sunday sermons inevitably put his congregations to sleep.

You see, what young Freeman really liked to do was carve pagan idols from driftwood. That was what he was doing the afternoon Mary first saw him standing along the banks of the Hudson, actually along the side of the driveway. Freeman was carving a two-headed serpent. And very early the next morning, after Freeman and the river and the serpent had disappeared, Mary went down the hallway to her little brother Barton's bedroom and told the boy he was destined to become a great sculptor. Although she would years later change her mind, Mary believed then that brother Barton was the ancestral reincarnation of Freeman Winslow.

Mary sat on the window seat twenty-seven years later, and once again she thought about her brother Barton. She could see those Georgia rednecks out in the driveway beating up her little brother. She could see his cargo van and his large painted sculpture. She knew Barton was scared and badly hurt but the pain and the fear would pass. In the long run Mary knew the beating would help the young man define his art, define his place in history. Something similar, she knew, had happened to Freeman. He had been forced to leave old Elizabethtown after certain elders in the church became aware of his "no longer subdued desire to serve Satan." That was how they defined Freeman's creative bent. They saw Freeman's hammer and chisel driftwood carvings as works of the devil himself. Freeman, like his grandpapa Giles running from the goons sent by King James, escaped with no time to spare. The feathers had been plucked and the tar was on the boil.

The young man wandered west, across the colony, doing odd jobs, occasionally going to church but always out of a sense of guilt, never from a sense of conviction. In 1676, with winter coming on, he settled in the brand-new community of Burlington on the shores of the Delaware. He did not know the small island he could see from the town wharf was the same island where his grandfather and his aunts and uncles had been murdered three decades earlier.

Mary could see Freeman now, out on the front lawn, standing along the banks of the Delaware. That first winter he worked as a common laborer off-loading ships and helping construct a newer, larger wharf. In the spring a passenger ship arrived from England carrying sixty new settlers. Most were Quakers from the shire of York. Mary could see them standing there along the rail of the ship, getting their first view of the New World. Freeman saw them also. And then he saw her. But what, Mary wondered, was her name? That fine young woman Freeman would wed before summer turned to fall, what was her name? Ellen? Elaine? Evelyn? No, she said, something similar but something else. No, not Evangeline. She took another look at the woman standing at the rail, her grandmother seven or eight generations back; a slim and smiling young woman with clear eyes and a clear complexion and the clear conviction that God did indeed dwell inside her soul. Freeman fell in love with her even before he helped off-load her two weighty trunks. One contained her plain, simple, Quaker clothes, *and the other contained money she had inherited from her father, money she intended to use to buy a fertile strip of land and start a farm. Eleanor, said Mary, yes, that's it, Eleanor Lane, soon to be Eleanor Lane Winslow. But first Freeman had to convince young Eleanor and the other members of the Quaker community that yes indeed, he did genuinely and sincerely desire to join the Society of Friends. Of course what Freeman really desired was Eleanor as his mate, was Eleanor in his bed, was Eleanor on her back; but lest we think ill of him for these lustful desires, let it be said right here and now that in the years to come Freeman Winslow would prove himself an exceptional Quaker, a fine Friend, a man who raised his children to believe in the Inner Light. Freeman came to see the Quakers and their simple, direct communion with God as both honest and noble. Far more noble, he felt, than those self-righteous Puritans. In his later years old Freeman even occasionally stood up at meeting and gave a rousing discourse on the power of all men and all women to hear from within the voice of the Almighty.*

One of the things Freeman liked best about the Quakers was they didn't give a damn if he carved or what he carved. He could carve till his heart was content. He could carve dragons and serpents and even men with hooves and horns. His Quaker neighbors might not have liked his carvings but they never plucked the chickens or fired up the pot in response to his creative outbursts. They tolerated him, viewed him not as good or evil but simply as another of God's many children. And when the time came for Redemption, they welcomed Freeman into their tight-knit society with open arms.

Mary waved farewell to Freeman, told him she would see him soon, and then she went over to the bed to lie down. She had not slept well on the plane from London and she could feel the jet lag seeping deep into her bones. Within seconds she was sound asleep. She dreamed the Westminster Abbey's boys choir sang inside her head. Leading Evensong were those two little boys of Evangeline's who stood in the front row singing high and sweet and clear.

Actually John and Paul were singing. But they were not singing psalms. They were singing "Old MacDonald's Farm" as they followed their mother out the door of the cottage, across the tennis court, and past the swimming pool. John carried a pot of steamed brown rice and Paul carried a pan of sautéed mushrooms with onions. Evangeline led the way with a large bowl of fresh garden salad. She added the animal refrains whenever the boys reached the end of a stanza.

Upstairs Ginny heard the singing through the open window. She got off the bed and crossed the room. She saw the trio coming across the lawn. She heard their singing and their laughter. She sighed, shook her head, and went back to the telephone.

Henry had reluctantly climbed the stairs to his old bedroom. He took a long cold shower in the third-floor bathroom where Bobby had cut off all his hair twenty-one years earlier. Henry could still see the hair in the sink and on the floor as he rubbed himself dry. As always he avoided even glancing at himself in the mirror. When he started to dress he realized he had not packed any clean clothes. His forest ranger uniform, the one he had been living in for more than forty-eight hours, smelled of sweat and grime. He thought about asking Joseph for a shirt and a pair of pants but Joseph was taller and thinner. No way would his clothes fit. So Henry decided to borrow some duds from the Wild One. He knew this would probably piss the old man off but he had no choice. He needed something to wear to the hospital.

Henry crept back down the stairs and along the hall to the sitting room just off the master bedroom. Three double-door closets occupied an entire hallway between the sitting room and the master bath. Henry found women's clothes in the first two closets, probably, he figured, belonging to the Wild One's new wife. In the third closet he found his father's rack. He chose a blue button-down shirt, a navy blue blazer, and seersucker slacks. He slipped on the slacks, buttoned up the oxford, and pulled on the jacket. The clothes fit perfectly. They could easily have been tailor-made for his own six foot, one-hundred-and-ninety-pound frame. He stole a quick look at himself in the full-length mirror. *Jesus*, he thought, *who the fuck's that asshole?* But before heading downstairs he slipped on a pair of thin cotton socks and Wild Bill's finest and favorite pair of Brooks Brothers patent leather loafers.

Joseph had showered, shaved, and snorted several thin lines of cocaine before heading downstairs. He hoped to reach the kitchen and maybe make a pass at Evangeline before the others started to reappear. But when he pushed open the swinging door and walked into the kitchen he found Rosa and Emily and John and Paul all singing *"Old MacDonald's Farm,"* and Evangeline snorting like a pig and baying like a horse. They all just laughed at the strange face he made and went right on singing. Joseph thought about going back up for another line of coke but decided that might not be a real good idea. Instead he filled a tall glass with ice, then raided the liquor closet off the dining room and poured Wild Bill's best bourbon to the brim.

Henry, as Bobby, looking very much like a younger version of the Wild One, reached the kitchen next. The singing stopped. Everyone took a double take. "Jesus," declared Joseph, "the old man rides again."

Henry managed a smile but then he took up his position in the corner and waited for whatever might happen next to happen.

"We can eat whenever you want," said Evangeline, "it's all ready."

"Then let's do it," said Joseph, "I'm starved."

"I'll go get Ginny and Mary," said Emily.

"No need for that," said Ginny, entering the kitchen in a fresh print dress, her teeth freshly brushed, her hair freshly combed, "I'm here now and Mary's sound asleep. I just looked in on her. We'll wake her before we leave for the hospital."

"But maybe she's hungry," said Joseph.

"Mary's never been much of an eater," said Ginny, taking her place at the head of the table. "Besides, if she's hungry we can stop on the way and get her a hamburger."

Joseph sipped the bourbon. "I don't think Mary eats meat."

"Then we'll find her something else."

The coke kept elbowing Joseph in the ribs, demanding he pursue the argument. But the bourbon held him steady, ordered him to put a lid on it.

Emily helped Evangeline put the food on the table. They sat down. The Winslows went after the chow like a pack of starving wolves.

Evangeline cleared her throat and asked, "Do you mind if we say grace?"

The Winslows stopped their furious movements quite suddenly and, for just a moment, they stared at sweet Evangeline. Some of their mouths hung open. Obviously grace was not a big part of their daily ritual. They had all been brought up reasonably well however. Their mother had taught them table manners and religious tolerance. Besides, who but a crazy person would object to someone desiring to say grace? Evangeline smiled and folded her hands. So did John and Paul. "Thank you, Lord," she said, her head now bowed, "for this feast and this day, and for the safe arrival of the family members around this table."

The Winslows waited. They thought there must be more. But that was all Evangeline wanted to say. "Amen," said Joseph.

"Amen," said the others.

Chapter Fourteen

●

Wild Bill lay in his hospital bed, alone and already sick of being bedridden, and wondered about the accuracy of his memory. Like that autumn morning some thirty years ago when he'd been sitting at the kitchen table just after dawn and out of nowhere those ten wild turkeys had walked up onto the back patio and started eating the sunflower seeds Virginia had put out for the finches and the chickadees. The kids started coming down for breakfast before heading off to school. Ginny and Mary and Henry and Bobby. Wild Bill told them about the turkeys. The kids looked out the window but saw nothing but a couple of sparrows. "Where did the turkeys go?" they asked. "Oh, you missed 'em," the Wild One said, "they're gone, long gone. Off gettin' ready to be some family's Thanksgiving feast." But now he wondered if the turkeys had really been there. *Or did I just imagine those turkeys, something to tell the kids, something to get them stirred up?* He couldn't remember. He couldn't be sure. He thought those turkeys had come up on the patio. He thought he'd seen them. *But maybe not. Maybe those turkeys had just been more of those damn mourning doves, always hanging around the feeders crapping and cooing and driving all the smaller birds away.*

For years the Wild One had been aware of his memory slipping; he forgot little things like his wallet and his dry cleaning and his kids' names. But far worse were the ambiguities; he could no longer remember which version of an event was the accurate version. The past was open to debate. *Did I knock Little Eddie down on his wedding night? No, I wouldn't have done that. I might've wanted to but I wouldn't have actually done it.*

Ever since Evangeline had left the hospital a few hours earlier,

Wild Bill had been slipping in and out of slumber and back and forth across time. He'd spent quite a while out in the western part of the state with the old Burlington branch of the Winslows. But now he'd jumped ahead a couple hundred years to those days just after he had buried his father back in the fall of '45.

Those had been tough times, maybe the toughest of his life. Not only had he lost most of his family to either death or emotional disease but it looked like he might lose the Winslow Compound as well. He had no job and no prospects of a job. He knew with his family connections and his college education and his excellent military record he could find something, but the salary would be miniscule, not nearly enough to pay off the debts incurred by Charles and Shady. And just to add fuel to the fire, he had winter coming on and almost no heating oil in the tank and an oil man who refused delivery until at least some of the several hundred dollars he was owed was paid. And of course the baby, the Wild One never for a moment forgot the baby. Virginia was due in just a few short months.

Wild Bill did not share these problems and anxieties with his young wife however. That was not his way. He kept everything inside, bottled up, stored away. How could he bring his new wife to this beautiful estate and then tell her there was no money, not a dime; in fact, they owed a quarter of a million dollars? How could he tell her that? He couldn't, and so he didn't.

For many days after he had put his father in the ground Wild Bill got up with the sun, put on his best suit, and walked the five miles down to the Far Hills train station. He walked not only to rid his body of its endless nervous energy but also because only one of the many family cars still ran and he did not want to leave Virginia up on the hill without transportation.

All day long he would ride the train back and forth between Far Hills and Hoboken. He would buy a round-trip ticket and the conductors would usually let him ride the rest of the day for free. They knew him. And they knew he had served his country for three years in the South Pacific. They knew he was a vet who had been through some tough times.

Wild Bill Winslow wasn't just sitting there on the train staring out the window feeling sorry for himself however. Occasionally he did some of that on a particularly bad day but most of the time he sat there thinking up ways to strike it rich, to make a killing. Winslow Cordage, he knew, was out. One day he had gotten off the train in Hoboken and walked over to the enormous factory old Crazy Legs had built half a century earlier. But the new owner was a nasty son of a bitch who told Wild Bill that his old man had been a stinking drunk. The Wild One thumped the bastard on the chest with his index finger and told him if he ever called Charles Winslow a stinking drunk again he'd bust his freaking head wide open. After that it seemed pretty clear the Winslows were out of the rope business for good. Unless of course Wild Bill started a whole new cordage company, which he had no intention of doing because first of all he had no capital, and second of all because he didn't know the first thing about making rope. The only thing he knew about rope was that it had made his grandfather, who might really have been his father, a wealthy man, and a length of it had made his father, who might actually have been his brother, dead.

Many entrepreneurial ideas came to Wild Bill during his days riding the Gladstone–Hoboken line. But the same two problems always put a whammy on his brainstorms: money and ignorance. He had virtually no cash and he knew next to nothing about almost everything. He had majored in American history at Lehigh so his educational skills were of little value. He had played a spirited tight end on the varsity football team but no way could he make it in the pro league. He knew how to hit a topspin forehand and how to drive a golf ball. He knew how to lead a bird and cast a fly. He knew how to drink whiskey and dance the Charleston. He knew how to kill Japs and stay alive in a war zone. He knew how to treat malaria and make the ladies laugh. But he didn't know how to make money. He had never learned that skill. There had always been plenty of money. And it was assumed there always would be plenty of money. (*We should remember the guy was only twenty-five years old. He had been raised in the lap of luxury. Excluding his three-year hitch with the United States Marine Corps the Wild One had never held a job or worked for wages.*)

Then one morning, a mile or so west of Summit, Wild Bill saw a crew of men framing out a new house. He could hear them pounding nails, shouting obscenities, sawing wood. He got off the train in Summit and walked back along the tracks until he found the house. For over an hour he watched the men work. They were installing roof rafters. One man cut the rafters down on the ground. Two others hauled the cut lumber into place. Then another man, must have been the boss because he kept barking orders, secured the rafters with nails and an endless stream of cuss words. The whole process fascinated the Wild One. The four-man crew worked in perfect unison, each one responsible for a single task, to get the job done quickly and efficiently.

Back on the train his brain went to work. All the way to Hoboken he visualized places along the tracks where land could be cleared, where houses could be built, where entire developments could be constructed. Recently he had read a magazine article about the growth of the suburbs. The author had predicted the late 1940s and the 1950s would be years of urban desertion. Families would be buying more and more cars and moving away from the cities, out into the country. New roads would be built, new schools, new shopping centers, new homes, lots and lots of new homes. These urban pioneers fleeing the cities would need housing. And not just brick apartment buildings but single-family dwellings with a picket fence and an attached garage and an acre of grass. This, the author wrote, would be the dream of every American family. The Wild One believed that dream and everywhere he looked out the train window he saw that dream transforming itself upon the landscape. Like anthills rising from ashes, he imagined he saw crews of men pouring concrete and erecting walls and installing doors and windows and toilet bowls.

By the time Wild Bill, now on his return to Far Hills, passed that new house west of Summit, the roof had been raised. The four-man crew sat out in the bright autumn sunshine laughing and eating their lunches out of metal lunch pails. The Wild One envied their work and their camaraderie. He missed his brothers and his youth. But as that train sped westward and that new house disappeared from view, Wild Bill found reason to smile. He made a fist with his right hand and pounded it into the palm of his left hand. *This is it goddammit,* he told himself, *this is definitely it.*

As soon as the train pulled into the Far Hills station Wild Bill hopped off the steps onto the platform and headed home. For the first time in weeks he had spring in his step. He ran a good deal of the way, even up those steep switchbacks on Old Post Road. He felt like a kid again, a college kid getting ready for the new season.

He opened the front door and stepped into the front hall and right away he heard the music. The music seemed to fill the entire house. He could not tell where it was coming from. It sounded like it came from everywhere.

"Virginia!" he shouted, but she did not answer. He looked for her in the living room and the dining room and out in the solarium. He couldn't find her but he could still hear the music. "Virginia!" He went up the wide front stairs, two at a time. The music grew even louder and more distinct. Down the hallway past his sister Helen's locked door the Wild One raced. And as he neared the master bedroom where he and Virginia had recently taken up residence, the music approached a crescendo. It was wonderful, beautiful, exhilarating. He could hardly believe his ears. And then he stood in the doorway and saw his pregnant young wife standing on the other side of the bedroom in front of those floor-to-ceiling windows fiddling as though her fingers were on fire. She had her back to the door so she could not see him. Plus she was far too involved with the music to hear his arrival. The Wild One waited silently while the music peaked then trailed off into a slow pulse and finally stopped. She was startled by his applause.

"My God, Virginia! What was that?"

"You didn't like it?"

"Like it!? It was incredible, unbelievable!" The Wild One was smiling broadly and moving toward his wife. "Christ, you never told me you could fiddle. What was it?"

"Mozart," she said proudly. "The opening movement from his Twenty-ninth Symphony."

"Mozart! Jesus!" He still smiled but at the same time he had tears in his eyes, tears running down his cheeks, tears streaming off his chin. "My God, Virginia, play it again! Play it forever!"

Tears came to Wild Bill again as he lay in his hospital bed and recalled that day in November of '45 when he had first heard his wife play the violin. He had begged her to play more but only after he promised to listen from out in the sitting room did she bring the instrument up under her chin and begin again. For the next several hours he sat out in the sitting room smiling and weeping and thanking some God he did not really know or have faith in for giving him a wife who could not only cook and laugh and make love but who could play Mozart on the fiddle as well.

Virginia's mother, who died before Virginia became a teenager, had been an excellent violinist. Her dream was that one day her only daughter would play with the New York Philharmonic. Every spare dime the Mullers had went into Virginia's musical training. She was gifted, extremely gifted, that much was obvious from the age of seven, but she had one rather pressing problem, a sort of tragic flaw: the audience. Young Virginia Muller could not stand to play in front of an audience. Even her own music teacher made her nervous. At her first recital she fainted from stage fright. At her second recital her right hand grew so shaky she could hardly hold the bow. More than once it fell right out of her hand. Virginia ran off the stage, tears running down her face. Several months later she tried again but with the same results. She suffered from acute stage fright. Alone in her room she could play like an angel but put the poor girl out on stage and she might as well have been there to mop up the floor after the performers had finished for the evening. By the age of twelve, just a few months before her mother's sudden and inexplicable death, the Mullers made the decision to discontinue Virginia's musical education. She could play the violin all she wanted in the privacy of her own bedroom, but never again would demands be made upon her to play in front of an audience.

Wild Bill sat out in the sitting room and listened to the music. The music cleared his thoughts, made him feel strong and powerful. He knew the music was a sure sign that his decision to build was a good decision, a sound decision, the right decision. He had nothing to fear. He had the music. He had Virginia. He had the energy and he had the guts. Now all he had to do was work, work his ass off.

And so early the next morning, instead of putting on his suit and walking down to the train station, Wild Bill pulled on some old work clothes, dug out the boundary map of the Winslow Compound from his father's desk, and spent the morning walking the property line. By noon he had made his decision; the first real business decision of his life. He went back to the house for lunch and to find the chain saw his brother Henry had bought before the war.

It might be a good idea to pause here for a few moments and take a look at this chunk of real estate Crazy Legs had purchased in 1888. He called it the Compound. It contained three hundred and twenty acres, most of which in 1945 was still covered with forest. Really only about twelve acres surrounding the house had been turned into lawns and gardens. There was a thirty-acre field out behind the hay barn where Crazy Legs had for a while grown alfalfa. But when Wild Bill made his survey in November of '45 that hay field was nothing but a tangle of weeds and groundhog holes. Most of the rest of the Compound was covered with white oaks and northern red oaks, sugar maples and silver maples, black walnuts and American chestnuts, flowering dogwoods and mountain laurel, white ash and black ash, eastern white pines and northern red pines, eastern hemlocks, and even a stand or two of black spruce.

The property was shaped like an enormous irregular rectangle. It ran straight along the ridge road for almost three-quarters of a mile. Plenty of frontage for someone desiring to subdivide. Then the line followed the lay of the land more or less straight back for a good half mile on both sides. Up along the road the land was high and flat but then it began to dip, gently at first, then more steeply. On the east side it bordered the Middleston estate. On the west side it ran for a while along the Englehard line but then it met up with the switchback road running up the mountain. It was here the Wild One decided to build his first house. He knew his decision to chop off a piece of the Compound would probably cause Crazy Legs to turn over in his grave. But it was either give up a small parcel down in the southwest corner or else face losing the whole damn shootin' match. And the thing was, Crazy Legs wasn't even dead. He was still going strong at eight-two; Wild Bill just didn't know it yet.

Forty-five years later the Wild One could still see himself as he trudged through those wet, dreary November woods carrying that massive cast-steel chain saw, its blade as dull as a butter knife. One of the original Homelites, it must've weighed thirty-five or forty pounds. But the Wild One knew the saw worked because back in the barn he had, after nearly a hundred pulls on the cord, finally managed to kick the engine into operation. But within seconds of beginning to fell his first tree, a small red oak, he realized the teeth on the blade needed sharpening. So he tramped back to the barn, and finally, after a forty-minute search, he found the appropriate file. He hiked back to the job site, sharpened the blade, and went to work. He brought down that red oak and a good-sized silver maple before the saw ran out of fuel. Then back to the barn for the gas can which he knew he should've brought along when he went back for the damn file. He refueled the saw but then couldn't get it restarted. He pulled and pulled on the cord until finally he pulled the line right off its spindle. Then he cursed and kicked the saw and the blade spun around and bit through his pants into his calf and the blood spurted out all the way back up to the house, nearly three-quarters of a mile away; all of it uphill through wild roses and brush and brambles. . . .

The Wild One smiled, as hindsight will allow one to do, and then he dozed while still remembering that first day, his first day on the job, his first day as a builder. Then he was asleep, sort of asleep, his eyes half-closed, and he saw his ancestor Freeman Winslow more than three hundred years earlier on *his* first day on the job, *his* first day as a farmer, *his* first day building a brand-new house for himself and his new bride Eleanor. Freeman owned a dull ax and a shiny new crosscut saw and a beautiful view of the Delaware River a few miles north of Burlington. Freeman, like Wild Bill, had never cut down a tree before. In his first hour on the job he split the handle of his ax when he mishit the trunk of a rock-hard shagbark hickory. In his second hour on the job, while sawing through the soft wood of an old and gnarled eastern white pine, Freeman failed to angle his cut. Halfway through the trunk the blade got pinched by the weight of the tree. Freeman couldn't move the blade an eighth of an inch in either direction. He couldn't drive it in and he couldn't pull it out. He tried pounding a wedge into the side of the cut but one good blow with his already split ax handle broke the wood right in two. Then it started to rain, really rain. Great sheets of water swept out of the sky. Then thunder and lightning exploded over the river. Freeman ran for cover. He ran all the way back to Burlington where his new wife Eleanor was safe and dry in their rented rooms. She welcomed her man home and while he put on dry breeches she made him some tea and something to eat. After supper, the storm still close, the newlyweds made love. It was the first time they'd ever made love in the middle of the afternoon. They didn't realize it during their tussle but during that storm their eldest, who would nine months and a few weeks later be brought smiling to the Society of Friends Meeting House on Delaware Street in Burlington bearing the name Henry Lane Winslow, was conceived. They named the boy Henry Lane in memory of Eleanor's father whose hard work, unfortunate death, and generous bequest had made their family farm in the New World possible.

The storm lasted for two days. For two full days the rain fell in torrents. The muddy banks of the Delaware overflowed. Roads were ruined, crops and houses destroyed. Over nine inches fell from the heavens. And on the third day, when Freeman finally returned to his homestead, he found his brand-new crosscut saw still pinched under the weight of that giant white pine, its not-long-ago-gleaming iron blade now brown and corroded with rust.

But Freeman, like his descendant in the middle of the twentieth century, persevered. He refused to let a little thing like ignorance hold him back. He overcame his ignorance first with hard work and then with a shrewd ability to get other people to do the work for him. In the last decades of the 1600s, with peace and prosperity sweeping the proprietary colony of New Jersey, Freeman Winslow became not only a successful farmer employing as many as thirty hired hands, but he also started one of the colony's first profitable sawmills. He learned everything he could about cutting and milling trees into lumber. Freeman became an affluent and well-respected man in the community. Others sought his council and advice both in business matters and in church affairs. He became, like his wife, a devout Quaker, a Child of the Light. Not too many days went by that Freeman did not silently thank his wife for unlocking the heavy shackles of Puritanism.

Eleanor gave birth to a dozen babies. Seven died before their fifth birthday. Another died at the age of eleven from a rattlesnake bite. Of the four children to reach adulthood, one was, of course, Henry Lane, who would sire the Winslow line into the eighteenth century.

The Wild One awoke to the emotional pull of nostalgia. He knew well the story of the Burlington Winslows before the Revolution. As a kid he'd heard some of the legends from old Crazy Legs, and years later he had learned some of the facts from his daughter Mary. He knew the Burlington Winslows had been held together by the land for four generations before being ripped apart by a war for economic independence and self-rule. Four generations lived in the same house, under the same roof, on the same swell of good earth. Four generations lived their lives on the banks of the Delaware. From Freeman's first felled tree in 1679 to the disastrous fire fueled by frenzied Patriots in 1776, the Winslows held their ground. One hundred years of relative calm. *It was the goddamn land held them together,* Wild Bill told no one but himself, *the goddamn land and the strength of the family line. That much I know for sure; that much I know is true.* . . .

"Excuse me," asked the nurse as she entered his room, "did you say something?"

Wild Bill brought himself back. "I said you got a great-looking behind, sweetie, and if you mosey on over here I'll give it a squeeze that'll make us both happy."

"The hell you will," she said without smiling.

"Why not?" the Wild One asked. "Don't you want to make an old man happy?"

"You have visitors," she said, checking his chart, "a whole busload. Try hard and maybe one of them will make you happy."

Chapter Fifteen

Their next disagreement concerned the mode of transport to the hospital. Once again it was Joseph and Ginny who faced off. Emily sided with Ginny. Mary sided with Joseph. Henry, as Bobby, kept his mouth shut. Not only did he want to avoid making enemies but this whole thing about going to see the old man had him stepping on thin sheets of plate glass.

After supper Evangeline had herded the Winslow children out the back door, insisting she and John and Paul would wash the dishes and tidy up the kitchen. "It's getting late," she said, "it's after seven already."

So the five siblings and little Rosa went out the back door and gathered in the driveway. "So how are we getting there?" asked Joseph.

"I hadn't thought about that," answered Ginny.

"I guess we'll just have to make a selection from Wild Bill's auto mall," said Joseph.

"That'll make him happy," mumbled Henry, who, as a teenager, had busted up more than one of the family cars.

"He'll never know," said Joseph.

Almost to himself Henry added, "Oh, he'll know, believe me, he'll know." Like that time before Henry had his driver's license. He decided to borrow the family car one night after everyone had gone to bed and drive down to the shore with a couple of his buddies. They went to Seaside, partied, drank beer, got home not too long before dawn. Everything went fine. No problems. But that night at dinner Wild Bill casually asked, after passing the potatoes, "So how'd the car run, kid?" Henry answered by turning bright red and dropping the bowl of potatoes on the floor. A couple of hours later Wild Bill showed up at the door of the third-floor bedroom. Henry was in there checking out the new *Playboy*. The Wild One didn't bother to knock. "Take it out again, kid, before you're legal and without my permission and I'll nail you by your accelerator foot to the barn door." He turned to leave, then added over his shoulder, "And don't pull your jerky too often, boy, you'll go blind."

"So which car should we take?" asked Ginny.

They ended up taking Evangeline's Nissan pickup because they couldn't locate the keys to any of the cars in Wild Bill's fleet and Ginny absolutely refused to ride in Bobby's, really Henry's, 1964 Ford F-100. The three sisters sat in the cab with Emily behind the wheel. Mary didn't have a driver's license and Ginny didn't know how to drive a manual transmission. The brothers sat in back with little Rosa huddled between them.

"So Bob," asked Joseph as the pickup pulled out of the driveway onto the ridge road, "how's life in the Adirondacks treatin' you?"

It may have still been spring but that infamous New Jersey heat and humidity were already working overtime. Evening had arrived but the air felt more like early August at high noon: hot and steamy. Thunderstorms had been predicted by local weathermen, but they had been making similar predictions all week.

The air felt clammy and close in the bed of the pickup. Henry could feel the sweat developing in his armpits. "Pretty good," he answered, "I can't complain."

"So what do you do up there for excitement?"

Henry, as Bobby, managed a smile. "Well, let's see. In the spring we barbecue black flies, in the summer we raise mosquitoes, in the fall we complain about the coming of winter, and in the winter, well, we just try to keep from drinking ourselves to an early grave."

Joseph laughed. So did Rosa. "No, really, what do you do up there for kicks?"

"Well hell, I don't know...we go fishin' and huntin' and—"

"Bobby Winslow, a hunter? I know Henry used to go hunting with Wild Bill once in a while but Mama always called you the pacifist of the family."

Henry shrugged, mumbled, "You gotta stay alive." He wanted to tell his kid brother right then and there, right there in the back of that pickup with his little niece listening, that he in fact was not Bobby Winslow but the long-thought-dead Henry Winslow. But of course he couldn't tell them, not right then, not right there. "Most of the meat we eat I bring down with my shotgun. Hunting's a primitive pleasure. Especially when you gotta do it to put food on the table. Course sometimes we get say a family of 'coons or a stray fox or a coyot' botherin' the garden or the garbage or the cats or the kids, and then I go out and shoot 'em just to be rid of 'em. Not to eat 'em understand, but just to be finished with 'em."

Joseph listened, nodded. "Kids? As in plural?"

"Right."

"I knew you had one, a girl. How many others do you have?"

"One other girl. Plus a third one in the oven. I'm hoping for a boy this time."

Joseph whistled softly. He sat back and tried to deal with the fact that he didn't really know at all this guy, his brother, sitting beside him.

"Are they like me?" asked Rosa. "Are they my age?"

"Constance is just about your age. Katie's a little older."

"How come I never saw them?"

"Well," answered Henry, as Bobby, and then couldn't think of anything to say, "I don't know. Just because I guess." He turned away from his niece and his brother and looked out at the trees rushing past along the side of the road.

A pretty substantial pause followed before little Rosa said, "Oh well, maybe I'll see them soon."

Up front Ginny and Emily chatted across Mary. "I can't believe Bobby actually came," said Emily. "I was shocked when I first saw him."

"Me too," said Ginny. "Doesn't he look funny in those clothes? He's the spitting image of Daddy when Daddy was that age."

"He's so serious. I can't believe how serious he looks all the time."

"I think he's pretty uncomfortable. I mean, none of us have laid eyes on him since Mama died, and that's almost fifteen years ago."

Emily glanced in the rearview mirror at her older brother. "Well, I hope he loosens up some pretty soon. He's been staring at me ever since I got here. He's got a set of eyes on him like the old winos wandering up and down Park Avenue."

"Maybe, Emily," suggested Mary, her sarcasm vaguely concealed, "he's just in awe of his little sister's beauty."

"Oh aren't you funny, Mary?"

This brief exchange cut off the flow of conversation for the next several miles. The three sisters stared straight ahead and listened to the air conditioner hum. While a thousand miles away brother Barton lay drowsing in a hospital bed just outside of Waycross, Georgia, with painkilling narcotics floating through his bloodstream and Beethoven's Third Symphony pounding against his temples. While two hundred miles away brother Edward listened to Mendelssohn's Piano Concerto No. 1 and made the decision without his wife's knowledge to head south once Samantha had fallen asleep. While hundred of millions of phantom light-years away sister Helen, who some thought should have been Mary, and brother Bobby, who everyone still thought was Henry, made plans to visit the old homestead just to see what mischief might arise. While three hundred or more miles away stepmother Bettina spoke at great length long distance with her great and good friend Millicent from Newport, Rhode Island, and learned that Millicent's third husband Lawrence had just run off to Monaco with their Polish chauffeur Stan. While less than a dozen miles away father Willy called his darling Angel and told her he loved her and worshipped her and longed to be in her arms, tight against her sweet sweet breast. While that same darling Angel asked her Billy Boy not to say such things, someone might be listening at the door. He laughed and whispered something about her sweetspot. She ignored him, told him they were on their way and that he should be pleasant and polite; they had all traveled many miles to see him. He assured her he would be the benevolent papa and then he told her again he loved her and worshipped her and would be doing everything in his power in the days and weeks ahead to make his Angel his wife and those boys his legitimate heirs.

As soon as the nurse whose butt he had tried to pinch left the room, Wild Bill, with an incredible amount of pain and discomfort, pulled himself up and out of that hospital bed and hobbled over to the door. The guy had a busted ankle, a dislocated shoulder, and a couple of hard-boiled-egg-sized bumps on top of his head, but still he hobbled over to the door. He pulled it open a hair and peered up and down the corridor in search of his offspring. All day he had wondered who would show, who would make the trip. He had started to ask Evangeline on the telephone but then decided to wait. He wanted it to be a surprise.

The Wild One watched and waited and tried to ignore the pain pounding against just about every muscle and joint in his body. And then, finally, just when he thought he might have to greet them from bed, he saw them, six of them, a regular army, coming slowly and cautiously down the hallway, not in formation but sort of ragtag; Ginny leading the way, and all of them trying, except little Rosa, not to stare into the open doorways of the sick and disabled; all of them glancing at the numbers over the doors, draw ing closer, their mouths closed, their faces taut, serious, almost solemn. The Wild One ducked back into his room, lowered him self facedown onto the floor, paused until he felt sure they were nearly upon him, and then, beating back the pain, he raised him self up on his one good arm into the push-up position. With his broken right ankle raised off the floor and the arm connected to to his dislocated shoulder hanging limp at his side, Wild Bill Winslow had to perform three excruciatingly painful push-ups before Ginny and Joseph stuck their heads through the doorway.

"Daddy?"

"W. B.! Christ! What're you doing?"

Then, all at once, the others reached the doorway. They strained to see what had their siblings all riled up. Emily and Mary peered over their older sister's shoulder, little Rosa between Joseph's legs, and Henry, as Bobby, in back, over everyone else's head. They all stared in disbelief at their father, the Wild One, whom they thought closer than not to death's door, flat out on the hard linoleum floor, doing push-ups of all things.

Wild Bill did two more just for the show of it, and then, purging the pain from his face, he struggled to his feet. It hurt too much to smile even though that's what he wanted to do. "Why hell's fire," he boomed, "now what's that damn cat dragged in?"

"Daddy," demanded Ginny, "what are you doing out of bed?"

The Wild One felt just about ready to collapse. He worked his way back toward the bed. "Hell, child, I'm just gettin' a little exercise is all. A man'll shrivel up and die lyin' around on his butt all day."

Ginny entered the room. She stood a few feet from her father. She tried to help him but some sort of invisible wall kept them apart, prevented them from actually touching. "We just saw the doctor, Daddy. He told us you need complete bed rest for at least a month."

The others continued to stand in the open doorway with both their eyes and their mouths hanging wide open.

"You're not even supposed to get out of bed for a week. You have to give your ankle and your head time to heal. You have a concussion. You were unconscious." Young Virginia was positively beside herself. "And we walk in here and you're doing push-ups!"

Wild Bill had made it back to bed by this time. He used all the strength he could muster to get himself settled. Then, his mission complete, he took a deep breath and asked, "So, how the hell is everyone? I didn't expect all of you to show up just because I took a little tumble down the back stairs. You might think I'd gone and died or something."

A pretty fair pause filled the room while everyone sought to reestablish their equilibrium. "The doctor, Daddy," said Ginny, finally, "I'm trying to tell you what the doctor told us."

"I've already heard it from the horse's mouth, kid. But what does he know? Thinks he knows every damn thing. Tells me he went to Harvard. You think I'm going to trust some punk doctor from Harvard?"

"You're not twenty years old anymore, Father," lectured Ginny, climbing that invisible wall, reaching the bedside, and pulling the sheet up over the Wild One's arms.

"You're telling me."

"I'm telling you what the doctor told me—told us—and he says you're not supposed to do anything for the next several weeks."

"Ginny, hey," said Joseph, taking a couple steps into the room, "give the guy a break, he was just doing a few push-ups."

"Twenty-five, if you're interested," lied the Wild One, just to see if maybe he could raise a little ruckus.

"You did twenty-five push-ups?" asked Emily. "God, after talking to the doctor I thought we'd walk in here and see you lying there with all kinds of tubes and wires and stuff sticking out of you."

"Not this old-timer, kid," said Wild Bill. He knew now the push-up display had been a bad idea. The pain raced through his body as though he were being tortured with a cow prod.

Little Rosa stepped past her aunts and uncles and mother and crossed to the bed. "Hi, Grandad," she said, "I'm glad to see you're not so sick as maybe you could have been." She climbed up onto the bed, hugged the big man as best she could around his broad shoulders, and then she kissed him flush on the lips.

The Wild One winced from the pain in his shoulder, but then he smiled and kissed his granddaughter back. "Thanks, Rosie. You're a good kid, one of a kind."

For a long moment the others did nothing. Undoubtedly they all felt the pull of paternity, the need to give their father a warm, physical greeting. But none of them seemed capable of acting on their desires. They had for far too long been conditioned not to touch.

Finally Emily, the youngest, crossed to the bed, but only to take Rosa by the arm. "Grandad's been injured, Rosa, you have to be careful. He needs special attention."

"Horse shit," growled the Wild One. "My granddaughter can climb up on top of me and give a hug any old time her little heart desires. You might do the same, Emily. I promise I won't bite you."

Emily hesitated, then leaned over and kissed her father quickly on the forehead.

"What the hell was that," he boomed, "a goddamn gnat? Did a gnat just light on my forehead? If you're gonna do it, do it. Don't do it halfway. Halfway's like half-assed, nothing but a waste of time and talent."

Henry remembered hearing that line before, or at least a variation of it, years earlier, back when he was still in high school. The Wild One had come to one of his football practices. He'd watched from the sidelines for half an hour or so and then, right in the middle of a scrimmage, he walked out onto the gridiron after a third down and long. He walked right past the coaches and the other players, right up to his son, right up to his son's face mask and said, "If you're gonna block, boy, block. Don't block halfway. Blocking halfway is like kissing ass and football ain't about kissing ass."

Henry wanted to tell that story but after mumbling an inaudible word or two he remembered Bobby had never played football. So he clammed up and tried to fade into the background.

But the Wild One had ears like an eastern white-tailed deer. "What's that? You there in the back, what did you say? Who is that stranger anyway? Step up and be accounted for, man."

Fuck you, dude, thought Henry. He took a cautious step or two into the hospital room.

That's when Wild Bill saw the duds. "Nope," he said, shaking his head, "I don't know who you are, but that coat and that shirt and those pants and them fancy patent leather shoes sure look familiar. We must shop at the same store."

Henry decided to laugh. The laugh fizzled but he did manage to take a few more steps toward the bed. "Hi, Dad," he said, sticking out his hand, "I was in kind of a hurry to get down here. Forgot all about packing any clean clothes. So I thought it might be okay if I borrowed some of your—"

"That voice," shouted the Wild One, "that voice, I know that voice. Could it be, is it possible that this formidable individual standing over me is one of my offspring, in fact my oldest surviving male heir?" The Wild One reached out his hand. Henry, as Bobby, took it. Wild Bill squeezed. Henry squeezed back. Both were surprised by the other's strength but neither was willing to show it. The Wild One squeezed a little harder. Henry retaliated. While the others watched and waited. All of them, even little Rosa, felt the tension. No one said a word. The squeezing business continued. Father versus son. Man versus man. Ego versus ego. Henry wanted the squeezing to stop because he knew he had an unfair advantage. Not only was he thirty years younger but his father had just been hospitalized. He was impressed with the Wild One's strength but at the same time he knew if he really wanted to he could break every bone in his father's hand. Wild Bill too wanted the squeezing to stop, partly because of the pain but mostly because it represented everything he wanted to avoid. *Cooperation and reconciliation, not confrontation.* That was Wild Bill's theme for this reunion. He wanted to heal old wounds, bury old hatchets. But even as he reminded himself of this he kept squeezing. It was like the push-ups. He wouldn't give up, wouldn't give in. *This is gonna be a bitch,* he told himself. *Maybe you can't teach an old Marine Corps dog new tricks.*

So both father and son wanted to stop squeezing but neither would be the first. It finally took little Rosa to ask, "Why are they hurting each other, Mommy?" before father and son laughed and let go.

Then Wild Bill, trying like the devil not to rub his hand, said, "Damn nice grip you've got there, boy. It's hard to believe you're the same kid who used to be afraid to come out of the house. I think in a fair fight you might even be able to lick the old man."

Henry smiled but thought, *I could bust you in two old man, break every goddamn bone in your body.*

The nurse with the fine but untouchable buttocks appeared at the door, and immediately up went her hackles. "What's this? You can't all be in here at the same time. You think this is a motel room or something? Two visitors at a time. No more than two at a time. That's the rule. The rest will have to wait out in the lounge."

"Take it easy there, honey," said Wild Bill. "Your blood pressure's going through the roof. This is my family, part of it anyway. They've come a long way to see their old man and about the only way they can handle me is in a group, en masse. Security in numbers. Get it? So why don't you take those sweet buns of yours out into the hallway and pretend like you never saw this mob."

But the nurse, who'd had a domineering father and a first lover who had been orally fixated, despised men, especially men who pinched her on the ass and told her what to do. So conflict ensued, resulting in the expulsion of all but two Winslows at a time from the Wild One's room. Emily and young Rosa visited first.

"So, kid," Wild Bill asked his youngest, "how's everything? How's the big city treating you?"

Emily had not yet told the others her news. She wanted the Wild One to be the first to know. "I think I got a part," she said.

"Not another commercial for feminine douche, I hope."

"No, Daddy, this is a real part."

"I'm listening."

"Well, there was this guy, see, who wrote these plays like three hundred years ago. I think you've probably heard of him. They sometimes call him The Bard."

"Yeah?" Emily had his attention now.

"Well, he wrote this one play about this king. And this king had these three daughters."

"Yeah?"

"And one of the daughters was named Cordelia."

"Yeah?"

"Yeah. And, well, now some people have gotten together and decided to put this play on again. Over in Central Park. And they're pretty sure they want me to play Cordelia."

"Pretty sure?"

"Real sure," said Rosa. "Mommy's gonna be Cordelia. She wants us all to call her that."

The Wild One smiled at his granddaughter. He was happy for the brief reprieve. "This isn't one of those 'Don't call us, we'll call you' things?"

"No, Daddy, I saw the director this morning. He told me I'm on top of the list. He wants a fresh face... I have to call him tomorrow."

Why King Lear? Wild Bill wondered. *Why not* MacBeth *or* The Merry Wives of Windsor *or* A Midsummer Night's Dream? *Why* Lear?... Long ago he had promised himself he would never see that play again. It was *Lear* they had seen the night of the accident. And it was Cordelia Wild Bill and Virginia had been talking about when that Rolls-Royce had rolled up onto the sidewalk outside of their Fifth Avenue apartment. The Wild One had been wondering aloud why he could not have a daughter whose love was pure and simple and uncompromised. And Virginia, not a full minute before she ceased to live, told her husband, "We get the love we deserve, Will." Those were her last words. Wild Bill remembered those words and then he realized he had to say something, something positive, something encouraging. "Well that's great, kid, really great. I mean it. We'll keep our fingers crossed.... It's an excellent part."

Emily assured herself the strange look in her father's eyes had something to do with his fall down the back stairs. She had expected him to react with far more enthusiasm. "You'll be there opening night, right? I'll make sure you're front row center."

Wild Bill nodded. He wanted to ask his daughter if she knew her mother had died less than an hour after watching a performance of *King Lear*. But instead he smiled and answered, "I'll be there, kid. Don't worry about that. I'll be there come hell or high water."

Emily smiled her best little-girl smile.

"Now why don't you take Rosa down to the cafeteria and buy her a milkshake. And on your way down send in a couple more of those boneheaded brothers and sisters of yours."

So Emily and Rosa said their good-byes and hope-you-feel-betters and see-you-tomorrows and then in came Ginny and Mary. Mary gave the Wild One a hug and a kiss on the cheek. "Hello, Father."

Wild Bill returned the embrace. "Well well, who have we here?

Our Old World emissary? Hello, Mary. Visited any of the family ghosts lately?"

Mary smiled. "Sounds to me like you were very nearly one of the family ghosts, Father."

"No way, not me, kid. You know the old saying, 'Old soldiers never die.'"

"Yes, I know it. But I like the second part better: 'They just fade away.'"

"I don't plan on fading away either. When the time comes I'm going out with gusto."

"Like Crazy Legs?"

"Well, maybe not exactly like Crazy Legs. But no way will a flight of stairs do me in."

"No, I suppose not. It wouldn't be fitting."

"Be downright cowardly."

"Let's not forget grandfather Charles, Father. God rest his soul."

"Always has to be one in the crowd, Mary. Keeps the rest of us on our toes."

"Hmm."

"Anyway, I'm glad you've come. Will you stay a while?"

"I'll stay until it's all out in the open."

"That may take some time."

Mary thought it over. "Yes, I suspect it will. But then, it's been a long time coming."

Ginny had been listening from over by the window. "What's going on? What are you two babbling about? You both sound so ominous."

"We're talking about things," said Mary, "that we don't really need to talk about."

"What does that mean?"

The Wild One, recovered now from his push-ups, let loose one of his better laughs. "We're talking about things we already know, Ginny, old girl. And if there's one thing your little sister Mary hates to do it's talk about things she already knows. So tell us something we don't know. Tell us how that Jewish baby doctor of yours is."

"Aaron is fine, Daddy. He even sends his best. Why, I don't know."

"Because he loves his father-in-law. Thinks the world of me. Sees in me the essence of honesty and integrity."

"He sees in you a bigot and an anti-Semite."

"No longer, girl. Not me. Once, maybe, but no longer. I've turned over a new leaf, seen a new day shine. Had a talk with God and He told me not to give a damn about a man's race, creed, or color."

"Oh yeah," asked Ginny, "so what happened? Did you have a religious experience while falling down the stairs?"

"Nope. We had our little chat long before that. I've seen the angels, kid. And they look pretty good to me."

"I think maybe they shot you up with some kind of hallucinogenic painkiller, Father."

The Wild One let loose with another booming laugh. "They shot me up with the most powerful painkiller of all."

"Oh, and what's that?"

"Stick around, maybe you'll find out."

"What's that supposed to mean? More of these things you know and I don't?"

Wild Bill shrugged his shoulders. "Anyone heard from that loving wife of mine?"

"Evangeline said she spoke to her," answered Ginny. "Supposedly she's on her way."

"Ah yes," whispered the Wild One, "Evangeline."

Ginny and Mary traded looks.

"She let us use her truck," said Mary. "We couldn't find the keys to any of the cars."

The Wild One drifted off for a moment but then, "The keys, yes. You can find them hanging on the back of the closet door in the front hall. And please, use the cars, even the Benz. I don't give a damn. Use them and enjoy them."

Another silent glance passed between Mary and Ginny.

"Oh, by the way," said Ginny, after a moment, "Barton would be here also except he's had a small accident."

"What do you mean, a small accident?"

Ginny told her father about the telephone call from Georgia.

Wild Bill listened and as he listened his face changed. It turned from a smile to a frown. And then his tone made a hundred-and-eighty-degree turn. "Are you telling me your brother's in some hick hospital in the Deep South and none of you have made arrangements yet to go down there and get him out?"

"Daddy," insisted Ginny, "there's nothing we can do. The nurse told me to call in the morning. We can talk to Barton's doctor then and get a firsthand report on his con—"

"Bullshit," interrupted the Wild One. "The first rule of war is, when your buddy goes down you get him out of the line of fire."

"What?" asked Ginny, her expression one of disbelief.

Mary watched quietly, said nothing, believed all.

"You heard me," said Wild Bill.

"He's not in the line of fire, Daddy. He's in the hospit—"

"Bullshit." The Wild One pulled himself up with his good arm and settled back against the headboard of the bed. "Send those two jerkoff sons of mine in here. I've got a few things to tell them."

Ginny tried to protest but Mary was already out the door. "Don't argue," she said, "we'll see him tomorrow."

Ginny fumed all the way down the hallway. "I swear to God, sometimes I hate that man."

Mary said nothing. She knew hate was as primeval as survival. The smart money never would've mentioned Barton's accident to the old man.

The moment Joseph and Henry, as Bobby, entered the room the Wild One launched his attack. "Both you jackasses knew your brother was beaten up by rednecks down in Georgia?"

Innocently, they both nodded. "Yeah," said Joseph, "sure, we knew about it."

"And you made no plans to go down there and bring him out?"

"Christ, Dad," said Joseph, "it's not like the guy's in Beirut or El Salvador or something. The Civil War ended a hundred and twenty-five years ago."

"Bullshit."

"Yeah, okay, bullshit. But actually I did suggest when we first got word of the accident, and Bobby here backed me up on this, that one of us fly down there and at least give Barton some moral support."

"Yeah, so why didn't you?"

"Ginny nixed it. She said first we should—"

"What do you mean, Ginny nixed it? You let your damn sister order you around? What are you, some kind of faggot? I want you two on a plane to Georgia first thing tomorrow morning. We're talking here about your own brother, not some stranger. Now get the hell out of my sight and don't come back till you've got

Barton with you. I don't care if you have to bring him home on a stretcher."

They headed for the door without a word.

"Jesus H. Christ," the Wild One added, loud enough to be heard out in the lounge, "I sure hope peace prevails, that the commies keep thinking democracy is the only game in town. I'd hate to rely on those two jerkoffs to defend this country."

Joseph laughed all the way down the hallway. He poked his brother in the ribs. "Hey, Bob, welcome home. Nice to see things have changed, huh?"

Henry, as Bobby, seething but trying hard not to let it show, just shook his head and kept on walking.

Chapter Sixteen

Maybe one of the reasons the world's so screwed up, and I think, reader, you know what I mean when I say this, is because, for all of mankind's technical genius and superabundant brainpower, he still hasn't learned to harness the flapping of his lips. We babble like babes all through our lives. We cry and scream and shout and make demands. Like the Wild One's reaction to news of Barton's hospitalization. Let's face it, the guy overreacted. And he knew it, couldn't deny it. Immediately after his sons had left his room, he wished he had busted his jaw in that fall down the back stairs. That way he would not have been able to talk; therefore he would not have been able to so quickly lose his temper; therefore he might not have alienated his kids ten minutes after their arrival. You stupid a-hole, he told himself, you'll never learn.

His mind wandering, his thoughts of sweet Evangeline mixing with memories of his long-lost Virginia, the Wild One dozed. He dreamed the two women were one. It was Evangeline who stood in the kitchen preparing supper that evening in the autumn of 1945 when he walked in bleeding after cutting himself with the chainsaw. It was Virginia he saw at that moment he opened his eyes after falling down the back stairs. It was Evangeline who cleaned and wrapped the cut on his calf. And Virginia who sat sleeping in the chair beside his hospital bed last night when he awoke startled and disoriented. Evangeline who stayed up most of that chilly autumn night listening to his ideas and his dreams. Virginia who listened to those ideas and dreams revisited and redefined.

And then, thinking sleep surrounded him but actually fully awake, the Wild One remembered more about the early days of his budding construction empire. Day to day, week to week, even month to month, it seemed like little happened, nothing much got accomplished, a few windows were installed, a couple doors hung, maybe the bathtub hooked up to the plumbing. But then one day that house down in the hollow in the southeast corner of the Winslow Compound stood complete and ready for occupation. The Wild One had learned plenty during its construction. He had never imagined building a house would be so complicated, so detail oriented. Subcontractors had performed most of the construction stages from framing and roofing right through plumbing and painting and electric. But Wild Bill had been on hand every step of the way: mixing concrete, pouring footings, pounding nails, ordering materials, obtaining the proper permits from town hall, organizing work schedules, and otherwise dealing with the daily crises that inevitably arose. He had designed the house himself and then had the plans drawn up by a professional architect in Bernardsville. The house sold just after the framing had been completed, about four months after the Wild One had cut down that first red oak. A young couple, about the same ages as Wild Bill and Virginia, first saw the new house while out for a Sunday drive. Their names were Bowen and Patricia Blackwell. Bowen, like the Wild One, had served in the United States Marine Corps in the South Pacific. The month before enlisting in the Corps Bowen had finished his law degree at Columbia University. Now, the war over, he was ready to start his own practice. The Blackwells were also ready to buy their first house. They made Bill Winslow an offer that very Sunday and within a few weeks a contract had been drawn up and signed.

Bowen and Wild Bill hit it off immediately, a pair of ambitious young ex-leathernecks with the same dream: money, power, family, and peace. Not too long after they signed the contract on the house, Bill Winslow became Bowen Blackwell's first client. And for the next thirty-six years Bowen advised Wild Bill on the complex and sometimes ruthless legal strategies of real estate law. He would no doubt be advising him still if not for the plane crash in the summer of 1981. While flying to their summer house out on Martha's Vineyard in their small Cessna along with Thomas and Pamela Pennington, Evangeline's parents, a furious thunder-

storm blew up out of the Atlantic. The plane went down somewhere over Nantucket Sound. None of the bodies were ever
recovered.

But for three decades Bowen Blackwell helped make it legally
possible for Bill Winslow to execute his plans for huge single-
family subdivisions, vast condominium complexes, office buildings, shopping malls, even a luxury high rise along the Hudson
in Hoboken complete with marina on what had twenty years
earlier been the site of Winslow Cordage. In return Wild Bill
had paid Bowen Blackwell large sums of money, hundreds of
thousands of dollars over the years; enough money, the Wild
One would joke when he went to Bowen's office for counsel,
to pay for the Blackwell's house on the Vineyard plus put his
four brainy kids through college. But Wild Bill knew the
money had been well invested. The hundreds of thousands he
had paid Bowen had solidified projects that were later worth
millions.

Now, from the security of his hospital bed, he saw the Blackwells
carry their new brass bed into their new house, up their new brick
path under the canopy of maple trees, up the front porch, and
through the front door. Wild Bill helped Bowen put that bed
together, safe in the knowledge that Bowen's money was now in
his bank account. The Wild One, mainly because he had already
owned the land, made a profit on that first house, not a huge sum
by any means, but a profit nevertheless; enough to keep the
creditors at bay for at least a few more months. And by that time
he knew he'd be finished with another house, a bigger house, a
better house, a more expensive house. And he'd keep building
them until he didn't owe the sons of bitches a nickel, until the
sons of bitches owed him.

The night Bowen and Patricia moved into their house in the
late spring of 1946, the Winslows and the Blackwells toasted the
occasion with a bottle of cheap champagne. They all stood in the
middle of the living room, stood because the Blackwells had a
brand-new house and a brand-new brass bed but no chairs, no
sofa, no other furniture whatsoever. Wild Bill worked the cork
from the bottle. Finally, the pressure released, the cork popped
and blew across the room. They all laughed. Wild Bill poured.
They drank. "Welcome to Far Hills," he boomed, his voice
echoing through the empty house which still smelled of paint and
polish, "the finest little town in America."

Virginia felt the baby kick. She drank a little champagne. The baby kicked again. She said maybe the time had come. They all started to panic, most of all the new father who couldn't find his wife's coat or the front door or the car keys. But the panic subsided and the right things were done and in the middle of the night, after a long and painful labor, the Winslows' oldest, Virginia, named of course for her loving mama, later nicknamed Ginny, popped into the world wide-eyed and looking kind of worried.

Forty-four years later and she still looked worried. Worried this time, as always, over things she could not control. She still had not been able to reach anyone at the house in Bel Air. It was 10:13 P.M. eastern daylight time. That made it just after seven out in California. *Where could they be? Aaron should be home from the office by now. And those kids. Where are those damn kids?* Ginny sighed and hung up the receiver.

She wondered what to do next. It had been a long and trying day. She was hot and sticky and tired. Even with the windows wide open the air in her room felt warm and clammy. *I can't believe he never put central air in this house.* She knew the others were downstairs, still talking, no doubt, about Wild Bill, about those push-ups and the way he had freaked out after hearing about Barton. But she did not feel like going back down. In some ways she did; she didn't want to feel left out. But in other ways she had no desire at all to rejoin her siblings, to add to the unrelenting hysteria generated by the Wild One. After all, she had heard it all before. A measurable amount of her life had been spent discussing her father with her mother and her brothers and sisters. She'd spent hours at a time dissecting him, analyzing him, verbally castrating him, raking him over the family coals, occasionally, at a weak moment, even defending him. Tonight she decided to keep her own counsel. Something Mary had said on the way home from the hospital, something about the Wild One reaching for a new awareness, made Ginny wonder if maybe this trip home was about more than just Wild Bill's fall down the back stairs. But she did not feel as though it was something she could talk about, not yet anyway, so she decided to take a bath, relax, maybe call home again later, before turning off the light. She would see the others in the morning.

*   *   *

Actually, the only Winslows left downstairs were Joseph and Henry, still acting out the role of Bobby. Emily had taken Rosa up to bed soon after they returned from the hospital. Rosa was afraid to stay upstairs in that big house all by herself so Emily had to stay with her. Mama fell asleep even before her daughter. Mary had a scotch and soda and then went off to bed not long after Ginny went up to call home. That left the guys. They sat around the kitchen table sipping Wild Bill's bourbon and looking at the road map of Georgia. After they located Waycross, Joseph called various airlines to see if they could get a morning flight to Savannah. Eastern had one at ten-thirty, Piedmont one at eleven. USAir had one at nine but it was booked. They had another one at noon. "No thanks," said Joseph, "too late." Delta had several flights going through Atlanta but most of those were full also, except for one leaving Newark at six-forty. Joseph passed this information on to his older brother. "Makes no difference to me," said Henry, as Bobby, "I'm up early every day anyway." Joseph could not remember the last time he'd been up before nine but he figured it was for Barton so he booked two seats on the six-forty flight and hung up.

"Looks like we'll be getting up pretty early, bro'," he said.

Henry nodded. "First day of summer, isn't it?"

"Tomorrow?"

"Yeah."

"I don't know. I think maybe day after tomorrow."

Henry sipped his bourbon. "Yeah, I guess you're right."

Joseph reached into his pocket, pulled out a small plastic vial. "Want some coke, Bob?"

"Cocaine?"

"Yeah."

"You've got cocaine?"

"Rarely without it."

Henry thought this over. "I never did it."

"Are you shittin' me?"

Henry, as Bobby, shook his head. "Nope. To tell you the truth I've never even seen it. Not in real life anyway. I know some people who grow their own grass though. They've been growing it for years. Sometimes I smoke a bone with 'em. Not too often. Irene doesn't like it much. She thinks it turns the brain into something resembling a rotten tomato."

"Well, bro', Irene's not here now, so what do you say you and me snort a few lines?"

Henry, as Bobby, shook his head. "I think I'll just sip my whiskey, Joe. This suits me fine. But you go ahead. Don't let me stop you. I'm not one to keep a man from doing what he wants to do."

Now Joseph thought it over. "Ahh, the hell with it. I won't sleep a wink if I start snorting this crap now. I'll stick with the brown. Probably ought to go to bed pretty soon anyway. We'll have to get up around five."

"Best time of the day," said Henry. "Not a soul around."

Joseph wanted to say, *No one with any sense anyway*, but he decided to forgo the slight. After all, the guy sitting across the table from him was his brother, his older brother.

They finished their whiskeys, turned out the lights, and went up to bed. Joseph went to the room he had once shared with Barton. Henry went up to the third-floor room he had long ago shared with Bobby. They wished each other good night after agreeing to rendezvous in the kitchen no later than five-thirty the following morning.

Edward, who had never shared a room with anyone in the big house, could not sleep. He did not want to sleep. He wanted to be on his way. But he had to be patient. He had to wait for Samantha to fall sound asleep.

After their evening stroll around the liberal arts quad, Edward and Samantha had stopped for an ice cream cone and then gone home. They had listened to some Mendelssohn and then gone to bed to read. At eleven-twenty Samantha had turned out her light and said good night. Edward put aside the book he had not been reading and switched his light off a few minutes later. At eleven-thirty Samantha's breathing grew calm and steady. By eleven forty-five she was sound asleep. Her husband whispered her name, received no reply. He listened to her sleeping for a long time, until well after midnight. Then he slipped out of bed, pulled on his Levi's and his sneakers and his sweatshirt, and went out into the kitchen. He turned on the light over the sink and sat down at the small wooden table. He wrote his wife a note:

Samantha,
    You were fast asleep. I didn't want to wake you. I have

some things I need to do. I'll be in touch. Try not to
worry.

Love,
Edward

Little Eddie Winslow stood up, found the field binoculars on
top of the refrigerator, and turned off the light. He hesitated just
a moment, then left the apartment. A few minutes later, his
thoughts swirling, he drove fast through deserted downtown Ithaca
and then south along Route 96.

Barton Winslow could not see his brothers Bobby and Joseph
saying good night in the upstairs hallway of the big house in Far
Hills. Nor could he see his brother Edward driving wildly through
the darkness. He could not see them but he could feel their
presence. Barton incorrectly nurtured the idea that his siblings
had learned of the beating he had endured at the hands of those
Georgia rednecks and had banded together to come to his defense. He imagined them calling one another long-distance,
spreading the word, discussing what to do, gathering at some
Georgia airport, renting a car or two, and traveling overland to
where he lay bruised and battered in that sterile and narrow
hospital bed. He envisioned their reunion as the first step in a
whole new beginning for the offspring of William Bailey and
Virginia Winslow.

Barton had never understood the disintegration of the family.
He did not know why they had all become so alienated from one
another. Even as kids Barton thought they often seemed more like
enemies than friends, more like strangers than siblings living
under the same roof, in the same house. Barton had never
connected these impressions with his own misbegotten ambitions.
He had always assumed his father, the Wild One, deserved the
lion's share of the blame for the family's divided condition. His
mother's sudden and unexpected death had certainly aggravated
the situation but Barton believed the family had begun its long
descent into self-destruction years before that runaway Rolls-
Royce laid his mama to rest. Not only had Wild Bill rarely showed
love or sympathy but he seemed to take pleasure in the pursuit of
divide and conquer.

Like that summer up in Maine, Barton recalled, *when he taught
Joey and me how to sail.* It was not enough to simply teach the

boys how to rig the boat and operate the rudder and beat against the wind. No, the Wild One had to teach them how to race and how to compete. But it was never enough to just race for the sake of racing; *no, we had to win, we had to come in first, second best didn't make the grade.* Not that Barton ever even came in second. Usually he was last, dead last. Often he was still out on the water trying to get around those final markers long after the other racers were back at the marinas joking and laughing and hauling in their sails. His brother didn't have a problem with competing. Joseph liked to race. He liked it because he was good at it. He liked it because sometimes he won and even when he didn't win and Wild Bill rode him, he just told the old man to take a long hike on a short pier. The Wild One might knock Joey down on the dock for sassing him but Joseph never cared much about that either; he bounced back like one of those vinyl punching bags, got back on his feet and told the old man to take his best shot. *Why couldn't I do that? Why did I always just stand there looking stupid? Why couldn't I stand up to the old man?* Barton lay in his hospital bed, his eyes wide open, his brain working overtime while outside his window the cicadas kept screaming at the darkness.

And finally, late that summer, after too much pain and too many defeats, Barton sailed his small sailboat up onto the shoals at the entrance to Blue Hill Bay. He steered straight for the rocks during a strong easterly, kept his sail taut and filled with wind. It was the best tack of his young life. At full speed he hit those rocks. The fiberglass hull split and cracked like the shell of a walnut. Within seconds the sailboat had disappeared beneath the waves...

Barton did not yet know about his father's fall down the back stairs. Had he known he would have been the first one to head for home. He blamed the Wild One for being less than perfect but nevertheless he loved his old man; and without the old man he knew the resurrection of the family would never happen.

The important thing, Barton knew from his study of Zen, was the whole. *Without the whole there is nothing; seven wandering Winslows are like a solar system without a sun.* He knew this despite his fanatical pursuit of destiny as foreseen in Mary's dream. The more he became isolated by his sculptures and his ambitions the more he longed for the bosom of his family. Barton knew his sun, and the sun of his siblings, was the Wild One. Wild Bill had the power to create night and day. *His satellites can orbit for eons but until we acknowledge the power of the sun our revolutions will be nothing but aimless wanderings...*

His father, he remembered, never even asked about the sailboat after Barton had made it safely back to shore. The old man was just relieved the boy had not gone down with his ship. A tear spilled out of Barton's eye. Moments later the young man fell asleep while waiting for the sun to rise.

Chapter Seventeen

———————————————— • ————————————————

The clock beside Mary's bed said 10:57 but her watch said 3:59. In London it was almost four o'clock in the morning. Normally she would be sound asleep at this time, dreaming her quiet, vivid dreams of long ago. Mary loved to sleep, to crawl deep beneath a great pile of pillows and bedclothes and give herself over to the mysterious workings of her subconscious. She sometimes slept as much as twelve hours a day. But she never considered this time wasted. She saw it as a time of rejuvenation and exploration. It was while asleep that she usually met the Winslows of the past. But now, partly because of the jet lag and partly because the room was so warm and stuffy even with the windows and the door wide open, she felt too exhausted to sleep. Her body wanted to sleep but her mind was wide awake; her thoughts troubled and chaotic. Lying there upon her childhood bed, Mary tossed and turned and tried to regain control of her thoughts as the night wound its way toward the dawn.

Of the seven surviving Winslow children born of Wild Bill and Virginia Winslow, Mary undoubtedly had the finest formal education. Her early years, like those of her brothers and sisters, had been spent at Far Hills Country Day School. From there she went to Kent Place School for girls in Summit, New Jersey. At Kent Place she was educated in science and history and the classics. Mary enjoyed history the most. She connected with it. When her class studied the American Revolution Mary knew more about New Jersey's role in the war than her instructor. At the time she did not know the origins of her knowledge.

She liked to dress in the fashion of the period the class was studying: coarse woolen skirts and blouses during the colonial period, ankle-length dresses and petticoats during the Civil War, short skirts and fur collars during the Roaring Twenties. She developed a reputation for being a little strange, slightly eccentric, but her tiny size and quiet voice and forlorn smile made her appear harmless; inquisitive but utterly harmless.

After graduating from Kent Place in 1966, Mary went up the Hudson River valley to Poughkeepsie, to Vassar College. At that time Vassar accepted only female students. This was one of the primary reasons Mary chose the school over Swarthmore, Penn, or Cornell. Her years at Kent Place had left her socially unavailable to men, and since what she thought she wanted most out of college was a sound understanding of Western civilization, she felt an all-girls school would suit her best.

Mary had known for a long time, really since the death of her older sister Helen, which was her earliest and most vivid memory, what her purpose was on the planet. She had been conceived, born, and delivered into adulthood in order to confirm the metaphysical realities of reincarnation. No small chore, but nevertheless one she undertook with fire and determination. More than anything else, her formal education convinced her the universe and virtually everything comprehensible in it operated on some kind of cycle. Repetition, measured in seconds or minutes or hours or days or years or even eons, was inevitable. Just as the bars of Beethoven's *Unfinished Symphony* eventually begin to repeat, an ancestor once told her in a dream, so too does the moon revolve around the earth and the earth around the sun and the reproductive cycle of the simple sponge around the tides and temperature of the ocean water. Variations occur, Mary believed, but these variations had more to do with the imperfect nature of the universe and its maker than in any flaws inherent in the cyclic system. The universe, and everything in it, Mary considered finite; therefore repetition was a basic law of nature. This conclusion led Mary to believe that the number of souls in the universe must also be finite. The human race itself was reproducing on some sort of cycle. Life, she concluded, was not linear at all but circular: birth to death, and then right back again to birth. Mary did not accept many of the theories of reincarnation as rendered by certain religions and religious cults. Men did not return as dogs and dogs as fleas and fleas as horses. The dead returned in kind. Man was a product of his ancestors. She believed she was a product of her parents and her grandparents and all the Winslows who had ever lived. She was her ancestors. The only differences concerned time and place. And so to understand herself and her family, and to be capable of anticipating the future, which she saw as the fundamental and primary aim of all thinking creatures, Mary sought out those characters from the past to whom she was biologically and emotionally linked.

Mary's first three years at Vassar were intellectually stimulating and spiritually revealing but socially stale and uneventful. She spent most of her time alone with her books and her ancestors or with a small circle of acquaintances, mostly young ladies from New York City who liked to smoke grass and drop acid and discuss which force would prevail: world peace or nuclear annihilation. But at the beginning of her senior year a change occurred beyond her control: the ruling body of Vassar College, in a bold attempt to bring the school into the latter half of the twentieth century, opened its doors to young men with the proper academic qualifications. At first Mary simply ignored the endless parade of smiling puppies crisscrossing the campus that fall. But then one night in late November, an early snow covering the frozen ground, Mary met Kenny, a sophomore transfer from the University of Pennsylvania.

We don't want to get too involved with Kenny Waterson but he plays an important role in Mary's development so you should know at least a little about him. Kenny tried to get accepted to Vassar straight out of high school but was told he would have to wait another year. He waited patiently down in Philadelphia, earing a 4.0 G.P.A. and excelling on both the swim team and the debating club. But more than anything Kenny wanted to go to Vassar. He wanted to go there because Debbie Howell, daughter of Andrew Howell, the filthy rich blue jeans and denim designer, went there. You see, Kenny wanted in the worst way to be a hotshot fashion designer. And scoundrel that he was, he had long ago decided that Debbie Howell was his ticket into that sphere.

Kenny Waterson and Debbie Howell had attended the same New York City prep school. Debbie, however, was two years older than Kenny so she had never acknowledged Kenny's existence. But like any good stalker, Kenny was patient, and totally ruthless. He stalked Debbie all the way up the Hudson River valley, all the way to Poughkeepsie. When he arrived there in the fall of '69,

Debbie was a senior majoring in Timothy Leary. She loved to hallucinate and tear down the status quo. She had a tattered ticket stub proving she had been to Woodstock a few weeks earlier, and so of course she saw herself as a direct descendant of the rock-and-roll God.

Mary and Debbie hung around together, rolled and smoked reefers together, went cruising together, listened to the Jefferson Airplane and Crosby, Stills, Nash, and Young together. They were buddies, college buddies. Mary and Debbie did not really like each other, had a great deal of uncommunicated animosity for one another, but college is a place where one needs allies, and so an uneasy alliance had developed between them.

Kenny played his hand quietly, skillfully. He did not just barge into Ms. Howell's room and spill his unconditional, eternal devotion. No, he put all of his intellectual and athletic skills on display for everyone on campus to see, and along the way he made sure she was aware of his presence. Then, when the time was right, he made his move. It happened one night at a small party attended mostly by people tripping their brains out on bright yellow blotters of electric sunshine. Kenny didn't know Debbie was tripping. He had never done acid and it was really far too dark in the small, smoky room to see how dilated her pupils were. For like five hours the guy made the moves on the fashion designer's daughter. Debbie laughed and smiled a lot; not at Kenny's witty remarks but at the strange colors floating around his face and at the weird shapes his head kept making whenever he opened his mouth.

Kenny got nowhere with Debbie but later that same night he met Mary. He was tall and broad and handsome, and always quick with a smile and a compliment. He said things to her that no young man had ever said before. He told her she was beautiful and sexy and feminine. At first he said these things because he wanted in the worst way to bed her. To Kenny, Mary was like those thin, gorgeous models in the magazines; the ones he craved like a drug. He tried every trick he had ever learned but Mary allowed him to go only so far. They kissed deeply while Kenny ran his hands over every inch of her smooth, pale skin. More than once he even poised naked and erect over her, but there Mary drew the line. There would be no penetration, not that night, nor any other as far as Mary was concerned. She had vowed to herself to remain celibate until the day she was married, not for any moral or religious reasons, but because she had this secret fear, the same secret fear possessed by several of her female ancestors: that loss of virginity meant loss of innocence, and loss of innocence led to a lifetime of looking through a window of darkness into a bleak and uncertain future.

Kenny might well have given up on this silent and sexless prima donna but for two things: his ego and the fact that a mutual acquaintance had told him Mary's father was worth millions. And so with Debbie Howell a dead dream, Kenny made the conscious decision to pursue Mary Winslow all the way to the altar, if necessary, in order to partake of her well-protected pussy and her Daddy's well-endowed credit line. Surely, he reasoned, father Winslow would want to back his son-in-law's ambitious plans to develop the country's largest line of designer jeans.

The relationship between Mary and Kenny went on for over two years, until the summer of 1972 when Kenny graduated from Vassar. During those years Mary pursued a master's degree in early American history at Columbia University, but her heart and mind remained north in Poughkeepsie. She had to repeat several courses before she finally earned her degree. Nearly every weekend for two years she drove north on the Taconic State Parkway to the apartment across from the campus where Kenny lived. Mary paid for the apartment with money she received from Wild Bill. The Wild One did not know of course that his daughter was using the money for this purpose. Had the Wild One known he undoubtedly would have kicked the crap out of Kenny Waterson.

A few days after Kenny graduated, he and Mary drove down to Far Hills and announced their engagement. Wild Bill and Virginia had known for some time about young Waterson so they were not surprised. Still, the Wild One did not much like this young intruder, but Virginia found him pleasant and polite, and she could see her daughter was in love, so for a change Wild Bill kept his mouth shut. He even offered his soon-to-be son-in-law room and board, plus a job for the summer mixing concrete and hauling lumber at one of his new subdivisions. It looked then like plans for an early autumn wedding would carry through.

But on an unbelievably hot and steamy August night, with the mercury hovering near ninety, with the humidity so high the shutters were sweating, the Wild One, on his way to bed, just happened to wander past young Waterson's bedroom at a rather inopportune time. Kenny was using Ginny's bedroom since Ginny was, as usual, out on the west coast failing as an actress. Ginny had a phone beside her bed, of course, and that night Kenny was on the phone when the Wild One walked by. The idiot thought he had closed the door but the attic fan, trying to suck the warm, wet air through the house, had blown the door partway open without Kenny realizing it. He had his back to the doorway as he babbled blindly on.

"No, man, no luck yet," Kenny said to his buddy on the other end of the line, "but unless I get me some sweets soon I swear to God I'll fuck that bitch right into the next century on our wedding night. Sometimes I thinks she's as dry as the goddamn Mohave Desert."

Needless to say, this snippet of chitchat kept the Wild One from moving on down the hall to the confines of the master bedroom. He stood there frozen, his ears like a couple of cantaloupe quarters.

After a short pause Kenny said, "Hey, man, lemme put it to you this way: the cat's in the bag. I'm so far up her old man's ass I'd need a flashlight to find my way out. I had to play it real cool because I could tell right away the guy was one of those macho soup brains who would think any man who wanted to design clothes must be some kind of faggot. So I've been coming on real heavy with this man-to-man masculine bullshit, you know, pounding nails, building houses, that kind of crap. But whenever I get the chance I tell him there's big money to be made in dry goods. He's totally into money. He's got this real super hard-ass role he plays but, man, I'll tell you, when the time comes he'll roll over like a—"

Wild Bill never heard the analogy. He slipped quietly into the bedroom and closed the door. Kenny heard it close. He turned around. His face went white. He hung up the phone without saying so long. "Watch out," said the Wild One, "here comes the hard ass." He crossed the room without the passage of time and hit Kenny Waterson on the chin with a right uppercut that lifted the young man with the big dreams right off the floor. No sooner was he back on the floor when another blow caught him in the solar plexus. His back exploded into the wall and he slumped down into the corner like a sack of potatoes tossed off a produce truck. The Wild One was on top of him in a second, lifting him by the collar and landing several left jabs squarely on his jaw. Blood spurted from the corner of Kenny's mouth. Another punch or two followed before orders for immediate removal from the Compound were issued. Wild Bill watched the bleeding Waterson boy pack his gear and then escorted him down the back stairs and out the back door. They encountered no one along the way. It was dark: no moon, no stars, just the heat and the humidity. Kenny had no wheels and none were offered. Wild Bill walked a step behind, his hand on the back of Kenny's collar. He pushed him and shoved him and occasionally gave him a good, swift kick in the ass. This went on until they reached the end of the long drive. Along the way the Wild One told the young man never to set foot in Far Hills again. He also told him that any attempt to contact Mary would result in permanent physical injury. At the end of the driveway, right there between the bald eagle and the turkey vulture, Wild Bill gave his no-longer-to-be son-in-law one last kick in the butt and told him to disappear. Kenny, having never before experienced the strong arm of scorn, decided wisely to go quietly away and conserve his losses.

Wild Bill went back to the house and up to bed. He never mentioned his midnight run-in with Waterson to anyone, not even to his wife. He knew she would find some way of blaming the entire incident on him.

Mary was heartbroken. She could not believe her young love had run off without reason or explanation. At first she felt sure the Wild One had said or done something to drive Kenny away. She especially thought this true after she found blood on the carpet in Ginny's bedroom. But Wild Bill insisted he knew nothing about Waterson's disappearance. He claimed the boy had left without even collecting his last paycheck. Mary finally accepted her father's denials. She told herself Kenny had been an unfaithful and therefore undeserving suitor. She was better off without him. He had come into her life, taken control of her emotions, and then thrown her aside. *And this,* she told herself, *will never happen again, ever.*

Less than a week after Kenny's disappearance, Mary went into New York to visit her old college pal Debbie Howell. She was walking alone up Fifth Avenue when she thought she saw him across the street. She crossed at the next block and made her way back through the crowd. Her heart began to pound. She wanted to turn away, leave it alone. But suddenly she was right behind him, right on his heels. She took a deep breath and tapped him on the shoulder. She thought for a moment she might slap him across the face. But then he turned around. His face was still swollen and bruised from the awful beating he had taken from the Wild One. Mary caught her breath. Her eyes opened wide.

So did his. "Stay away from me," he pleaded. "I don't want that crazy fuck coming after me again." Kenny turned and made his way quickly through the crowd.

Mary watched him go, watched him disappear. She did not even try to follow him or stop him. She hated her father at that moment, more than she had ever hated anyone in her entire life. She hated Kenny Waterson as well. She hated all men, every last one of them. And so right then, right there along Fifth Avenue, right outside of Tiffany's, at the tender age of twenty-three, Mary told herself to have nothing more to do with men. They were liars and deceivers; little boys in big, ugly, powerful bodies. They could do nothing for her but hurt her, stand in her way, hold her down. *I have far more important pursuits to occupy myself than the petty emotional crimes of dysfunctional bullies.*

Mary lay there on the soft, narrow bed with the windows open but nothing but warm, wet air seeping into the room. The unwanted memories of Kenny Waterson made the room seem ever warmer. She threw off the thin cotton sheet and tried to clear her thoughts. But she saw Kenny again, poised above her, and the desire to touch herself became almost unbearable. . . .

During the post-Kenny years, Mary focused more and more on her family's past. She entirely retraced the Winslows' New Jersey lineage. Over the next decade she visited every museum and historical site in the state in the hope of uncovering details of the New World Winslows. Little by little, generation by generation, she pieced together a chronology. The Wild One supported her endeavor, partly because he too recognized the connection between past and present, but also because he did not want his Mary hurt ever again. If he could insulate her from harm and harassment, he would. Of course he did this, as always, with direct financial assistance; with money, lots of money; which was something, but certainly not everything the young woman needed.

But lying in bed, unable to sleep, Mary was not thinking about the money. Money was just a means to an end. It had no enduring significance, no ability to solve the complex problem of time elapsing.

Finally Mary shook off her sexual frustrations and made the leap back. She sat upon the front porch of that huge, sprawling clapboard house on the banks of the Delaware just north of Burlington. Four generations of Winslows sat there with her; including the family's patriarch, old Freeman Winslow, who rocked slowly on a wooden rocker while puffing on a corncob pipe and only offering his advice when asked directly. Born in 1649, he was ninety-seven years old that summer morning Mary came a-calling, maybe the oldest living human of European descent in the thirteen colonies. His boy, Henry Lane Winslow, closing in rapidly on sixty-five, sat next to this father whittling on a piece of hickory and saying even less. The one doing most of the talking, which wasn't much, was Henry Lane's only son to reach manhood, thirty-three-year-old Robert Bailey "Jawbone" Winslow. They named him Robert Bailey after his mama's papa. A few years later they nicknamed him Jawbone because, relatively speaking, he talked a blue streak.

Mary said nothing in this crowd, partly because in those days women did not say much in the company of men, even Quaker men. But mostly she kept quiet because they couldn't hear her anyway since she wouldn't even be born for another two hundred years.

Resting on a blanket between Mary and Jawbone were the most recent additions to the line of New World Winslows: a pair of healthy infant males; twins: Robert Bailey Winslow, Jr., and his little brother, Henry Lane Winslow II. They had been born a few months earlier, on the first day of spring, 1746. Their mama, nineteen-year-old Anna Carlson Winslow, thirteen years her husband's junior, had given birth to those two seven-and-one-half-pound babies, and the next morning she'd gone out to the barn and milked the cows and fed the chickens.

By 1746 the Winslows owned land up and down the Delaware for most of a mile in both directions. Close to six hundred acres, Jawbone reckoned, with close to half of it under till. The Winslows had been on that land for almost seventy years. The land had brought them prosperity plus a prominent role in their local west Jersey Quaker community. Old Freeman was a highly respected elder at the Meeting House. Once he'd even been sent to Philadelphia for the important Annual Meeting where he had met and bought a pint for the aging but still boisterous William Penn. Henry Lane and his wife Rebecca had been among the first colonists to not only condemn slavery but to grant both their slaves and their indentured servants unconditional freedom. A majority of Quakers on both sides of the Delaware soon followed suit.

Today, however, Henry Lane's son Jawbone was not thinking about the Annual Meeting or the plight of the Colored. He was worried about the new governor and this latest tax increase and the Indians and the French and six or eight other issues which he feared might soon disrupt the family business and therefore the family's tranquility.

"Tain't worth the trouble to worry yourself over what you cain't control, Jawbone," said Henry Lane. "Tain't that right, father Freeman?"

Freeman took a long pull on his corncob, rocked a time or two, and then nodded his head.

"Maybe that's so," said Jawbone, "but I have to think about what might happen sometime not too far down the road."

"You do all the thinkin' you want, son," said Henry Lane, "just don't do any doin' 'fore you stop and reckon your options with your papa. Now tain't that what you always 'vised me, father Freeman?"

Freeman took another long pull on his corncob, rocked a time or two for effect, then nodded his head. "That's true, son, I did. But there comes a time when a man has to do what he has to do. Some men get to live lives that don't demand much disruption. Other men tain't quite so fortunate. Others got to do things they might not regularly do."

"But father Freeman," said Henry Lane, "even during times of disruption we Quakers keep calm, calm and quiet. Quakers ain't fighters."

Freeman thought this over for quite a spell. "That be the hope, son," he said, finally, "that be the dream. To follow the Inner Light. But you see, that beam a light sometimes gets busted. Sometimes the Outer Light draws a brighter bead."

They all sat there for a long while not saying a word, just looking out across the fields at the river. The river kept flowing by, changing, but always the same. Then the twins started to cry, and within seconds those brothers were grown men, identical in every way but attitude. They were engaged in a knock-down-drag-out argument right there on that same front porch but Mary knew the outcome of the argument so she closed her eyes and turned away. She knew then, lying there on the sheet wet with perspiration, why the Wild One wanted to see them, why they had all been summoned home. It was more, she knew, than the fall down the back stairs. It had to do with the land, with the family's future on the land. But nothing more would come, so she drifted into a light sleep which carried her fitfully toward the dawn.

Chapter Eighteen

Ginny did not share her sister Mary's passion for the past. She had absolutely no desire to reconstruct history in order to understand the family's past in the hope of being able to foresee the family's future. Ginny did not see herself or her siblings as the consequence of events and circumstances which had transpired generations and centuries ago. Nor did she see herself or her siblings as progenitors of twenty-first century Winslows. Life was what it was: here and now, the day-to-day struggle to get out of bed, make the coffee, get the kids off to school, stay out of the maid's way, hope for a break, go shopping, keep hubby happy but never fully satisfied. Sure, she would prefer the glamorous life of a Silver Screen queen, but barring that faded fantasy Ginny wanted security. She did not want or need to question the realities of a slightly falsified life. She was a good mother, a loving if somewhat selfish wife, and so what if she would've dropped both roles in an instant had some big-time Hollywood producer offered her the female lead in the sequel to *Gone With the Wind?*

Ginny lay in bed, the same bed she had slept in as a child, and dreamed she was the new Scarlett O'Hara standing on the front porch of Tara, strong and proud and beautiful. She was surrounded by her loyal slaves, including the faithful Mammy, who had just promised to remain forever, even if those dirty Yanks won the war. But suddenly a strange sound could be heard in the distance. It was an engine racing at full speed, full throttle. Everyone on the set grew silent. And then they saw it: a small red sports coupe screaming up Tara's front lane. The coupe, a Porsche Targa, kicked up a cloud of dust and came to a noisy halt right at the foot of those porch steps. Out of the driver's seat stepped the

Wonder Boy himself, Clark Gable, dressed impeccably as Rhett Butler, and smiling broadly from ear to ear. Ginny gasped. Her heart fluttered. But then, out of the passenger seat climbed her own real-life daughter Madeline. The frail fifteen-year-old had gained weight, lots of weight. "My God, Maddy," shrieked her mother, "you're pregnant!" And then, before she could come fully awake, Clark turned into that slovenly gigolo Stu. A moment later the couple climbed back into that Porsche and drove off into a painted landscape of a fire-red Georgia sunset.

Ginny sprang off the bed. She glanced quickly at the clock but failed to register the fact that it was just after four A.M. She dialed the number of the house in Bel Air. It took Aaron several rings to answer. He sounded like a man who had been fast asleep. "Yes? . . . Hullo? . . . Yes?"

"Aaron, finally, where have you been? What took you so long to answer? Where are the kids? I've been calling for hours."

"Ginny?"

"Yes, Ginny. Your wife. Remember me?"

"Yes, of course. . . . What is it? . . . It's the middle of the night."

"I don't care if it's the middle of next week. Where've you been? And where are the kids?"

Aaron was wide awake now. "In bed, I suppose. Although actually, Gin, I haven't checked in the last fifteen or twenty minutes."

"Don't be funny, Aaron. Go check now."

Aaron did not argue. He had been dealing with Ginny's insecurities for many years. For him they were part of her charm, part of the reason he loved her. She needed him. So he held the receiver away from his face, covered the mouthpiece with the palm of his hand, and waited at least a minute. "Okay," he said, finally, "I checked. They're both fast asleep."

"You're sure?"

Aaron had had a long day. But he knew his wife had no doubt had a long day as well. "Want me to look again?"

"No, but I do want to know where you all were earlier. I must've called fifty times. I've been worried sick."

Aaron thought about making something up to really get his wife going, but he knew that in less than six hours he had to be at the hospital to remove the tonsils from the throat of some soap opera queen's spoiled stepdaughter. "We all went out for dinner, Gin," he told her. "Maddy and Adam were watching TV when I got home from the office so I asked them if they wanted to go out and get some Chinese food and they said okay."

Ginny thought about this. "No sign of Stu?"

"Nope, no sign of Stu."

Ginny told Aaron about her dream and then Aaron asked Ginny about the Wild One. "We only saw him for a few minutes. He seems pretty good, better than I'd expected. But I'll find out more in the morning and let you know."

"Okay."

"You'd better get back to sleep."

"Yeah, you too," said Aaron. "And don't worry about the kids, Gin. They'll be fine, really. I promise."

"I know," she said, softly. Then, after a moment, "I love you."

"I love you too."

Finally they said good night and hung up. Ginny lay in bed looking for signs of dawn and wondering if Aaron and the kids had really gone out for Chinese. Adam, she remembered, hated Chinese food. But then, just as the eastern sky began to brighten, she fell into a light, unsettled sleep.

Unlike Edward and Barton and Mary and Ginny, Evangeline slept like a baby in the arms of her mother. She almost always slept well and woke up rested. Her mother had once told her that night was a reflection of day; if she had good thoughts and did good deeds she would have sweet dreams and be watched over by angels.

After the Winslows had left for the hospital in her Nissan pickup, Evangeline cleaned up the kitchen. John and Paul helped. When they were finished they walked out across the front lawn to gaze at the evening sky. And when the colors had faded they headed for the cottage. They took turns reading from *The Adventures of Huckleberry Finn*, the part when Jim and Huck discover a dead man. Before too long John and Paul started to fall asleep on the living room floor. Evangeline sent them off to wash their faces and brush their teeth. A few minutes later the two boys pulled on their pajamas and climbed into their double bed. Evangeline tucked them in and kissed her boys good night.

Just before Evangeline turned out the light Paul asked, "When will Uncle Bill be able to come home from the hospital, Ma?"

"Oh, I'd say in a few days. Maybe less, knowing him."

"Can we go see him?" asked John.

"Do you want to?"

"Sure we do," they both answered.

"Then we'll go see him tomorrow."

"Maybe we could bring him something," said Paul, "like when he brought me that fishing pole last year when I had my 'pendix out."

Evangeline smiled. "Sure, we can bring him something. He'll like that."

"Maybe some goldfish or something."

"I thought you were the one who wanted goldfish."

"Yeah, well, I thought he might like some too."

She laughed. "Parental manipulation? From a five-year-old?"

"What?"

"Nothing," she said, "go to sleep." She turned off the light and gently closed the door. Back out in the small living room, Evangeline switched on the stereo and inserted The Beatles' *Abbey Road* into the CD player. She skipped ahead to track eight, adjusted the headphones over her ears, and started the music. She sat in that old wooden rocker, the same oft-repaired rocker where Crazy Legs Winslow had suffered his nonfatal heart attack. The Wild One had brought the rocker down to the cottage soon after Evangeline and the boys had taken up residence nearly four years ago.

Before they had moved to the cottage, the small family lived a stone's throw from the Delaware River just north of Frenchtown. There they lived in the same renovated carriage house where Evangeline had been born and raised by her parents Thomas and Pamela Pennington. The Penningtons were the gardener and caretaker on an old and well-established seventy-five-acre river estate. Originally they had worked for an old New Jersey family named Dayton who had owned the land since the 1700s. But in 1960 the Daytons sold the property to Bowen and Patricia Blackwell. The Blackwells took one look at the beautiful gardens and asked the Penningtons to stay. The Penningtons agreed. A year later, in the summer of 1961, their only child was born. They named her Evangeline.

Two decades later, on the day before her twentieth birthday, Evangeline waved good-bye as her parents and the Blackwells lifted off the grass runway at Sky Manor Airport outside of Pittstown. The Penningtons and the Blackwells were off to the

Vineyard for a long weekend. But a few hours later the small Cessna crashed into Nantucket Sound.

Wild Bill Winslow attended the memorial services for the dead. The first service was held for the Blackwells at the Presbyterian Church in Frenchtown. The pastor and then several members of the congregation lavished religious praise on the deceased. The Wild One sat there thinking people were saying things they did not really mean, did not really believe. He had never known Bowen Blackwell to go to church except maybe on Easter Sunday. When the service ended Wild Bill paid his respects to the Blackwells' children.

The service for the Penningtons was held in Quakertown at the Friends Meeting House. Wild Bill sat in the rear of the small, simple house of worship. He had never been to a Quaker meeting before. No one seemed to be in charge; there was no pastor, no pulpit. Thirty or forty others sat quietly on the narrow wooden pews. The Wild One spotted Evangeline sitting alone in the front row. Occasionally someone would approach her, take her hand, whisper something in her ear. There were no speeches or sermons, no eulogies or elegies. And then it ended. The people started to file out. Wild Bill waited outside for her to come. He told her how sorry he was and how much he would miss her parents. She wept on his shoulder.

He had known her all her life. He had watched her grow up. At least a dozen times a year the Winslows visited the Blackwells for parties and picnics and holidays. The Penningtons were always invited to these affairs. They worked for the Blackwells but they were also very good friends. Evangeline and Emily had often played hide and seek with Jeannie Blackwell in the Blackwells' big old colonial overlooking the Delaware.

The relationship between young Evangeline and Wild Bill began to change when he held her while she wept. He wanted to comfort her, make her feel secure, but at the same time her firm breasts and slender hips aroused him, made him aware that she had become a woman, a lovely and sensual young woman. He caught himself, told himself he was a disgusting old man. He had recently turned sixty-one. She had only a few days earlier turned twenty. Her parents were dead. His best friends were dead. But when finally her crying subsided he wiped her tears and told her to please call if there was anything she needed, anything at all.

A month passed. August arrived dry and hot. The Blackwells'

oldest son moved onto the estate. He assured Evangeline she could
stay on in the carriage house and continue her parents' work.

She called him one Saturday afternoon that first week of
August. He was on his way out the door when the phone rang.
He almost did not answer it. He was on his way to Bar Harbor for
his annual visit. She asked him how he was. He said fine. She
wondered if he might like to come down the following day for a
picnic along the river. "I just feel like we're missing those things
this summer," she said, "and it makes me sad and lonely." He told
her he would be happy to come, honored. After they said
good-bye he called Bettina. He told his wife he would not be
coming north anytime soon.

The next day, a warm and breezy summer afternoon, they sat in
the shade of the big willow along the riverbank. They ate fried
chicken and the year's first ears of corn on the cob. They drank a
bottle of white wine. The Wild One told some jokes. Evangeline
laughed. They walked together on the dirt path running beside
the river.

"Maybe I could go to the Meeting House with you sometime,"
he said.

She looked into his eyes. "That would be nice."

"Maybe next Sunday."

She smiled and held his hand.

It was Christmas, actually Christmas Eve, before they first
made love. Wild Bill drove down to give her a present: a
brand-new stereo system. He knew she loved music and the old
record player in the carriage house had long ago given its best
performance. They hooked up all the wires, plugged in all the
right cords. Evangeline put a record on the turntable, *Let It Be* by
The Beatles. While McCartney sang "The Long and Winding
Road" Evangeline and Wild Bill danced. He kissed her and
wondered why you had to grow old before you learned how to
hold a woman the way she wanted to be held. He missed Virginia
right then, wished he could bring her back and tell her he loved
her. A tear rolled down his cheek, probably the first tear he had
shed since her funeral. Evangeline wiped it gently away.

She sat in the wood rocker listening to the music and remembered.
She could still feel Billy Boy's tears on her breast as they lay naked
together on her bed in the loft of that old carriage house. She
could still see the moonlight streaming in the window. She could

still hear that great horned owl screeching somewhere down along the river. He had stayed the night, and most of Christmas morn.

After she and the boys moved into the cottage Billy Boy often came for supper. After the meal he liked to sit in the old rocker and listen to Bach and Beethoven and The Beatles while bouncing those two growing boys on his knee. Occasionally, after the boys had gone to bed, he would bounce her on his knee. Sometimes he still did. It always made her smile.

She smiled now. It had been two long days. It seemed to her like a month had passed since she had found him at the bottom of the stairs. But it looked like he would be okay; like he would be just fine in a few weeks.

Evangeline had listened to *Abbey Road* a thousand times but each time it sounded new. The more she heard the songs the better they made her feel. She knew by heart every note, every rhythm, every pause, every pulse, every lyric; but always she heard something fresh, something she had not heard before. She did not have to think about the music. It just happened. She could think about Billy Boy and John and Paul and all the rest of it. The music flowed through her thoughts and through her desires until she was filled with the music, that simple rock-and-roll music.

And when the music ended she turned off the power, brushed her teeth, took off her clothes, and stood in front of the open window. A warm, dry breeze blew through the room. Evangeline was thankful for any breeze at all. She saw a sliver of waning moon setting in the western sky. "Thank you, Lord," she said, "for helping create this day. And thank you for making John and Paul and me Children of the Light, Friends without enemies or adversaries. Thank you for Billy Boy who gives more than he takes. And thank you for helping him fall so this reunion he has wanted and needed for so long could finally come true." She took a long, deep breath. Then she ran her fingers gently over her hair and down her face and across her shoulders and over her breasts and along her hips and between her thighs and down the length of her legs. She took another deep breath, let it out slowly, and climbed into bed. She closed her eyes. A moment later, she was sound asleep. And all night long her dreams stayed sweet while the angels hovered overhead.

Wednesday, June 20, 1990 . . .

Chapter Nineteen

———————————————•———————————————

If you had really good eyes, the kind of eyes Ted Williams must've had, you might've been able to see him up there through the dim gray light in that hour just before dawn. But to see him you would've needed some reason to look, some reason to think he might be up there; up there in the woods hiding, peering through his binoculars, keeping tabs, taking notes, building himself into a mental frenzy that told him violence looked like the only way out.

Neither Henry, as Bobby, nor Joseph saw him as they left the house a minute or two before half past five. They had no reason to think he might be up there. Joseph was tired and cranky and already complaining about the heat and humidity.

"Doesn't it ever cool off or dry out in this goddamn climate?"

Henry shrugged. "Been like this up in the Adirondacks for weeks."

"Goddamn greenhouse effect."

The two brothers stood outside the back door. Back up in the woods he could not hear what they were saying. He saw their heads nod in agreement just before they walked across the driveway and into the garage. He heard but could not see a car engine start, and then, a few seconds later, he saw a small low-slung sports coupe back out of the garage and swing down the long drive, its headlamps bouncing off that dim gray light.

There had not been enough light for Edward to be sure who he had seen outside the back door. Through his binoculars it looked like Joseph and Bobby but it might have been Bobby and Barton or Barton and Joseph. His brothers, definitely, but which two? Not that it really mattered. He hated the whole lot of them, or thought he did. They'd turned on him when he needed them. They'd looked the other way when he went down for the count.

Edward had decided the night before, while listening to Horowitz play Mendelssohn, that this little reunion of the Winslow clan had been set up to force him back to the institution, back to the loony bin. He felt certain they had come together to put him away. That bit about Wild Bill falling down the back steps was just a hoax, a scam, a way of getting Edward to let his guard down, to lure him out into the open. But he wasn't falling for it, no way. He was on to their schemes. Yessiree, Little Eddie had their number. Including Samantha's. He wasn't sure yet but he had a sneaking suspicion she might be another of the old man's lackeys.

From atop the old deer perch in that tall black ash at the edge of the wood, Edward could see virtually everything from the back door of the main house all the way down across the yard to the large wooden barn at the edge of the abandoned alfalfa field. He could see the back stoop and the side of the garage and the swimming pool and the tennis court and most but not all of the cottage. He could see the outside of the cottage but not the inside. Inside it was dark, dark and quiet. The main house was dark also except for a single light burning in the kitchen window.

As a kid Edward used to watch the house from that same deer perch. The perch had been built by Crazy Legs in the last decade of the nineteenth century. Crazy Legs thought it might be fun to shoot a buck, drag it home, and throw it at the feet of his innocent young wife, Caroline. Caroline was city born and city bred and from the moment she moved to that castle in the Jersey countryside she was an unhappy woman. She suffered every single day from the quiet and the solitude. But it was the life her husband wanted so she kept silent and did her duty. She ran the house, kept the servants in line, made sure Crazy Legs was satisfied sexually and digestively. And she prayed daily for God to make her pregnant.

Finally, after more than three years of marriage, her prayers were answered. Charles was born on a cold winter night in January of 1892. He was small and frail and he very nearly killed his mother while crawling through the uterine window. Caroline recovered but never again would she possess one hundred percent of her health.

While Charles was still a babe, Crazy Legs built the deer perch and shot his one and only buck. He sat up on that narrow wooden platform one cold November morning, freezing his ass off and waiting for his prize to calmly pass. And finally it did: a twelve-point buck with a big, proud head and an impressive set of antlers. Crazy Legs, never a man to let his emotions get the upper hand, had to force himself to raise the gun. But finally he did. He sighted the heart of the beast along the two oily barrels. Time passed. The deer stood perfectly still. The man thought he might not be able to do it but as soon as he had that thought he pulled the trigger, both triggers. Then came the blasts and the animal kicking and falling and the man screaming. Yes, screaming. But to cover his screams he climbed down out of that tree, his manhood bulging through his swelled-out chest. He crossed over to his prize, avoided its still-open eyes, and thought for an instant he might even cry. But of course he didn't cry. No way. Not John "Crazy Legs" Winslow. He got hold of himself and pretty soon he had dragged that big buck down out of the woods, across the cold brown earth, and right up to the foot of the back stoop.

The caretaker and Crazy Legs's driver came out of the shadows to see what the boss had brought home. The three of them stood there talking about what a great wall mount the head would make when suddenly Caroline appeared at the back door. She had on a flannel robe and a woolen shawl. Her face looked pale and gaunt. She opened the door, started to ask what was going on, then saw the dead deer. She fainted straight away. Crazy Legs caught her a split second before she hit her head on the slate stoop. He carried her up to bed. Less than a month later she passed away, not from having seen that dead deer but from having suffered for so long with sadness and isolation. Her husband never hunted again. He put that Remington double-barrel twelve-gauge shotgun away in a closet somewhere and forgot all about it.

Edward knew the story of his great-grandmother's death. She had been just twenty-seven. He also knew the story of his great-grandfather's late-life decision to abandon his family and his home and his business and start again someplace far away where no one knew him. That story had reached mythological status in the family. Crazy Legs was a legend. The way he had raised himself out of poverty, overcome polio and had practically no formal education. The way he had built Winslow Cordage and that great estate in Far Hills. The way he had accumulated wealth and power out of nothing. And then the way he had one day announced out of thin air that it was all a giant load of crap. And then the way he had packed a small leather satchel and walked through the front door without looking back.

Sure, Edward had heard the story. He, like his brothers and sisters, had been swept up in the tale all through their youth. Edward had especially liked the part when Wild Bill had gone down to see Crazy Legs in British Honduras in the late '40s when word came the old man was dying. That part had always sounded to Little Eddie like a grand adventure, and it had been one of the millions of reasons the young lad had worshipped his papa. But he wasn't thinking about that now, not consciously anyway. He was thinking he should sneak down to the house for a look around before the dawn burned off the haze. But then a light snapped on in the cottage and Edward sat frozen watching for some movement on the other side of the window. He did not see Evangeline get out of bed, go into the other bedroom, and kneel beside Paul who was muttering in his sleep. He did not hear her comfort the boy, "You're just dreaming, sweetie, just a bad dream. Wake up and go back to sleep." He thought he saw her pass through the living room, a silhouette against the shadows. But a moment later the cottage was again shrouded in darkness. Edward decided to make a move on the house.

The Wild One too saw Evangeline pass through the cottage. But his vision was part of a dream pulling him toward the dawn. Most of the rest of the dream was reality. Like the morning the letter arrived. Saturday, January 22, 1949, the fifth day of a record cold spell. For five straight days the temperature had barely climbed out of the single digits. Schools were closed. Cars wouldn't start. People without sufficient heat were dying in urban tenements and rural shacks.

Wild Bill had stirred in the middle of the night and heard water running. After a five-minute search through the dark mansion he found the source of the water. A pipe had burst in the basement and the basement was now a huge indoor cement pond three feet deep and getting deeper every second. Wild Bill stared at the water, considered for a moment walking out the back door and never looking back, but then, of course, he waded into that frigid subterranean swamp for a look around. It took him the rest of the night and most of the next morning but finally he got the broken pipe repaired and the sump pump sucking the now four and a half feet of water out of the basement.

Late in the morning, when he came up out of the cellar for something to eat and a cup of coffee, he found the letter beside his cup. It carried a British Honduran postmark dated December 12, 1948. The letter had taken nearly six weeks to reach the house. It was addressed simply: The Winslows, Far Hills, N.J. U.S.A.

Wild Bill could hear the kids crying upstairs as he opened the envelope. Little Helen was just two and Ginny almost three. And another one, the Wild One knew, due before the first thaw. He sat there sipping his lukewarm coffee and thinking much more about the responsibility of three kids and that big house and his new subdivision than about this strange and unexpected letter from someplace he had never been.

> Dear Mr. Winslow,
>
> My name is Gustave Frederick. I am writing in regards to your relative, Mr. John Winslow. I believe you know him as Crazy Legs.
>
> John has been a guest in my house since early September. It is my belief your relative is dying. I inform you of this not because he is in any way a burden to me but because I feel his family should be aware of his condition.
>
> Please feel free to write to me at the address below, or, if time is as short as I fear, simply come. As a relative of John Winslow's you will be welcomed in my home with open arms.
>
> Very sincerely yours,
> Gustave Frederick

Wild Bill read the letter a second time. During his third reading Virginia walked into the kitchen carrying babies on both hips. Another invisible one hung prominently off her belly.

"Everything okay in the basement?"

The Wild One did not hear the question. He rubbed his eyes with one hand and held the letter aloft in his other. "I have to go to British Honduras," he said, slowly, "and I think I should go right away."

*   *   *

Well, Wild Bill went to British Honduras all right; left less than forty-eight hours later, soon after the banks opened Monday morning. But I can tell you, the trip did not play real well at home. Virginia, normally calm and steady and undemanding, acted as if her husband was going off to fight the Japanese for another three or four years. They had a pretty good battle raging when Jimmie Maxwell pulled up to the front door in his Checker. Jimmie was there to drive Wild Bill to Newark Airport so the Wild One could begin his long journey to the small town of Punta Gorda on the Caribbean Sea.

"I'll be back as soon as I can," the Wild One called through the cold after he threw his bag into the trunk. He'd plundered their small savings to make the trip but he thought the expense was justified. He couldn't let his grandfather die all alone in some godforsaken corner of Central America in the house of some guy named Gustave. *I have to go,* he told himself, *I have no choice.*

"Don't bother, damn you," shouted Virginia from the front door. "Don't bother coming back." Ginny and Little Helen were where they had been two days earlier. They seemed permanently attached to their mama's hip. Sometimes she wondered where she'd attach the new one once it arrived. "Stay a year," she screamed into the cold, "stay forever. I don't give a damn." And then she stepped back into the front hall and slammed the front door so hard the whole house shook. A few moments later Auntie Helen, looking more than ever like a family ghost, made one of her rare appearances at the top of the stairs to ask if an earthquake had just hit the Garden State.

It took Bill Winslow forty-eight hours, three planes, a boat, two buses, and a cab to reach paradise. The first thing to hit him was the warmth. After all the intense cold in the northeast it felt good just to unbutton his shirt and feel the sweat run down his arms. Then there was the beautiful young lady with the chocolate skin (of Mayan descent he found out later) and the shy smile who welcomed him to the house and made him a tall, cool drink of coconut and rum.

"Mr. Frederick be with you soon," she said.

"Fine. Thank you."

She smiled and went away.

Paradise was a plantation on the Gulf of Honduras a mile south of the small fishing village of Punta Gorda. The main house sat on a low bluff two hundred yards back from the sea. The house was a sprawling one-story whitewashed concrete structure with high ceilings and slow-moving fans in every room. Most of the furniture was white wicker with feather cushions. The house was very quiet, and spotlessly clean.

Outside the grass grew thick and green. There were flowers and shrubs and fruit trees. The Wild One saw lemons and grapefruits. A badminton net hung between two orange trees. On the grass lay several badminton rackets and a couple of shuttlecocks. But no one played. No one was around.

Beyond the well-tended lawn, away from the sea, the forest began. It was thick and dark and to Wild Bill it looked impenetrable.

"Hello. Mr. Winslow?"

The Wild One turned and saw a small, elderly gentleman wearing crisp white pants and a crisp white shirt and a rose-colored ascot. "Yes. Hello."

"Gustave Frederick," said the old man through a thick German accent.

"Bill Winslow." They shook hands.

"How wonderful of you to come. I was beginning to think my letter had reached no one."

"It took six weeks, sir, but I finally received it."

Gustave smiled. He had a soft, gentle smile, like one of those statues of Buddha, thought the Wild One. "I'm glad. And I'm glad you could come. Your father will be pleased."

"My father? Oh no, Crazy Legs is my grandfather."

Gustave seemed not to hear this. He had the Wild One by the elbow and was leading him across the room. "Come, he's awake. You should see him now before he goes back to sleep. He sleeps many hours every day since the stroke."

"Stroke?"

"Yes. It very nearly took him."

They passed through a wide hallway, lined on both sides by oil paintings of tropical landscapes. "So, how is he?"

That smile again. "Strange, quite strange. But you will see for yourself in a moment."

Gustave Frederick pushed open a door and when Wild Bill looked into the room he saw Crazy Legs seated in a wicker rocking chair wearing nothing but a pair of cut-off pajama bottoms. The old man had been born in 1863. *That*, calculated the Wild One, *makes him eighty-five years old. Jesus, he doesn't look a day over fifty. Still has a pretty good crop of hair both on his head and on his chest.* The chest looked a little concave but the arms still looked strong. Wild Bill wondered if maybe the letter about his being so sick was just a ploy to get the attention of the family.

He walked right up to the old man and stuck out his hand. "Hello, Grandfather. You may not remember me but I'm your grandson, your middle grandson, Will, or Wild Bill as you dubbed me back in the twenties."

Crazy Legs looked carefully into Wild Bill's eyes. A moment passed and then a deep furrow showed itself in the old man's brow. "Enough nonsense, boy," said a deep, gravelly voice which seemed to originate way down in the belly of old Crazy Legs. "We got ourselves a battle to fight, a war to win. No time for nonsense. Nuthin' I hate more than nonsense. Seems most soldiers today know nothing but nonsense. Young whippersnappers like yourself think time's for wastin' but believe you me it ain't. Time's for workin' and fightin' and kickin' the crap outta them Rebs."

Wild Bill turned around and looked at Gustave Frederick, but all he got for his look was another of those Buddha-like smiles.

"Stand at attention, boy," snapped Crazy Legs. "I got my orders. Now you'll get yours. General Meade thinks Lee is tired of these skirmishes we've been fightin' for the last two days. He thinks Lee's about ready to attack, a full-blown attack, probably on our right flank. If that happens there'll be hell to pay tomorrow morning. This quiet burg'll be turned into an inferno. And we'll be right smack in the middle of it, boy, right smack in the middle of the shit. Meade's thinking right flank but some of us think Johnny's coming right down the middle, straight across that open field you see under the moonlight." Crazy Legs took the time to point at the wall. "And if they do, we're gonna have to stop 'em, boy, me and you and those greenhorn buddies of yours from western Jersey. If we let them Rebs through there'll be nuthin' between them and President Lincoln. Follow?"

Crazy Legs paused, waited for a response.

Gustave Frederick whispered in Wild Bill's ear, "Just say, Yes, sir, Colonel."

"What?"

"Yes sir, Colonel. Just say, Yes sir, Colonel."

"Yes sir, Colonel."

So every time Crazy Legs paused, Wild Bill said, "Yes sir, Colonel."

Crazy Legs went over the entire battle plan in great detail. His battalion, part of the Second New Jersey Division, would play a vital role in the third day of fighting at the Battle of Gettysburg and he wanted his men prepared.

Old Crazy Legs had taken on the persona of his long-dead father, Colonel Barton Henry "Gentleman Bart" Winslow. Gustave told Wild Bill that except for occasional moments of lucidity, John was Barton at all times, and more often than not it was the night of July 2, 1863.

"Why," said Gustave, "I don't know, but he certainly dwells on that one particular evening more than any other."

The Wild One explained. "Barton was John's father, the father he never knew. Colonel Winslow died on the morning of July third. He rallied his regiment and met Pickett's Charge head on. He went into battle armed with nothing but his saber and his armor-plated testicles. The family has probably exaggerated his role somewhat over the years, but legend has it that Gentleman Bart's troops were responsible for turning back Longstreet's men at the high-water mark. Without his heroism the Confederate army would have broken through the Union line and marched all the way to Washington. At least that's the way we like to tell it. We like to think Barton saved the Union."

Gustave wore his little smile. "Pretty potent legend."

Wild Bill nodded. "The Colonel paid a price. He caught a Rebel miniball with his stomach and bled to death right on the battlefield. Lincoln later gave him the Medal of Honor. Which didn't do Barton's young wife Dorothy much good. She was a twenty-two-year-old widow with an infant baby. You see, Gustave, on the same day Gentlemen Bart died in battle, little Johnny here was born in a one-room shack in Lamington, New Jersey."

Not much happened during Wild Bill's first three days in paradise. He sent Virginia a telegram assuring her he was alive and well. He went swimming in the sea. He drank rum and coconut juice. He thought about the pleasures of bedding the young Indian girl who made the drinks and served the meals. He dreamed about deserting his post, leaving his wife and kids, forsaking the house and the busted pipes and the debts and the small subdivision he'd just started in Bernardsville. He stood at attention in front of Crazy Legs whenever the old man beckoned his lieutenants. But not once in those three days did Crazy Legs show the slightest interest in the fact that Wild Bill was family. The old man just babbled on and on about those Rebel bastards and how for their belligerence they were going to pay the price come the dawn.

Wild Bill took the evening meal with Gustave. It was during these meals that the Wild One learned a little but not much about what his grandfather had been doing since he had left more than twenty-five years earlier.

"I met your father in Key West in 1937," said Gustave. "John was anchored in the harbor trying to decide where to go next. We had a few drinks and decided to make a sailing trip together. We crossed to Havana and after a few days of drinking and gambling we sailed for Kingston, Jamaica. But on the western coast of Cuba we ran into a tropical storm, damn near a hurricane. We only lived to tell about it because of your papa's keen sailing ability and his intense desire to survive."

Wild Bill had stopped telling Gustave after the first day that Crazy Legs was his grandfather. He was far more interested now in Crazy Legs the sailor. "So what happened?"

"The wind kicked up so fast we barely had time to draw the sails. I was just about swept overboard and surely would've been if not for John Winslow's ability to pilot a sailboat in a tropical storm and save a man's life at the same time. One courageous son of a bitch, your old man. He fought that storm for six hours. By the time it ended we'd been blown way off course, to the southwest we figured. And sure enough, not long after the sky cleared we saw land in the direction of the setting sun. We anchored just down the beach from here, right outside Punta Gorda. That's when I told your papa I'd gone far enough."

"How do you mean?"

"I mean I was done running. I'd been running from the Nazis since thirty-three. I decided to stay right here. Eventually I bought this place. I like it here. The weather's good most of the year. And although you can't see them from the house, I've got several hundred acres of sapodilla trees out back. You know what sapodilla trees are good for, William?"

Wild Bill shook his head.

That smile. "Not much for thousands of years. But then someone found out the tree produces chicle. From chicle they make chewing gum. So while my countrymen are back home bombed and obliterated because they listened to that crazy little Austrian wallpaper hanger, I'm thriving here in the tropics off the goo oozing from my sapodilla trees. A funny life, wouldn't you agree, William?"

Wild Bill did indeed agree. "But what about Crazy Legs?" he asked. "Did he stay here in Punta Gorda also? Or did he move on?"

"As soon as his boat was repaired he headed out. Probably for Key West. Maybe Havana. Your papa didn't like to stay in one place too long. Liked to move on, you know, William, didn't like the moss growing between his toes. Liked to go to England, I remember that. Had some family there I think. But me, I stayed right here. Occasionally, maybe once a year, maybe every other year, he'd drop by for a few days, maybe stay a few months. Of course he was always welcome, because as I told you, William, your papa saved my life. That's close to twenty years ago. Twenty years and counting I owe that old man who's lying in there trying to figure out who he is and where he's going."

Wild Bill thought this over but said nothing.

Two days later, in the middle of the afternoon on another warm and sunny Caribbean day, Crazy Legs passed away. But before he did he fought his way back to the present for a few brief moments.

Wild Bill stood at attention before the Colonel who sat in his rocker wearing, as always, his pajama bottoms. The Colonel kept pounding his fist against the arm of the rocker. "We've got to fight the good fight, man. I've seen too many of our troops turn on their heels and head for the hills at the first sign of trouble. And I've seen those dirty Rebs laughing at us, calling us yellow-bellies in blue. That has to stop, man, and stop come dawn. I talked to Meade about this problem and he put his arm around my shoulder and asked me what we could do about it. And do you know what I told the General, boy?"

"No sir, Colonel, I don't," answered Wild Bill.

"I told him we oughta shoot our own men if we see 'em running from the fight. Shoot 'em down like dogs."

"And what did the General say to that, Colonel?"

"He said . . . he said . . ." But Crazy Legs never finished. He moved on and never went back to the war. His face turned white and his body began to tremble. Right away Wild Bill thought about the time all those years before when he'd sat on his grandfather's lap on the rocker in the sitting room just off the master bedroom. He thought the old man was about to have another stroke.

And he was, but not for a few more minutes. Suddenly Crazy Legs stopped shaking and a bit of color returned to his face. He looked around the room, kept opening and closing his eyes, trying to figure out where he was and what he was doing there. Then he fixed his gaze on the Wild One and stared hard at the young man for at least a minute.

"I know you," he said, finally. "You're Wild Willy, terror of the Winslow Compound. What the hell are you doing here? And by the way, where the hell are we?"

"We're in British Honduras, Grandfather. At the house of Gustave Frederick."

"That old Kraut. I should've let him drown." This made the old man smile. "And what about you? What's your excuse?"

"I just came to see you."

"Why? Did you think I was dying? Did you want something from me? Maybe my money? Well you're outta luck, Wild Willy, there ain't no money left, not a dime. That stupid-ass son of mine lost it all in the Depression. Me, I saw the Depression coming and got the hell out."

Wild Bill waited for the old man to finish. "I just wanted to see how you were getting along, Grandfather."

"I'm doing fine, boy, just fine. Been all around the world. Seen just about everything worth seeing. Mostly bullshit . . . How 'bout yourself? Betcha were involved in that world war, weren't you?"

"I played a small role, yeah."

Crazy Legs twitched for just a moment, as though a jolt of electricity had raced through his body. "I never did get to take part in one of our country's wars. Biggest regret of my life."

"Why Grandfather? You should feel lucky. War stinks."

Crazy Legs struggled with some pain. "I suppose you're right. I suppose it does." His eyes wandered far away.

"You okay, Grandfather?"

"Yeah, sure, I'm okay. . . . Let me tell you something, boy. Take it with a grain of salt but listen anyway."

"Sure Grandfather, go ahead."

The old man drifted off again but eventually came back. "Go for it, kid. Give it every goddamn thing you've got."

"Go for what, Grandfather?"

"Whatever. That part doesn't matter. Maybe it's money, maybe it's sex, maybe it's power. Who gives a shit? Just go for it. Don't go halfway. Don't do anything halfway."

The Wild One nodded. "Right, okay."

"But don't expect it to do much. Don't expect it to do you any good. Don't expect it to make you happy or bring you friends or make you immortal."

"Then why do it, Grandfather?"

"Because, boy, you've gotta do it. You've got no choice." The color quickly began to run out of the old man's face. Sweat began to pour off his brow. "I'll tell you what, Willy my boy, why... why don't you take this old..." His hands began to tremble and the legs began to twitch. His whole body grew stone rigid, and then relaxed. "... take this old man... take this old man home." Crazy Legs pushed the final words out and then he collapsed on the floor and never got up again.

Wild Bill woke up in his hospital bed and saw Crazy Legs lying there on the hard, cold floor. *Don't expect it to do you any good. Don't expect it to make you happy or bring you friends or make you immortal.* The first light of another new day filtered through the dusty hospital window. "I'm goin' home," the Wild One told the empty room, "I'm gettin' the hell out of this dump today."

But not, he knew, for at least a few more hours, so he settled back and pulled Crazy Legs off the floor. Gustave Frederick gave Wild Bill the money to bring Crazy Legs back to the States. He said it was the least he could do for the man who had saved his life.

It took three days and a pretty good tussle with the customs people over in New York to get the dead body back to Far Hills. But finally the Wild One returned home. Eighteen days he had been gone on his sojourn to Central America. Virginia forgave him the moment he walked through the front door. What else could she do? It's tough to stay mad at a guy who has just hauled his dead grandfather four thousand miles on buses and boats and planes.

The same undertaker Helen had hired in '45 to work on Charles prepared Crazy Legs for burial. They buried him very early on Sunday morning, February 20, 1949, up in the still-small but ever expanding family graveyard. Crazy Legs, founder of Winslow Cordage and builder of the Winslow Compound, was given the center plot. His wife Caroline, the first to be laid to rest there, lay beside him. Also present were Charles and Shady and their youngest son Robert. More were on the way.

It started to snow during the service. Just a few flakes at first but pretty soon a regular blizzard. The mourners finished up and made their way back to the house. Before they got there Virginia screamed with pain and announced the new baby was on its way. The fifteen-mile drive to the hospital took over two hours. The car slipped and slid and several times very nearly crashed. Virginia moaned and groaned in the back seat. Wild Bill winced every time he heard his wife scream. He kept telling her to hang on, just a few minutes more. She hung on, somehow. Maybe Mary didn't want to make her debut in the back seat of that old Chevy wagon. She waited until Mama was safely inside the hospital, warm and dry and tended by a staff of doctors and nurses. Only then did she break the seal and show her face. Her eyes were wide open and alert. She seemed to know exactly what was going on, exactly where she was and what she was doing there.

Burials and births, thought the Wild One, *burials and births*. And then, the dawn exploding beyond the window, he dozed, and in his dream he found Evangeline padding barefoot and naked across the cottage floor.

Edward made his way down through the early morning gloom. He moved slowly, cautiously, his eyes constantly watching the house for signs of light or life. He crept up through the brambles and the wild roses behind the garage. Twice he drove thorns into his flesh but he pulled them out and pinched the wound until the pain passed.

He stood at the northwest corner of the garage and peered around the corner. Still the house was dark except for that one light burning in the kitchen. Edward did not know who was in the house but he felt sure it contained several of his siblings and quite possibly his father. Little Eddie knew his father was not in any hospital. That part he knew was a lie.

He went down on all fours and slipped around the corner and through the open door into the garage. He did not dare turn on the overhead lights. But he could see well enough. He was not looking for anything special, just whatever might come in handy while he decided on a course of action. He took a hatchet off the workbench plus a spool of twine and a pocketful of twenty-penny nails. He searched through the Range Rover and the Mercedes-Benz 250 Sports Coupe. From the Rover he took the first-aid kit. From the Benz he took nothing, but he had to control an urge to tear to pieces with his hatchet the plush leather seats of that sleek roadster.

Outside the dawn began to break. Edward decided he had better get back to the cover of the woods, back to his perch. He studied the house before making his getaway. No signs of activity. He was just about to make his move when he noticed the old Ford F-100 for the first time. He saw the New York license plates and wondered who owned the pickup. Little Eddie took a long look at the battered body. The sun reached out then across the wide front lawn and bounced a beam of light off the rusty steel. And that's when Edward saw it. Hanging there in its rack across the rear window: the shotgun, the old Remington double-barrel twelve-gauge shotgun. Edward saw it and he knew right away he had to have it.

He went down on his belly and crawled across the macadam drive. When he reached the side of the truck away from the house he straightened up and tried the door. It creaked but it opened. He wasted not a second. His arm went in and pulled the gun off the rack before anyone inside the house had time to breathe. Only Mary shuddered, but in her early morning sleep she had no idea why. Edward silently closed the door and crawled with his weapon back to the garage. Once able to take a good look at it, he recognized the shotgun immediately. It had originally belonged to Crazy Legs, the gun he had used to bring down that buck. Charles had only shot the gun once, at a family of raccoons who had been upsetting the garbage cans. When the Remington kicked it knocked Charles right on his butt. He put the gun away and never touched it again. Wild Bill found it in the back of one of the hall closets in the early '50s. He cleaned it, oiled it, and used it to shoot ducks and pheasant until he gave the gun to his son Henry on Henry's fifteenth birthday, much to the dismay of the boy's mother. Edward knew the gun belonged to Henry. "But Henry's dead," Edward mumbled at the dawn, "so who owns the gun now? Must be the same guy who owns the truck. Must be

Bobby. Gotta be Bobby." But Edward had a hard time imagining Bobby with a shotgun.

He opened the barrels, checked the chambers. Empty. No shells. Inside, in her sleep, Mary breathed a sigh of relief.

But Little Eddie found a handful of shells in an old box under the workbench. He filled both chambers. Mary awoke with a start, gunfire exploding all around her. Little Eddie stuffed the rest of the shells into his pockets, slipped out of the garage, and headed for the hills.

Chapter Twenty

———————————●———————————

Mary sat up in bed and glanced out the window. She thought she saw someone moving through the underbrush up behind the garage. But the flat, early morning light made it difficult to see. She decided the figure must be Crazy Legs heading for the woods to shoot himself a buck. She shrugged, yawned, and went back to bed, back to sleep, back to her dreams.

For the next two hours, until nearly eight o'clock, the big house made not a sound. The Winslow womenfolk did not stir. Rosa and Emily slept arm in arm in Emily's double bed. Ginny probably would have slept until noon had the telephone not startled her slumber. The first ring she barely heard but the second ring exploded like a gunshot. In less time than it takes to raise an eyebrow, Ginny woke up, sat up, grasped her surroundings, and concluded young Madeline had been gang raped by Stu and Stu's crack-smoking cronies. Stu had never smoked crack but Ginny did not believe that.

She practically tackled the telephone. "Yes! Hello? Aaron? Is that you, Aaron? What is it?

"Hello?" asked a calmer but not exactly soothing voice on the other end. "Is this the Winslow residence?"

Ginny realized her scenario might have been a bit premature. She looked around to see if anyone had noticed. All was quiet. "Um, yes it is."

"Who is this?"

Ginny looked at the receiver and frowned. "Who is *this*?"

"This is Samantha Tuttle-Winslow . . . Edward's wife."

Ginny had heard all about Samantha but had never met the woman. "Well this is Ginny Cohen, Edward's sister."

A moment of silence before Samantha asked, "Is Edward there?"

"Not as far as I know, but I certainly would think he should be."

This gave Samantha pause. "Yes, well . . . perhaps he's on his way."

"You mean you don't know?"

"Actually, no. We were discussing whether or not to come. But last night, before we went to bed . . . we hadn't really made up our minds." Samantha hated the defensive tone in her voice.

"Perhaps Edward made up his own mind."

Samantha decided the conversation could only grow uglier. "Perhaps." And then, after a moment, "I think maybe I'll call back in a few hours to see if he's arrived. He may just have gone out for an early morning drive."

"Time will tell."

"Yes."

Another pause.

"Well," said Ginny, "call later. Maybe he'll be here."

The two women said good-bye then replaced the receivers simultaneously with a distinct bang. For the next few minutes they sat on the edge of their beds and mentally ripped apart their sister-in-law. Samantha got over it first. She decided to get dressed, go to the office, work through her morning appointments, and then see if Edward had surfaced. If he still was unaccounted for she would pack a bag and drive to Jersey.

Ginny, unaware of Edward's tenuous mental stability, hoped her little brother was coming home to see his father. Certainly she knew Eddie had been through some troubled times, but self-absorption in her own West Coast melodrama had kept her from fully understanding her brother's situation. In her mind Edward was just another guy who had been through some tough times, a rough divorce. She knew dozens of people in L.A. going through the same hell. Some of them handled it better than others. But she had no idea Little Eddie blamed her, at least in part, for his misfortunes. Had she known she would have wondered why. She had not even been around when the whole thing with his wife and kids happened. She'd been three thousand miles away, on the other side of the country.

Ginny stopped thinking about Edward and his icy wife Samantha when a little picture in the back of her head shot forward and she saw Stu taking credit orders for a roll in the hay with her sweet Madeline. Not long after her hubby paid the price.

"Yes," said a sleepy voice, "hello, what is it? This is Dr. Cohen."

"Aaron, it's me."

A short pause, long enough to glance at the clock: 5:07, pacific daylight time. "Surprise, surprise."

"I want you to pack up the kids and come east."

"What?" Aaron rubbed his eyes and sighed.

"Just for a few days."

"Ginny!"

"I need you here."

"You mean you need the kids there."

"I need you all here."

Aaron tried to stay calm. "What's happened?"

"Nothing's happened," she snapped. "I just think it would be better if we were all together right now. I think it's important."

Aaron sighed. He found it impossible to muster a sense of humor. But he knew his wife, her anxieties and her eccentricities. "It won't be today, Ginny. No way. I have two operations this morning."

"What about tonight?"

"You're pushing."

"Well?"

"I'll have to call you this afternoon."

"I might be at the hospital with Daddy."

"Then I'll try again. Just relax."

They said good-bye. Ginny sat on the edge of the bed and let out a long, sad-eyed sigh. Through the window she saw the early morning sun reflecting off the swimming pool. She decided to take a swim, it was hot enough already. But first she wanted to call Barton. It was only 8:15 but she wanted to call when the others were not around. She dialed the number of the hospital in Waycross, Georgia. *So many hospitals,* she thought, *so many sick people.*

"Good mownin'," said a female voice, "Waycross General."

"I'd like to speak to Barton Winslow, please."

"Kinda early, ma'am. Mr. Winslow probably still be sleepin'."

Ginny sighed again but not so desperately this time. "Would you please check. It's very important I speak with him."

"Awright, ma'am, just a minute."

It took more like five minutes but finally Barton's voice came across the wire. "Hello?"

"Barton?"

"Yes, who's this?"

"It's me, Ginny. . . your sister."

"Ginny?" Barton sounded surprised but really he was not surprised at all. This was exactly what he had expected. "How did you find me here?"

And so began a quarter of an hour of explanations. Barton told all about his encounter with the rednecks and Ginny told all about Wild Bill's fall down the back stairs. He told her he was feeling much better and would be discharged from the hospital as soon as he spoke with the doctor. She told him the Wild One was doing pretty well also but that he would probably not be discharged for several more days. Barton immediately interpreted the whole chain of events as premeditated, as definitely some kind of positive omen. He could hardly contain his joy when Ginny told him how everyone had arrived the day before, everyone but Edward, "but even he," she said, "might be on his way."

"I'll be there as soon as I can," said the youngest of Virginia's sons. "I just have to find out about my van and then I'll be on the first plane north."

"You feel well enough to travel?"

"I feel like someone ran over me with a steamroller but that's not going to prevent me from getting home."

"I know Daddy wanted Joseph or Bobby to fly down there and make sure you were okay."

"Tell them not to bother. I'll get myself up to Newark and then maybe someone could come to the airport and pick me up."

"Definitely, but you take care. Do what the doctor tells you to do. And if you run into any problems just call."

"I'll call as soon as my plane gets in."

No sooner had Ginny set the receiver back in its cradle than the ringer shattered the silence. She scooped it back up before it had a chance to ring again. "Yes? Hello?"

A soft, calm voice followed a short pause. "I'm sorry to bother you so early in the morning. I certainly hope I have the right number."

"Yes? So?"

"My name is Irene, Irene Biddford—"

"Yes?"

"Biddford-Winslow. I'm Bobby's wife."

Ginny paused while she tried to place yet another brother's spouse, another spouse she had never met.

"This is the Winslows," asked Irene, "isn't it? William Winslow?"

"Yes, yes it is," said Ginny. "I'm sorry, I was just . . . never mind. I'm Ginny. Bobby's sister. We've never met. How are you?"

"I'm just fine, thank you. I'm just a little concerned about Bobby is all. That old truck he drives. I just wanted to make sure he made it down there okay."

"Oh, he made it, Irene. We all made it. Most of us anyway. In fact I can see Bobby's truck sitting out in the driveway. He must still be sleeping. Everyone's still sleeping. Almost eight-thirty and this house is as quiet as a morgue."

"I don't want you to wake him. Just tell him I called, and of course we send our love."

Ginny remembered Bobby had two little girls but she couldn't remember their names. "I'll tell him, Irene, just as soon as I see him."

"Thank you. . . . How's your father?"

"Pretty well, thank you. Better than I think any of us expected."

"That's good news. I've never met your father but I've heard a lot about him."

"Anything good?"

"Well, mostly good. Some maybe not so good."

"I'm surprised there's any good at all. Bobby and father were not exactly peas in a pod."

"It's strange," said Irene, standing there behind the counter at Merlin's Tackle Shop, "when we were first married Bobby rarely mentioned his family at all. But lately, and I mean the last few years, he's been talking more. Especially about your father. I try to get him to open up because I know there must be some things in the past that keep him from you all. But I don't push. He has to do this on his own."

Ginny actually took a moment to reflect. "You know, Irene," she said, finally, "this may be impossible but I just had an interesting idea."

"An idea?"

"Yeah, I think you ought to pack a suitcase and put those kids of yours in the back seat of the car and drive down here." Ginny could hardly believe she was saying this. The last thing she wanted was more people hanging around the house. "I think it's time you met Bobby's family."

"I'd like nothing better, Ginny, but—"

"No buts, Irene, just do it. It's not often we're all in the same place at the same time."

"But you see, we don't have a car. Just the truck and—"

"So rent one."

"I don't know if we could afford that. I'd have to talk to Bobby about that."

"The hell with Bobby. Just do it. Surprise him. Surprise all of us." Ginny really had it going now. "I'll loan you the money for the car. You can pay me back sometime."

The two women passed the idea back and forth for another few minutes. Pretty soon it was no longer a matter of if Irene would come but when. That same day, just as soon as she could line up a car and get the kids ready, was the decision they finally reached.

Ginny hung up the phone feeling quite pleased with herself. She had too many things to do, too many things to worry about, "But maybe," she whispered to herself, "just maybe everything will work out. I just have to figure out where everyone will sleep. I have to get the kitchen organized, buy some food, call my agent, see if he can postpone the toothpaste audition, call the hospital, see what time we can visit Daddy, call Aaron, insist he bring the kids east . . ."

Chapter Twenty-one

———————————————•———————————————

The cottage screen door opened and closed with a bang. Evangeline stepped out onto the deck. She raised her arms and stretched. Edward heard the door slam, raised his binoculars, and brought her into focus. Edward knew Evangeline, had even played volley-ball and softball with her at the Blackwells' estate along the Delaware. But he looked at her now and had no idea who she was. She wore running shorts, running sneakers, and a tight, navy blue T-shirt. He watched as she bent over and touched her fingers to her toes. Then she placed her hands against the side of the cottage and pushed back on one leg at a time. He could see the long, thin muscles in her thighs and calves. Her legs reminded him of Christine, of making love to Christine, of putting his head between Christine's breasts and wanting to cry but not. And then she was off: across the tennis court, around the pool, onto the driveway. He lost her for a moment as she passed between the garage and the house but then he saw her running down the drive. She had long, fluid, graceful strides. As Edward watched he forgot all about hate and vengeance and revenge. But then she was gone, around the first bend in the road, and Christine was gone, and his mother was gone, and the boys were gone, and Edward brought his true purpose back into focus by fixing his binoculars on the back door of the big house.

Ginny pushed open the door and stepped out into the morning. He did not recognize her at first; it had been years since he had last seen her. But he knew it was one of his sisters, either Mary or Ginny. She wore a cotton robe and kept her arms wrapped tightly around her chest. *Definitely Ginny*, thought Edward as he fiddled with the focus knob, *no doubt about it*. He knew she had married a baby doctor and lived in California and had kids. That reminded him again of his own kids, the kids he no longer had, and this time the memory aggravated him to the point where he thought about aiming the shotgun at his sister, even if he didn't actually pull the trigger. But instead he just followed her across the lawn with the glasses. *There's plenty of time to act,* he decided. *Right now I just have to be patient, lay low, figure out what's what and who's who.*

Ginny stood at poolside and dipped her toes into the water. After all the severe heat the pool water was almost tepid, but to Ginny it felt cool, almost cold. She kept the pool water back in Bel Air at eighty-five degrees.

She found the thermometer tied to the ladder in the deep end; the same place the thermometer had been for as long as she could remember, since her long-ago youth. This tiny testament to continuity brought a mixture of sadness and joy to her thoughts. Ginny had mixed emotions about her childhood. As an actress and a wife and a mother she longed to remember her youth as a time of simple pleasures and carefree adventures. But as a middle-aged woman emotionally ravaged by time and its influences, she knew her youth had been a difficult time filled with regrets and missed opportunities. She sighed and pulled the thermometer up out of the water: seventy-nine degrees.

At forty-four she was still in excellent shape; thin and firm even in her thighs and buttocks. She swam and did aerobics and played tennis (a game the Wild One had taught her years ago) at least twice a week. Ginny stayed fit partly because her friends stayed fit and partly because she lived in southern California but mostly because she still believed Success and Stardom were right around the corner and no way did she want a saggy butt and flabby thighs on the cover of *People* or when she made her first appearance on the "Tonight" show. She wore a tight one-piece bathing suit under the robe. She removed the robe and dove gracefully into the crystal clear water.

Crazy Legs had built the original pool in the 1890s. It had been rebuilt a couple times since and each time it had been made larger. It was rectangular in shape, almost ninety feet long and fifty feet wide; an enormous concrete pond halfway between the back stoop and the tennis court. There were two diving boards, both had been installed by the Wild One. There was a one-meter board for those seeking the simple joys of diving. And a three-meter board for those more adventurous souls who liked to propel themselves up into the air, swirl and spin and flip, and then slice open the water with a splash. Wild Bill had considered installing a ten-meter diving platform but his insurance man had talked him out of it.

Ginny was midway through her tenth lap when Evangeline slowed to a walk and started across the lawn. She waved and smiled as Ginny approached the end of the pool.

Ginny considered ignoring the wave and making her turn, but that, she knew, would be extremely rude. *Still, who does she think she is, strutting across the lawn like that, all smiles and arms and legs and with practically no clothes on?*

Evangeline was sweaty but barely breathing hard from her three-mile run. "Good morning, Ginny. Did you sleep well?"

Ginny smiled back without even realizing it. "Yes, pretty well."

"That's good. Looks like another beautiful day."

The smile disappeared. "Looks like another hot, sticky day to me."

Evangeline nodded but kept on smiling. "So did you have a nice visit last night? With your father, I mean."

Ginny wiped the water off her brow. She wanted to be cool and aloof but somehow Evangeline's manner made that impossible. "He was in much better shape than I'd expected after our phone call the day before yesterday."

Evangeline remembered her small lies and her anxious tone of voice on the telephone. "I'm sorry," she said, "I didn't mean to alarm you or make you think he was worse than he really was. Those first few hours, when he was unconscious, were pretty scary."

Ginny saw the emotion in Evangeline's face. "No, I didn't mean it that way. You did the right thing. The doctor told us that for a while he was in real danger."

"Yes."

"But I don't think any of us could quite believe it when we walked into his room and found him on the floor doing push-ups."

"Push-ups!" The alarm in Evangeline's voice gave them both pause for several seconds.

"Yes, push-ups. I'm sure he did it just to show us that a little

thing like a fall down the back stairs doesn't slow Wild Bill
Winslow down. Still, seeing a seventy-year-old man with a concussion and a sprained ankle and a separated shoulder doing
one-armed push-ups left us all speechless."

"I can understand why."

Little Eddie watched all this through his field glasses but much
to his displeasure he could not hear a single word the two ladies
said. He felt certain they were discussing his institutional
incarceration.

*Actually the two ladies were trying, without being obvious, to gain
some small morsels of information. Ginny wanted to know if Evangeline
had ever slept with her father, but of course she could not simply ask
such a thing. In fact, the whole idea of a sexual liaison between the two
seemed totally preposterous to Ginny, but nevertheless . . .*

*Evangeline's inquiries were far less personal but she too tried to get
answers without asking direct questions. She wanted to know when
Ginny and the others were going back to the hospital. She wanted to
know because she wanted to take her sons to visit Billy Boy but she did
not want to take them when the others would be there.*

*So they played this conversational cat-and-mouse game until finally
Evangeline decided to take a more honest tact.*

"I thought I'd take the boys over to see your father this morning.
They've been bugging me to take them ever since the accident."

This opened the door for Ginny. "I guess they know Wild Bill
pretty well?"

Evangeline hesitated but only for a moment. "Yes."

"John and Paul must get to see a lot of the old boy."

Just about every evening, Evangeline wanted to say, but she
satisfied herself with, "They see him from time to time. He's been
real good to them."

"I'm sure he has." Ginny pulled herself up out of the water,
dried her arms and legs with a towel, and pulled on her
robe.

Evangeline took the opportunity to change direction. "I was
listening to the weather this morning. It's supposed to reach the
mid to upper nineties this afternoon."

"It was incredibly hot in the house last night. I can't believe Father never installed central air-conditioning."

"There's a"—Evangeline started to say there was an air conditioner in the master bedroom but she caught herself in time—"a fan in the attic to draw air through the house."

"Yes," said Ginny, missing the dropped beat, "that's been there for an eternity. But believe me, it doesn't do much. It was on all night long and all it did was make a lot of noise."

Evangeline nodded and quickly moved on. "By the way, not that it's any of my business, but I just wondered about the car I saw in the drive this morning."

"Car?"

"Yes, early this morning, around five-thirty. Paul woke up from a nightmare and I went into the kitchen to get him a glass of water. That's when I saw the headlights."

"I wonder who it could've been?"

"I couldn't see the car, just the headlights. It seemed to be pulling out but I'm not even sure about that."

Ginny turned and looked across the lawn at the driveway. "It looks like all the cars are still here: the Mercedes, Bobby's truck, the Range Rover. I don't know. . . . Years ago we used to have a milkman who came at the crack of dawn. Do you still get milk delivered?"

"Not since I've been here."

"Well that's strange. I'll ask the others. As far as I know they're all still sleeping."

Upstairs, in the back bedroom, Emily and Rosa were wide awake. Actually mother and daughter inhabited Lear's castle in the British countryside. Lear, played by young Rosa in a peculiar bit of casting, has demanded his three daughters pledge their eternal love before he divvies up his massive kingdom. Goneril and Regan, without pause but certainly with a degree of hypocrisy, have expressed their complete and unwavering daughterly devotion. Cordelia, played of course by young Emily, does not feel fit to lie or deceive. . . .

EMILY: Okay, Rose, you say, "Cordelia, tell me you love me. Speak."
LEAR: Cordelia, tell me you love me. Speak.

CORDELIA: Nothing, my Lord.

EMILY: Now say, "Nothing?"

LEAR: Nothing?

CORDELIA: Nothing.

EMILY: Okay now, "Nothing will come of nothing. Speak again."

LEAR: Nothing will come of nothing. Speak again.

CORDELIA: Unhappy that I am, I cannot heave my heart into my mouth. I love your Majesty according to my bond, no more nor less.

EMILY: All right now, "Cordelia, better mend your speech at least a little, lest you mar your fortunes."

LEAR: Cordelia, mend your speech or else mar your fortunes.

EMILY: Good, Rose.

ROSA: Thanks, Mommy.

CORDELIA: My Lord, you have begot me, bred me, loved me. I return those duties back as you are fit. I obey you, love you, and most honor you. Why have my sisters husbands, if they say they love you all? Perhaps, when I shall wed, that Lord whose hand shall take my plight shall carry half my love with him, half my care and duty. I shall never marry like my sisters, to love my father all.

ROSA (looking out the window at her Aunt Ginny swimming): Mommy, can we go swimming?

EMILY: In a minute, Rose. Now say, "But goes the heart like this?"

LEAR: But goes the heart like this?

CORDELIA: Ay, my good Lord.

ROSA: Now can we go swimming?

EMILY: One more line, sweetie. Say, "So young and so untender?"

LEAR: So young and so untender?

CORDELIA: So young, my Lord, and true.

ROSA: Okay, Mommy, let's go.

Emily sighed and hugged her daughter. She felt like she was beginning to understand Cordelia's conflict. "I can do this part, Rose, I can do it. All they have to do is give me the chance. I can play this bitch, this Miss Goody Two Shoes."

Rosa raced down the front stairs and out the back door just as Ginny remarked to Evangeline about the others still sleeping. "Hi Aunt Ginny, hi Aunt Evangeline," she shouted as she jumped up onto the high dive and plunged feet first without fear into the water.

Evangeline smiled. Ginny frowned. Emily soon joined them at poolside. Before long they were discussing the mysterious car.

"I didn't see any car," said Emily. "At five-thirty I was sound asleep."

"I'm sure," said Ginny, "everyone else was also."

"Quiet as a church in there now," said Emily. "Not a sound or a soul around."

"Oh well," said Evangeline. "I'm sure it was nothing. Someone probably just made a wrong turn."

"Probably."

It took another half an hour but finally Emily realized her Jaguar was not in the garage. She rushed into the kitchen where Rosa and Ginny and Mary sat around the table eating toasted hamburger buns they'd found in the freezer and sipping hot jasmine tea they'd found in the back of one of the cupboards. There wasn't a whole lot to eat or drink. Wild Bill didn't do much shopping. He ate most of his meals out or down at the cottage.

"Someone stole it," shouted Emily. "Someone stole the Jag!"

Well, this announcement, as you can easily imagine, caused quite a commotion. First they all rushed out to the garage for a look, then they stood around in the driveway discussing the various scenarios. Emily told them about the weirdo in the VW Cabriolet, about how he had known where she lived. Ginny felt sure he'd stolen the Jag. Mary had reservations. She kept insisting there must be some other explanation. The keys, she said, were inside in the front hall where Wild Bill kept all the keys. How, she wondered, would the weirdo in the VW know where the keys were? I don't know, said Emily, I don't know. . . .

And on and on. Until finally it took the innocence of youth to ask, "Maybe Uncle Joseph and Uncle Bobby went for a ride."

The ladies rushed inside but found not a trace of their brothers.

"They've gone to Georgia," announced Mary, "they've gone to get Barton."

This conclusion led Ginny directly to the telephone. She called the hospital in Waycross, and as the tiny twists of fate sometimes turn, she learned that Mr. Winslow had been discharged not fifteen minutes earlier.

The DC-9 touched down at Savannah International Airport at the exact moment the conversation between Far Hills and Waycross came to a close. Joseph and Henry, as Bobby, left the airplane and entered the terminal at about twenty minutes after nine in the morning. They went directly to the Hertz rent-a-car desk where Joseph used his Winslow's West American Express card to procure him and Henry a Ford Thunderbird. No economy cars for Joseph. That wasn't his style.

By quarter to ten the brothers were heading south on Interstate 95, brother Joseph behind the wheel, brother Henry behind the map.

"We'll go south to Brunswick on I-95," said Henry, as Bobby, "then head west to Waycross on Route 84. Looks like about a hundred miles. Probably take a couple hours. We should be there by"—he glanced at the digital clock on the dashboard—"by noon or a little after."

Joseph smiled and nudged the accelerator a little closer to the floor. The Thunderbird was in the fast lane traveling on cruise control at eighty-two miles an hour. Brother Joseph had already made a few calculations of his own. He figured to be in Waycross by eleven o'clock, and hopefully, as long as there were no hassles at the hospital, halfway back to Savannah, with Barton in the back seat, by noon.

Barton hoped to reach Savannah by noon also. But first he had to get out to Homerville and pick up his van. There was a Trailways but not for a couple hours so he decided to take a cab. It cost him sixty-two dollars to make the twenty-seven-mile trip but no way was he going to leave his vehicle and his painted sculpture at some filling station in some crummy little southern crossroads town. His friend up in D.C. had wired him five hundred dollars, so he had plenty of cash. He reached Homerville just as his brothers turned off I-95 and headed west on U.S. Highway 84.

The filling station owner, a dirty little man with stubble on his chin and a mouthful of rotten teeth, charged Barton one hundred and twenty-five dollars to tow the van up from Edith and another forty dollars for two days' storage. Barton paid the money, filled the tank, and drove away. All he wanted to do was get out of Georgia and get home. Ever since the call from Ginny his heart had been pumping a little faster than normal. He could not remember the last time he had felt so excited. He tempered his excitement with thoughts of the Wild One battered and broken in the hospital, even though Ginny had assured him the old boy was going to be just fine. He could not believe that in a few hours, by the end of the day, he would be sitting around the kitchen table of the old house in Far Hills with Bobby and Joseph and Mary and Ginny and Emily and who knew who else? Maybe their wives and husbands and kids, maybe everyone'd be there. *The more*, he thought, *the merrier.*

Driving north and then east through Argyle and Manor, and then back through Waycross, Barton kept trying to imagine how everyone would look, what everyone would say. It had been so long since he had seen some of his siblings. There were so many things he wanted to tell them, so much emotional baggage he wanted to unload. *But*, he wondered, *will they listen? Will they care? Will they hear me if I tell them I love them?* He assured himself they would. "That's what this is all about," he said right out loud, "this coming together of the family; it's a resurrection, a rebirth." He nodded, then moved to select some Bach for the stereo. But the Bach was gone. All the cassettes were gone. So was his radio and his tape player. And his paints and his brushes and his tools and his clothes. But he told himself he didn't give a damn. He told himself that none of that stuff mattered now.

Like many dreamers and artists, Barton's expectations far exceeded the province of possibility. He wanted miracles in a world choked by reality. But for the time being I think we should let the young man have his dreams. There's no need to let him see the symbol of reality speeding toward him at more than seventy miles an hour. Let's protect him for a while longer. I mean, who knows? Maybe miracles do happen. We can't slow Joseph down but at least we can divert Barton's eyes.

Joseph's got that Thunderbird's pedal to the metal. And he's coming fast and furious, roaring down Highway 84 like a man on a mission. . . .

The Ford Thunderbird and the Chevy cargo van shot past one another a mile east of a little Georgia town coincidentally named Hoboken. Joseph looked right up into the eyes of the driver of that van, his own brother's eyes, but all he saw was a guy with a bandage around his forehead and a goofy smile on his swollen face.

Chapter Twenty-two

———————————●———————————

Family comes from the Latin word familia *which originally referred to the servants in a Roman household. Now we define family as the fundamental social group of society, as a group of persons of common ancestry. By ancient and modern definition I think we can safely call the Winslows a family, an American family. They are White Anglo-Saxon Protestants descended from Old World stock. It is their kind that came across the north Atlantic, slaughtered the Indians, tamed the land, fought the wars, built the big bankrolls and the railroads and the capitol buildings and the national debt. For many generations the Winslows, and families like them, controlled the land and the people and the industries and the government. They spread west from the banks of the Atlantic, and like locusts they devoured everything in their path.*

Times change.

Wild Bill knew times had changed. And he feared many of those changes. Chaos bordering on lawlessness had become the most prevalent component of modern American society. *Too many goddamn cultures, too many immigrants, too much violence, too much welfare, too much greed and graft. The whole thing's turning to shit right before our eyes.*

He was wide awake in his private hospital room now, had just devoured his breakfast of bacon and eggs and juice. *The New York Times* lay spread out across his lap but he could not bring himself to read any further. *Nothing but cop killings and racial attacks and child abuse and water contamination and drug addiction and this AIDS stuff. Jesus! It's enough to make a grown man cry.*

He threw the newspaper on the floor and turned his thoughts to the family, to the Winslows past, present, and future. Off and on all morning long he had been thinking about Virginia, about how she had been the glue that held the family together. *For thirty years she did the job. For thirty years she put up with me, put up with my ego and my bullshit.* He shook his head. *Like that time we went to Carnegie Hall to hear Beethoven's Third*... Virginia had procured the tickets to hear Bernstein conduct the London Philharmonic through sheer force of will. *Two tickets, seventh row center, I'll never forget. I got there late, had to go straight from Hoboken.* For six months the Wild One had been working sixteen-hour days on the development project along the Hudson. He arrived at Carnegie Hall carrying his black leather briefcase.

Virginia met him in the lobby. She looked miffed. In less than ten minutes Bernstein would begin the music. "You're late."

"Sorry, I had car trouble. I had to come over by cab."

Her eyes said car trouble was no excuse. She looked at the briefcase. "Bring a little work along, did you?"

"I couldn't just leave it out in the street."

They went into the hall and took their seats. While Virginia read the program Wild Bill opened his briefcase, glanced at some contracts. He scribbled notes and more than once reminded himself to call Bowen Blackwell in the morning. Then the lights went down, the hall grew silent. Bernstein marched out onto the stage. The audience responded with applause. He bowed, turned, and faced the orchestra. He raised his arms and the music began. The Wild One had heard the Third Symphony many times on LP. Virginia had played a recording of it for him just the night before. He tried to relax, tried to find the rhythm of the music. But the contracts beckoned. They kept whispering to him from inside that black leather briefcase. *Read me, read me.* He began to fidget, to shake his legs. Beethoven's first movement seemed to last forever.

Finally it ended. The audience stirred but remained hushed. Virginia produced a small flashlight from her purse. She turned it on to study her program before the second movement began. As she was putting it away he nudged her arm and asked if he could see the light for just a moment. She narrowed her eyes but handed it to him. At first he just held the flashlight in his hand, rolled it between his fingers. But after a few minutes, the slow, depressing pulses of the second movement rattling his ears, he could not resist. He switched on the light and very carefully opened the briefcase.

Virginia turned immediately. "What are you doing?"

Like a little kid with his hand in the cookie jar he replied, "Nothing."

She scowled at him and turned away, back to the music. He tried to turn off the light, to close the case. He knew the ramifications. *Sure, I knew she'd be pissed off.* But like a junkie he could not resist. *I had to know the specs for the electrical contractors. I had to know right then.* So he read on. Quietly, cautiously, he turned the pages. Her looks sent shivers down his spine. The music of Beethoven's *Eroica* exploded in his ears . . . The Wild One read until the batteries on that small flashlight went dead.

"Why," she asked him then, with more sarcasm than he thought she could muster, "don't you go out and buy some new ones?"

Those were her last words to him for more than a week.

The Wild One laughed about it now but there had been no laughter then. *I can't believe I did that to her. Besides the kids, music was the most important thing in her life. Jesus, I can't believe half the shit I did.* But he made up for some of it; at least he tried. After the Hoboken project was completed he traded the huge penthouse overlooking the Hudson for the apartment on Fifth Avenue. He had planned to keep the penthouse because it occupied the same real estate Winslow Cordage had once occupied. But Virginia wanted the apartment in Manhattan because she wanted to be closer to the museums and the theaters and the concert halls. So he agreed to make the deal, to make the swap. *But if I hadn't agreed, if I hadn't swapped the penthouse for the apartment,* thought the Wild One for maybe the one millionth time, *we wouldn't've been on Fifth Avenue that night. We wouldn't've been walking along the sidewalk when that drunken maniac in the Rolls-Royce* . . . He sighed and rubbed his temples and forced himself not to finish the thought.

Wild Bill Winslow knew his wife never would have allowed the family to deteriorate the way it had. She would have used all of her powers to hold the family together, to keep the children close. His own reasons for reconciliation were many, but deep down he knew he had to do it for her. She deserved nothing less.

For years the Wild One's connection to the past had been negligible. His old man (no matter if Charles or Crazy Legs was his father) had not given a damn about the family or the family's past. Charles hadn't given a damn about much of anything beyond hobnobbing with the rich and fogging his apathy with alcohol. Prohibition was the cruelest wind to blow through his life. Crazy Legs had never been a great believer in the past; both his parents had died before his tenth birthday. So like father like son: Wild Bill had grown into manhood without much appreciation or respect for the past. He felt a certain obligation to it, as evidenced by his trip to Punta Gorda. Although in many ways that trip was a journey of self-indulgence more than an odyssey of selfless devotion. He needed a reason to escape the mounting pressures of family, and what better excuse than a family member in distress. No, it was later in life, after financial success had been assured, that the Wild One began to read the lessons left by those who had come before. And only recently, since Evangeline had come into his life, had he decided to act upon those lessons to preserve the legacy for those still to come.

For a time after the death of Virginia and during the early years of his marriage to Bettina, Wild Bill had played with the notion of abandoning his children, of writing them out of his will. *They don't do shit for me, barely give me the time of day. So why,* he'd asked himself repeatedly, *should I give them anything? All they want from me is my money! If I didn't have money they would've told me to go to hell a long time ago.* Most of them only made token appearances, usually when they wanted something; and others, like Eddie and Henry, had totally absolved themselves from the family. *If this is the way they want to act,* he'd tell himself in bed at night when he couldn't sleep, *then to hell with them.* He continued to support several of his offspring financially but almost every day during the early 1980s he considered cutting them off at the knees, blowing them off without warning. Barton, Emily, Joseph, Mary—they were all in one way or another dependent upon Wild Bill's wallet, and he was growing sick and tired of them sponging without the slightest show of appreciation.

His desire to separate himself from his children grew considerably when Evangeline arrived on the scene. During their first two or three years together she had no idea she had this effect on him. He rarely spoke about the kids and when he did it was usually something informational, not emotional, something to do with a marriage or a birth or a divorce. But later the Wild One began to talk more and more about the distance between himself and his children. One night, Evangeline would always remember, he told her he was changing his will, cutting out not only Bettina but all seven of his children as well. That night was the beginning of the change. Evangeline slowly and patiently opened the Wild One's eyes. It took months but she showed him without ever pointing that to forsake his children was to admit his entire life had been a waste of energy, a pointless meandering. And in time he saw she was right: without connections the paths become cluttered with nothing but chaos. Her own parents were dead but she kept them alive with her thoughts and her words. And here he was trying to kill off the living.

He lay in that hospital bed thinking about Evangeline and hoping she would come before any of the others. He needed her to come and reassure him, tell him everything would work out fine, work out the way he had planned. . . .

And then the warm room and the steady hum of the silence pushed his eyes closed and sent him wandering. He traveled back through the years and over the lush, green, rolling hills of Jersey to that big house on the banks of the Delaware just north of Burlington. It was the middle of the night of July 4, 1776, and that old wooden house fueled its own flames as though soaked with a thousand gallons of high-octane gasoline. Patriots for the cause of Independence had marched on the house after midnight and set it ablaze. Imagine the scene: chaos, confusion, fear. More than two dozen men and barely grown boys armed with muskets and torches and conviction. They surrounded the house in the darkness and ordered all those inside out. The inhabitants, seven Winslows strong, refused to budge; the patriarch, Robert "Jawbone" Winslow standing at the front door demanding the intruders retreat, calling them treasonous scoundrels, petty criminals, disciples of the devil himself. But the mob heard barely a word. They were overcome with the day's declarations from Philadelphia. They were out for trouble, out for blood. Glass shattered, clapboards splintered, shutters burned. Within minutes the flames owned that old house. The Winslows had no choice but to flee. One hundred years under the same roof and in an historical instant, because of events way beyond their control, their lives were irrevocably changed.

The good Winslows of Burlington had been labeled Tories, supporters of the Crown, of the hated King George III. They had housed British troops, sold the British army meat and corn and lumber. They had been to parties in Burlington and Philadelphia where high-ranking redcoats had been in attendance.

All of this did not escape the notice of local supporters of an independent America; of those who wished to break the ties between the colonies and Mother England. These associations between the House of Winslow and the British army were easy enough to explain, but when tempers rise common sense is often lost. The Winslows housed British troops but only because the law of the land ordered them to do so. They sold food and lumber to the redcoats because they had food and lumber for sale and the redcoats had money. It was an economic relationship; politics had nothing to do with it. Jawbone was not a political man. "We're Quakers," he kept insisting right up until his Day of Judgment, "we're beyond this petty struggle to decide who will make the laws and force those laws upon the people; we are God's people, belonging neither to the King nor to these self-appointed emissaries who call themselves Patriots."

It sounded good but it didn't save his hide. A shot rang out of the mob as Jawbone led his brood out the front door and across the front porch where he had sat since his youth with his father and his father's father and his own twin boys, Henry Lane and Robert junior. The musket smoked, and an instant later Jawbone fell from the porch, mortally wounded. The Wild One saw his ancestor fall but the fall did not shake Wild Bill awake; it made him remember even more.

He was there the next day when Henry Lane and Robert junior argued for hours amidst the smoldering timbers and the ashes and the decimation of the family homestead. Their father was dead. Their house was destroyed. The American War for Independence was just beginning.

Henry Lane wanted nothing to do with the struggle. He pleaded the case of Quaker neutrality. "Quakers do not take sides," he insisted, "Quakers do not bear arms." His argument sounded strong and just, but in fact Henry Lane was a closet Loyalist. Not only did he believe the Union Jack would quickly crush the rebellion, he secretly hoped the victory would come sooner rather than later. He wanted the preservation of the status quo. As the eldest member of his generation of Winslows, a full seven minutes older than his identical twin brother, Henry Lane knew he would control the family's vast land holdings and financial fortune. He did not want some stupid war, especially one so totally motivated by economics, upsetting his plans for expansion and ever more prosperity. He wanted the redcoats to squash the rebels, to nip the voice of dissent in the bud. Adams and Stockton and Jefferson could be tarred and feathered and locked in the public stocks as far as he was concerned.

His little brother held a somewhat different point of view. For months Robert junior, nicknamed Mad Dog after a childhood skirmish with a some-said-rabid mongrel mutt, had been warning his father about possible repercussions if the Second Continental Congress meeting in Philadelphia passed a resolution demanding sovereignty from Britain. Mad Dog never said it out loud in his father's house but he secretly hoped that resolution would come, and come soon with the full force and fury of blood and guts. Who knows precisely why, but Robert Winslow junior had dismissed the Quakers as a bunch of pantywaists before his thirteenth birthday. His opinion of Henry Lane was that Henry Lane was a jackass, a jackass and a yellow-bellied coward who wouldn't fight even if someone threw mud in his face. Robert would fight at the drop of an unwanted nickname, and because of his combative nature he was almost continually in his father's doghouse. But now Jawbone was dead and Mad Dog could think and say whatever he chose to think and say.

The twins had recently turned thirty. They had both lived those thirty years under the silent, heavy hands of not only their father but also their grandfather and even their great-grandfather, Freeman. That morning, under a gray July sky, smoke and ashes blowing in the summer breeze, the two young Winslows unbound their chains and struggled to become men. Henry Lane was determined to rebuild the family's home and protect the family fortune. He kept insisting, while his mother and sisters looked on, that nothing would change, the winds of rebellion would blow away and life would soon be back to normal. Robert junior could see his brother had their mother's support, and he knew nothing he could say would change her mind. These men calling themselves Patriots had burned down her house and murdered her husband; no way was she about to side with that rabble. But Mad Dog had decided long before, back when he'd first read an account of the tea party in Boston Harbor, to join the cause for Independence. He had made this decision partly out of a political conviction but mostly because he had the makeup of a rebel, the personality of a fighter. No matter what the status quo, he had a desire to break it down and create something new.

So as that July afternoon faded into dusk and the arguments

wound around only in circles, the Winslow womenfolk began to fix up a corner of the barn for sleeping and for preparing meals. They had hours before given Jawbone back to the earth, buried him in the family cemetery out behind the barn. "You're either with us or agin us," said Henry Lane. Robert junior spit in the dust at his brother's feet, turned on his heel, and walked away. Wild Bill, his dream more vivid than the long pull of reality, watched the distance between the brothers grow. He did not know what to do. He did not know which way to turn. . . .

Evangeline stood over the bed and saw the frown cross his face. His eyes and brow narrowed. He looked worried and confused. She wanted to bend down and kiss his lips but with her boys at her heels she decided to keep the kiss to herself. He opened his eyes then and the frown turned instantly into a smile.

"A bad dream?" she asked.

"An old family squabble," he answered.

"I see."

"I didn't know which side to take. It was confusing. I didn't know if I should stay home or go to war."

"War?"

"Yes," he said, "the War for Independence."

Evangeline nodded and smiled. She let the moment pass. "I found a couple of soldiers down in the lobby. When I told them I was going up to see the famous William Bailey Winslow they asked if they could tag along."

John and Paul, quiet and hesitant on their first visit to a hospital since delivery day, stepped up to the bed. "Hi Uncle Billy."

Wild Bill's smile spread across his entire face. "Well I'll be a son of a gun. Come on over here, boys, and give this old buzzard a hug."

They did just that, climbing onto the bed and giving the Wild One the best bear hugs he'd ever had. He held them tight, first John and then Paul and then both of them together. They wanted to know when he was coming home and when they were going fishing. He said he was coming home real soon and that they'd go fishing first chance they got. But Evangeline said no way, you're staying put until the doctor says different, and no fishing for at least a month. He said he could rest at home. She said she'd heard about the push-ups. He laughed and grabbed her by the waist. When the nurse walked into the room a few minutes later all four of them were wrapped in an embrace. The nurse felt immediately the emotional pull of this family scene: the injured grandfather with his daughter and her two young sons. She stepped quickly back into the hallway to give them a few more moments together.

Chapter Twenty-three

●

Unlike the nurse, an emotional RN with strong family ties, Mrs. William Bailey Winslow probably would have thrown up had she witnessed that scene at Morristown Memorial Hospital. Bettina had no stomach for outward displays of affection.

She stirred slowly on that huge king-size bed in her Sheraton Hotel suite just outside of Portsmouth, New Hampshire. The clock beside the bed read: 10:43. Checkout time was eleven but that had never stopped Bettina from holding on to a room until late in the afternoon if she felt like it. If they wanted to charge her for another day, she didn't give a damn; it wasn't her money. She rolled over and tried to go back to sleep but eleven hours of slumber was as much as her body could stand. After a few minutes she sat up, switched on the light, and picked up the telephone. From room service she ordered coffee, juice, an English muffin, and a single soft-boiled egg. Then she dialed the number of her friend Millicent down in Newport. She wanted to know how Millie had slept her first night without her third hubby Lawrence, the one who had recently run off with their Polish chauffeur, Stan.

The phone rang a dozen times or more before someone answered. It was the maid, Sylvia. "Yes, hello? Tattersall residence."

"I would like to speak to Mrs. Tattersall."

"Who is calling, please?"

"Bettina Von Culin." Bettina liked the sound of Von Culin better than Winslow, thought the name had the ring of class, and so she used it whenever she could get away with it.

"I am afraid Mrs. Tattersall will not be able to come to the phone."

"And why is that? Is she still asleep?"
"No."
"Has she gone out?"
"No."
"Well then?"

Well, it took a while but finally Sylvia told Bettina why Mrs. Tattersall could not come to the phone. Millicent, you see, was dead. She had consumed half a bottle of Gilbey's the night before and then gone to bed and swallowed an entire bottle of Demerol. Sylvia had found her a few hours ago, white as a sheet and dead as a doornail. The police had already been to the house and the body had already been carted away. The day before Millicent had laughed with Bettina about her hubby running off with Stan the chauffeur, but when push came at shove and Millie had to deal with the silence and the solitude of that big house in Newport, she decided the matter was actually more depressing than she had originally thought. So she decided to take immediate action. Booze and barbs did the trick.

Bettina listened to Sylvia weep but when the knock came at the door bearing her breakfast, Bettina cut the maid short, said so long, and hung up the phone. Millicent's sudden suicide certainly bothered Bettina. She never would have thought her old friend would take such drastic action. She drank her coffee and ate her muffin and decided Millie had taken the whole thing too seriously. Lawrence had always been a schmuck; demonstrating his sexual preference for Stanley only added to his long list of inferior qualities. *If he'd been my husband,* Bettina told no one but herself, *I would've sued the faggot for divorce and taken him to the legal cleaners for every penny he possessed. Millicent was weak,* Bettina concluded, *weak and petty and far too emotional to lead the good life of upper-crust America.*

She finished her breakfast and picked up the telephone. She had more important things to concern herself with than dead friends, especially ones who couldn't take the heat. She told herself that seemed callous but as the phone began to ring she reassured herself by concluding that there was nothing more she could do for Millicent anyway.

"Good morning, Morristown Memorial Hospital."

"Yes, good morning, I'd like to check on the condition of Mr. William Winslow."

"Just a moment, please." When the receptionist returned she told Bettina that Mr. Winslow's condition was stable and improving.

"Stable and improving," repeated Bettina, enunciating clearly the final word.

"Yes, stable and improving," said the receptionist. "Would you like me to connect you to his room?"

Bettina considered this for several seconds. "No," she said, finally, "that won't be necessary."

She hung up the phone and sat down on the edge of the bed. The recovery of Wild Bill was much more on her mind now than the demise of her old friend Millicent. She considered returning to Bar Harbor; there didn't seem to be any reason to drive all the way to New Jersey if the old bugger was on the road to recovery. But she felt the need to keep up appearances. She knew his kiddies would no doubt be there, some of them anyway, and so she decided to make the trip. It took her most of an hour to shower and shave her legs and fix her face and get dressed, but by one o'clock she sat behind the wheel of her Cadillac Allanté heading south down Interstate 95.

Samantha's office was above a bakery on State Street just off the Ithaca Common. She had been there for nine years, since before Edward even. It was a small office with a waiting room not much bigger than a walk-in closet, a tiny cubicle for her receptionist, and a pretty good sized therapy room with two overstuffed tweed chairs and a three-cushion tweed couch for those patients who felt the need to become horizontal. There were two squeaky clean double-hung windows on the front wall that looked out over the west end of the Common. Samantha had a thing about clean windows. She washed them at least twice a week, inside and out. And she had the furniture in the room positioned so that no matter if the patient chose the couch or the other chair, Samantha could see out the windows. Whenever she grew bored with a patient's problems she liked to look out the windows at the shoppers walking in and out of the stores and sitting on the wooden benches eating ice cream cones and hot dogs.

The young lady on the couch this morning had been boring

Samantha for weeks. A Cornell coed, she spent most of every session complaining about her narrow-minded parents and her narrow-minded peers and her narrow-minded professors. Samantha had sessions ago stopped listening. She looked out the window and thought about Edward. She wondered where he was, what he had in mind. *No way,* she told herself, *is he going down there to make amends, to make peace with his siblings and his father. He'd need me for that. No, he has something else in mind, and I doubt if it's anything much good.*

Her wristwatch alarm went off at the top of the hour, drawing Samantha back to the therapy room. She pretended to write down a few notes on her pad. She then told the young coed her problems could certainly be overcome with a lot of determination and perhaps a few more sessions. She suggested two appointments a week, "until the two of us can work this thing out." The young coed nodded in agreement. Less than a minute later Samantha had her out the door and on her way. Over the years she had mastered the art of getting rid of patients. She had even considered designing a course on the subject for students studying to become emotional therapists.

As soon as she had the door closed she called the apartment. It rang four times and then her own voice answered. "Hello, this is Samantha. I'm not here right now but if you leave your name and . . ." She waited for the message to finish and then, after the beep, she said, "Edward, if you're there would you please call me right away. Please. It's very important."

She waited five minutes. Edward did not call back. And how could he? He had no telephone out there in the woods on his deer perch. Samantha tried the house in Far Hills. The phone rang at least a dozen times. She was just about to replace the receiver when a little kid's voice answered. "Hullo?"

"Yes, hello, this is Samantha Tuttle-Winslow. Is Edward there please?"

"I don't think so," said Rosa.

"Who is this?"

"This is Rosa."

Samantha did not know who Rosa was. "Is this the Winslows?"

"Yes."

Samantha sighed. "Is there someone else there? A grown-up?"

"They're all out in the car. Mommy and Aunt Ginny and Aunt Mary. We're going to the hospital now to see Grampa."

"I see," said Samantha, "but your Uncle Edward's not there?"

"Uncle Joseph and Uncle Bobby were here but we think they went to see Uncle Barton in Georgetown."

"Georgetown?"

"Yes, Georgiatown."

Samantha had little patience for children. "Okay, Rosa . . . Would you do me a favor? Would you please tell your Aunt Ginny something?"

"Okay."

"Tell her I haven't found Uncle Edward and that I'll be coming down there later this afternoon."

Rosa waited for the rest.

"Okay, Rosa? Will you tell her?"

"Yes."

"All right, Rosa, good-bye."

"Good-bye." Rosa hung up the telephone and ran out the back door and jumped into the front seat of the Mercedes.

Samantha buzzed her receptionist. She said she would see her next patient but the remainder of the day's schedule would have to be canceled. So would everything for the next few days. "I have an emergency. I have to leave town for a while."

Irene didn't have to rent a car after all. The folks up in Blue Mountain Lake might be a pretty independent lot but they pull together when a neighbor needs a helping hand. Irene had called the house in Far Hills from the telephone in Power Merlin's tackle shop. Lots of folks who lived on the lake used Power's phone. When he got his monthly bill from AT&T he just added whatever long-distance calls folks had made to their accounts. Once in a while he got burned for a random call but usually the system worked pretty well.

Power's sister-in-law Aggie was there sipping her morning coffee when Irene called New Jersey. Aggie always seemed to be on hand whenever something out of the ordinary happened in Blue Mountain. She didn't exactly eavesdrop on the conversation between Irene and Irene's sister-in-law, but when the call ended she had a pretty good idea that Irene needed to get down to Jersey on family business. The two women talked it over, Aggie's mouth doing most of the moving, and within fifteen minutes Irene had herself a free set of wheels. Aggie's husband, Digger Merlin, ran the service station in Blue Mountain. Digger pumped gas and fixed engines and tried as best he could to straighten bent bumpers and take the dings and dents out of battered fenders. About a year ago some state politician from over in Albany had been up in Blue Mount with some woman who most folks speculated was not his wife. Well, this pol smashed up a real nice late-model Buick Regal on that hairy turn along Route 30 just north of the Adirondack Museum. The pol and his mistress didn't get hurt too bad, just a few bumps and bruises, but Digger had to go up and haul that Buick back to his garage with his wrecker. The car sat out back for most of the summer. Then one day the title to the car arrived in Digger's mailbox along with a note from the pol saying, "Thanks for everything and I'd just like to forget the whole incident and why don't you keep the car?" Which Digger did. He fixed it up as best he could, registered and insured it, and used it for leisurely weekend drives up to Saranac and over to Lake Placid.

Which was undoubtedly the reason he balked when his wife told him to lend the car to Irene Winslow. But Digger had long ago learned that peace was best served by granting Aggie her every wish. So he drove that Buick over to brother Power's tackle shop, went inside, and personally handed the keys to Mrs. Winslow. By this time Irene had gone back across the lake to collect the kids and pack a bag and lock up the house (mostly from vacationers who felt they had the inalienable right to trespass inside quaint lakeside cabins). Katie and Constance could hardly contain their excitement. Neither of them had ever been farther than Utica. All of their friends were on hand to see them off. In fact, most of the town had gathered once again outside Merlin's to see this second wave of Winslows set off on their journey south.

The kids waved out the back window of that fancy Buick as Irene pulled onto the highway and headed east on Route 28. She had money and sandwiches and a full tank of gas and a good map and Ginny's directions to the big house in Far Hills. But nevertheless she felt the pull of apprehension. She was not at all sure this was the right thing to do. It had been such an impulsive decision. She rarely made impulsive decisions. She worried how Bobby would react. She worried about meeting his brothers and sisters and father. And most of all she worried about the new baby. The doctor had assured her just last week that she had at least three more weeks before the baby arrived. But Irene felt like the baby could come at any time. She drove along, remembering how both Katie and Constance had come suddenly and without warning. Neither had been a problem. She probably could have given birth to those two girls right in her bedroom. *But in a Buick,* she wondered, *somewhere out on the New York Thruway? Or down in New Jersey in some strange hospital room with some strange doctor?* These thoughts troubled her but she pressed on, her swollen belly pressed against the steering wheel. She drove fast through North Creek and Warrensburg. By noon she had reached the Northway and started the long haul south to the Garden State.

The doc remembered suiting up, pulling on the latex gloves, walking into the operating room, saying good morning to his assistants. He remembered telling the little girl to relax, "Everything will be fine, it'll all be over before you know it." He remembered her mouth wide open and his big hands going in to begin the job. But the rest was a blank. He could not recall actually connecting with the tonsils, making the incisions, pulling the tonsils out, closing up the incisions with sutures. He sat in his office at the hospital smoking a cigarette and admitted to himself that he had done the operation on autopilot. *But it must've gone okay,* he thought, *because after the close I got a "Job well done" from the RN in O.R.* But still the whole idea of doing a tonsillectomy and not remembering doing it sent a shiver of fear down Dr. Cohen's spine. "This is the way you screw up," he said out loud to himself, "this is the way you get sued for malpractice and lose every damn thing you've worked for." He took another pull on the cigarette and tried to relax. Aaron was not really a smoker but occasionally after an operation he liked to kick back and light one up. He kept a pack of Larks in his desk drawer for just those occasions. The tobacco was stale and harsh but he didn't care, barely noticed. The same thing that had been on his mind during the tonsillectomy was on his mind now while he smoked: Ginny. *How,* he asked himself, *am I going to swing a trip east? I'll have to rearrange my whole schedule.* But he knew he would find a way. It was all part of the deal, part of the compromise. He knew she would do the same for him. He sat back and dialed up his travel agent.

"Yeah," the agent assured him, "I can get you and your kids on a flight tomorrow morning to Newark. No problem. Economy class or first class, Dr. Cohen?"

"First class."

"Okay, first class it'll be. Can I get you a car? A hotel? . . . A car, fine. Economy or—a Caddy, okay. Great, fine, a Sedan de Ville. Call you A.S.A.P."

Aaron hung up and called the house. It took twenty or twenty-five rings but finally Adam answered the phone. "Yeah?"

"Is that the way you always answer the telephone? 'Yeah?'"

"I was sleeping," snapped the boy's snotty voice.

Aaron glanced at his watch. It was almost nine-thirty (pacific daylight time). He had to be back in O.R. in less than half an hour. "We're going east tomorrow."

The boy was not happy. "What? Why?"

"Because I said so, that's why."

"Shit," the boy mumbled. "I gotta lotta stuff to do, Dad. Ya think I could skip the trip, like stay home?"

"No, I don't."

"I could look after the house."

"You're only twelve years old."

"Thirteen."

"Whatever. You can't stay home alone. Is your sister there?"

"I think she's sleepin'."

"No I'm not." Madeline walked into the master bedroom of the house in Bel Air and grabbed the phone away from her little brother. "Hi, Daddy. It's me. What's up?"

"We're flying east tomorrow."

"Hey, that's great. I could use a vacation."

Aaron sighed again. *Fifteen years old and she needs a vacation.* "I'm not sure what time we're leaving. Probably in the morning. I'll be home for dinner. We'll talk about it then."

"Okay Daddy, bye."

The telephone rang as soon as Aaron put it down. It was the travel agent.

"What do you mean, nothing tomorrow morning?" asked Aaron.

"Nothing at all," said the travel agent. "Tomorrow afternoon at four or I can get you on a dinner flight tonight leaving at seven."

Aaron sighed and swore under his breath. "I'll have to call you back."

"Right. No problem."

Aaron hung up and headed for O.R.

* * *

Before we head back to Jersey there's one more family I'd like to check on. They don't have much to do with the rest of our story, not directly anyway, but indirectly they play an extremely important role in the events which will transpire over the next thirty-six hours. I'm talking of course about the Sullivans of Kittery Point, Maine. You remember them: Todd and Christine and their three sons who were once the sons of Edward and Christine, William and Edward, Jr., and Henry.

Let's see if we can find them. They've gone out to Fort McClary for a picnic on this, their first day of summer vacation. There's a whole group of other kids and moms out there also. Fort McClary's an old coastal defense rampart once used by the United States Marine Corps to discourage the British navy from sailing up the Piscataqua River during the War of 1812. Its view of the Atlantic and the Isles of Shoal made it an excellent place to build a bulwark. Now the fort is a favorite place for Kittery Point picnickers. The moms love the desolate vistas and the kids love the slippery cliffs.

Mama Sullivan and her three boys look like a pretty happy bunch. Christine knows most of the other moms, and the boys look like they have loads of friends. I hate to say this but probably the best thing to ever happen to this foursome was getting out from under the burden of Little Eddie Winslow's psychosis. I suppose I could throw some tragedy into their lives, maybe have young Henry slip and fall off the rocks and crack his head open and drown in the snarling sea. But that would be pure fabrication. These kids are okay. They're going to make it. Maybe they won't find a cure for cancer or bring down the house at Carnegie Hall or score the winning touchdown in Super Bowl L, but I have the feeling they'll wind up being decent, relatively well adjusted middle-class white people.

They don't know their true biological father is sitting up on that deer perch above the big house in Far Hills. They don't know he has a gun. They don't know he's sick and pissed off at the world and glaring through his binoculars at his three sisters and his niece as they drive off in the Wild One's German luxury sedan. They don't know all the crazy, violent thoughts floating around in his head. They don't know any of this stuff, and yet they are partly responsible for it. Maybe Little Eddie Winslow never had his screws properly adjusted but when he slipped over the edge and lost his boys those screws got tightened down way beyond the stress point. If he had somehow held on to those boys I don't think he'd be up in that tree. I don't think he'd have a loaded shotgun at his side. I don't think he'd be contemplating patricide.

None of this is to suggest his actions are their fault. I'm not interested in blame so much as cause and effect. I'm interested in the interconnectedness of the universe. I doubt we will visit the Sullivans again during this narrative but nevertheless those boys will be nearby at all times. They'll be out there in the woods hanging on the periphery of their Daddy's thoughts. Every move he makes will at least partly be motivated by a desperate need to avenge the unjust devastation of his small branch of the Winslow family tree.

Chapter Twenty-four

———————————————•———————————————

"So who was it, Rosie?"

"Some lady."

"Some lady?" asked Emily. "What lady?"

"Samantha."

"Samantha?" Emily buckled her daughter's safety belt and put the Benz into drive. "Who's Samantha?"

"Samantha is Edward's new wife," answered Ginny from the back seat.

"Oh, right," said Emily, "I knew that."

Ginny leaned forward as the car sped down the driveway. "What did she want, Rose?"

"She wanted to speak to Uncle Edward." The kid was more interested in the push-button window than her conversation with Aunt Samantha.

"Leave the window alone, Rosa," ordered her mother, "I have the air conditioner on."

"So what did you tell her?" asked Ginny.

"I told her Uncle Edward wasn't here. I didn't know I had an Uncle Edward, Mommy."

"Yes you did, Rose. You just forgot."

"So what did Samantha say?"

Rosa stopped playing with the button that operated the passenger-side remote-control mirror and turned around. "She told me to tell you she was coming later to see us."

"I knew it," said Ginny as she sat back in the seat, "I knew she was looking for some reason to come here."

Mary, sitting beside her older sister, was not surprised. She knew everyone connected to the situation would be there before long. She had known that much ever since Lois Chilton had appeared at Westminster Abbey with news of the Wild One's fall.

Mary listened as Ginny related the conversation she'd had earlier with Samantha. Ginny said very little Mary did not already know. The thing that puzzled her was the whereabouts of Edward. She wondered where he was. Why he hadn't arrived. What role he would play once he finally did arrive. She knew all about Edward's emotional roller coaster ride, but she had no idea her brother had become a madman.

"Really, Emily, that's not nice," said Ginny, snickering.

"Maybe not but it's still pretty funny."

"And probably true."

"What's that?" Mary asked.

"You've been drifting off again, Mary," said Ginny. "Our little sister has just suggested that perhaps Edward married Samantha so he could receive free therapy for life."

Mary glanced from one sister to the other. "And that's funny?"

"I was just kidding, Mary. God, you take everything so seriously."

"Why? Because I don't believe in ridicule?"

Emily kept her eyes on the road. "Oh, I thought maybe it was because you hadn't had any in so long."

Ginny turned and looked out the window, tried to wipe the smile off her face.

Mary nearly shot back a counterinsult but instead said, "I've never even met Samantha. I'm not about to start making her the brunt of insensitive jokes."

"None of us have met her," said Ginny. "They've been married for four years and no one in the family has ever laid eyes on her."

"So is that her fault? She's probably very nice."

"Not from what I hear," said Emily.

"Oh, and what do you hear, little sister?"

Emily could not resist. "I've heard she keeps Edward in a cage and only lets him out to feed and do the deed."

Ginny giggled like a schoolgirl but muffled it when Mary said, "That's atrocious. How would you like it if someone spoke about you that way?"

Emily was about to answer when she heard Rosa ask, "Mommy, what's the deed?"

The back seat passengers grew silent while Emily thought about her response. "Oh . . . it's nothing, Rose. Mommy was just pretending, trying to get Aunt Ginny to laugh."

Rosa nodded and switched her attention to the radio buttons. Like most kids her age, she had a rather short attention span. The adults in the car, however, allowed the conflict to dictate the mood the rest of the ride to the hospital. They did not utter another word.

"Hey, look," shouted Rosa, "it's John and Paul."

"Where?" asked Ginny and Emily at exactly the same time.

"Over there, with Aunt Evangeline."

Sure enough, there they were, coming out the front door of the hospital and heading across the visitor's parking lot. Emily swung the big Benz into an empty slot right beside Evangeline's pickup. Evangeline waved and smiled. The Winslow women waved back and pushed open the doors. The three kids greeted each other like long-lost pals. They all jumped into the bed of the pickup and started to play some game that had no name and no rules but which the three of them understood perfectly.

The four women jockeyed for position. It may have been unintentional but within a few seconds the Winslow sisters had Evangeline surrounded. At least she felt surrounded. They exchanged pleasantries.

So, you've been up to see him?

Yes, I took the boys up. They've been bugging me to bring them over.

And how is he?

Evangeline started to say frisky but decided feeling better would sound less intimate.

That's good.

Says he's ready to go home.

That doesn't surprise me.

Me neither. But he really should stay another few days.

At least.

Blah blah blah blah blah. The words coming out of their mouths had next to nothing to do with the thoughts going on in their heads. Evangeline felt defensive and wondered what they really thought. Emily looked over her old childhood chum and wondered if she knew the whole story here. Ginny felt pretty certain her father had bedded this . . . this teenager. And Mary just stared as she tried to fit together this latest piece of the puzzle.

And then Evangeline, "Well, I know he's anxious to see you all, so I won't keep you."

And Ginny, "I guess we should go up."

And Emily, "I want to go in just to get out of this heat. It must be a hundred out here."

"At least."

And then the good-byes and Evangeline asking if there was anything they needed at the store and Ginny saying no, she had to go shopping later anyway, but please keep an eye out for any new arrivals, i.e. Samantha, Irene, Aaron, etc.

Finally waves and see-you-laters before the two teams went their separate ways.

And then the sisters, not even out of the heat yet, changed their tune. Ginny, as the eldest, sang the first verse. "Do you get the feeling something's going on between that young lady and our dear old father?"

Emily sang the refrain. "I most certainly do. And I think it's that old dirty deed again. Did you see her eyes light up when I asked how he was today?"

Mary certainly had (she rarely missed an expression or an intonation) but still she chose to sing in a different key. As they crossed the lobby and stepped into the elevator she said, "I really don't think it's any of our business."

"Of course you don't," said Emily, "but that's only because we think maybe it is."

They were not the only ones going up. An old lady wearing a black hat and carrying a bamboo cane stood at the rear of the elevator.

"I think it's definitely our business," said Ginny. "I mean after all, half a century must separate them. If Evangeline is having some kind of"—Ginny glanced over her shoulder, then lowered her voice—"some kind of relationship with . . . with him, then she must have some ulterior motive."

"Such as?" asked Mary.

Ginny threw an irritated look at her sister. "Such as money, of course."

They reached the third floor and the doors opened. The old lady with the cane and the black hat said, "Excuse me," and stepped out. Before the doors closed she turned and smiled. "Money and sex make the world go 'round, girls. That's a fact of life."

The Winslow sisters did not smile back. They rode the rest of the way in silence. Minutes later they were at his door. He lay in bed flipping through the pages of the *Wall Street Journal*. "Grampa!"

shouted Rosa. She ran across the room, jumped onto the bed, gave the old boy a hug.

"Oh, man," said the Wild One, "I needed that. Hugs like that make a man feel young again. Why don't you and your momma come out to the country to live and it'll be your job to give this old geezer a hug every time he looks a little glum?"

"Okay," agreed Rosa. "What's glum?"

"Glum? That's like sad, unhappy, you know."

"I've never seen you sad, Grampa."

"That's because whenever you're around I'm not."

None of the three sisters smiled. They did not understand or trust this small but significant moment of intimacy between Wild Bill and Rosa. They stared at the old man and the little girl and tried to recall a similar moment from their own childhoods.

"So," asked the Wild One, "any news of Barton?"

Ginny filled him in on Joseph and Bobby's trip to Georgia and how Barton had already been discharged from the hospital.

"I'm not surprised," replied Wild Bill. "It's just more miscommunication. Something this family has long been famous for."

Then Ginny told him about the call she'd had from Bobby's (really Henry's) wife. "Unless she changes her mind she should be here this afternoon."

"High time we met those Adirondack mountain folks," said the Wild One. "Now all we need is Little Eddie and that bride of his to join our little party."

"They're coming too," said Emily.

"What's that you say?"

"Edward and Samantha are coming also," said Ginny.

"Edward! Coming to see his old man? You must be joking?"

"Nope. Samantha's coming anyway. We're not sure yet about Edward. No one seems to know exactly where he is. He's temporarily disappeared."

This news distracted Wild Bill immediately. The idea of Little Eddie unbound troubled him. He had never admitted it to anyone, just vaguely to himself, but his middle son frightened him. *Scares the crap out of me if you want the truth, even more than those crazy Japs did during the war.*

"Aaron and the kids might be coming also," he heard Ginny say.

"Great," he said, shaking off his vision of Edward hiding behind the shrubbery with a machete. "Bring 'em on, I want everybody assembled. I'm getting out of this dump sooner than later, and when I get home we're gonna have us—"

"Do you really think," Ginny asked, "you're ready to leave the hospital so soon?"

"Damn right I'm ready, girl. And as soon as I get home we're gonna have us a party and talk some things over. I have a few things I want to say. I don't get to see any of you all that much so I don't want to waste this opportunity when I've got you all here together."

"So what is it, Daddy?" asked Ginny. "What do you want to tell us?"

Wild Bill sat up high and straight in his hospital bed. He wore a pair of lightweight summer pajamas, brand-new. Evangeline had bought them for him when he had first been admitted to the hospital. He didn't own any pj's of his own. He'd been sleeping in the buff since they mustered him out of the Corps back in '45. "Nope, not here," he said. "I want everyone present, and I want us to be at home, where we belong."

"Sounds like pretty serious stuff, Daddy," said Emily.

"Nothing serious about it, kid."

"Mysterious then."

"Nope, not mysterious either. Just want to talk is all. Get a few things off my chest."

Several seconds passed before Ginny said, "We saw Evangeline out in the parking lot."

This announcement immediately sparked the Wild One's attention. "You did, did you?"

"Yeah, her and the kids."

"John and Paul," added Rosa.

"Right," said the Wild One, "John and Paul."

The daughters waited for more.

The old boy did not disappoint. He drifted away for a few moments but then, "I'll tell you something about your old friend Evangeline, Emily."

"What's that, Daddy?"

"She saved your old man's hide."

"How do you mean?"

"I mean I'd probably still be lying at the bottom of the back stairs if not for that young lass." He almost said something about how none of his kids had been there to help, almost said, *I would've died right there on the floor if I'd waited for any of you to come to my rescue,* but he managed to back off. He managed to keep his mouth shut.

"I guess it was pretty lucky she found you," said Ginny, sounding sincere but really just probing for more details.

Lucky my ass, thought the Wild One. He very nearly launched into a tirade about how Evangeline had saved his life years before she'd found him at the bottom of the stairs. *She,* he thought, *saved my life from booze and boredom and a shitty marriage and a whole slew of selfish kids.* But he kept this to himself. He wanted to tell them but feared his own wrath. "Lucky? I suppose. Sure. Why not? If you believe in that stuff."

"I just meant," said Ginny, "that . . . well . . . that it was lucky she was there when you needed her."

Wild Bill thought it over. "There's no doubt about that," he said. "She was definitely there when I needed her."

Chapter Twenty-five

The big Thunderbird pulled up in front of Waycross General Hospital a few minutes after eleven o'clock. "Let's go, bro'. Let's bust Barton loose and get the hell outta Dixie before the sun gets any higher in the sky."

Henry, as Bobby, followed Joseph up the wide set of concrete stairs and through the automatic glass doors. He felt, as the older brother, that he should take charge but Joseph marched across the lobby, straight up to the reception desk. The woman behind the desk, gray hair and a painted smile, watched them coming.

"Good morning, ma'am," said Joseph. "My name's Winslow, Joseph Winslow. This here is Bobby Winslow. We've just come all the way from Aspen, Colorado, to see our little brother Barton. If you could just direct us to his room, we'll mosey on down and see him."

The smiling, painted mouth opened. "I'm afraid that's impossible, Mr. Winslow." The voice was thick with the South.

"And why's that, ma'am?"

"Because your brother is no longer with us, Mr. Winslow."

"Say what?"

"Mr. Barton Winslow checked out a little after nine o'clock this morning."

"Are you sure?"

"Oughta be. I did the paperwork. A real nice young man, your brother. Said he had to get up to New Jersey to see your father who's had some kind of an accident."

Joseph looked a little confused so Henry jumped into the void. "Did he say how he was traveling? Driving? Flying?"

The smiling lady shook her head. "No, I'm afraid he didn't,

Mr. Winslow. But he was in an awful hurry. Very excited. Of course, we could ask the doctor. He might know."

"Is he available?"

"Be back probably around three o'clock. Went up to Athens to a conference on the AIDS virus. A terrible thing, this AIDS virus."

"Three o'clock!" repeated Joseph. "Jesus, we'll be halfway back to the Garden State by then."

"Sorry, Mr. Winslow. I could have the doctor call you."

Joseph shook his head, turned, and started for the door. "Come on, Bob. Maybe we can make the two-fifteen flight to Newark."

Henry thanked the receptionist and hurried after his brother. "What's the big rush, Joe? If we don't make that flight we'll get a later one. I need something to eat anyway."

Joseph pulled open the door to the Thunderbird. "Let's roll, bro'. I've got something better than food." He climbed in behind the wheel and slammed the door. As soon as Henry closed his door, Joseph pulled away from the hospital, leaving behind the smell of burning rubber.

Back out on Highway 84 he announced, "What a waste of time. I coulda been back at the house makin' the moves on Wild Bill's gardener."

"Evangeline?"

"Yeah, a real sweetie that one. She was good-looking as a kid but she really bloomed into a beauty."

"I wouldn't mind making the moves on her myself."

Joseph looked at his brother and laughed. "Not you, bro'. You're a married man, remember? Two kids, a house, probably a dog and a cat, the whole picture."

Henry thought it over. "And another kid on the way."

"That's right. That's what you told me."

Henry, as Bobby, nodded. "Pretty soon too. Could be just about any day now."

"No shit? You're fucking crazy, three kids. I'm not having any, ever. World's too fucked up to bring kids into it."

"I don't know. Probably no more fucked up than it's ever been. Besides, I like kids. I like the way they need you . . . and trust you . . . And I'd like to have a boy, you know, a son."

Joseph glanced at his brother and rolled his eyes. "Sure, Bob, I know. I know exactly where you're coming from. Now what do you say we keep this trip from being a total bummer and take a little detour on the way back?"

"Where to?"

Joseph reached into his hip pocket and brought out his small plastic vial. "Into the land of the real thing, bro'."

"You're gonna do cocaine and drive?"

"Do it all the time. This stuff makes you drive like a combination of Grandma Moses and Mario Andretti. Plus with this special snorter I can snort a line without taking my eyes off the road. Just shake, tip, and snort."

Henry, as Bobby, declined to participate for maybe a dozen miles but finally he gave in to the temptation. "You only go around once, brother," Joseph kept telling him. "Might as well go for the gusto. Besides, a few lines ain't going to turn you into a freaking addict."

So the brothers partook of the crystalline narcotic alkaloid, and after just two or three lines Henry felt this uncontrollable urge to tell his brother his deepest, darkest secret. By the time they reached Brunswick and started north on I-95, the surviving twin could hardly contain himself. In less than half an hour the drug had completely broken down his defenses. He felt like God had touched his shoulder, whispered in his ear to speak the Truth. He could hardly believe he had been masquerading as another person for over twenty years. He also had a huge boner, probably the biggest boner he'd had in a decade.

Henry snorted another line. The fine white powder shot up his nasal passages and slammed into his brain like a baseball bat connecting with a high fast one. BOOM!

"Want to hear something funny, Joe?"

Joseph had his seat all the way back and the accelerator all the way to the floor. "Sure, bro'. Lay a good one on me."

"I'm not your brother Bob."

"No?" Joseph smiled and glanced across the seat. "Then who the fuck are you? William Fucking Tell?"

Henry could barely feel his tongue or his teeth. "No, I'm Henry. Your brother Henry."

"Oh yeah, right. And I'm our big sister Helen."

"No, Joe, really." As soon as he said it, Henry realized how absurd it sounded. For twenty years he had wondered what it would be like to finally tell someone, to actually let the words spill out of his mouth. Now that he had he found it almost impossible to believe. It sounded ridiculous, him saying he was Henry and not Bobby. But this huge boulder had been lifted off his chest and no way was he about to let it slide back into position.

"Hey bro', listen, I believe you."

"Good, because it's true. Bobby went to 'Nam in sixty-nine, not me. He took my place. I was chicken shit, couldn't go, wouldn't go, was getting ready to go AWOL to Canada. Bobby said he'd go. I let him. I let him go."

"Christ," said Joseph, "I never saw coke fuck anyone up like this before. No more lines for you, dude. I'll be driving you straight to the nuthouse. Next you'll be telling me you're the reincarnation of old Crazy Legs or something."

Henry, as Henry, didn't hear a word his brother said. "Bobby bought it from those gook bastards. He didn't have a chance. He didn't even know how to discharge his weapon. It's his body they shipped back from that stinking jungle. Not mine. It's Bobby who's buried up on the hill next to Mom and Helen. Not me. Do you hear me, Joe? Do you hear what I'm telling you? I'm telling you something here that I've been itching to tell someone for twenty-one years; twenty-one long and miserable fucking years."

Joseph pulled onto the shoulder of the interstate and turned off the engine. He took a long slow look at his brother. "Look man, are you shittin' me, or what? Because if you're shittin' me, I don't want to hear it. I can't deal with shit that's this far off the fucking wall."

"I'm not shitting you, Joe. It's the truth. I'm Henry."

"Wow."

They sat there for it's tough to say how long, ten maybe fifteen minutes, without saying a word. They'd look at each other for a while, then for a while they'd look out the window at the cars and trucks racing up the interstate, then they'd look at each other again for a few seconds. Who knows how long they might have sat there if that Georgia state trooper hadn't come up to the window and asked if they had mechanical trouble.

"No sir," said Joseph, that vial of coke barely concealed in his breast pocket, "no trouble at all. Just pulled over to change drivers."

The cop wanted credentials but after a few minutes the Winslow brothers were on their way. They waited for the cop to pass and then they both snorted another line. They relaxed for a few miles before Henry told his tale. He told it starting with the part where he got tossed out of college for breaking that professor's leg during the antiwar rally at Lehigh. He told about boot camp on Parris Island and how he got assigned to the infantry and about that night up in the third-floor bedroom when Bobby shaved his head and offered to change places. He told the whole story, every painful detail of it. Most of the time Joseph just listened and nodded and drove the car. A couple times he asked questions for clarification but Henry didn't miss much; he knew the story pretty well after twenty years of never letting a day go by without thinking about it.

They made the 2:15 flight with only minutes to spare. Even before they buckled their seat belts the flight attendant closed the hatch and the plane pulled away from the gate, rumbled out onto the runway. The DC-9 couldn't have been more than half-full; mostly salesmen in rumpled suits and loosened ties anxious to get airborne so they could order a drink.

Joseph and Henry did not see their brother in the seventh row window seat when they walked down the aisle. Barton sat slumped against the fuselage, his eyes closed, his mind deep in thought about the future of his creative outpourings. He had reached the airport before noon but this was the first flight he could get to Newark. He had almost decided to drive north but knew the trip would take at least fifteen hours. He did not want to wait that long to see his father, to see his brothers and sisters. So he had left his van in long-term parking, his painted sculpture locked up safely, he thought, in the back.

Barton thought about the sculpture. He knew it was a reflection of the way he viewed his life. It was a pessimistic view; one filled with dragons and demons. He had always believed that to create lasting art it had to come out of suffering; the happy, contented man could create nothing of validity. Life was essentially pain and true art had to come from life, so it followed that the more he suffered the more powerful would be his creation. But Barton was sick and tired of suffering for his art. He was sick and tired of spending 95 percent of his time all alone in this pursuit of perfect expression. *Couldn't I*, he wondered as that plane soared toward the heavens, *be happy and still be creative? Is that so much to ask? I've learned my craft. Can't I rely now on my imagination for inspiration? Do I have to live like a recluse? Do I have to give every last ounce of my energy to those chunks of wood and pieces of Sheetrock? Can't I rejoin the world and still get my work done? Can't I smile and laugh like other people? Acting strange and hiding out doesn't set me apart; the work does that, it always has. And maybe I'm not a homosexual, maybe I just thought I was. Maybe I've got the whole thing turned upside down, inside out. Maybe...*

The urge to urinate brought him back to physical reality. He started to get up but saw the Fasten Seat Belt sign still glowing over his head. He sat down and waited for the sign to go off.

A dozen rows back Joseph and Henry had settled in for the flight north. Joey needed another line and, like Barton, he was waiting for the seat belt sign to go off so he could slip into the head and break out his vial. The vial had only a few lines remaining so Joey kept hoping his brother wouldn't ask for more.

Henry had forgotten all about the cocaine. A far more powerful stimulant had entered his system. He felt like he could have flown back to New Jersey without the aid of jet engines. He felt like he could have made the flight under his own power.

"So what do you think," asked Joseph, "we going to tell everybody or what?"

Henry had to struggle to sit still. It would be an understatement to say the guy felt energized. But spilling his guts again, to the rest of them, to the rest of the family? *Now hang on a second here, slow down.* "I don't know. Maybe—"

"What do you mean, you don't know? You have to tell them. You can't go halfway, bro', not after all this time."

Henry blew a long breath out of his lungs. "I want to tell them, I really do. I especially want to tell Wild Bill. But Jesus, Joe, some of these other people might not handle it as well as you did. They might look at me like I'm some kind of murderer or something."

"Bullshit, Henry. They're your family."

More air blew out of Henry's lungs. His legs twitched and he rubbed his hands together hard enough to strike a spark. "I don't know, man, I just don't know."

The plane leveled out and the seat belt sign went off. "Well you think it over, bro'," said Joseph, "while I take a leak." He stood up. "Be right back."

Henry was far too involved in his own thoughts to see his little brother Barton walk by. But walk by Barton did and then he entered the lavatory right next to the one occupied by his brother Joseph. Barton relieved his bladder while Joseph drew another line into his nasal passages. Barton washed and dried his hands while Joseph checked himself out in the mirror and smiled. "Lookin' good, dude, lookin' good." They both opened the narrow doors at the same time and stepped out. They bumped shoulders.

"Excuse me," said Barton.

"No prob—," began Joseph, then, "Barton! Shit!"

Those two brothers who were so close in age but so distant emotionally, physically, and intellectually wrapped their arms around one another and held tight. Barton had tears in his eyes. Joseph had a runny nose. He told his little brother about the flight down, about driving to Waycross, about the lady with the painted smile. He spoke rapidly, his head moving all over the place. After every couple words he sniffed.

Barton nodded and smiled and listened and had this feeling like everything was going to turn out okay. "I can't believe you flew all the way down here to see me," he said at least half a dozen times. "I told Ginny to tell you not to come."

"Yeah, we figured you must've talked to her. But we left before Ginny talked to you."

"Who's we? Did Bobby come with you?"

"Yeah, well, no . . . not exactly."

"What do you mean?"

"Let's check it out."

They headed back down the aisle to where Henry sat still lost in his dilemma. "Yo, bro', wake up," said Joseph, "look who I found hanging around in the smoking section."

"Who?' Henry turned. "Barton!"

"Bob!" Then to Joseph, "I thought you said it wasn't Bobby."

"Did I say that?"

"Yeah."

A pause, then, "I'm not Bob, Barton." And so began the story of Henry's true identity all over again. Barton had a far more difficult time adjusting to this assault on his perception of reality than Joseph. It took over an hour for him to become fully assimilated to this new version of the truth.

Except for brief inquiries about the Wild One's condition and the general welfare of various family members, Henry's journey through adulthood as Bobby dominated the conversation all the way to Newark International Airport. Barton was far more curious than Joseph had been about how Henry and Bobby had changed identities without anyone knowing and without anyone ever finding out.

"Mom knew," Henry said. "She knew almost right from the start. But she said nothing, told no one. For a long time I didn't understand why. But at her funeral I realized she kept silent because she knew I had done something I would have to suffer through and deal with on my own for the rest of my life. She wasn't punishing me so much as leaving me free to make my own way."

"But no one else knew?" asked Barton. "Not even Wild Bill?"

"As far as I know she never told him."

"So no one else knows but Joey and me?"

"That's right. No one. Not even my wife. She thinks I'm Robert Giles Winslow. She never even met Henry Winslow."

"She will now."

Henry looked at his brothers. "I don't know about that. I've been thinking on it. I've told you guys. I feel like I have to tell the old man. If I don't tell the old man I think the pain will go on forever. But everyone else, I don't know. I'm not sure I see the point. Irene never knew Henry so she wouldn't know the difference anyway."

Joseph and Barton nodded. No one said anything for most of a minute.

"Whatever you want to do, Henry," said Barton.

"Henry," said Henry, "I like the sound of that."

"Yeah," said Joseph, "it's your call. We'll keep our mouths shut till you tell us one way or the other."

"I'd appreciate that."

They sat there looking at each other and nodding and sort of smiling as that jet airplane made its final approach into Newark. Whenever a truth is revealed between people it changes those people and their relationship. No doubt this happened between the Winslow brothers. Henry had taken them into his deepest confidence. He had told them something he had lived with for twenty years. Joseph and Barton had listened and asked a few questions, but neither of them had copped a single attitude. They took it like brothers. They did not pass judgment or inflict condemnation. They knew he had paid his dues and would go on paying probably forever.

These three brothers who had for so long been alienated from one another, who had grown into manhood divided, who seemed not to possess a single common thread, proved without effort or energy that the old adage about blood being thicker than water is in fact a truism. They didn't made a big deal about it, even Barton managed to keep his eyes dry, but something had changed between them, something important, something profound. They didn't discuss it, didn't even try too hard to understand it. All they knew as that plane pulled up to the gate and the passengers started to file off, was that they were brothers, born of the same flesh, descended from the same line.

They walked off that plane and through the terminal side by side: three pretty tall, pretty good-looking white dudes. They didn't look like trouble. They didn't look like fairies. They didn't look like drug addicts or murderers or impostors or artists. But they did look like brothers. Anyone could see that. You could see that a mile away.

"Let's go check out the old man," said Joseph.

"Yeah," said Henry.

"Yeah," said Barton.

Chapter Twenty-six

Bettina reached the hospital late in the afternoon, several hours after the three sisters and young Rosa had gone back to the big house in Far Hills. She reached her husband's room maybe fifteen minutes before Evangeline's return and half an hour before three of his sons arrived in the XK-140. She stepped into the room after two brisk knocks on the wide-open wooden door. Her husband sat against the headboard of his bed. His face was hidden behind a copy of *Real Estate Week*. He had a scowl on his face as he heard the knock and lowered the paper.

"Don't you look happy."

The scowl deepened when he saw who had arrived. He folded the newspaper in half and tossed it on the floor. "Interest rates are bouncing around like schoolgirls. Housing starts are down. No one's buying but the rich. Realtors in this part of Jersey say no one's even out looking. The market's dead, as dead as it's been in twenty years."

"So are we going broke?"

"We may be able to hang on for a few more months."

"Funny man, funny man." Bettina crossed to her husband, bent down, and kissed him on the cheek. "They told me you were in a bad way. I came as quickly as possible."

"I'm sure you did, Bettina."

"I expected to find you knocking on death's door."

"Sorry to disappoint."

"Don't be silly. I'm glad to see you looking so well. Except for that cast on your leg you look whole and healthy."

"Yup, whole and healthy. No reason, really, for you to drive all the way down here."

She shrugged and sat in the chair under the window. She opened her pocketbook and rummaged around until she found her pack of cigarettes. "Do you mind if I smoke?"

"I do mind, yeah. You know I hate cigarette smoke."

She gave him a look, sighed, and dropped the pack back into her purse. "Yes, right. How could I forget?"

Wild Bill thought about going back to his newspaper but knew it would solicit nothing but sarcasm. So he did nothing, said nothing, wondered why she had come and what she wanted.

"I'm surprised your cherubs aren't here showering you with love and affection."

"They've come and gone."

"So soon?"

"They'll be back. They're staying at the house."

"I hope they haven't occupied the master bedroom."

"Why? Do you plan on making a rare appearance there?"

She let out a little laugh. "Thought I might."

"How touching."

"Well," she said, reaching back into her bag for what she did not know, "isn't this a pleasant visit."

Unbeknownst to Bettina and Wild Bill, sweet Evangeline had just stepped off the elevator. She had a smile on her face and a vase filled with just-picked daisies in her hands. John and Paul had helped her pick the flowers. They were back at the house now swimming with Emily and Rosa. Evangeline had told Emily she had a few errands to run but Emily felt sure the hospital was her eventual destination.

She did not hear Wild Bill say, "You know, Bettina, I think it's time we talked about a divorce."

She missed that line but just as she was about to come bouncing into the room she heard Bettina's response, "Let's not be silly, dear. We don't need to talk about that, not now, not ever."

Evangeline heard the voice, stopped short of the door, and pressed herself against the wall just outside the Wild One's room. *I can't go in there now. I'll have to come back later.* She told herself to walk away, not to listen, to leave them alone.

But she heard Billy Boy say quite clearly, "No, Bettina, we do need to talk about it. We need to talk about it now. This marriage stinks. In fact it sucks. It's a charade. And I'm telling you now that I want out."

"This is a lovely way to greet your wife. I drive all the way down here to see you, and you say, hello, how are you, I want a divorce."

"Don't hand me that crap, Bettina. You probably prayed to the god of greed that the fall I took would finish me off."

She removed a cigarette from the pack, placed it between her lips, and lit up. She took a long, slow drag, then blew the smoke in the direction of the bed. "You're a cruel man, Bill Winslow, a cruel and crazy man."

"And you're a selfish, sexless bitch, Bettina."

She allowed herself another little laugh. "Then we're a perfect match, dear heart, a match made in heaven."

This was as much as Evangeline could take. Not only did she feel like a spy standing there eavesdropping, but she could not stand to hear the things they were saying to one another, the way Billy Boy was treating his wife; she couldn't stand it, not a moment longer. She turned and walked quickly down the hallway. Evangeline hated conflict, despised confrontation, found no value whatsoever in condemnation.

She did not get to hear Bettina add, "I do take offense, however, to that remark about being sexless. I think I could put together a fairly lengthy list of suitors who would dispute that claim."

Wild Bill knew all about the suitors. A private investigator had been on the job for over a year. "Why don't you marry one of them, Bettina? Then you and I can go our separate ways."

"But why would I do that, dear? Marriage is such a burdensome institution. It ruins all the fun. Remember the sex we had before our wedding day? No, I see no reason to get divorced. I have things pretty much how I want them. You support me, supply me with both a summer and a winter residence, pay the bills, take care of all my financial concerns. Good God, why would I divorce you?"

"Maybe because you make me sick and I hate the sight of you."

"Those feelings are certainly mutual, but very much besides the point, don't you see?"

"I'll give you the house in Maine."

"Of course you will, but it's rather cold and dreary there in the winter."

"Maybe I'll throw in the house on Captiva as well." *But that,* he knew, *would be tough; that had been Virginia's house.*

Bettina took another drag, then blew the smoke toward the window. "Now that is an interesting proposition. We might also talk about the apartment in Manhattan. I was pretty much expelled from there when little Emily needed a refuge. But why are we talking like this? All these homes take a small fortune to keep up every year. There's maintenance and repairs and electric bills and of course those blasted taxes. I think maybe—"

"I think maybe you'll just have to collar one of your beaus to help pay the bills."

She shook her head. "No, I don't think so. I think for now we'll just leave things as they are. I mean after all, you're here and I'm there. We don't really have much to do with one another. You can sleep with anyone you want. I don't give a damn. Really, if you think about it, it's an excellent arrangement."

Bill Winslow knew his wife had a price. He just didn't know yet how high that price might be. But he did know it would undoubtedly be one of the tougher negotiations of his life. He also knew he had to keep Evangeline and John and Paul as far away from those negotiations as possible. *If the bitch finds out about them she'll strip me clean. Sue me for infidelity and mental cruelty and every other goddamn thing her lawyers can think of.*

Speaking of Evangeline, she walked out the front door of the hospital with her head hanging low. She felt sad and troubled. Her daisies drooped in the late afternoon heat. She did not see the Winslow brothers climb out of the XK-140 and stride across the parking lot.

"Flowers for me?" asked Joseph.

Evangeline lifted her head and tried a smile. "Actually for your father, but he has a visitor."

"And who might that be?"

"Bettina."

"Ahh, his loving wife . . . our darling stepmother."

Evangeline took Barton's hand. "Barton, hello. I'm so glad you made it. We heard about what happened. Are you all right?"

Barton blushed. Evangeline was the first girl he had ever kissed. It happened one night after a picnic down along the banks of the Delaware out behind the old carriage house. It was just one brief adolescent kiss but he had never forgotten the sweet, moist taste of her lips. He squeezed her hand and smiled. "I'm okay."

"I've never met this Bettina," said Henry. "What's she like?"

"A bitch, brother," answered Joseph. "A blood-sucking parasitic bitch." Then he turned to Evangeline. "Excuse my language, but sometimes you have to tell it like it is."

Evangeline lowered her eyes.

Barton gave her hand another squeeze and asked, "So how is he?"

"I think he's about ready to break loose. He's getting pretty antsy up in that hospital room. This is probably the longest he's been in bed his entire life."

"No doubt about that," said Joseph. "He must be ready to jump clean out of his skin."

"He wanted to go home today but the doctor ordered him to stay at least until tomorrow."

"A tough old warrior. Hard to hold down. But the sight of Barton here will cheer him up. Want to ride along?"

Evangeline tried to hide her smile. "No, I better get back to the house."

"Okay, suit yourself. We'll see you back at the ranch."

By the time Evangeline had reached her Nissan the three brothers had arrived on the fourth floor. They walked side by side, Henry in the middle. Their strides were long and confident.

Back in the Wild One's room, the impasse between husband and wife continued. He considered telling her that if she hung around till he died she would find not a scrap in his last will and testament. But he decided not to take that tack. He expected to live at least another twenty years and no way did he want her hanging around all that time.

So she smoked while he simmered, and outside the heat shimmered off the sidewalks. Almost six o'clock now but the mercury still hovered close to ninety-five. A smoky blue-gray haze kept the humidity close and just below the saturation point. The room was cooled artificially but the heat wave had lasted so long and been so severe that no air conditioner made could drive off the oppression.

Joseph didn't bother to knock. He just walked right in and let his mouth go to work. He brought himself to attention and saluted the man lying in bed. "Mission accomplished, sir! Prisoner sprung from Andersonville, sir!" He flicked his salute and turned back to the door. "Front and center, Private Winslow, front and center!"

Barton smiled and shook his head and stepped into the room. "Hello, Father."

The Wild One forgot all about his wife. "Barton, my boy! Is that you?"

"Yes sir." Barton crossed to the bed. He had already decided not to hold back. He gave his father a hug that had only been bettered by young Rosa. A tear fell from his eye when his father hugged him back but as soon as the embrace ended he wiped the tear away. "You okay?"

"Never better, Barton, my boy, never better. And what about you? They tell me a bunch of redneck Rebs jumped you and beat the tar out of you."

"It's true, they did. But I'm all right now. A few bumps and bruises is all."

"I can see you're a little swollen around the eyes. But I'll tell you what, son. Just as soon as I'm fit, we're going down to Dixie and kick the crap out of them Rebs. Those two jackasses standing over by the door are coming along with us. Right, boys?"

Joseph saluted. Henry, as Bobby, just nodded.

"That big son of a bitch," said Wild Bill, pointing at Henry, "is going to lead the charge."

Bettina stood up, reestablished her presence in the room.

The Wild One thought about ignoring her entirely but instead said, "I think you boys know Bettina."

Henry shook his head but no one noticed. Barton nodded but held his ground. Joseph nodded and crossed to her. He took her hand, kissed it, and said, "You're looking lovely, Mother, just radiant."

A moment's silence was shattered by one of Wild Bill's famous laughs. It shook the room for the better part of ten seconds. When it ended Bettina was over by the door.

"Going somewhere, dear?" asked her husband.

"Yes, I'm going home. I thought I'd check into the master bedroom suite for a few days. It doesn't look like you'll be sleeping there anytime soon." She turned and brushed past Henry without even acknowledging his presence.

"I'll be there sooner than you think, woman," shouted the Wild One as his wife marched down the corridor. "And I'll be looking for some satisfaction, for some of that sweet puddin'!"

The four Winslow men yucked it up for quite a while over that one; really had a belly laugh at Bettina's expense. Finally Henry, as Bobby, said, "I guess that was your wife."

"It sure was, boy. A fine figure of a woman. How'd you like her?"

"Seemed like a real charmer."

"Yup. One of the truly memorable acquisitions of my life."

That one solicited another laugh before Joseph said, "We saw Evangeline outside. Now she would be a fine acquisition."

"You saw Evangeline?"

"Just a couple of minutes ago."

"So where is she?"

"She went home. Didn't want to bug you and Bettina."

"She knew Bettina was here?"

"She had a vase full of daisies for you, Dad," added Barton.

"Well I'll be a son of a bitch. I can't believe she left without saying hello." Wild Bill wondered if Evangeline had overheard any of his conversation with Bettina.

"I think," Joseph said to his brothers, "young Evangeline is sweet on the old boy."

Henry and Barton chuckled, as though such an idea was ridiculous.

"Well I'll tell you boys something. I'm sweet on her as well. I'm going to marry that young filly."

"Oh yeah, right Pop," said Joseph, "and did I mention lately that next month I'm piloting the space shuttle on a mission to Neptune."

"Don't be a wiseass, boy."

"Hey, W. B., I was just joking. But really, that young lass needs a stud to rein her in."

"Don't talk about her like she's a piece of meat."

The tone in the Wild One's voice totally altered the mood in the room. The brothers all felt it. They exchanged glances. Henry and Barton wondered what had happened. Joseph knew exactly what had happened. *The old man's getting some, or else he's wanting it bad enough to fight over.* He decided to push a little harder to see if he could find out which scenario was the accurate one.

"Hey, Pop, really, I didn't mean anything by it. It's just that I think I know what a young babe like that needs."

"You don't know shit from shinola, boy. And you definitely don't know the first thing about what that young lady needs."

"She needs the lovin' of a strong young bull. I can see it in her eyes."

"Yeah? Well why don't you shut the fuck up now before I come over there and stick my fist in your mouth."

He's doin' her, thought Joseph, *he's done her.* He held up his hands in defense. "Hey, okay, Jesus, take it easy. I was just jivin'."

"Yeah," said the Wild One, "well go jive someplace else. It's time you three got the hell out of here. The doctor told me to rest."

"But Dad," said Barton, "we just got here."

Wild Bill tried to calm himself. *I'm way the hell out of line here.* "I know," he said, "but I'll be going home tomorrow. Then we can have ourselves a proper visit. I'm as jumpy as a chicken on the cutting block in this dump."

"Okay," said Barton, "if that's the way you want it."

"That's the way I think it oughta be."

Henry, as Bobby, stepped forward into the room. "Hey Dad?"

"Yeah, Bob?"

"There was something I wanted to say."

"Yeah? Go ahead."

"Well, it has to do with, uhh, with..."

"With what?"

Henry thought about it. "Forget it. It can wait."

Wild Bill sat up rigid on the bed. "Listen, Bob, if you have something to say, go ahead and say it."

Henry shook his head. "No, I'd rather wait till you get home."

The Wild One nodded and relaxed. "Right, no problem."

Henry stood right at the edge of the bed now. "So we'll see you tomorrow?"

"Right, tomorrow. We'll talk a few things over." There was silence in the room until Wild Bill added, "I want one of you back here to pick me up bright and early. Say nine o'clock, at the latest."

"Don't worry," said Joseph, "I'll be here. I'll pick you up in the Benz."

Out in the corridor, on their way to the elevator, away from the Wild One's hearing, Joseph thumped Henry on the chest. "Why didn't you tell him? Shit, I kept waiting for you to tell him."

"Yeah," said Barton, "me too."

"I couldn't," said Henry. "I don't know why, I just couldn't. I'll do it tomorrow after he gets home, after he settles in."

"Pussy," said Joseph as the elevator doors opened.

Henry stopped. A scowl crossed his face. *I'm no pussy, pal,* he almost said. But then he realized the comment had been made in jest. His brother had only been joking. And then he realized a lot had changed in the past twenty-four hours. *Twenty-four hours ago I might've punched his lights out for calling me a pussy.* But now he followed Joseph into the elevator, thumped his little brother back on the chest, and said with a smile, "I'll tell him when I wanna tell him, faggot."

Which upset Barton, but not enough to ruin the newfound camaraderie between this trio of Winslow males.

Chapter Twenty-seven

———————————————•———————————————

Ginny's shopping cart overflowed with meats and breads and fruits and vegetables and all kinds of goodies like cookies and ice cream. She was just beginning to unload the groceries onto the checkout counter when she saw him walk through the automatic glass doors. She stared, couldn't quite believe her eyes, decided it must be someone else. Then he looked straight at her. She glanced away, busied herself with the bananas and the Purdue Oven-Stuffer Roaster. When she took a quick look around a few moments later he was gone.

She paid cash ($189.24) for the food and pushed the cart out into the parking lot. She was in a hurry now; she did not want an encounter with her old high school lover, Scottie Johnston. The heat on the black asphalt was oppressive. Ginny felt the perspiration under her arms and behind her knees and along her brow. She began unloading the bags into the back of the Range Rover. She glanced over her shoulder, through the large picture windows covering the front of the store. There he was again: in the checkout line. Yes, it was definitely him. He had less hair on his head than he did back in the '60s and more girth around his waist, but otherwise he looked pretty much the same, sort of crazed and stupid, like a lot of rich boys who get ahead without half trying.

She packed the last bag into the back of the Rover and closed the hatch. She pushed the cart out of the way, unlocked the door, and climbed in behind the wheel. In the rearview mirror she could see him now leaving the store with his brown bag, coming toward her, his hand raised. She started the engine, put the Rover into Drive. But a Mercedes blocked her way. She slammed the transmission into Reverse, backed up, nearly ran Scottie Johnston over.

He scurried out of the way. "Hey, Ginny!"

Ginny pretended not to hear. She shoved the Range Rover back into Drive and hit the accelerator. All the way to the big house in Far Hills she ran the air conditioner full blast. She did not even bother trying to figure out why she had so desperately wanted to avoid the boy who had stolen her virginity.

Little Eddie watched his sister through the binoculars. Mary walked out the back door and across the driveway. She entered the garage and for a few minutes he could not see her. Then she came out of the garage carrying what looked to Edward like pruning shears. She walked around to the back of the garage, through a tangle of underbrush, and up through the field directly toward where Eddie sat on his deer perch. He very nearly panicked, almost jumped out of that tree and took off into the woods. But Mary stopped in the middle of the field and began cutting wildflowers. She cut a thick bunch of poppies and foxglove and golden yarrow and then headed away from Eddie's perch, across the field along the slope above the cottage. He watched her every step of the way. She walked past the cottage and out beyond the old barn, through the overgrown alfalfa field, and up the low rise to the family's small plot of graves. She was now a long way off, three or four hundred yards at least, but Eddie could still see her clearly through the glasses. Seeing her there kneeling in front of the headstones made him think of his mother. He did not like at all the idea of Mary being so close to her. He thought about the shotgun, about unloading a round of shells in Mary's direction, about driving her away from the family burial site. But he reminded himself the time had not yet come for action; before he made his move he first had to discover the whereabouts of Wild Bill.

Mary felt Edward's presence but she misinterpreted the aura as something emanating from the past, not the present. She placed a few wildflowers on top of each of the graves: her mother, her sister Helen, her brother Henry, her Aunt Helen, her Uncles Robert and Henry, her grandparents Charles and Martha, her great-grandparents Crazy Legs and Caroline. She wondered who would join the group next, wondered if a fifth generation of Winslows was destined to someday join the dead at this same location.

She paused the longest over Henry's grave. That strong, aggressive, powerful, and competitive force which had surrounded her brother in life showed no signs of survival at his burial site. Instead she felt a quiet, steady murmur, confident but in no way confrontational.

She closed her eyes. She saw her twin brothers, one dead and one still alive. *Twins, she knew, are just divisions of cells very early in the cycle of reproduction. The birth of twins does not indicate the creation of two entirely separate human beings; it is merely a physical mutation: two bodies but nevertheless one psyche.* Like her ancestors Robert Winslow junior and his brother Henry Lane. *Had they been born with a single body,* Mary felt sure, *the family's history would have followed a very different path.*

Mary lay down in the grass beside her dead relatives, the late afternoon sun still high and hot on this the last day of spring. She drifted back to take a look, to better understand how events two hundred years ago had influenced the present. She hoped the past would provide some fresh insights into how her own brothers, one dead but one still living, might influence the future. . . .

The years 1776 to 1781, the years of the War for Independence, were tough years for the Winslows in the New World. Just as the colonies were divided in their support for King George and the throne, so also were the Winslow brothers divided. After their father Jawbone was killed by zealous Patriots, there was no one, not even their mother Anna, who could hold the twins together. Robert Winslow junior, a rebel since his youth, chose to fight. All his life he had longed for a fight and what better battle than a struggle for Independence.

Henry Lane tried to remain neutral. He kept the farm going, sold his goods to whichever side made the best offer. His fields were more than once occupied by soldiers from both armies. They slept there and fought there and died there along the banks of the Delaware. They burned his barns and slaughtered his livestock. They raped one of his little sisters and opened his old mother's skull when she tried to interfere. This attack on his family was the last straw, and the end of the Burlington branch of the House of Winslow.

In the early spring of 1779, Henry Lane packed up his mother and his sisters and as many of their belongings as their two remaining carriages could carry. They made their way across the Delaware and down to the city of Philadelphia. There they rendezvoused with other Quaker families who had seen enough of war. For two weeks Henry Lane tried in vain to find the whereabouts of his brother, but at the end of those two weeks the family sailed for England. One hundred and fifty years the family had struggled for a foothold in the New World, in New Jersey, but when that schooner sailed out into the Chesapeake and headed east, there was but one Winslow left, and he lived every day like it might be his last.

Robert had crossed the Delaware with Washington on Christmas night in 1776, and for his trouble he received a Hessian bullet in his left shoulder and frostbite on seven of his ten toes. He survived the winter with all but two of his toes (the two tiny ones on the ends) and a permanent stiffness in his damaged shoulder. He survived other winters as well: Valley Forge and two stops at Jockey Hollow, just a stone's throw from where his descendant now lay recuperating at Morristown Memorial Hospital. Robert fought at the Battle of Brandywine and the Battle of Monmouth. He fought at the Palisades and in Princeton. He fought wherever they ordered him to fight and always he fought like a madman. He loved to scream at the top of his lungs during battle and to taunt the rigid redcoats with barbs and profanity. Several times his superiors tried to promote him to the rank of officer but each time he rejected their commissions. He preferred to remain a sergeant, in the thick of the fray from dawn till dusk. Robert "Mad Dog" Winslow never received even a footnote in all the long histories of the American Revolution but it was the tough, ornery, hardheaded individuals like him who wore the British down and in the end gained a victory for the fledgling republic.

Robert was thirty-five years old when the war, for all intents and purposes, ended down in Yorktown in the autumn of 1781. He missed that battle, preferring as he did to do his fighting close to home. When news of peace reached him outside of Camden, he celebrated for several days at the nearest tavern. When the celebration waned he headed home, back to the family farm north of Burlington. He found nothing left. The house had been entirely destroyed by fire and neglect. The barns and chicken coops had been leveled. The fields grew nothing but weeds. The plows and disks and thrashers had all been left out to rust in the rain and snow. Robert stood staring at the destruction when some stranger with a musket and a pair of wild hounds drove him off the land, his land, the land his family had nurtured for four generations.

Robert walked into Burlington and inquired after his family. It was then he learned of their return to England.

The Continental army had not paid him in more than a year. He had maybe seven Continental dollars to his name. Seven dollars, a worn-out flintlock, holes in his boots, holes in his breeches, holes in his deerskin shirt. He was dirty and hadn't shaved in weeks. Folks stared at him as he walked down Main Street. "Is that a Winslow?" "Is that Robert Winslow, Jawbone's son?" "Have the Winslows been reduced to this?" "My God, the vagaries of war." Mad Dog just kept walking. He held his head high and marched out of town without looking back.

Mary marched along with him. "You okay?"

"Hell yes, that scum don't bother me."

"You won the war."

"Damn straight we won the war. Beat the tar out of those pompous, tea-swilling, red-jacketed swine."

Mary hesitated then asked, "So what now?"

"What now?" asked Robert. "Well I'll tell you, cousin, I've got to do the same things all men got to do. I've got to earn me some money, get me a woman, and raise me some kids, preferably some sons who'll help with the chores and carry on the family line. I didn't fight this war to watch the Winslows die out on this side of the Atlantic."

They walked for a mile on the dirt road north to Trenton. It was early November, cool and gray. The leaves were changing and the wind was blowing from the north.

"So," Mary asked after a time, "you're not worried about the future?"

Robert looked at her kind of funny. "Hell no. You?"

Mary almost said sometimes she was, but instead just shook her head. Then, after another pause, she said, "I best be getting back."

"Okay, cousin. Come see us anytime. We'll be here."

Mary knew they would: Robert and his wife Katherine Fox Winslow and their five daughters and one son, Henry Lane III, named for Robert's twin brother who "pussied out and sailed for jolly old England." Mary knew they would be there scratching out a life along the Millstone River in that old farmhouse north of Griggstown. She knew that part of the family story well: how

Robert had more or less forced the old-timer, Jeremy Fox, off his land after marrying the old-timer's granddaughter, Katherine. (All the other Foxes had been killed during the war.) For five years, from 1782 until 1786, Robert impregnated Katherine every spring. And every winter for five years Katherine delivered a baby girl. All were strong, healthy, beautiful babies; not a single problem or defect in any of them. But the arrival of each ensuing one only made Mad Dog more angry and less civil. He wanted a son and he kept telling his wife she would have to reproduce until she could "make a baby that had more than a hole between its legs." Nothing happened after 1786 until the spring of 1790. That's when Katherine's belly started to swell once again. On Christmas Day of that year she gave birth to a nine-pound baby boy after a labor so severe that more than once she begged God to let her die. But she didn't die, not for another seven days when some strange fever caught her and wiped her out in less than twenty-four hours. So Robert had the son he had long wanted but no woman to bring that baby up. He relied on his daughters, who did an excellent job of raising young Henry Lane, even if the boy was, at least in his father's eyes, "a sissy who liked cookin' and cleanin' and gigglin' better 'an plowin' and milkin' and cuttin' the heads off chickens."

Mary heard screams coming from down by the house. She sat up startled and peered through the heat and the haze. It was just John and Paul and Rosa running around the pool, jumping off the high dive, yelling and splashing. Mary shook her head and settled back.

She knew the tragedy of Henry Lane III. At the tender age of twenty-one, Henry Lane married a young farm girl named Lorelei Constantine. Lorelei was only seventeen when she stood all in white beside Henry Lane at the altar. It has been speculated that Lorelei was the most beautiful woman ever to wear the name Winslow. She looked, they say, like an angel—long golden hair and a face as calm and placid as a princess. She married Henry Lane because he was kind and sweet and gentle and knew exactly how to make her laugh. But less than two years after their wedding, and still, so say some, not a baby born, hostilities broke out with Britain. It had something to do with shipping and politics and economics, Henry Lane really could not have cared less. But father Robert, closing in on seventy and growing more ornery every day, wanted his boy to join the army and kill some redcoats. Henry Lane wanted nothing to do with war, but finally the old man forced the boy, through insult and physical injury, to join the fight and defend his country. So off went Henry Lane, up the Hudson River valley with the troops under the command of William Henry Harrison. The army entered Canada in early October 1813. It was cold and all Henry Lane wanted to do was desert his post and go back to his loving Lorelei along the banks of the Millstone. But that desire would never be because on the fifth of October, during the bloody Battle of the Thames, a British regular thrust his bayonet through Henry Lane's chest at the exact same moment the famous Indian chief Tecumseh hailed the Great Spirit less than a hundred yards across the field of battle.

Word of Henry Lane's demise did not reach Griggstown until Christmas. The news sent Lorelei into a deep state of mourning. She did not leave her room until the spring of 1814. In the summer of 1814 Robert realized that if he suddenly died the Winslow line in the New World would end. So what did the old soldier do? "What I had to do." He locked his daughter-in-law in her bedroom and forced himself upon her sexually until he was absolutely certain she was with child. It took all that summer and most of the fall before he saw evidence of copulation. But that did not end Lorelei's imprisonment. No, Robert had to make sure the baby was a male, so he kept her under lock and key for nine long months. And, thank the Lord, when the baby came it came with ease and sure enough, another Winslow male had come upon the earth.

It took Lorelei nearly a year to secure her revenge. Although she never actually considered what she did revenge. She considered it more a service to the rest of the females on the planet. Besides, she loved her baby, who was named William Giles, after her father and after an old Winslow name from the past which she had heard once and liked.

Mary accompanied Lorelei into Mad Dog's bedroom that night. She boosted the young woman's morale, assured her she had every right to carry out her plan. When Lorelei hesitated outside the old man's bedroom door, Mary held steady the hand that held the gleaming butcher knife. Lorelei crept into the room. She had practiced this scene a thousand times in the privacy of her own thoughts. "Go on, Lorelei, do it. Do it before he wakes up and sees you." And so she did.

She walloped that old rapist over the head with the blunt end of the butcher knife. And then, when she was sure he was knocked out, she positioned him on the floor just so. She then raised that razor-sharp blade high over her head and brought it down with all her fury. The blade severed Mad Dog's scrotum and his male projectile just as easily as a knife through soft butter. His body trembled and the blood came pouring out. Lorelei carefully bandaged the terrible wound and then left the room. She bundled up William Giles and the two of them, in the middle of the night, fled that house along the Millstone forever.

Mary gasped at the sight of what the butcher knife had done. She knew her ancestor had deserved his punishment. But at the same time she realized that had he not raped his daughter-in-law the family line would have ended and all that came after would not have come after.

She tried to follow Lorelei and William Giles through the night but more screams from down by the house and then car horns blowing and people shouting brought her back to the present. She sat up in the grass and saw that the afternoon had faded to evening. Dusk was beginning to settle. Long shadows from the trees beyond the graveyard reached across the field. Mary stood up, stretched, and headed away from the shadows, back in the direction of the house.

Chapter Twenty-eight

The horn blowing and shouting had to do with the long caravan of vehicles that pulled into the Winslow Compound looking and sounding like some kind of honky-tonk carnival show. They drove down that long drive one right after another. Nothing but chance and a tidy narrative collision brought them all wheeling in at exactly the same point in time.

Ginny led the troupe in the forest green British Range Rover. Behind the Rover, in her Nissan pickup, was Evangeline. After leaving the hospital she had taken the long way home to think through the words she had overheard outside Billy Boy's room. Right behind Evangeline was Irene in that borrowed Buick Regal. Katie and Constance sat in the back seat of the Buick and looked out the back window. They spotted their father crammed into that Jaguar XK-140 along with Uncles Joseph and Barton, but of course they wouldn't know Joseph and Barton were their uncles for another minute or so. When Henry saw his daughters he reached across the seat and started blowing the Jaguar's horn. That in turn started Irene blowing the Buick's horn, which, in a moment of frivolity, caused Ginny to abandon propriety and actually blow the Range Rover's horn a time or two. All this horn blowing caused Rosa and John and Paul to climb out of the swimming pool and shout stuff like, "The circus is coming, the circus is coming!" They went racing across the grass, Emily at their heels. The welcoming party stood at the edge of the driveway when the first car pulled up in front of the garage.

There was a fourth car in the caravan as well. It was a dark blue Cadillac Allanté carrying the infamous stepmother, Bettina Von Culin Winslow. After leaving the hospital Bettina had gone

shopping, found a lovely string of pearls, and charged the purchase on the Wild One's American Express card. Now she sighed
and shook her head at all the family fanfare but decided against
turning around and driving away. There were some things in the
house she wanted. And besides, she rather enjoyed the luxurious
master bedroom suite with its oversize Jacuzzi bath, its king-size
feather mattress, and its splendid view of the rolling New Jersey
countryside.

As she pulled up behind the Jaguar and watched the family
descend upon itself, she thought she might even seduce one of
those Winslow males, *fuck his brains out right there on his father's
bed. Maybe that big hunk with the sad eyes hugging that woman and
those two little girls. He looks prime for the picking. Probably hasn't
had any in months. Or maybe young Barton, although I've always
suspected he likes his own kind best. Forget about Joey, he's too stuck
on himself, probably has a dick the size of a golf tee. Jesus, look at them
all acting like they like each other. Makes me want to throw up. Ginny,
that phony bitch. And Emily. Tried like the devil herself to keep the old
bugger from marrying me. Almost succeeded too.* Then she was out of
the Allanté and walking slowly toward that assemblage of Winslows.
She put a smile on her face and pretended as though this moment
was the moment she had been waiting for all her life.

The Winslows did their best to ignore Bettina but she ignored
them ignoring her. She gave the women hugs and pecks on the
cheek. Ginny scowled, Emily turned away, and Mary, fresh from
the graveyard, vowed to herself never to let Bettina rest among
the family dead.

As dusk gathered and the heat tried to dissipate, Edward's eyes
swelled and bulged at the whirl of activity down on the driveway.
His binoculars swept from car to car, from face to face. He saw
them all, every last one of them, everyone but the one he wanted
most.

The kids gravitated to one another, sort of sniffed each other
out like a pack of friendly, domesticated hounds. They had no
need for introductions; their eyes told them all they needed to
know. Katie, the oldest at nine, assumed the role of leader. John
and Paul found this quite natural; they had been brought up by
their mom. Constance, small and shy, stayed close to Rosa who
held her hand and told her all about Shakespeare. The five of
them wandered off, first down to the swimming pool, and then
wherever the scent led them.

The adults made formal introductions. None of the siblings had ever met Irene. Ginny and Emily especially made a big fuss over their sister-in-law, partly to ignore Bettina but also because they were genuinely pleased to finally meet their brother's wife.

Ginny touched Irene's stomach and then gently slapped her brother's face. "You didn't tell us there was another Winslow on the way."

Henry, as Bobby, was at first disoriented at having Irene so close to his brothers and sisters. "Hey," he said, a smile radiating from his face, "I thought I told you, I know I told someone."

"Well it wasn't me."

Mary and Barton hugged and kissed and then stood side by side, shoulder to shoulder, like a devoted and inseparable couple. Joseph kept his eyes on Evangeline. She kept her eyes on the kids to make sure none of them fell into the water.

After maybe ten minutes of milling around outside the back door, Ginny remembered the groceries. "The ice cream's probably soup in this heat," she said as she opened the back of the Rover. So everyone grabbed a bag, except Bettina, and they hauled the groceries into the kitchen. The large quantity of food caused someone to ask if they were all moving in for the summer. "Ho, ho, ho," they laughed, "that's a good one." Although some of them, such as Henry, secretly hoped it might be true.

Once the frenzy subsided, Ginny took charge. "Hey, someone has to do it, otherwise we'll have nothing but chaos around here." She put Emily and Evangeline in charge of supper, "salad, fresh string beans, boiled new red potatoes, and applesauce. There's no time to prepare meat tonight, it's almost nine o'clock already." Which was just fine with Emily and Evangeline; they rarely ate meat or served it to their kids anyway.

While the two cooks washed and sliced and chopped, Ginny led Irene upstairs so the Adirondack side of the family could get settled. "You look just about ready to have that baby, Irene."

Irene just shook her head.

Henry, as Bobby, followed the ladies up the front stairs with the bags. Ginny headed for the master bedroom.

"Hey Gin," asked Henry, "where you going?"

"I thought you two could sleep in Daddy's room and we'll put the girls up on the third floor."

"I thought we'd all just sleep up there together."

"Nonsense. There's only two twin beds in that room. Come on, Irene, follow me."

They walked down the hallway, through the sitting room, and into the master bedroom where they found Bettina, already busy unpacking her bag. "Yes?" she asked, that phony smile plastered on her face.

"*You're* sleeping here?" Ginny asked.

"I thought I would, yes."

"I thought it would be best if Bobby and Irene slept here." Ginny went over the sleeping arrangements she had worked out while driving home from the grocery store.

"Well, that's fine, Virginia," said Bettina, "but where does that leave me?"

"I suppose it leaves you on the sofa bed in the den. I didn't know you were coming."

"Yes, well I have come, as you can see. And since this is my bedroom, I think I'll sleep right here. I hope that suits you."

"It doesn't suit me and this isn't your bedroom," snapped the oldest of Wild Bill's children.

Bettina shrugged and went on unpacking her bag.

"This is my mother's bedroom," insisted Ginny.

"Yes, I suppose it was."

"You bitch."

Henry, still Bobby but feeling a heck of a lot more like Henry, stepped between the two women. He put his hand on his sister's shoulder. "Come on, Gin, let's go. If this . . . this person wants to sleep here it makes no difference to us. There's plenty of room in this house."

They turned and left the room, Irene's mouth still hanging open as they made their way down the hall and up the stairs to the third floor.

Missing of course from the festivities were Wild Bill and his boy Edward. Little Eddie could quite easily have joined the party. All he needed to do was climb down off his perch, fight his way through the underbrush, and walk through the back door. He was, after all, a member of the family. He was a Winslow. This was his house too. These were his brothers and sisters. They wouldn't have ostracized him or criticized him, not for long anyway. Sure, he looked a little crazy from his sixteen-hour vigil on the deer perch and his six-year hiatus from conventional society. His eyes were bugged out from staring through those binoculars since dawn and his brow was permanently furrowed from so many years of scowling at the world. He looked kind of strange, a little wild, but so what? His family would have taken him in, consumed him, sucked him into their familial bosom. That's what families do. Even when they don't see each other for years, even when they have all this misconstrued animosity and hatred for one another they do it. It's just the way things are and always have been. But Edward could not see any of this. Most of his siblings did not see it either but they had never strayed quite so far as Little Eddie; no, not even brother Henry. Henry blamed himself for what had happened to his life. Edward blamed just about everyone but himself. He peered through those field glasses at the bodies walking in and out of the back door and all he cared about was the whereabouts of the person he blamed the most. "Where is the old bastard," he said right out loud, "where the fuck is he hiding? Why doesn't he come out where I can see him?"

Where was Billy Boy Winslow? Why sitting on his hospital bed calling Evangeline at the cottage for the tenth time since his boys had left and wondering where she was and why she didn't answer. He finally hung up and rang the nurse's call button. Down the hall at the nurses' station the nurse heard the ring and sighed. "What does that piggish man want this time?" It was the same nurse who had thrown Wild Bill's children out of the room the evening before. The Wild One had only ever used the call button once during his stay but this particular nurse felt that twice was once too often. She finished her patient report before responding to the call.

"It took you nine minutes to get here," growled Wild Bill, pointing at his watch.

"Sorry, Mr. Winslow, I was busy."

"What if I'd been dying?"

"Not much chance of that."

"You oughta be a traffic cop, not a nurse."

"I understand you're leaving us tomorrow."

"Sooner if I could."

She checked his chart, took his pulse. "I'd take it slow and easy if I were you. You'll be right back in here if you don't."

"Thanks for the advice. But I called you because I need to borrow twenty bucks."

"What?"

"I just realized I don't have any money with me, not a dime."

"So what do you need money for?"

"I want to... uhh, send some flowers."

"You're supposed to receive flowers in the hospital, not send them."

"Yeah, well I've always done things ass backward. Now cough up the dough. You lend me twenty tonight and I'll pay you back twenty-five tomorrow."

"That sounds like a pretty fair interest rate."

"Then we have a deal?"

"Let me get my purse." The nurse left the room.

Wild Bill watched her go, then he went over his escape plan one more time. It was a good plan: simple, straightforward, very little room for error. After the nurse gave him the twenty he tried Evangeline once more. No answer. "Dammit." He decided to settle down and get some rest. He knew it would be a long night... *He had no idea how long.*

Evangeline did not answer the telephone because she was sitting between her sons at the enormous cherry table in the Winslows' dining room. She had never eaten there before. Many times she had eaten at the small table in the kitchen with John and Paul and Billy Boy, but never before at the dining room table. She liked it. And she liked sitting among all those people, all those brothers and sisters. An only child, she saw only harmony in numbers. She kept hoping this was just the first of many meals the family would take together.

Henry, sitting across the table from Evangeline and between his two young daughters, kept hoping the same thing. He turned and smiled at his wife every few mouthfuls. Irene tried to smile back but the baby kicked so hard and so often that what she really wanted to do was cry.

Mary, sitting next to Barton, tried to remember the last time the entire family had taken a meal together. It, she felt sure, had been the night of their mother's funeral. She wondered if this meal was an omen that another tragedy was in the offing.

Barton remembered that meal also. He had cried often that night but he told himself he would not cry tonight. *Don't think back, you idiot, think ahead.*

Joseph glanced every few seconds down the table at Evangeline.

He felt tired and depressed after having snorted half a gram of cocaine in the past twelve hours. But he still had the curiosity to wonder about Evangeline and his old man. He found it hard to believe she had actually gone down with Wild Bill. He sighed and then he let a soft but perfectly clear, "Jesus," fall from his lips.

"What's the matter, Joseph?" asked Emily.

He shook his head. "Nothing. Nothing at all. Just a little tired I guess."

Ginny spent most of the meal studying Evangeline's two young boys, John and Paul. They looked so familiar, like old friends, old photographs. *My God*, she thought, *they look exactly like a couple of little Winslows.* She could hardly believe she had not noticed the resemblance before. She was tempted to say something, to just comment nonchalantly on this coincidence, and she very well may have had not the doorbell sounded, announcing someone's presence at the front door.

"Who could that be?" asked Emily. "I thought we were all here."

"Maybe it's Edward," suggested Barton.

"I doubt that," someone said softly.

No, it was not Edward but his lovely bride Samantha. The dining room was as quiet as a funeral parlor when Joseph, who had gone to answer the door, led Sammy through the front foyer and into the lion's den. None of them had ever seen her before but they all knew exactly who she was. A full minute ticked off the grandfather's clock in the front hall. No one said a word or made a move. The clock struck ten. They all silently counted off the hours. Outside, the last bits of stray light fell across the front lawn. Spring was almost over. Another summer had very nearly arrived.

"You must be Samantha," said Ginny, of all people, finally.

"Yes." Sammy smiled. She looked both frightened and relieved. "This place is quite a little ways off the beaten path. I thought for sure I was lost."

Several of the Winslows chuckled.

"Thought I'd never get here."

"I guess," asked Ginny, "you didn't find Edward?"

"No, I'm afraid I didn't. When I saw you all through the window I hoped he would be here among you."

"Fat chance," mumbled Emily.

"We haven't seen him or heard from him," said Ginny.

"In like six years," added Emily, sort of softly.

Joseph laughed and put his arm around his sister-in-law. "Hey, Samantha, listen, we're not always this unfriendly. Sometimes we're even worse."

"Shut up, Joseph." Ginny pushed back her chair, stood. "Have you eaten, Samantha? Can we get you something?"

"Yes . . . No . . . Thank you. I ate on the way down."

Joseph brought in another chair. "Here you go, Samantha. Take a seat while we finish up."

"Yes," said Ginny, "and we hope you'll stay. I was expecting you would. I have Edward's old room all ready for you."

"Which, by the way," said Joseph, "is my old room also. So I guess we'll be bunking together. But don't worry, I don't bite."

Samantha wasn't too sure how to take all this. She had half expected to find a den filled with devils. *But they all look pretty normal,* she thought, *except maybe that wiseass who answered the door.* She smiled and said, "I don't bite either. Unless provoked."

Several of the Winslows laughed.

"Joseph's just kidding," said Ginny. "Edward always had his own room. You won't have to share a room with anyone. We're going to put Joseph out in the loft over the garage anyway."

Joseph shot his sister a look. "The hell you—"

"So, Samantha," asked Mary, "where do you think our brother Edward is?"

Well, Samantha had absolutely no way of knowing but I happen to know that Little Eddie was right outside peering in the window. As soon as he had seen his wife climb out of her car he had abandoned his perch and made his way down to the house through the darkness and the underbrush. He crouched low, his eyes just above the window ledge. If someone at the table had looked out the window they probably would have seen his forehead shining there between his eyebrows and his short crop of hair. But no one looked; they were all too busy studying Little Eddie's wife. He was busy studying his wife also. So, he muttered to himself, the bitch is part of the old man's hit squad also. I knew it, I knew she was a freaking spy, a fucking traitor. I'll get her for this. I'll get her good.

* * *

"I really don't know," Samantha answered. "I really have no idea where Edward is."

No one could think of much to say after that. Soon after, the meal ended. The party broke up. Evangeline, with Barton's help, took her boys down to the cottage and put them to bed. They fell asleep before she turned out the light. Barton said good night and went back to the big house. Evangeline went to bed not long after. So did Emily and Rosa. Before she fell asleep, Rosa said to her mother, "This is nice, Mama. We ought to get Shakespeare and stay here all the time. I'll bet Grampa wouldn't mind."

Emily smiled but thought, *Yeah, but I would.* She felt lost in the shuffle downstairs, just the way she had felt as a kid. She was ready to go back to New York, ready to get to work on *King Lear.*

As soon as Rosa fell asleep Emily called the director. She had been trying to reach him all evening. She had her fingers crossed when he picked up the phone. "Yes?"

"Hello, this is Emily Winslow."

"Yes?"

"Um, Emily Winslow. I auditioned for Cordelia the other—"

"Oh yes, Emily...I expected you to drop by and see me."

"You told me to call...to call you tonight."

"I did? Yes, well...we've given the part to someone else."

Maybe it was her imagination but Emily thought she heard giggling in the background. "You did?"

"I'm afraid so. But you're talented, kid. Keep trying."

Emily said something. She was not at all sure what. A moment later she hung up the telephone. She sat on the edge of the bed staring out the open window. Tears filled her eyes and ran down her cheeks. After a time she dried her eyes, slowly took off her clothes, and slipped between the sheets. Rosa was there waiting for her.

Henry carried Constance up to the third floor. Irene and Katie followed. Katie settled on the floor on top of a great heap of thick blankets. Henry put Constance on one of the twin beds. Irene sat down heavily on the other one.

"I'm glad you guys decided to come, Irene."

"Me too. And I can't believe how nice your brothers and sisters are."

Henry, as Bobby Winslow, nodded. "Yeah, nice. Maybe a little strange."

"No stranger than you."

Henry smiled. "How's the baby?"

"Kicked the crap out of me all the way from Blue Mountain. I think he'd like to get out of my belly and get on with the chore of living."

"He?"

"Must be. The girls didn't kick like this. Sometimes I think I've got a whole soccer team inside me."

Henry sat beside his wife and rubbed his hand slowly and gently over her swollen stomach. "We'll name him Bobby."

Irene smiled. "I like that. Robert Winslow junior. After his father."

Henry nodded. "Yeah, after his father."

They sat there for a minute or two thinking it over, staring at her belly.

"Are you going back downstairs?"

"Maybe for a little while," he answered. "You?"

"Not me. I'm beat. It's tough going up and down those stairs when you're this fat."

"Then I'll stay too."

"No, I want you to go down and be with your brothers and sisters. You get to see me all the time. You never get to see them."

Henry nodded. "Irene?"

"Yeah?"

Henry held his wife's hands. Time passed . . . "It's pretty hot up here. You going to be able to sleep?"

"I could sleep inside a furnace when I get this tired. Now get out of here. I'll see you in a little while, or in the morning."

Henry kissed his wife and went back downstairs.

The dining room table had been cleared. Joseph, believe it or not, was loading the dishwasher while Mary wiped off the counters with a wet sponge. Bettina had already retired to the master bedroom without even so much as clearing her plate or saying good night. Ginny had taken Samantha upstairs to show her where she would sleep.

Henry walked into the kitchen at exactly the same time Barton returned from the cottage.

"Hey Bart, old buddy," said Joseph, "you were gone quite a while. Trying to move in on the old boy's territory?"

Barton did not find the remark funny. "Just trying to help her out."

"Right. You hear that one, Henry, I mean Bobby, old Bart's just trying to help her out."

Henry glanced at Joseph, then at Mary who had her back to them as she wiped off the stove. "Yeah, I heard."

The kitchen sounded pretty quiet for the next few seconds. Then Mary, without even turning around, said, "I was up at the graveyard earlier, paying my respects..."

The brothers all turned to listen; all the brothers except Edward, who had returned to his perch, and Bobby, who was dead.

Mary turned around then. She glanced at Joseph and Barton and then looked directly at Henry. "It was quiet up there," she said, "peaceful. But I heard some things. I heard a few rumblings."

"A few rumblings?" asked Henry.

Mary nodded, then crossed to her brother. She looked him in the eye. "You see, it doesn't really matter. It's much bigger than us. We play only a small, peripheral role. Our headaches and our bodyaches are nothing but a sideshow. The real show takes place in the womb and in the dark places we think about but never get to see."

Henry dropped his eyes, looked away. Barton glanced at Joseph. Joseph rolled his eyes and shrugged his shoulders.

Mary turned and went back to her wiping. When Ginny walked into the kitchen a few moments later, she saw her three brothers standing there with their mouths hanging open staring at their sister's back. "Who are you," she asked, "the Three Stooges?"

Thursday, June 21, 1990...
Summer Solstice

Chapter Twenty-nine

———————————————•———————————————

After midnight now on the shortest night of the year. Barely more than six hours between dusk and dawn. No wind, no moon, zillions of stars, billions of galaxies. Perfectly calm, perfectly clear. Constellations in every corner of the sky: Big Bear and Little Bear, Flying Fish and the Winged Horse, Orion and the Serpent's Tail. Shooting stars, super novas, exploding suns, lifeless planets. It's warm on earth, in the northern hemisphere anyway, in the northeast corridor of the United Staes of America, in the Garden State, in Far Hills, up at the Winslow Compound. It's extremely warm, almost stifling in that big house; especially now as those century-old stone walls begin to fold in upon themselves in anticipation of the approaching tempest.

You might think those Winslows would be fast asleep, snoring softly, dreaming pleasant dreams. They'd all had a rather long and emotional day. And they certainly all had reasonably good health (not a cancer or so much as a hemorrhoid among them), excellent medical coverage (supplied of course by the Wild One), full bellies, a demobilized military, capitalism on the march from Berlin to Budapest, and large quantities of U.S. dollars securely invested in some of America's leading companies; i.e., Exxon, AT&T, McDonald's, and IBM. They also had each other, but even with all of these advantages, the majority of Winslows could not sleep. Their bodies may have been exhausted but their minds were like lightning bolts slashing at the dark, damp night. Let's take a look:

We may as well first dispose of those few individuals who actually could sleep. Bettina, of course, but then she slept the night of the day her mother died. And Rosa, she slept like, well, like a baby. And John and Paul; a cyclone hitting the cottage wouldn't've shaken them from their slumber. And Katie and Constance: they slept with smiles on their *faces and love in their hearts. And their mother Irene: she awoke from time to time when the little human in her belly gave a swift kick to her kidneys but otherwise her sleep was sound and untroubled. But really I think that's about it; they're the only ones using the night for its intended purpose. Oh no, wait, check this out. Lying on the floor beside his wife: Henry Winslow. My God, the man is sound asleep. His face looks happy, relaxed, contented even. This could be the best sleep he's had since the night before news of his brother's death reached him down at Princeton more than twenty years ago.*

Emily couldn't sleep. She fell asleep for an hour or so after the phone call but then awoke because of the heat and because she had this terrible feeling her whole life sucked, her whole existence was a miserable failure and a waste of time. She felt this way because she would not be playing Cordelia in Central Park. The fact that the young lady who would be playing Cordelia had fucked the middle-aged director's brains out to get the part did not enter into Emily's estimation of her own worth.

Evangeline couldn't sleep. She lay in bed thinking about Billy Boy, remembering the terrible things she had overheard him say to his wife. He had never said such mean or hateful things to her in all the years they had been together. She had not thought he was capable. He had always been so kind and gentle and giving. But now she did not know what to think.

Barton couldn't sleep. Every time he closed his eyes he had this vision of the Roman Colosseum. The stands were packed with his sculptures. And they were all shouting, "Death to the Artist, Death to the Artist." And then he was in the ring, not with lions but with this huge creature with the body of a wildebeest and the head of Wild Bill. The creature chased him around the ring, laughing and heckling him, until finally Barton surrendered and opened his eyes. After a while he didn't even try to close them.

Ginny couldn't sleep. She kept calling Bel Air and not getting any answer. Along about 12:45 she turned on the light and looked for something to read. She had a whole shelf of books on the wall across from her bed. She went over and glanced at the titles. They were pretty much the same books that had been there when she was in high school. There were a couple of Hermann Hesse books, Salinger's The Catcher in the Rye, Slaughterhouse Five, Of Mice and Men, *a bunch of plays by Eugene O'Neill and Edward Albee, a few textbooks, her senior high yearbook, which she almost pulled out until she saw, at the end of the shelf, the family photo album she had put together as a teenager. She carried the album back to bed. There were pictures of her* mother and her father and all her brothers and sisters, even Little Helen and Bobby. There were pictures of the family at picnics and at birthday parties and on Christmas and the 4th of July. In most of the pictures the people were smiling, laughing, looking like they might even be having a good time. Then she saw a snapshot of Joseph and Barton sitting on the grass out by the swimming pool. They must've been about five years old, between five and seven, thought Ginny, about the ages of John and— She pulled the dusty photo out of the album and examined the image more closely under the light. The picture could easily have been taken of John and Paul that very afternoon and slipped into the photo album which so perfectly captured moments from the past. Ginny practically whistled out loud. She dialed the house in Bel Air once again. She had to tell Aaron. She had to tell someone. But no one was home. The Cohens were on their way east, tired and irritable from a long delay at LAX, but on their way east nevertheless. In fact, they were at that very moment passing directly overhead as that DC-10 made its final approach into Newark International Airport.

Joseph, not in the room over the garage but down in the den, couldn't sleep. Not only had all the cocaine thrown his equilibrium to the dogs, but that hide-a-bed mattress had a metal bar running straight across the base of his back. He felt like one of those Indian gurus who sleeps on a bed of nails. He tossed and turned for a couple hours then decided to make a move. He got off the bed, found his stash of weed, rolled a paper-thin reefer, and smoked the entire joint in three long drags. Then he went over to the floor-to-ceiling bookcase that filled the long wall across from the hide-a-bed. Joseph was not a big reader; maybe read a book or two a year, biographies of business tycoons and professional athletes mostly. He preferred magazines, especially slick ones with lots of color photographs of ski equipment, sports cars, mountain bikes, voluptuous naked women. But tonight he decided to find something good to read, something interesting. There must've been close to five hundred books on those shelves. Most of them had been there for years. Charles had been an avid reader. He liked fiction and travel books. Wild Bill read a lot also. He read mostly about American history. Other members of the family had been interested in politics, science fiction, philosophy, the occult; so there was a wide range of books on those shelves. Joseph pulled several of the volumes out, read the first few lines, put them all back. He worked his way from bottom to top. To reach the books on the higher shelves he had to climb a special ladder that ran along the ceiling on a steel track. It was on the top shelf, more than an hour after he had smoked the reefer, that he *finally found the book which gives this scene validity. It was just a skinny, nondescript book with a faded leather jacket sandwiched between two thick volumes on the Civil War. The book had nothing at all written on its spine, which may have been why Joseph decided to pull it out and take a look. He opened to the inside front cover.* The Personal & Private Diary of Martha Matthews Winslow. *Joey smiled and flipped to the first entry:*

September 13, 1916
    We finally did what we had been threatening to do since spring. We had to polish off an extra fifth of gin but at last the inhibitions broke down and the clothes came off. The six of us (I won't name names, except of course for yours truly and my Lucky Chuckie, that scoundrel) frolicked in the pool in our birthday suits laughing and giggling and touching whomever we felt like touching. It was absolutely fiendish. I nearly faint dead away just thinking about it.

Joseph read his grandmother's diary, from first page to last, in one sitting. It didn't take him long, maybe an hour. I could probably reprint the entire diary right here and many readers would find it very, well, very stimulating. There is, after all, a bit of the voyeur in all of us. But I think a total reprint is unnecessary. Martha's entries are interesting but nevertheless rather sparse and not of much historical significance, especially to this particular narrative. Months sometimes pass without a single entry. In fact, the only time she made an entry was the day after she got drunk and did something naughty, usually with her hubby and their rich, spoiled friends. It took them a while to get up the nerve but by late 1917 they were having wild orgies with piles of naked bodies and everyone doing exactly what they felt like doing. Joseph got a terrific erection just reading his grandmama's prose. Whether or not Martha was merely fantasizing is anyone's guess.
    Near the end of the diary he found an entry dated May 3, 1919. The first paragraph spoke of Charles leaving for France the previous day and the drunken bon voyage party they'd thrown for him aboard ship. She then spent half a page wondering when her Chuckie would return. And then:

    Crazy Legs came to my room last night. He barely uttered a single word. He tore off his clothes and jumped on top of me. I struggled, but I must admit, not for long and not with much aggression. It was delicious.

May 7, 1919

We did it again, me and papa-in-law. But it was not like that first wild time when reckless won out over reason. This time I felt guilty and dirty and I told him so. He told me he would not return. I feel I have made a terrible, woeful sin.

June 5, 1919

I have thought as much for a week now but yesterday Dr. Smithers confirmed my suspicions. I am with child. I cannot help but think that this child has been fathered by the father of my husband. In fact, it must be so. Timing crosses out all other possibilities. Woe is me! What am I to do? Where am I to turn?

And then, after several entries over the next few months in which Martha considered everything from abortion to suicide, she made one last swipe with her pen.

January 28, 1920

Three days ago the baby arrived, my second, an eight-pound boy. He caused me little pain and popped out with a smile on his face. Charles, home now after his long stay in Paris, says we should name this newest Winslow, William Bailey Richford. Sounds good to me.

Chuckie suspects nothing. Maybe I suspect too much. Maybe it was our final thrusts before he went abroad that made this baby after all.

There were no more entries. That was Shady's final written word on the subject. Joseph closed the book and, like his sister above as she stared at those old photos, whistled softly. He wondered who else knew about this skeleton in the Winslow closet. The diary sat up on the shelf for all to see, for all to read. But he had never heard a word about it, not a whisper. . . . And neither, fellow reader, had I. Not until that night I passed there with Joseph. As I said many pages ago, I thought as much was true but my ruminations on the subject were nothing more, speculations only. And so we see a case of fiction turning to fact, of rumor turning to reality. It's the kind of discovery that makes all the research worth the effort. But what does it mean? Does it mean anything? Does it change anything? Well, it means Charles and Wild Bill are actually of the same generation, brothers of different mothers but like fathers. It means Gustave Frederick was right when he kept referring to Crazy Legs as the Wild One's father. It means Wild Bill's sons are only the third and not the fourth generation of Winslows to be born and raised on that hilltop in Far Hills. Which means Wild Bill's dream of a fifth generation born and raised there, thus outlasting the four generations who lived along the Delaware north of Burlington, looks more like a pipe dream than a point of destination. But who knows? Maybe Joseph will keep his mouth shut, not allow this skeleton to run loose. But will a cover-up make it right? Does not knowing the truth preclude its existence? I don't know, but I doubt very much if Joseph will be able to hold his tongue on this one anyway. Why, he asked himself, would I even want to? This is great stuff. Everyone should know about this. But as the night wore on he thought about it more, and when the tempest finally broke he still had not made up his mind. He did, however, hide the diary up on the top shelf, not between those two thick volumes on the Civil War, but behind them.

Wild Bill made the call, then slipped out of his room a little after midnight. The corridor was quiet, the lights dimmed. He made his way past the nurses' station, the rubber feet of his crutches squeaking on the just-cleaned, still-wet linoleum floor. The nurse did not look up from her thick paperback romance novel. He hobbled past the elevators and down the back stairs in his pajamas. He saw no one. No one saw him. But when he reached the ground floor he found this sign on the door: Open Only in Case of Emergency. Alarm Will Sound. "Shit." He searched for another exit, found the same sign on all the doors. "What is this, a goddamn prison camp?" Finally, after deciding the driver would not wait, he walked straight down through the middle of the main lobby and out the front doors. He looked like a man who knew where he wanted to go. The night receptionist saw him but said nothing. No one said a word.

The taxi pulled up after he had been out on the curb for only a minute or two. "You the guy," the driver asked, "who wanted a cab?"

Wild Bill pulled open the back door. "That's right, that's me."

The driver had hair pulled straight back and greased down. A smoky cigarette hung off his lip. "Okay, no problem. It's just that it's like the middle of the night and I can see you're a patient so, like, I got to ask if it's okay with the people inside that you leave."

Wild Bill threw his crutches into the backseat, then pulled himself in with not too little trouble. "What are you," he asked, "the goddamn zookeeper or something? Drive the cab."

The driver watched him in the rearview mirror. "Okay, man, but just tell me that you ain't from up on Franklin Five."

"What are you talking about? Franklin Five?"

"Franklin Five, man. That's the psycho ward of the hospital. Where they keep the wackos. You ain't no wacko, are you?"

Wild Bill knew about Franklin Five. Little Eddie had spent some time up there on an occasion or two. "Come on, pal. Drive the cab. I'm in a hurry."

The driver put the car in gear. "You got money?"

Wild Bill waved the twenty. "Yeah, I got money."

They didn't say much during the drive out to Far Hills. The cabbie made good time until they reached the road that wound up into the hills. Then he slowed, took his time in the big bends. "Never been out this way before. You live up here?"

"I do, yeah," answered the Wild One, "seventy years."

"Seventy years, no shit? You must have bucks."

Wild Bill glanced at the meter. *$18.65, and still clicking.* He knew he'd just make it. "I have what I've worked for."

"Right."

They reached the top of the hill and turned onto the summit road. *$19.40.* "Next driveway on the right," said the Wild One.

"No sweat, man, I see it."

$19.70. The driver pulled the cab into the driveway, right between the eagle and the turkey vulture.

"Okay, stop here," demanded Wild Bill.

The cabbie stopped. The Wild One pushed open the door and struggled to get out.

"Sure you don't want me to take you the rest of the way?" the cabbie asked. "I can't even see no freaking house."

Wild Bill was out of the cab. He steadied himself on his crutches. "No, this is far enough." He handed the driver the twenty through the open window. "Here you go, you nosy son of a bitch. Keep the change."

The driver checked the meter. $19.85. "Hey, and fuck you too, old man."

Wild Bill turned away, right down the middle of the drive, right smack down the path of that taxi's headlights. The cabbie considered running the cheap old cripple over but decided it would be more trouble than it was worth. So he backed out of the driveway and raced away, leaving behind six or seven thousand miles worth of rubber off his Bridgestone radials.

The Wild One hobbled down the smooth macadam, those tall red maples casting shadows against the past.

Now I hate to admit this but I can see I've overlooked something, actually someone. I've been talking about who's asleep and who's awake for the last several pages, and I guess I just assumed Edward would be wide awake. I couldn't imagine him actually falling asleep; just goes to show you can't take anything for granted. You have to stay on top of things, keep a constant vigil. While Ginny looked at pictures and Joseph read Martha's diary and the Wild One made his way home, Little Eddie slept with his back against a mature white oak and his head drooped down against his chest. I really should have known. The guy had not slept more than a few hours over the past three days. After sneaking down to the house to check out his wife's arrival, he went back to his hideout in the woods and promptly fell asleep from sheer exhaustion. He looked like a harmless little boy on a camping trip slumped there against that oak tree. An empty can of pork and beans lay near his foot. A can of root beer lay crumpled at his elbow. Milky Way wrappers and empty bags of peanut M&Ms and a half-eaten box of powdered doughnuts littered the campsite. It all looked pretty innocent, except for that old Remington double-barrel twelve-gauge leaning against the tree right beside Little Eddie's head.

I don't know what woke Eddie up, maybe a rabbit in the woods or a noise in his head or maybe just that old train fate rumbling through the Jersey countryside. But whatever did the trick, just as Wild Billy Boy Winslow hobbled into the pool of light cast by the two bright spotlights on the side of the garage, Little Eddie opened his eyes. He immediately looked down in the direction of the house. And that's when he saw him; that's when he spotted his old man. His eyes grew wide. He grabbed the Remington and jumped to his feet.

* * *

The Wild One hobbled through the circle of light and into the shadows. Edward expected him to reappear at the back door but he never did. He went right past his wife's Allanté and the Jaguar and the Buick Regal and the Range Rover and into the garage. Little Eddie brought the binoculars to his eyes and scanned the darkness. "Where'd that old fucker go now?" The spotlights threw enough light for the Wild One to see his way around the garage. He went to the back wall to where he knew he had left those two Orvis fly-casting rods. But the rods were gone. *Sure they were gone; they were in that cabbie's basement out in Queens, the one who had brought Mary home from Kennedy.* Wild Bill looked around the garage but he knew the rods were gone, he knew he'd left them against the back wall. "Jesus H. Christ," he muttered, "home barely a day and already one of 'em has pilfered my fishin' poles?" He wanted the poles because he wanted to leave them outside John and Paul's bedroom so when they got up in the morning the poles would be there waiting for them.

Edward hurried to the edge of the woods and once again swept the field glasses back and forth across the driveway and the lawn. "He has to be there somewhere. The son of a bitch can't just disappear." And sure enough, the Wild One was somewhere. Little Eddie picked him up as a shadow slowly hobbling across the tennis court. Then he saw his father more clearly as Billy Boy crossed into the light thrown by the porch lamp near the front door of the cottage. Eddie watched his father climb the three stairs to the porch. "Where's he going? Why the hell's he going there?" Little Eddie had no idea but he watched his father turn the knob and slowly push open the door. He shook his head. "This doesn't make sense. He shouldn't be going there. But it doesn't matter. It doesn't matter worth a damn. I've got him now. I've got him exactly where I want him." Edward waited for his father to enter the cottage and close the door, then he made his move. There would be no more sleep for Little Eddie Winslow that night, not a wink.

Chapter Thirty

———————————————●———————————————

Mary saw the Wild One hobbling down the driveway also. She saw him from her bedroom window. But in the early summer starlight he did not look to her like Wild Bill. He looked like the Wild One's great-grandfather, William Giles, son of Lorelei Constantine Winslow, the young woman who Mary believed had been raped by her father-in-law, Robert "Mad Dog" Winslow. That rape being, by the way, another of the many incidents in this narrative which cannot be fully validated. There are some differences of opinion on the whole matter of Lorelei's relationship with her father-in-law. It is true that her husband, Henry Lane III, went off to fight in what we call the War of 1812, and that he died in Canada during that conflict against the British. But whether or not Lorelei was already with child before Henry Lane's departure remains open to question. Certain letters supposedly exist from Henry Lane to his wife which suggest the young soldier knew a baby was on the way. Mad Dog may indeed have tried to rape his daughter-in-law, may even have been successful; she was after all young and beautiful and extremely vulnerable. But this scene where she sneaks into his bedroom and cuts off his male member has the smell of something conjured up by Mary's wicked imagination. I don't think Lorelei had it in her to commit such a heinous act. Yes, Mad Dog was a tyrant and a bully. And yes, Lorelei, with the aid of Henry Lane's sisters, escaped her father-in-law's household as soon as William Giles grew old enough to travel. But did she club the old soldier over the head and then whack off his pecker with a cleaver? I suppose we could exhume Mad Dog's body from its wet grave along the Millstone, haul him over to some laboratory, hire some specialist to check for missing body parts...

*   *   *

Lorelei went to live with friends of friends on a vast estate along the Raritan River, not far from the county seat of Somerville. She raised William Giles on that estate. She raised him in a one-room cabin. She did sewing and weaving and housekeeping for the owners of the estate in return for a small weekly salary. It was an estate of over a thousand acres. The owners were an old New Jersey family, not as old as the Winslows, but the War for Independence had left them much better connected in this new century both politically and financially. Their name was Scottfield and they had a son, Todd, the same age as William Giles. The two boys grew up together and became fast friends. William Giles did not have the advantages of a private tutor and boarding school and a university degree from Princeton but he did get the opportunity to learn farming. In the mid 1830s, after the old Scottfields had died off and Todd had taken over the estate, he put William Giles in charge of crops and livestock. Young Winslow worked sixteen hours a day, seven days a week. He put more money than ever into the Scottfield coffers and in return Todd gave William several acres on which to build his own home. He built his house with his own hands and in 1839 he moved in with his aging-but-still-beautiful mother, Lorelei, and his brand-new bride, a Pennsylvania Dutch girl named Emily Schaffer. A year later, in the late fall of 1840, William Giles and Emily had their only son, their only child, a huge ten pounder at birth who they named Barton Henry after their fathers, Barton Schaffer and Henry Lane Winslow.

Barton Henry grew up like a member of the privileged class. Todd Scottfield, whose wife could not bear children, made sure young Winslow received a first-class education. By the age of sixteen the boy was ready for university. He told his father and his Uncle Todd that he wanted to attend West Point. And so he did. Scottfield supported the local representative with a great deal of money so the congressman happily arranged an appointment for young Winslow at the Point.

Barton Henry excelled as a student and a soldier. It was obvious from the beginning of his enrollment that he had leadership qualities. Although the youngest member of his class, he knew instinctively how to take charge, how to give orders, how to get men to do what they might not want to do. And he did it all with a subdued, almost gentle manner. He was an enormous man, as wide as Wild Bill and as tall as Wild Bill's son Henry. He had broad shoulders, a chest like a rum barrel, arms like oak limbs, and a stomach as hard as iron. In his cadet's uniform he looked like a soldier, like a commander. He was also, at least in the eyes of his superiors, a perfect gentleman. In fact, on the day of his class commencement in June of 1860, war fever sweeping the banks of the Hudson, the commandant of the Point introduced the class valedictorian as Barton Henry "Gentleman Bart" Winslow. The nickname stuck.

He was commissioned a lieutenant but when hostilities broke out after the incident at Fort Sumter his rank began to soar. He led a platoon at the first Battle of Bull Run which took thirty Confederate prisoners and captured more than a dozen pieces of artillery. They made the twenty-one-year-old Winslow a captain. A few months later, in October of 1861, during a skirmish with Rebel cavalry along the Rappahannock in Virginia, Captain Winslow took a slug in the shoulder, fell off his horse, and broke his kneecap. They sent him home to recuperate for the winter.

Barton Henry enjoyed those winter months in the bosom of his family. He was a war hero. Everyone told him so. One young lady in particular: Dorothy Anne Hayes. She and Barton had been acquainted as kids, and once he had even kissed her out in the hayfields during harvest. But during Barton's visit home from the war they did a lot more than kiss. Every chance they got the two youngsters stripped themselves bare and made love like a couple of wild animals. Barton Henry was twenty-one, Dorothy just twenty. They feared what their parents would say if they declared their desire to marry. So what did they do? They borrowed a buggy one cold day in January and rode over to Somerville where they bought a marriage license and found a preacher to make it legal. Barton Henry wore his uniform, his medals displayed prominently on his chest. No one dared question or caution the young soldier's matrimonial haste.

When they arrived home that evening Barton and Dorothy told no one what they had done. They decided it would be their secret until the war was over. Less than a month later Barton Henry had to rejoin his company. In the second Battle of Bull Run he showed his courage once again. He led his men against a company of Rebel sharpshooters in an attack which his superior officer called "an action well beyond the call of duty." They made the boy-soldier a major.

Three weeks later, in Maryland, outside a sleepy farm town called Sharpsburg, he further validated the claim that he was one of the roughest, toughest, bravest soldiers in the Union army. He led a charge across the small bridge spanning Antietam Creek and helped push John Bell Hood's Fighting Texans into a defensive position. The maneuver may not have gained a victory for the North but it helped stymie the Confederate army and turned back Lee's bold advance on Washington, D.C. Major Winslow took a hit near the end of the charge when a miniball crashed through his thigh. But shouts of "Gentleman Bart is down!" sang out across the battlefield and within minutes he had been carried back to the field hospital where doctors stopped the bleeding and bandaged the wound. The next day General George McClellan, who probably should have been chasing Lee's retreating army across the Potomac, personally made the twenty-two-year-old Winslow a colonel. As soon as the young colonel could travel they shipped him home for a month of R and R.

He spent every moment he could with his wife but others made demands on his time so days went by without their getting a single minute alone. He wanted to announce their marriage but she said no, the time was not right, her mother was sick with fever and her father would never understand. So Barton Henry kept his mouth shut. Only twice during his furlough did they find the time and the place to make love. The second time, out in one of the Scottfield barns on a cold damp November day, guaranteed the passage of the Winslow line for another generation.

Barton Henry went back to the war in December and passed the winter outside the capital drilling his troops and preparing for the spring offensive. Back home Dorothy wrote letters several times a week to her husband but not once did she mention the slow but certain swelling in her belly. Her mother died from fever that winter and her father went into a state of depression. He did not notice his daughter's condition. She agonized daily over what to do, over who to tell, over how she would ever be able to have this baby.

In the spring the armies fought at Chancellorsville. Stonewall Jackson lost his life and the Union army cheered. But Lee and his Army of Northern Virginia kept coming, kept advancing all the way to the Mason-Dixon Line. In the middle of June the Confederates swept across the Potomac, threatening once again to attack the capital. By the end of June two of the largest armies of the war had assembled outside a small Pennsylvania town called Gettysburg. On the first of July the fighting started and for the next two days it raged on practically without pause. Colonel Winslow had his men in the thick of the fight both days from dawn till dusk. He did not bother to sleep or eat. More than once he had premonitions of his own death but he laughed out loud each time they came. The generals kept telling their commanders that if the Rebs broke through, the war, and the nation, could be lost. Gentleman Bart fought on.

Dorothy fought on also. Finally, in her seventh month, she had confided in an old childhood friend. The friend took her in, gave her comfort and a place to sleep. Dorothy's own father did not even seem to notice her absence. Her labor started almost at the exact same moment the fighting started on July first. For two days she struggled with the help of a midwife to have that baby. For two days the baby struggled to stay in the womb.

By late afternoon on July third both Dorothy and her husband were well past the point of exhaustion. But neither would give up, neither would give in. The noise on the battlefield as George Pickett led his fifteen thousand Confederate troops across that open meadow sounded to Colonel Winslow like the end of the world. Not only were hundreds of cannons and mortars and parrots exploding their charges one right after another, but tens of thousands of men yelled and screamed from fear and pain and simple human outrage. Barton Henry met the Confederate charge head-on; didn't flinch for an instant at this totally insane confrontation of brothers and old friends and countrymen. He held his ground. He fought and killed and then died. And he did it all, he thought, for duty, for manhood, for the preservation of the Union and the glory of the family name.

His wife did it also. But she did it for life, for the preservation of her fetus, for the survival of her baby. She did it for herself and for her husband and for their future. She refused to succumb to the pain and the exhaustion. She pushed until she very nearly collapsed. But then, suddenly, all at once, the struggle ended: Barton passed on and the baby passed into the living world. For all his kicking and fighting he was not even that big, about five and a half pounds, looked kind of yellow and wrinkled and sickly. But he had a determined look on his pale face, sort of half-angry and half-amused, like "Stand aside, people, I'm coming through to get my fair share come hell or high water."

Dorothy named the infant John after her father. But her father would not recognize the baby as his grandson. He called his daughter a whore and her boy a bastard and forbade her from ever setting foot in his house again. Her insistence that her marriage to

Barton Henry Winslow was legal and sanctioned went unheard. He banished her. So too did the Winslows, Barton's parents, William Giles and Emily. They didn't like to do it but their only son had just been shipped home in a wooden box the day before this young lady arrived with a newborn baby claiming their son was the baby's father.

It was barely an hour after William Giles and his wife Emily showed young Dorothy to the door that Mary, up in her bedroom, saw William Giles, who was actually her own father, Wild Bill, hobbling down the dark driveway under those tall red maples. In Mary's mind the old man on the crutches was hobbling out to the barn to milk the cows and wash away his sorrows in a pint of whiskey he kept there hidden beneath the hay. He was on crutches because he had recently hurt his knee while plowing. His knee hurt and his head hurt and the pain in his heart made him want to die. He could not believe his boy was dead. He could not believe war had taken his only son. He wanted to die himself. And all the while he sat in the barn on the milking stool pulling on those cows' udders and sipping his whiskey, William Giles wondered if his boy's death meant the end of the Winslow line.

Mary of course knew it meant no such thing. She knew the marriage between Barton Henry and Dorothy was legal and sanctioned. She knew the infant John was a full-bred Winslow.

Dorothy had a difficult time bringing the boy through infancy and early adolescence with no husband and with no help from either side of the boy's family. For eight years she raised a young Winslow male (no small chore even in the best of circumstances) all by herself. And she would have carried on longer, for forever if necessary, had she not contracted the polio virus during the hot and humid summer of 1871.

Young John Winslow contracted the disease that summer also. The doctor all but told the mother that her frail, sickly child would not live through the winter. But even at the innocent young age of eight John Winslow was too thick-skinned and bullheaded to let some virus wipe out his chances for a full life. He came within a heartbeat of dying, but when the boy saw his mother suffering in pain he climbed out of bed, told God to go straight to hell, and then he put himself to work. Twenty-four hours a day for the next thirteen days he watched over his mama, fed her mouthfuls of soup, cooled her fever with damp rags, cleaned up her waste, and shook his fist at the power of the Almighty. She died in the middle of the night. He wept until dawn and all the rest of that day. And when darkness came again he buried his mama in an unmarked grave because he had no money for an undertaker or a preacher or a tombstone.

Before his tenth birthday young John was in Hoboken working twelve hours a day in the cordage factory. He slept in a dilapidated tool shed out behind the factory, along the banks of the Hudson, right near where young Freeman Winslow had once chiseled his wooden carvings of pagan serpents. The boy ate wherever he could find a place to sit down, whatever the other workers threw aside. He was tired and weak all the time. He had a permanent limp from his bout with polio. He would have that limp the rest of his life.

The owner of the factory, a cruel and nasty old man, and one of the reasons the federal government eventually passed child-labor laws, nicknamed young Winslow Crazy Legs. He told the boy if he worked like a dog for the next forty or fifty years he might one day own his own factory. Crazy Legs, never one to say much, just smiled and nodded at the Boss. But the boy had no intention of waiting that long. "I'm gonna own this shithole before you die, you fat old fuck," he mumbled to himself every night out in his shack, "and when I do I'm gonna make your kids lick my ass and clean up my crap."

Mary heard that and decided she had heard enough for one night. She looked out the open window once more at the darkness. The shadowy figure hobbling down the drive had long since disappeared. Mary went back to bed, settled her head on the soft down pillow, and fell fast asleep. Her slumber did not last long however, barely more than a few brief minutes. The storm was on the rise. Everyone in the family would soon be rousted from their roosts.

Chapter Thirty-one

•

The Wild One stepped into the cottage and quietly closed the door. He crossed the small dining room, his crutches squeaking against the hardwood floor. One step down and he stood in the middle of the living room on top of plush wall-to-wall carpeting. The first night of summer cast enough light through the large picture window for him to see the shapes of everything in the room: the sofa and the old wooden rocker and the antique wooden chest and the shelves of books and Evangeline's brand-new stereo system and the long, orderly line of compact discs. Wild Bill loved that room: its smallness, its tightness, its warmth, its intimacy. Sometimes he felt as though he could pass the rest of the evenings of his life in that room. But he knew it was not the room but the people in the room: John and Paul and sweet Evangeline. They were always so pleasant, so polite. They always had a kind word and a smile. And they were usually quiet, rarely confrontational, never impatient. They had no television set, and only occasionally did they play the radio. The outside world was not allowed into this room. This was their space, their sanctuary.

He crossed to the boys' bedroom door and slowly turned the knob. The door opened without a sound. He saw their young faces. They slept on their sides, their breathing soft and steady. He watched them and smiled and knew he loved them as much as anything he had ever loved in his entire life. And then she was behind him, her hands closing around his waist.

"Billy Boy, are you crazy? What are you doing here?"

He turned around, pulled the door to the bedroom closed. He could see she was happy but not quite smiling. "I missed you."

"I was awake missing you."

"So that's why I came." He put his arms around her back.

"But it's almost two o'clock in the morning. How did you get here? How did you get out of the hospital? Do they know you—"

He gently pressed his finger against her lips. "None of that matters, kid. Not right now anyway."

"Don't be so sure about that," she whispered.

"What does that mean?"

"It means I overheard some of your conversation with Bettina."

He looked at her in the dim gray light. "I was afraid of that."

"It was pretty ugly."

"What do you expect, dealing with her?"

"That's no excuse."

He wanted to argue, defend himself, tell her Bettina brought out the worst in him, but he knew she was right. "Yes, I suppose it was pretty ugly."

She wanted to say more, to make sure he understood how she felt. But she decided she had said enough. She knew it was better to say too little than too much; the Quakers had taught her at an early age the virtue of brevity. She kissed his finger then put her arms around his waist. "Do you want to sleep here tonight?"

"I hadn't thought that far ahead. I just wanted to get here." He had his arms wrapped around her shoulders.

They stood there like that, arm in arm, pressed close together, quiet and contented, while outside Little Eddie doused the cottage with gasoline. *Yes, gasoline, a five-gallon can of the explosive stuff. High octane.* Evangeline used it to run the John Deere field tractor. Little Eddie wanted to use it to burn his old man at the stake. Before he lit the match he peered in the dining room window. He could see through the dining room into the living room. His blood boiled when he saw his old man hugging Evangeline. *That slut,* he thought, *maybe I'll wait till they start fucking before I light this stinking whorehouse on fire.* But he feared the petrol would evaporate so he stepped back, ignited a blue tip, gave the tiny flame a moment to catch, and then he tossed the match against the cottage. The gasoline exploded. The explosion very nearly knocked Little Eddie off his feet. The backlash of flames singed his eyebrows. He regained his balance, caught a whiff of the burning hair, and sprinted for the cover of the trees.

"What the hell was that!" The Wild One broke the embrace, turned, immediately saw the flames. "Jesus Christ!" The entire east end of the cottage was on fire. The old dried-out wooden clapboards ignited like year-old kindling. He grabbed his crutches and hobbled across the living room to the dining room. Already he could feel the heat. No way could they get through the door: the fire had completely engulfed it. "Get the boys up, get 'em up! We gotta get 'em out!" he screamed but Evangeline had already made the move for the bedroom.

Up at the main house, little Rosa saw the fire first. She was in the bathroom getting a drink of water when she looked out the window and saw the flames. "Fire! Fire! Fire!" She ran up and down the hallway screaming at the top of her lungs. "Fire! Fire! The cottage is on fire! The cottage is on fire!"

One by one the Winslows sprang from their beds, raced down the stairs, and out the back door. Henry, from all the way up on the third floor and fast asleep when the alarm went out, was the first one to reach the scene. He sprinted across the lawn, past the swimming pool and over the tennis court. By the time he reached the cottage the flames had completely swallowed the tiny dwelling. "My God! Evangeline!" he screamed. "Evangeline!"

Henry thought he heard voices but the incessant roar of the fire easily stamped out any pleas for help.

The others started to arrive: Barton and Emily and Rosa. Then Ginny and Joseph. Irene and Katie and Constance. And Mary and Samantha. And finally even Bettina came slowly across the tennis court wearing a fine silk nightgown. It was tough to tell in that chaotic mix of starlight and firelight but it sure looked like she had a very smug smile on her face. A smile despite the fact that she did not even know yet Wild Bill was in the cottage.

Henry took charge. He was, after all, a fire fighter. He sent Joseph for some shovels and an ax. He ordered Emily to locate and hook up the garden hose. He told Ginny to find some buckets. He and Barton went for the door. They both kept shouting for John and Paul and Evangeline. There were no replies. At least none they could hear above the fire's roar. Henry tried to slip through the flames but the heat drove him back. Emily turned on the outdoor spigot and uncoiled a length of hose. But when the thin stream of water hit the flames the fire just laughed. It hissed and cracked and spit in her face, spit in all of their faces. They had to keep retreating from the fire's wrath.

Ginny and Mary found some old buckets, dipped the buckets in the swimming pool, and tried to form a bucket brigade. But by the time the buckets reached the cottage most of the water had either leaked or spilled out. The fire continued to laugh and scream. The asphalt roof shingles began to burn and melt.

No one knew what to do. They all shouted and screamed at once. Henry's authority broke down. Those Winslows raced around the outside of the cottage shouting and hoping to find a way inside. The fire burned out of control. Then, suddenly, they heard glass breaking. The large picture window in the living room cracked and then burst. The sound of shattering glass brought the activity out on the lawn to a halt. An instant later a single wooden crutch soared through the smoky air and landed at their feet. Before the crutch came to rest two small bodies rushed through the broken window. They cleared the flames and the smoke and then rolled onto the grass. Their bodies were wrapped in soaking-wet bath towels.

"Mama," shouted Rosa, "it's them, it's them! It's John and Paul!"

Indeed. Frightened out of their little minds they were, but okay now except for a couple of cuts and some smoke in their lungs. Then came their mother and father. Wild Bill hobbled through the heat; Evangeline held him steady. Their bodies also were wrapped in soaking wet towels. He had a crutch under one arm and his other arm around her shoulder. They came clear of the fire and the smoke and out into the afterglow in the middle of the lawn.

"Daddy!" one of the girls, either Emily or Ginny or Mary, shouted.

They were all out, all four of them, the entire family, and they were all okay. There was some bleeding and some coughing and some shaking, but this fire, already running low on fuel, would not claim a single victim.

It's at times like this I wish I'd gone into filmmaking. Sure, the cottage burning would look great up on the Silver Screen, but even better would be the faces of those Winslows as they watched the Wild One come hobbling through those red-hot flames. I'd pan back and forth through the crowd, picking up wide-open eyes and gaping mouths and dropped jaws. I'd have close-ups of Bettina's smug smile falling away, of Ginny and Emily's stares of surprise, of Henry's sigh of relief, of little Rosa's tears of joy running down her fire-red face. I'd give each of those Winslows a few silent frames to let us know how they feel about this latest turn of events. But alas, I have only my words. We have only our imaginations.

It took at least half a minute for the shock and then the relief to subside before Joseph shouted above the flames, "Jesus H. Christ, W. B., what the hell happened?"

The Wild One made sure the members of his no-longer-secret family were all right. Only then did he reply, "That's what I'd like to know, goddammit. Looks to me like the place was torched."

"Torched?" more than one of them asked.

"Goddamn right." The Wild One snapped his finger. "It went up like that. One second, nothing, and then, wham! it was like a bomb exploded, like we were inside a furnace."

They all turned for another look. The high point of the fire had already passed. The best burning was over. They tried again to douse the flames but there was little they could do. They brought more hoses, found more buckets, made holes in the earth and threw on shovelfuls of dirt. And eventually the fire succumbed to their efforts, but not before it made the cottage an uninhabitable shell of smoldering timbers and smoking ashes.

The Wild One stood there leaning on his one good crutch and holding Evangeline. "Don't worry, kid," he said, and he didn't give a damn if the others could hear, "we'll rebuild it. We'll make it exactly the same, only better."

"Kid?" Bettina said out loud but no one heard her. Or if they did they didn't let on.

Headlights appeared in the driveway. All heads turned to take a look.

"Who could that be?"

"Maybe the fire department."

"A little late."

"Did someone call the fire department?"

No one had.

Anyway it wasn't the fire department. It was the Cohens: Aaron, Madeline, and Adam. They climbed out of their rented Cadillac and stood under the spotlight mounted on the garage.

"Aaron!? It's Aaron," Ginny told the others. "Aaron! We're down here!"

But the Cohens knew that. They weren't blind. They had seen the flames. The three of them, practically asleep on their feet from their long journey east, met Ginny along the service line on the north end of the tennis court.

"You're here!" Ginny kissed her husband, hugged her daughter, tried to hug her son but Adam slipped away.

"Yup," said the Doc, "we're here, we made it. But what the hell's going on? We could see the flames and smell the smoke out at the end of the driveway."

"Arson," answered the Wild One, "that's what's going on. There's a goddamn arsonist among us. And almost a murderer as well."

The whole family gasped.

"Now wait a minute, Billy Boy," whispered Evangeline, "don't say that. We don't know yet what happened."

"Billy Boy?" Bettina turned on her heel and marched off across the tennis court. No one paid her any mind.

Wild Bill kicked the empty gas can. "I know what happened," he said, and then he took the time to study each of his kids. "I just don't know yet who made it happen."

"Hey, look, W. B.," said Joseph, "I'm sorry about the fire but fuck you. Don't look at me like that, like I'm guilty of actually doing something like this. Don't even think about it."

"Same goes for me," said Barton.

"And me," said Emily.

Henry, as Bobby, stood aside with his wife and kids. He stepped forward. "Let's take it easy. This is no time to start fighting. I think it would be better if we—"

Before he could finish Rosa raised her arm, pointed into the darkness of the woods beyond the cottage, and shouted, "What was that!? I saw something. What was it?"

They all turned to where she pointed. No one saw or heard anything. Several seconds passed.

"What was it, Rose?" asked her mother. "What did you see?"

"I don't know. An animal or something, I guess."

"Maybe a deer," said John. "Lots of deer around here."

The Winslows turned away from the woods, back to Henry who tried to pick up where he had left off. "Yeah, well, I just think we—"

"Oh my God!" This time the interruption came from Samantha. She had not looked away from the place in the woods where Rosa had pointed, not for an instant. She knew he was out there. She could feel him, smell him, almost reach out and touch his intensity.

"What is it?" The attention turned to Little Eddie's second wife.

"It's Edward," she announced, knowing that to keep it a secret would be both foolish and dangerous.

"Edward?"

"Yes," she answered, "I just caught a glimpse of him." She pointed into the woods, into the darkness. "But it was him. It was definitely him."

"I say we call the cops," said Joseph, after everyone had expressed their shock and their dismay at this sudden and violent arrival of the middle son.

"No cops," said the Wild One.

"What? Why not? The fucking guy tried to kill you."

Wild Bill pointed his finger at Joseph. "You watch your language, boy. And I'll tell you why no cops. Because Edward is your brother and my son. If he's out there we'll find him, we'll catch him. He's our responsibility. We're not going to have a bunch of cops with bloodhounds and spotlights stalking around in these woods. No way. This is our land. Outsiders will do more harm than good. Besides, it's high time you all realized that blood takes care of its own."

No one said anything until Joseph piped up again, "I think you're making a mistake. The guy's obviously crazy. He's gone over the edge. No telling what he might do next."

"You're right, boy," countered the Wild One, "there's no telling. So I suggest if you're worried about him slipping into your room tonight and slashing your throat, you go pack your bag and hightail it out of here. You've been running for thirty years; can't imagine why you'd want to stop now."

Joseph had several witty replies on the tip of the tongue but he couldn't seem to push even one of them out.

"And that goes," continued Wild Bill as he looked over his sons and daughters, "for the rest of you as well. Me, I'm staying put. And I ain't calling for reinforcements. The family's been on this land a hundred years. I've been here seventy. I'm not about to back down now." He put his arm around Evangeline. "Come on, kid. Come on, guys. Let's go up to the house and see if we can find some dry clothes and a place for you all to sleep."

John and Paul and Rosa and Wild Bill and Evangeline started across the tennis court. The rest of the Winslows hesitated, waited to see what their siblings would do, what their siblings would say.

Henry made the first move. "Come on, Irene, I have to get you back to bed. You look like you're about to have that baby right here on center court." The Adirondack Winslows, arm in arm, started back to the big house.

Mary and Emily followed close behind. Mary had been waiting a long time for this moment, for this showdown. She had been impressed with her father's grit and determination. Of course, she had expected nothing less. What she had not expected was violence from brother Edward. A confrontation, maybe; a display of anger, probably; but this kind of desperate violence? No, this was not something she had anticipated. She wanted to get back to the solitude of her bedroom to see if she could figure this one out, to see if she could come up with some kind of scenario regarding what might happen next.

Ginny rounded up her family and headed across the tennis court. "I've got beds all made up for you," she told them. "I'm so glad you've come."

The three of them, Aaron and Adam and Madeline, looked at her like she must be crazy, totally out of her mind, but they were too tired to speak, too exhausted to ask questions. They followed her up to the house without uttering a word.

That left Joseph and Barton and their sister-in-law Samantha. The fire had died. Only the embers remained. Barton continued to spray the hose on anything that looked red or hot.

"So what do you think, Samantha," asked Joseph, "is this guy dangerous or what?"

"What kind of stupid question is that?" asked Barton. "He poured gasoline on the cottage and lit it on fire. He knew they were inside, he must've known. He tried to burn four people alive. I'd say that's pretty dangerous."

"Yeah, I know, but, like"—and Joseph turned back to his sister-in-law—"like, do you think he's after all of us?"

Samantha took a deep breath and followed it up with a long sigh. "Only a week ago I wouldn't've thought so. Edward is often depressed but I haven't seen him violent or even particularly angry in over a year. I really thought he was beginning to make progress."

"Yeah," Joseph said, pushing, "so what do you think now, after witnessing this little crusade?"

Samantha took her time. She never had imagined she might one day side against her Edward. "I know he blames you, all of you, for the loss of his children. Ever since I've known him, he has expressed a great deal of hatred and resentment for all of you, especially your father. But frankly, I never thought it would come to this. I didn't think he had this in him. I thought I knew his capabilities."

"So, what you're saying is, you don't know what the hell the guy might do?"

Samantha shook her head. "I guess not. I guess I don't. . . . I would say that this is a worst-case scenario."

"No shit."

The cottage was nothing but a smoldering, smoky mess. Barton turned off the hose. "I guess it's over."

Joseph looked at the cottage, then at his brother. "I don't think so, bro'. I don't think it's even started yet."

Barton took a deep breath. Maybe a minute passed. "So what are you going to do, Joe?"

"Me? Shit. I don't know. I don't need this crazy bullshit, I can tell you that. But I guess I ain't going anywhere, not right away."

"No, I guess not."

So those two Winslow brothers, with their sister-in-law between them, headed back to the house. "Back to Fort Winslow," said Joseph, as he scanned the darkness for signs of his renegade brother.

Just as Wild Bill and Evangeline reached the back stoop with John and Paul and Rosa, Bettina opened the back door and stepped out carrying her leather overnight bag. She looked rather discombobulated. Her hair went every which way, the buttons on her blouse looked as though they had been misaligned, her skirt hung wrinkled and twisted from her anorexic hips. Only her lips had been touched by artificial enhancers, and it was obvious a shaky hand had applied the rose-colored lip gloss. Someone should've reminded Bettina about her attitude toward her old dead friend Millicent. Bettina, in the heat of the moment, had lost her cool. "A pig and her pimp," she announced as she slammed the door. She spit her *p*'s all over those being accused.

They stopped and stared at her.

"You wanted a divorce, pal," she said, smoke pouring from her nostrils, fire from her lips, "well you've got it. But believe me, you're going to pay and pay dearly. I don't know what's going on between you and little Miss Bimbo here but I think I've got a pretty good—"

"Easy, Bettina," said the Wild One. "Just slow down. Watch your mouth."

"Go to hell!" Bettina swung her leather overnight bag at her husband. He blocked it with his crutch. She took a moment to regroup. "Fine," she said, "I'll slow down. We'll talk about it in court. Maybe I'll subpoena these two little tykes here as evidence of my husband's infidelity."

"Don't make a fool of yourself, Bettina," said Wild Bill. "You'll get your fair share."

Other members of the family began to arrive from the cottage. They stopped to listen to Bettina's digressions.

"You're goddamn right I'll get my fair share. And more. Much more. You're all a bunch of lunatics, burning down houses. Maniacs. This place is a madhouse. An insane asylum. I wouldn't pass a night here if my life depended on it. You keep this house, Bill Winslow, it's yours. I wouldn't live here for all the gold in Fort Knox."

"How 'bout all the tea in China?" *I think the old boy was smiling.*

"Screw you."

"Let's not be hasty, Bettina."

More Winslows arrived.

Bettina spit more fire and stepped off the stoop. They made plenty of room for her. "No," she said as she headed for her Allanté, "I won't be hasty. I'm going to take my time and get what I want, get what I deserve. So you"—and she turned to face her husband—"you best prepare yourself for a long and bloody fight. I'll take it all, Bill Winslow. I'll take everything I can get, every damn penny. You may as well kiss it all good-bye."

But first I'll kiss your ass good-bye, he wanted badly to reply but he held his tongue in consideration of Evangeline and the boys. He hobbled across the drive on one crutch and opened the door for her. He had this image of himself opening his wallet and finding nothing inside but a couple of faded one-dollar bills. The image made him feel good. It made him feel young again.

Bettina threw her leather overnight bag across the seat, brushed him aside, and settled in behind the steering wheel. She turned the key. The engine roared. The Wild One leaned inside so his words would not be overheard. "You've made me very happy tonight, Bettina," he whispered, "the happiest you've made me since the day we married. You've made me the happiest man alive."

"Go fuck yourself, Bill Winslow."

He smiled down at her, taunting her to punch him in the nose. "Oh, I don't think that'll be necessary."

"Get away from the car. You'll hear from my lawyers."

"Fine, and you'll hear from mine." Wild Bill grabbed her arm so she could not put the car in gear. "You'll get plenty, Bettina, much more than you deserve. But you won't get it all, no way. I've got the goods on you as well, lady. I know every roll in the hay you've taken from Bar Harbor to Captiva for the last year and a half. It's not a pretty picture, so watch yourself. Don't get greedy."

She leaned forward and bit his hand. He screamed and pulled away. She slammed the Allanté into gear. The car lurched forward. The still-open door sent the Wild One reeling. The steel-belted radials squealed. Wild Bill spun around. He landed facedown on the macadam. Evangeline rushed forward. So did several of the others. But the Wild One came up laughing and waving good-bye as his wife sped away down the long dark drive.

Chapter Thirty-two

Once the Allanté was out of sight, Wild Bill turned and faced his family. They all stood there in the porch light, young and old alike, waiting for the Wild One to speak. He could feel the pain in his separated shoulder and the busted ankle trying to swell inside the plaster of Paris cast. But the pain, like the image of the empty wallet, made him feel good, made him feel strong, made him feel young. "There goes our first deserter."

No one made a move.

"Anyone want to join her?"

No one said a word.

"Good."

Slowly they started to file into the house through the back door. Ginny led her brood through the kitchen and the dining room and up the front stairs. Emily and Rosa followed close behind. Then Mary and Samantha.

"Having a good time?" Mary asked.

Samantha, assuming sarcasm, smiled. "Wonderful."

Henry helped his wife inside then told her he'd be right back, "I have to get something from the truck." But he didn't need anything from the truck; he wanted to see if that old Remington twelve-gauge was still hanging in the window rack. When he found it wasn't he whistled softly, then stood in the driveway for a long minute staring into the darkness. "Where are you, you crazy fool?" he asked quietly of the night. "And what in God's name do you think you're doing?"

Irene and Katie and Constance were halfway to the third floor by the time Henry reached the kitchen. The only ones left downstairs were Joseph and Barton. They had the refrigerator door wide open and a whole pile of deli meats out on the counter.

"Hey bro'," asked Joseph, "want a sandwich?"

Henry shook his head. "No, no thanks. Where's W. B.?"

Joseph unwrapped a thick pile of red roast beef. "He took his little family up to bed. Do you believe him? That sly old fox. Seventy years old and pumping that sweet young piece of ass."

Henry didn't want to think about that right now. He headed across the kitchen. "Don't go to bed, you guys. I'll be back in a few minutes."

"We'll be here. If I'm gonna die tonight I'm going down with a full belly."

Henry found Irene slowly climbing the stairs to the third floor. He helped her the rest of the way and then settled her back in bed.

"Hey, Dad," Katie asked from her pile of blankets on the floor, "is it always so crazy around here?"

He went over and kissed her on the forehead. "No," he said, "not always. Now go to bed. Get some sleep."

"Who's Edward?" asked Constance.

Henry sighed. "Edward? He's your uncle, sweetie."

"Oh."

Henry crossed back to his wife. "Sorry about all this, Irene. I had no idea—"

She looked up at him and shook her head. "You don't need to explain, Bobby. Really."

"I don't know. I think maybe a lot of things need to be explained."

She took his hand and placed it on her belly. He felt the baby kick. "This little guy's coming," she said, "in a very big hurry."

"Do you think we should do something? Find a doctor? Call the hospital?"

She shook her head. "No, let me just get some sleep. I'll see how I feel in the morning."

He kissed her and held her and then, after the kids had fallen asleep, he said, "I have to go see the old man for a few minutes. I'll be back as soon as I can. Don't wait up."

She smiled. "Don't worry, I won't."

He went back down the narrow stairway and along the hall to the master bedroom suite. The door to the sitting room was closed. He knocked lightly.

After a moment the Wild One pulled open the door. "Yeah?...Bob. What is it?"

"I need to talk to you for a minute."

"About what?"

"About Edward."

"Right. Hang on a second." The Wild One left the door open a crack and went through the sitting room to the bedroom. Henry took a quick look through the opening. The couch in the sitting room had been turned into a bed. It was covered with sheets and blankets. *Evangeline,* he thought, *must be sleeping in the big bed with the kids, his kids.* Indeed she was. Indeed they were. The Wild One had insisted.

After maybe two minutes he returned. He hobbled out into the hallway and closed the door. "Okay, what's up?"

"Well..." Henry hesitated.

"Come on, boy, it's late. Tomorrow's going to be a hell of—"

"I think Edward has a gun."

"What?"

"Remember that old Remington double-barreled shotgun?"

"Sure I remember it. Originally belonged to Crazy Legs. Haven't seen it for years."

"That's because I've got it."

"You've got it?"

"Actually I had it. Now I think Edward's got it."

"Wait a minute," demanded the Wild One, "slow down. Why did you have it?"

"Because you gave it to me...I mean you gave it to Henry...and he gave it to me...just before he left for Vietnam."

Wild Bill took his time, thought it over. "I remember giving the gun to Henry. A long time ago. Back when he was a teenager. He wanted to hunt squirrels and rabbits out in the back woods. But now you're telling me he gave the gun to you?"

Henry nodded quickly. "Right...That's right."

The Wild One took a long look at his son. He decided not to push it. "Okay, so where's the gun now?"

"That's the thing."

"What do you mean?"

"I'm pretty sure Edward has the gun."

Wild Bill's eyes narrowed. "And why the hell do you think that?"

Henry, as Bobby, explained about the gun disappearing from the pickup. "I know it was there when I got here."

"I'll be a son of a bitch. . . . I wonder if he's the one who stole my fishing poles as well."

Henry remembered his bet with Mary. He decided not to mention anything about the cabbie who had made off with the Wild One's fly rods.

"What about shells?" asked the Wild One.

"What?"

"What about shells? Did you have any shotgun shells in the truck?"

"I don't think so but there might've been a box under the seat."

"Or he might've found some in the garage. Probably best to assume he has some."

Henry nodded.

Wild Bill leaned against the wall, rubbed his eyes. He took another long look at his son. "Okay," he said, after maybe half a minute, "I want you to get Joseph and Barton and that baby doctor out of bed. Meet me down in the kitchen in a few minutes. Try not to roust the womenfolk or the kiddies. No sense getting everyone all riled up again."

Henry had some trouble getting Aaron away from Ginny, but by fifteen minutes after three o'clock in the morning on this the day of the summer solstice, the menfolk had assembled around the old wooden table in the kitchen. The Wild One explained about the shotgun.

"So what you're telling me," Dr. Cohen reiterated, "is that your son is somewhere outside this house wandering around with a shotgun which may or may not be loaded and which he may or may not be thinking about using to wound or possibly even kill certain people inside this house, certain members of his family with whom he has some kind of long-standing and irrational feud?"

Wild Bill nodded. "I think that's about it, Doc. I think you've summed up the situation pretty clearly, thank you very much."

Aaron shook his head as though he could not quite believe the situation. "So what, if you don't mind my asking, is it you want me to do?"

"Well first of all," began the Wild One, "I wouldn't blame you if you packed up your kids and drove that Caddy back to Newark

Airport and caught the first plane for Bel Air. That's up to you. This isn't really your fight. I think your wife's right in the middle of it but that doesn't mean you are."

Aaron thought it over. "I can tell you one thing: I'm not pulling out of here tonight. I'd have a rebellion on my hands if I tried to get those kids back in the car. So I'm here at least until sometime after the sun comes up. I'll talk to Ginny. If she wants to stay, we'll stay."

Joseph gave Aaron a lightweight jab to the shoulder. "Atta boy, Doc."

Aaron shook his head some more. "I just don't want to see anyone get hurt. After all, we're reasonable people."

"Don't be so sure, Doc," said Joseph. "But listen, if you decide to split for the airport, let me know. I might need a ride."

"You won't need a ride, boy," said the Wild One.

"No? And why's that?"

"Because you're not going anywhere until this thing's resolved."

"Oh yeah?"

"Yeah," growled the Wild One. "Now listen up, all of you. I know you all want to go back upstairs and get some sleep but the way I see it, that's a luxury for the women and children right now. There's nine different doors into this house, plus maybe three dozen windows. We're going to go around and make sure every door and every window is locked up tight. I want you to divide into two teams. Bobby, you go with the Doc, and Barton, you keep an eye on your brother."

"Who the hell are you," asked Joseph, "the Colonel?"

Wild Bill ignored him. "I want the basement checked. I want the south porch and the sun room checked. I want all doors and windows locked. After everything's secured two of you patrol the front of the house and two of you the back of the house. Stay inside but keep moving. Try not to linger in front of any windows."

"W. B.," asked Henry, as Bobby, "do you really think this is necessary? I mean do you really think the guy's out there getting ready to take potshots at us?"

"I don't know, so that's why it is necessary. But if you don't think so, just go down and take a look at the cottage, or what's left of it."

Henry shrugged and nodded.

Joseph, "I still think we should call the cops."

Wild Bill, "Good for you. Now let's get moving."

But Joey wasn't quite ready yet. "And what about you, Colonel? Where are you going to be?"

"I'll be upstairs. Unless he uses a ladder there are only a couple of ways in on the second floor. The most obvious one is up the trellis and onto the flat roof outside the master bedroom."

"So you'll be up there guarding your sweet?"

"You're out of line, boy."

"So shoot me."

The Wild One let it pass. "I'll check all the windows upstairs. If I hear or see anything I'll holler. You all do the same. And don't worry, in a couple hours it'll be dawn. We'll find him then." Wild Bill turned and started out of the kitchen.

Joseph could not resist. "Have a nice sleep, Grandpa."

The Wild One turned. "Believe me, boy, I won't be sleeping, I've got too many reasons to stay awake, wide awake. Maybe you'd best find a few reasons yourself."

"So Bobby," asked Dr. Aaron Cohen of Bel Air, California, "what about this brother of yours? I mean, is he really capable of shooting at us?"

The two men were down in the basement checking the cellar windows. Henry pulled on each one, made sure the latch was secure. "I don't know, Doc. I haven't seen the guy in years. I know he had some hard times, but shit, I never thought he'd end up like this."

They started up the stairs. Henry switched off the light.

"So what happened to him? I know he got divorced and all, but so do millions of other people." Aaron was not normally inquisitive but he had this strange desire to know more about his potential executioner.

Henry was not the best guy to ask. "Again, Doc, I don't really know. I haven't exactly been in the bosom of this family for the last twenty years. Had a few problems of my own . . ."

They reached the top of the cellar stairs and went through the kitchen. Aaron peered out the back door into the darkness. It must have been eighty-five degrees inside with all the doors and windows closed and locked but the Doc suddenly shivered. "The idea of him out there really gives me the creeps."

Henry took his time, then said, "Yeah, I know what you mean." Then, after a moment, "Say, Doc, you're a baby doctor, right?"

Aaron looked at who he thought was Bobby Winslow. The

strange glint in the young man's eyes did not reassure him. He could still hear Wild Bill's wife, just before she roared away in her Allanté, shouting something about this place being a madhouse, an insane asylum. Aaron wondered if it might be true. He wondered if maybe he should go upstairs, wake up his family, and get them the hell out of there before the bullets started to fly. "Well," he said, "I'm a pediatrician, not an obstetrician."

"What's the difference?"

"I take care of young children. I don't take mothers through pregnancy or deliver their babies."

"Right." Henry rubbed his chin. "I get it."

The Wild One had his .45-caliber pistol at the ready. As soon as he had returned to the bedroom he'd taken the gun from the locked drawer of his bureau and inserted a full clip. *No way,* he told himself, *am I going to let that crazy son of a bitch come in here and hurt these kids. No way. I'll shoot the crazy motherfucker first. I'll shoot him right between the eyes.* He saw with his own eyes closed the cottage burning and Evangeline and John and Paul escaping within an inch of their lives.

Wild Bill had bought the handgun some twenty-five years earlier, back in the early '60s. He bought it when they started having the race riots in Newark and Camden and then as close as Plainfield. He used to lie there in bed beside Virginia, wide awake and waiting for the hordes of poor, pissed-off black men to come rampaging out of the cities and valleys. He fully expected the Compound to come under attack. At the time he felt pretty certain the country was on the brink of revolution. The revolution never came, at least not the one he had anticipated, the one fraught with violence and bloodshed and change. No, that revolution never came but he held on to the handgun anyway. It had only been fired once, at the pistol range where he had purchased it. He cleaned the gun once or twice a year but he'd only ever pulled the trigger on that one occasion. The idea that he might actually pull the trigger with the barrel pointed at his own son made him for just a moment consider turning the pistol on himself and blowing his brains across the room.

He sat on the leather armchair with his broken leg up on the leather ottoman. He had the chair turned so he could see, just by rotating his head, all the glass windows and doors circling the room. Behind him on the king-size bed Evangeline and the two boys slept. He could hear their breathing slow and steady. All he wanted to do was crawl in beside them, hold them tight, close his eyes, and go to sleep. But the danger outside seemed real. It felt close and extremely volatile. So he kept his eyes open, his ears alert, his head moving, and his right hand in constant contact with his weapon.

"Been a long day, huh Joe?"

"A long day that ain't over yet."

"Oh, I don't know," said Barton. "I mean we're still awake and all but I really don't think Edward's going to do anything. If he wanted to shoot at us with that shotgun he could've done so when we were all standing out in the open watching the cottage burn."

"Maybe," said Joseph, "I don't know. I don't know what the son of a bitch wants."

Barton shrugged. The two brothers sat on opposite ends of the long sofa in the living room. They had secured all the doors and windows in their patrol zone. For over an hour they had walked back and forth through the front of the house, their eyes constantly peering out the windows for any sign of movement. There had been none. They had seen nothing. Now they had settled down to rest on the sofa. They had all the lights turned out. Beyond the wide picture window which covered most of the front wall of the living room, the brothers could just begin to see the long sweep of front lawn as the first light of a new summer beat back the shadows. They could see the silhouette of Lady Godiva streaking on horseback through the New Jersey countryside. They could see the fountain and the outline of the tall red maples lining the driveway.

"I think," said Barton, "he wants our attention."

"What?"

"I think Edward wants our attention. I think he wants us to sit up and notice him, notice his pain and his suffering."

Joseph let out a long, audible sigh. "Jesus H. Fucking Christ!"

"I know," said Barton, "I know."

What Barton did not know, and would not know for several more days because it would take the authorities that long to identify the wreckage, was that his own personal fortunes were taking a peculiar turn even as he spoke. Down at Savannah International Airport, a young man and a young woman in their mid-twenties were sneaking around in long-term parking looking for cars to burglarize. The couple were members of some weird religious drug cult which believed in the daily ingestion of synthetic hallucinogens and the complete destruction of all modern art. As far as I can tell, nothing but pure coincidence, although surely fate must've had a hand in it, delivered those two loonies to the passenger side door of young Barton's Chevy cargo van. They jimmied the door, slipped inside, and immediately went to work on the glove box and the ashtray and the floor mats. Barton was rather meticulous about his van however, and they found only a couple of dimes and a few pennies. But then they crawled into the back and found the painted sculpture. It flipped them both out. They might just as well have encountered Lucifer himself. The young woman screamed. The young man kicked at the monster with the skill and dexterity of a kung fu master. But the sculpture stood firm, refused to budge. He kicked some more. She hammered on it with her fists and elbows. Some of the paint began to chip off but the plywood and Sheetrock laughed at their attack. They both heard the laughs and went into some kind of psychedelic frenzy. "Burn it," she shouted, "burn it to the ground!" And so he did. They scrambled out of the van, ransacked several garbage cans for anything that would burn, and stuffed their torchables into the gas tank. Using the front page of that day's Atlanta Constitution *as a fuse, the young man struck a match, ignited the newspaper, and the two of them fled for cover. Less than half a minute later that Chevy cargo van blew sky high. An old woman in downtown Savannah who had just gone to the front door to let her cat out later said the whole skyline north of the city "lit up like the Fourth of July."*

Back in Far Hills Barton shivered when the van blew, but he had no idea why, figured it had something to do with events close at hand.

"I don't think the worst is over," said Joseph, "I think we're just getting started."

Barton shrugged off the shiver. "Why? If we can just bring Edward back into the fold we'll be a family again. All of us together."

Joseph laughed. "Gimme a break, bro'. This family's got so much bullshit in its closets we couldn't dig it out with a backhoe."

"You mean like Henry?"

"Yeah I mean like Henry. Think about that one. For twenty years the guy's been pretending he's somebody else."

"I think it's kind of sad."

"Sad, maybe, but fucked up nevertheless. And this thing with Edward. Christ, the next thing you know he'll take a shot at the President or the Pope or Mick Jagger. Fucking family will make the newspapers and the evening news then. And what about Wild Bill? The guy has another whole life that none of us even knew about. And check this one out. Before the fire hit the cottage I was reading this diary. I found it on the bookshelf in the den. It was written by W. B.'s mother—"

"Martha?"

"Right. And in it she says her father-in-law—"

"Crazy Legs?"

"Yeah. It says he knocked her up and that he's really Wild Bill's father."

"What?"

"I'm not shitting you, that's what it said."

"That Crazy Legs was W. B.'s father?"

"Right."

"What else did this diary say?"

Before Joseph could tell Barton about the orgies they heard a noise in the front hallway. They both sprang to their feet. They both expected to see brother Edward standing there, the Remington twelve-gauge pointed at their chests. But it wasn't Edward; it was sister Ginny looking sleepy and disheveled in her nightgown.

"Where is Aaron?" she demanded. "What's going on? Why are you two still up? When did it start getting light out?"

Upstairs Ginny's sisters slept. So did the youngsters: Rosa and Katie and Constance and John and Paul. Evangeline lay still but wide awake. She could see Billy Boy sitting in the leather armchair but she did not call to him. She needed to try to sort out what had happened and why. Nothing made sense. All of her worldly possessions had suddenly been snatched away. *Why? What has happened? What have I done? Or have I done nothing? Is all of this for some reason we do not yet understand?* She closed her eyes and searched for the Inner Light. *God*, she reminded herself, *does not punish. We punish ourselves. Just as we glorify ourselves. I should just be thankful we all escaped the blaze.*

* * *

Samantha was certainly thankful everyone had escaped the blaze. She lay awake staring out the window at the approaching dawn. She blamed herself for what had happened. *I should've seen this coming. I live with him day in and day out. I should've known something like this might happen. But I was blind. I believed him, every word he said. But now I see these people are not demons; they're just like everyone else. What a blind, selfish fool I've been.* She knew she had to find Edward, reel him in, calm him down, bring him back to earth, back to reality. She knew he needed help, more help than she could provide. She went back to bed. She needed rest. It would no doubt be a long day.

Another whole group of Winslows, however, were just starting to wake up, to rise from a deathlike slumber. The dead, so far as I have been able to ascertain, usually only ascend from their burial pits for special occasions. Normally they prefer to keep their own counsel, bide their time, let the eons pass without disruption. Those Winslows buried up on the hill have pretty much adhered to these practices over the years. A new arrival may ascend more frequently to check out what's going on in the material world. He or she might make daily visits to see how their husband or wife or brothers or sisters are getting along without them. But soon enough these visits grow weekly, then monthly, then biannually, then annually as the dead person realizes that in the material world, as in all the other worlds, the more things change, the more they stay the same. Bobby, for instance, used to check out his brother Henry several times a day in the weeks following his return as a corpse from Southeast Asia. He wanted to make sure his brother was suffering plenty for his act of cowardice. But after a while that grew boring and undignified. And after Henry moved up to the Adirondacks Bobby gave up visiting his brother almost entirely. Contrary to popular opinion, you see, the dead cannot simply snap their fingers and reappear across town or in another state or in another time zone. They have to travel just like you and me. So by the time Nixon and Kissinger finally brought the boys home from 'Nam, Bobby had pretty much stopped getting his kicks by watching his brother sweat. Instead he played the violin and read the works of Rousseau and Kant and Wharton (spiritually of course since violins and books do not exist in that world).

Anyway, this summer solstice seemed like a pretty important day to the ten Winslows buried in the family graveyard. They could feel the earth above them trembling with heat and fear and confusion. They didn't all rise up at once and swoop down on the burning cottage however. One by one, in their own good time, they made their way down off the hill. Most of them felt the time had come for another member of the family to join their ranks. Some thought it might be the Wild One, others thought Edward, still others thought Henry. But they had no way of knowing for sure. The dead know nothing more about the future than the living.

Virginia watched the cottage burn. She said a prayer for those inside. She wanted Willy and his new young family to escape the blaze unharmed.

Robert and Henry, Wild Bill's brothers, the brothers-in-law Virginia never knew, watched the cottage burn also. They watched it away from their sister-in-law partly because they were shy about girls and partly because they did not want her to see them rooting for their brother to burn. Neither of them had ever understood why Wild Bill got to live when they had to die. This is a common complaint among the dead. They never think they should have to go. They always figure it should be the other guy. But I think some power beyond our grasp had a hand in this decision. Of the three brothers, Wild Bill was the one with the biggest balls, with the guts to get the job done, to carry on the Winslow mission in the New World.

Let's see, who else watched the cottage burn? I don't think anyone. I think the rest of them drifted down to the big house after the fire died and the living returned to bed. Charles and Martha arrived together, their interest in events based more on boredom than on the trials and tribulations of history. You see, Chuck and Shady had lived a shallow life. They hadn't worked much, hadn't read much, hadn't traveled much, hadn't even cooked or cleaned much; they hadn't really done much of anything except drink and fornicate. And since the dead don't drink, not even mineral water, or screw, Charles and Martha entered the world of the dead totally unprepared for the endless passage of time. For them, this madness down at the big house was like one of their grand cocktail parties back in the Roaring Twenties: a time to think they were having fun, a time to believe they were leading useful lives.

The two Helens reached the big house at the same time but not together. The elder Helen, Wild Bill's little sister, never socialized with anyone. She lived dead much the same way she had lived her last years alive: silent and tormented. Did she suffocate her niece, Helen junior, with a pillow? Did she think she was suffocating Mary? I've tried to get the answers to these questions but Helen senior is as tight-lipped as a

Benedictine monk. The only thing I can tell you is that once when I asked her why Mary had to be eliminated her eyebrows arched and her eyes for a moment flamed. But I suppose the truth will forever remain a mystery.

One thing which is not a mystery is Helen junior. She died, as we know, at five. She died before her soul had been soiled by the material world. She lived the death of an angel. She had wings but preferred not to fly. She liked to walk, slowly. She did everything very slowly and patiently, as though time meant nothing at all, as though she had all the time in the world.

Last to reach the big house was its creator, John "Crazy Legs" Winslow, and his wife Caroline. Crazy Legs, like his great-granddaughter, rarely rushed. He had lived too long and seen too much to rush. Sometimes he wished his old buddy Gustave, down in Punta Gorda, had never sent that letter to Wild Willy. Sometimes he wished Gustave had just tossed his dead body into the ocean so that his soul could have drifted forever across the seven seas. But the living have this assertive way of taking over the destinies of the dead, so Crazy Legs had years ago contented himself with being buried on the hill beside his wife. He saw a certain beauty in this notion of continuity, but if pressed on the matter he would tell you that really it was all a bunch of bullshit. He gave in to his wife's desire to visit the big house but only because he wanted to see who might get their ass kicked in this latest Winslow family squabble.

So as dawn on this the longest day of the year unfolds, the House of Winslow is indeed crowded with both the living and the dead. I mention the dead only in passing, simply so you will know they are on the scene, watching events unfold. You can, if you wish, pretend they do not exist. But I think it's sort of nice to know the dead are watching, keeping tabs, maybe getting a chuckle or two out of all the craziness and self-righteousness and piety. The dead, unlike the living, usually don't take themselves too seriously. They've been through the tough part.

Chapter Thirty-three

————————————————•————————————————

The dawn came and Edward didn't. He was miles away, down in the center of Bernardsville at the coffee shop having a cup of hot java and a plate of scrambled eggs with whole wheat toast. After lighting the cottage on fire he had slipped into the woods to watch the building burn. It's easy enough to imagine him crouched there in the underbrush staring out of the darkness. He saw his brothers and sisters and in-laws and second wife come hurrying across the lawn from the main house. He saw them trying to douse the flames. He saw the escape of Wild Bill and his paramour and her two kiddies. He saw it all, and all the while he watched he had this fiendish grin on his face. Little Eddie became so absorbed in the chaos and confusion he had caused that he lost track of himself and tripped over a dead log. He stumbled and snapped a dry branch in half. That's when Rosa first heard him. Minutes later, the whole clan peering into the darkness, he decided to make a run for it. Secretly, he hoped they would chase him, catch him, subdue him. He ran the whole length of that vast Winslow track of land in the rolling hills of north central New Jersey. He ran through woods and across overgrown fields, up hills and over streams. He ran through the darkness but all the hours he had spent on that land in his youth made the nighttime passage possible. Edward had no trouble finding his way. He knew every bump and ripple on that land, every rise and every swell. Finally he reached his car, parked in the woods along an old Jeep trail just off Lake Road. He waited long enough to know they had not pursued.

Edward drove all the way to Summit, some twenty miles, before he pulled into the train-station parking lot and fell asleep stretched out across the front seat. While his brothers patrolled the house Edward slept. And when he awoke not long before dawn he put the car in motion and headed back toward Far Hills. He stopped in the center of Bernardsville and was waiting outside the door when the woman who ran the place opened up the coffee shop for the early birds.

While Edward ate his wet eggs, brother Barton settled back in the overstuffed tweed swivel chair in the corner of the living room to listen to some music. Dawn had broken. The summer sun had climbed over the horizon. Joseph and Ginny had gone off to bed to find an hour's sleep. Barton had assured his brother he would keep the watch, he would not leave his post. He did not think, however, a watch was necessary. Barton did not believe Edward would come storming into the house, firearms a-blazing. He found that scenario totally inconceivable. He just wanted to relax, hear some music, some music his mother had liked. For the last couple of hours he'd had her on his mind; a mixture of nostalgia and curiosity. He wondered how she would've handled this trouble with Edward.

Virginia felt her youngest son's ruminations and so after a quick trip through the bedrooms to see who was sleeping with whom, she settled in the living room between Barton and the stereo system. Barton flipped through the dozens of LPs stacked neatly on shelves in the corner of the living room. There must have been two hundred record albums, mostly classical LPs Virginia had bought over the years. Most of them had not been played since her death. Barton considered a piano concerto by Schubert, a violin sonata by Grieg, various symphonies by Beethoven, Mozart's concerto for flute, but each time he reconsidered and kept flipping. Virginia had something specific in mind and she was using all of her motherly powers to influence her son's decision. He very nearly pulled Vivaldi's *The Four Seasons* from its sleeve. Virginia would have loved to hear those opening violins, but it was not the music she wanted. She pushed her son to keep searching. He did. And finally he flipped to the LP she had been waiting for: Johann Sebastian Bach's *Brandenburg Concerto #1*. Barton hesitated but only for a moment. He drew the LP from the sleeve and carefully placed it on the turntable. He wiped off the vinyl with the record cleaner and turned on the power. So not to awaken those still asleep, he set the controls so he could listen to the music through headphones. He placed the headphones over his ears and gently settled the tonearm onto the record. After just a moment those first extraordinary notes radiated through his body. A thousand times or more he had heard those strings and woodwinds and horns pushing and pulling, rising and falling and blending, and never once had the music failed to arouse in him something magical, something very close to Divine. It was, his mother had often said, the music of the King of Kings. A gentle smile broke across his face at the exact moment tears welled up in his eyes. He reached over and turned up the volume control on the amplifier. The music, music written nearly three centuries ago, took hold of Barton and lifted him off that chair, levitated his body and swept him around the room as though he were a babe rocking in his mama's arms. His mama did indeed hover close by. She too was absorbed in the music. But she did not allow Bach to carry her all the way away. She had something more in mind.

The initial allegro movement ended and the much slower and more controlled adagio movement began. Virginia knew from the many times she had both listened to and performed the movement in the privacy of her own bedroom that the adagio would last approximately three and a half minutes. She had to work fast.

Had she been able, Virginia would simply have pushed the proper buttons herself. But the dead do not have hands or legs or noses or elbows. They have no body parts at all. Fortunately she had a son who had been brought up listening to Bach. Barton knew very well what was coming. The thing he enjoyed most about the slow second movement was the way the third movement exploded at the conclusion of the adagio. He was ready to fly again, ready to float away. He sat up high and straight and smiling and weeping all at once in that tweed chair. And then, just as the adagio closed, and without even realizing his hand was in motion, Barton reached out and touched the buttons Virginia wanted him so strongly to touch. And a moment later that third movement, undoubtedly inspired by some authority higher than man, filled the living room, filled the whole downstairs, filled that whole gigantic house. Barton did not even know it. He had his eyes closed and his head moving and the headphones pressed close against his ears. He heard the music deep down in his soul but he could not hear the music bouncing and vibrating off the walls of his childhood home. Everyone else in the house could hear the music however; even the Adirondack Winslows way up on the third floor. The oboe and the tiny piccolo reached up to them and opened their eyes and made them smile without even knowing why. Irene and Katie and Constance had never heard those notes before, but as if Bach were some old-time country minstrel beckoning them to the county fair they rose up out of bed and followed the notes down the narrow steps, along the hall, and down the wide front stairs. Along the way they met a whole lot of other Winslows, and a handful of Cohens as well. Barton, with a little help from his mama, had the volume turned way up, almost as loud as it could go. It sounded incredible, wonderful, perfectly clear and crisp; as well it should have on those custom-made ten-thousand-dollar German speakers.

Sixteen of them stood there in the front hallway one step up from the living room. Sixteen sleepy-eyed but nevertheless smiling human beings stood there and stared into the room and tried without saying a word to understand why the music played. They could not see brother Barton. He sat with that tweed swivel chair turned away from them, turned toward the wall. They could not see him and he could not see or hear them. But the music kept playing. And they all kept listening.

The dead arrived as well. They could see Virginia over by the stereo and they knew immediately she had orchestrated this family gathering. They hovered here and there, smiling and tapping their nonexistent feet and bobbing their nonexistent heads in time with Bach's God-given melody.

And then the Wild One hobbled onto the scene. It took him longer than the others to reach the bottom of the stairs with that twenty-five-pound plaster of Paris cast stuck on his leg. "What the hell's going on down here?" he shouted above the music, but his voice more curious than authoritative.

"Don't know," came the replies.

Wild Bill stepped through the crowd and down off the landing into the living room. "Well who turned it on? Someone must've turned it on."

"Don't know," came the replies.

"What do you mean, you don't know? One of you must know. One of you must've done it."

But the music reached even higher and swallowed the Wild One's words. The room had nothing left in it but the music; all else disappeared. The violins and the trumpets and the oboe and that piccolo, oh, that piccolo, carried the early morning light on their wings. . . .

Virginia smiled. So did her children. None of them could hear that music and not think of their mother, their mother who had given them so much more than any of them realized or were willing to admit, their mother who had introduced them to this music, who had told them, because she believed it was true, that we all contain good and evil and we just need to suppress the evil and celebrate the good. And her children's spouses smiled. And her grandchildren whom she had never met smiled. And Evangeline smiled. And John and Paul smiled. They couldn't help but smile. The music made them smile. Edward could have swept into the house at that moment and blown them all away with that shotgun and they all would have died with smiles on their faces.

Then the allegro third ended and for a moment the room grew incredibly quiet, utterly silent, as still as a Quaker Meeting on Sunday morn. It was as though the House of Winslow had suddenly turned into the House of God. No one said a word or made a move. A certain truth had overcome them all. Then Barton rose off his tweed chair, his headphones still in place. He moved to the turntable to flip the LP for the menuetto. That's when he saw them, all of them, standing there, staring at him. And he knew the creators of the Tao were right: *The world may be known without leaving the house; the further you go the less you will know. The Wise Man knows without going, sees without seeing, does without doing.*

The music and the mood faded as the sun rose higher in the solstice sky. Wild Bill took charge once again. He ordered breakfast made and search parties formed. "We're going out after him," he told the living, "and bringing him back."

"But he has a gun," Joseph reminded him.

"What?" Ginny demanded.

"Edward has a gun?" asked Emily.

"How did he get a gun?" Ginny further demanded.

"What kind of gun?" asked Samantha.

"A shotgun," answered Joseph.

"Good God."

The goddamn Japs had guns too, was the Wild One's reaction but he kept the thought to himself. "We *think* he has a gun. We're not absolutely sure. And even if he does I doubt very much if he'll use it. That old piece of scrap metal probably wouldn't fire even if he had the guts to pull the trigger."

Henry knew perfectly well the Remington would fire. He had just killed a couple of pesky coons with it the week before last. But he decided not to mention the coons. Some of the assembled were spooked enough already.

"Well I'll tell you," said Joseph, who was much more concerned with voicing his own attitudes than with shoring up sagging morale, "just because you think that gun might not fire ain't good enough for me. You think I'm going out in those woods to look for a guy who has obviously flipped his switches? Well forget it because I ain't. I'll say what I said last night: call the cops. Let them handle this. Let them bring the crazy son of a bitch in."

The others held their tongues. They waited for the Wild One to snap the neck of this dissenter.

But Wild Bill took his time, decided not to snap. He took a quick look around, made some judgments on who might be on Joseph's side and who might be on his side. He knew if they called in the cops it would only lead to the further alienation of the family. *If the cops come to get him,* he thought, *we might just as well write the S.O.B. off forever; he'll never come back to us, never.* The Wild One was not prepared to let that happen. *But who,* he wondered, *will back me up? They're all a bunch of goddamn jellyfish. They got backbones made of rubber. I don't know if I can count on any of 'em.*

But then, much to the Wild One's surprise, Ginny said, "No, Daddy's right, Joseph. Edward is our responsibility. He must be a sick young man to do what he did. We need to find out why. We need to help him, not turn our backs on him."

No one said anything for several seconds because no one could quite believe these words had risen from the mouth of sister Ginny. But indeed they had, and everyone, including Ginny's dead but nevertheless beaming mother, had heard them.

And then, in another blow to the oddsmakers, Emily spoke up. "I agree with Ginny. I don't think Edward wants to hurt us. He might think he does but really he's just trying to—"

"What are you all of a sudden," demanded Joseph, "a goddamn shrink or something?"

"Let her finish," said Ginny.

"That's all really," said Emily. "I just think he might need us a lot more than he knows, a lot more than any of us knows."

"I think you're absolutely right, Emily," said Samantha. "I think Edward needs all of you very much."

"Then why," asked Joseph, "did he try to fry the old man?"

"That's a complex question. Why do so many of us hurt the people we love?"

No one had an answer for the in-law psychologist but they all took some time to think it over. They were home now, all the sons and daughters, more home than any of them had been in a long time. Even Mary felt an emotional attachment that she thought had died years ago. It suddenly dawned on her that she could no longer be merely a spectator, dissecting the past, interpreting the present, forecasting the future. History was unfolding right before her eyes. She could not avoid participation. The family was breaking new ground, traveling to places it had never been before.

"Okay, look," and it was Henry (as Henry, even though most of the people in the room still thought it was Bobby) and not William Bailey Richford, who offered this rousing oratory to help rally the troops, "we can do this. We can bring him back. We don't need any outside help. We can bring him in, talk him down, do whatever needs to be done. Sure, the guy has a gun, he's done some crazy stuff. Some of us are scared. We're all scared. No one wants to get shot." And then the old Marine who had ducked his duty, deserted his post, really came to the fore. "But sometimes you have to take a chance. And I think this is a good time for all of us to take that chance. We have to do it for him, and for us." Henry took a deep breath. Everyone, including Wild Bill, waited for the rest. "We're going to divide up into three groups and comb the property. I'll go out with Emily. Ginny, you go with Joseph. And Mary, you go out with Barton. W. B.'s in no shape to be tromping around in these woods so he'll stay behind here with the others."

Wild Bill thought about overriding this final order but he knew his son was right: he would only slow down the operation. *Besides,* he thought, *it's high time the son of a bitch took charge. I've been waiting twenty years to see it happen. I can't go and stomp on him now . . . Shit, maybe Virginia was right, maybe he'll drive these pansies into the next century after all.*

"What about me?" asked Samantha. "I'm not staying behind."

Henry thought about it. "I figured the brothers and sisters should take care of this, but you're right, you're his wife, you should be out there with us."

"Count me in on a team too, Bob," said the Doc, "I'm not a real fan of this macho stuff but I'd feel like a real heel back here with my wife out there."

Ginny looked at her husband. "Don't be ridiculous, Aaron."

"I'll be ridiculous if I want to be . . . And count Adam in as well. He's got good eyes and good ears and he's quick on his feet."

"No," said the boy's mother.

"Yes," said the boy's father, and everyone in the room knew from the tone of Aaron's voice that Adam would go along on the search for Uncle Edward.

"Okay," said Henry, after an appropriate pause, "we'll go in three groups of three. Samantha, you go with Ginny and Joseph. Aaron will go with Mary and Barton. And Adam, you come along with Emily and me. Everyone agree?"

Everyone did not agree but no one disagreed, at least not out loud. The orders stood. They ate some toast and drank some juice and then the search parties filed out the back door. It was not yet eight o'clock in the morning but already on this first day of summer the mercury had climbed to ninety. You could feel the heat on the small of your back and taste it on the tip of your tongue. You could smell the heat in the air and see it in the sky and feel it rising from the earth right through the soles of your shoes.

They carried no weapons, not even sticks or stones. Some went east, some went west, some went south. Some went with fear, others with confidence. They agreed to rendezvous in the northeast corner of the property, near the old abandoned barn foundation, at ten o'clock.

Each of the three search teams handled their duties in different ways. Ginny, Joseph, and Samantha walked down the driveway to the road and then along the road to the open field in the northwest corner. Joseph had chosen this route for his party because most of the time they would be out in the open, not susceptible to sniper fire from up in trees or behind buildings. He insisted on complete silence and constant movement; no stopping, no talking. He set a wicked pace, almost a slow run. And he didn't walk in a straight line but rather serpentine. Ginny put an end to this nonsense before too long. By the time they walked between the eagle and the turkey vulture she was already winded and perspiring. "Ease up, Joseph, this isn't a foot race. We're not out here for exercise." Silently Samantha thanked Ginny for slowing Joseph down and straightening him out. Her duties as a psychologist did not leave her much time for exercise. Even after they had settled into a slow but steady ramble, Samantha could feel her heart pounding away in defiance. For the first mile or so she wished she had just stayed back at the house. During the second mile she wished she had stayed up in Ithaca. By the end of the third mile she wished she had never heard of Edward Winslow or the Winslow family.

Across the way another in-law fared not much better. Doc Cohen played some sluggish doubles on weekends but regular exercise had never been his forte. An L.A. man born and bred, Aaron could deal with orange air and throat-clogging smog and temps in the triple digits, but this humidity was killing him. By the time his team had reached the first rise at the entrance to the pine forest he looked as though he had just boxed ten or twelve rounds with Joe Louis. Sweat poured off his beet-red face. His breath came in short, frantic gasps. He must have asked himself at least twice every minute what the hell he was doing out there. Poor guy. His family didn't have these kinds of problems. Sure, they were all a little oppressed, slightly neurotic in an American-Jewish sort of way, but his sister was a lawyer and his brother a banker. They got together a time or two a year and talked about their vacations and their investments. They certainly didn't chase each other around in the woods while waiting for their chests to be blown open by stray shotgun shells. The Doc thought about turning back but rejected the idea because of how it would look later in the eyes of his wife and kids.

His teammates did not seem to suffer from the same afflictions. Barton led the way, blazed the trail, stomped down the briars and the brambles for his sister and his brother-in-law. He, unlike Joseph, did not fear his brother's wrath. He felt sure Edward wanted to be found. Every minute or two he cupped his hands around his mouth and shouted, "Edward! Edward! It's me, Barton. I just want to talk!"

Mary wished her brother would stop shouting, not because she feared Edward and his armaments, but because she felt all the noise would only drive the renegade deeper into the woods. The only way she thought they would find him was through persistence and stealth, by practically stumbling over him in the woods. Although privately she doubted they would ever find him unless he wanted to be found. She floated through the undergrowth, oblivious to the thorns and the heat and the humidity. Her light airy frame barely made contact with the earth when she walked. And she walked so much; miles every day in London and out in the English countryside. She thought about her eventual return to London but knew now it would be some time before she renewed her search for the Old World Winslows.

Henry led his troops over the middle ground. He and Emily and Adam went out across the tennis court, passed the smoldering wreckage of the cottage, and down the grassy path to the old barn. They walked around the outside of the barn, and then inside in the no-longer-used horse stalls and up in the hayloft. There were no signs of Edward. They did not say much as they quietly searched the barn, but they made their presence known by clearing their throats and shuffling their feet.

Up in the loft Henry boosted Adam up into the rafters where young Cohen crawled up into the cupola and out onto the barn's steeply pitched roof.

"Be careful up there, boy."

"No problem, Uncle Bob."

Henry recoiled at the inaccuracy. "See anything?"

"I can see all kinds of stuff, miles in every direction. Looks like a thunderhead off to the west, but I don't see . . . wait a minute . . . that must be Mom and Aunt Samantha and Uncle Joseph, out along the road."

"Yeah. Anything else?"

Adam took a slow look around. He liked it up there. He liked the view and the green hills. Everything back in L.A. was so flat and dead; nothing but concrete and steel. He wished he could sit up there all day long with a thick reefer and a couple of ice-cold liters of Dr. Pepper. *I'd like to just sit here,* he thought, *and get stoned and watch that storm come rollin' into town.* "I can see Dad and Aunt Mary and Uncle Barton way up in the woods in the other direction."

"But no sign of a solitary man?"

Adam took another look. "Nope, I guess not."

"Okay, kid, let's go. Time to cover some ground."

Over the next hour the three teams covered a lot of ground. They tramped over most of Wild Bill's two hundred acres. But none of them saw anything to indicate the whereabouts of brother Edward. They rendezvoused as planned a little before ten o'clock down at the old barn foundation in the northeast corner of the property.

"He's disappeared," said Ginny.

"Maybe it wasn't even him," suggested Emily.

"No," insisted Samantha, "it was Edward. Believe me, it was him. I saw him."

"Okay," said Henry, "let's head back to the house, cool off, get something to drink, maybe go out for another look later."

No one suggested anything different. They started back to the house on pretty much the same line Wild Bill had walked forty-five years earlier on that autumn morning he began work on his first house. The tall pines and towering hardwoods did not look all that different now. They crossed a stream, almost dry from drought, and then up a low rise. The in-laws lagged but kept moving. Then up a higher, steeper pitch to the thickly wooded high ground above the house. Barton led the way. He spotted the empty can of pork and beans. Mary almost stepped on an empty bottle of root beer (even as a kid Little Eddie's favorite flavor of bellywash). Soon they had all arrived on the scene and discovered Edward's discarded trash: an empty tin of Spam, an almost empty box of doughnuts, empty bags of M&Ms and Milky Ways and Wise potato chips.

"This sick fuck," said Joseph, "has been up here laying for us. Look at the view he has of the house. Christ, he can see everything that happens, every move we make. He's probably been sitting up in that deer blind for the last couple days taking notes."

Henry nodded. "I wouldn't doubt it."

"Sure looks like," added Barton.

"I know," said Mary, "that he used to come up here when we were kids."

"He did?"

"Yeah, I remember several times when it was time for dinner if we couldn't find Edward Mom would send me up here to look for him. She knew he liked to sit up here by himself and watch the house."

"Jesus, Mary," asked Joseph, "why didn't you tell us this earlier?"

"I just remembered."

"He could've been up here taking potshots at us as we stepped out the back door."

"Easy, Joe," said Henry. "Let's just be glad we found this place. Now we know for sure he's been here."

"But where is he now?" asked Ginny. "And will he be back?"

"He'll be back," said Samantha, quietly.

They all stood there thinking it over, not saying anything, not a word, staring at the trash, the trash of a wild man.

Chapter Thirty-four

The brothers and sisters did not find Edward because Edward was holed up on the second floor of the Bernardsville Library. He sat among the stacks with his head buried in Poe's "The Murders in the Rue Morgue." He had been reading close to an hour but had only reached the third page of the story. He had to keep rereading the lines over and over before they made sense, before the words on the page penetrated the petrified walls of his brain. Little Eddie could not concentrate. He kept muttering under his breath, something about the price sinners have to pay, and enunciating quietly but very clearly some particularly graphic obscenities. It was not a pretty scene.

Once already the assistant librarian had been sent up to ask the young man sitting in the far corner to please refrain from making any unnecessary noise. "This is," she told him nicely, "a library." Edward looked away from the Poe. He peered over the top of the short story collection. He saw a woman standing there but he had no idea why or what she wanted. She gasped ever so slightly and returned forthwith to the safety of the reference desk. The muttering and the cussing continued.

Several patrons complained. They called the man's behavior an outrage. More than a few left the premises entirely. The head librarian and her staff discussed what to do about the young man up in the stacks.

"He smells," whispered the assistant who had been up to visit. "I don't think he's bathed in weeks."

Actually it had been only a few days since Little Eddie's last shower but in all that heat and humidity his body had poured out an incredible amount of perspiration. Stress had not done his pores any little bit of good either.

"Do you think he's homeless?"

"In Bernardsville? Good God," said the head librarian, "things can't have fallen that far."

"Maybe we should call the police."

"I'd hate to do that to the poor man."

"But he's saying the most awful things."

The head librarian nodded.

Above, Edward was on the move. He had torn several pages out of "The Murders in the Rue Morgue," crumpled them up into tight little balls, and thrown them into a dusty corner. "Crap," he mumbled, "pure, filthy, stinking, unadulterated crap."

The only other person left on the second floor, a recently retired hardware-store owner who had never said a mean word to anyone in his entire life, earmarked his book on safe investments for retirement and hurried to the relative safety of the floor below. That left Little Eddie all alone.

He roamed through the stacks pulling books randomly off the shelves. He glanced at the titles, stared at the pictures of the authors on the back covers. "Jackass," he muttered. "Jerkoff. Asshole. Slut. Dickhead. Scumbag. Whore." The photographs turned into his siblings right before his eyes.

Below, they heard the books crash to the floor. There were not that many, only a few, maybe a dozen. But each one sounded like a small explosion, like a tiny bomb had fallen on the safe, quiet, superaffluent burg of Bernardsville. More of the remaining patrons voiced their disgust and then marched out in a huff. Later they would spend hours discussing the maniac in the library. They would speculate on the nature of his craziness and conclude finally that society in general was fast falling into a state of anarchy and decay.

The head librarian knew what she had to do. She had to do her duty. She picked up the telephone and called police headquarters.

Above, Edward spotted the word *slaughtered* on the spine of a book. The word drew his attention immediately. He pulled the book off the shelf. The front cover of the book, in gold letters against a solid black background, read: *"I, Pierre Rivière, having slaughtered my mother, my sister, and my brother. . ."* The book was subtitled *A Case of Parricide in 19th Century France* but Edward did not bother with the subtitle; the title was enough; the title was all he needed, all he wanted. He read it over and over and over again. The words excited him, mesmerized him, even quieted him down, made him as silent as a ghost. The book under his arm, he crept back to his chair in the corner.

Below, they breathed a sigh of relief as the bombing attack came to an end. But the deed had already been done: the long arm of the law was on the march.

Above, Edward found the full confession of Pierre Rivière on page 54. He read the first line of the confession slowly many times: *I, Pierre Rivière, having slaughtered my mother, my sister, and my brother, and wishing to make known the motives which led me to this deed, have written down the whole of the life which my father and my mother led together since their marriage . . .* Edward tried the second line once or twice but it did not sink in, it did not make sense, it did not suit his needs. So he concentrated on line one and line one only. He read it until he had transformed it into something of his own making, something of his own creation, of his own volition. He turned Pierre's words into his own personal confession. And now when he read the words on the page they sounded like this: *I, Edward Winslow, having slaughtered my father, my father's whore, my sisters, my brothers, and my double-crossing wife, and wishing to make known the motives which led me to this deed, have written down the whole of the life which my shitty father and my perfect mother led together since their marriage . . .*

Edward focused all of his energies on this original interpretation until he heard a familiar voice from below. The voice sounded low and deep and authoritative. It sounded to Little Eddie like his papa's voice, like the voice of Wild Bill.

"So where is he?" asked the voice.

"Upstairs," answered a woman's voice, a soft voice, a gentle voice, his mama's voice.

"I'll go up and have a talk with him."

"He's really been very quiet since we called you. He hasn't made a sound. Maybe he's just had a bad day or a fight with his wife or something silly like that."

"Maybe. I'll find out."

By the time the cop found Eddie in the far corner several things about Eddie had changed. He no longer stared at the *Pierre Rivière* book. That book had been stowed away, behind some other books, not to be found again for years. Edward had a new book now, something light and benign, something classic and conventional. The young man had also tucked in his shirt, pushed the hair back off his face, and formed his mouth into a simple, engaging smile.

"Good morning," said the officer.

Edward casually glanced over the top of his book. He was somewhat surprised to see a cop instead of his father but he did not let the surprise show in his eyes. "Good morning."

"Everything okay?"

"Yes, everything's just fine. Thank you."

Below, they all listened with strained ears.

The cop noticed Eddie's eyebrows, actually his lack of eyebrows. "What happened to your eyebrows, son?"

Edward reached up and touched his brow. Most of the hair had been singed off when he tossed the match onto the cottage. "Oh," he said, and smiled, "last night, when I was trying to light the charcoal in the grill . . ." And he shook his head. "Stupid."

The cop nodded. "I did that once."

I doubt it, thought Edward.

"So," asked the cop, "what are you reading?"

Edward turned the book so the policeman could see the cover. *The Adventures of Huckleberry Finn.* Edward widened his smile. "Huck Finn. I bet I've read this book a dozen times but I still get a kick out of it."

The cop nodded. "I always liked that one myself."

"I especially like it after a bad day. It lightens things up."

"Had a bad day, have you?"

Edward shook his head and sighed. "Try a bad few days. A bad week would be more like it. Goddamn business is going down the tubes. It's this whole Japanese thing. We just can't compete with 'em. But I think I've got it worked out. If I can't beat the bastids, I'll join 'em."

The cop laughed. "I know what you mean, pal, but it's like this: some folks downstairs seem to think you've been causing a ruckus."

Edward got his head shaking again. "Probably been muttering under my breath. I do that sometimes. I ought to know by now to stay home and do it in the privacy of my own bedroom."

The cop knew he had to ask. It was his job. "Do you live in town, sir? Could I see some identification?"

Edward explained that his family lived in Far Hills and that he lived in Ithaca, New York, where he was the owner-operator of a small company which manufactured precision medical equipment. He sounded calm and reasonable and responsible. He handed the officer his driver's license.

The cop looked it over. "Winslow? You related to Bill Winslow, the builder?"

"Sure am, I'm his son. I'm on my way over to see the old boy right now as a matter of fact. I'm hoping he'll come through with some fresh investment capital." Edward smiled. So did the cop. But right away Edward wondered if he had gone too far. He wondered if his father had called the cops because of the cottage. He worried that maybe an APB had been put out for his arrest.

The cop immediately silenced his worries. "Shit, I'm sorry about this, Mr. Winslow. Things go a little out of the ordinary and downstairs the people get panicky. It's like that in a small town."

"No problem," said Edward. "I'm sure I was out of line. I get like that sometimes."

"We all do."

"Well, I'm leaving now anyway so on my way out I'll apologize for any trouble I caused."

"That'll be fine."

Edward followed the cop down the stairs. Everyone below immediately became very busy, as though they had not all been hanging on every word from above. No one looked up as Edward walked by. He followed the cop past the card catalog and the magazine rack and the new books. He walked right up to the front desk and waited for the head librarian to stop pretending like she was searching for some important piece of data on her computer screen. "I'm sorry if I caused you any mischief, ma'am. I certainly didn't mean any harm."

The librarian, an older woman with half glasses whose own children had not turned out as she had hoped, managed a little smile. "Oh, that's all right, it's nothing. We were just worried about you is all."

Edward thanked her for her concern and said good-bye. He followed the cop out the front door. In the parking lot they shook hands. "Say hello to your father for me."

"I sure will."

The cop climbed into his police cruiser, the radio already barking out his next assignment.

Edward waved as the patrol car pulled out into the street and accelerated away. As soon as the cruiser disappeared Edward crossed the parking lot to his car. He took a quick look around, made sure no one was watching. He unlocked and opened the trunk. His gear had not been disturbed. The binoculars, the shotgun, and the small pile of shells were right where he had left them. . . .

Chapter Thirty-five

———————————————————————•———————————————————————

Back at the big house, while Eddie mumbled and the search parties searched, all was not quiet. Far from it in fact. The circus started with a row between Madeline and her grandfather. The youngster from southern California wanted to go swimming. The Wild One told her she could not go swimming, she had to stay inside.

These orders did not please the baby doctor's daughter from Bel Air. "But it's so hot in here. It's like a sauna."

Madeline and Wild Bill and the others who had stayed behind sat or stood in the big kitchen. The Wild One sat at the head of the table where he could see out the kitchen windows. "It's not that hot."

"But it is. It's like an oven in here."

"Quit complaining, girl."

"It's like being inside a furnace."

"Stop your grousing."

But Madeline figured she just needed to give another little push. She decided to use the same tactics on Grandad that she used on dear old Dad. "Come on, Grandfather, just a quick dive and then right out again. Just to cool off." She crossed to where he sat, put her hands on his shoulders, and rubbed the muscles still sore from the fall down the back stairs.

"No."

"But why not?"

"Yeah, why not?" asked Rosa.

And Katie.

And Constance.

And John and Paul.

"Because I said so," snapped the Wild One, "that's why." His tone was not friendly. Most, if not all, of those present took a step away from where he sat.

After a moment Irene and Evangeline corralled the younger kiddies and herded them from the kitchen through the dining room into the living room. "Come on, guys," said Evangeline, "I have a game we can play."

Madeline, her support waning, sulked. "I don't know why you won't let us go swimming. I think it's stupid. I think it's selfish."

Wild Bill kept looking out the kitchen windows. He had been looking out the windows since the search parties had disappeared into the hills. He felt old and useless sitting there bruised and broken. "Shut up, girl," he barked at his granddaughter, "just keep your mouth shut. You whine just like your mother used to whine."

Madeline stopped breathing. She did not take a breath for nearly ten seconds. Then she began to cry, just a few wet tears. She wiped the tears away and screamed, "Oh, oh, you go to hell, you . . . you old fart."

Wild Bill turned away from the window but all he saw was his granddaughter's back as she marched out of the kitchen. She went up the front stairs, down the hallway, and into her bedroom. The Wild One heard the door slam. The whole house shook from the explosion of anger. Wild Bill sighed. All his life he'd heard doors slamming in that big old house.

He felt for the handgun tucked into the waist of his lightweight khaki trousers. Earlier Evangeline had carefully split the seam of the right pant leg so that Billy Boy could pull the khakis over his cast. But she did not know her man was packing a .45. Had she known she would have been both angry and afraid. She would have pleaded with him to put the gun away.

Virginia was already angry and afraid. She knew her husband had the gun. Upstairs she had watched him tuck it into his khakis. She had never wanted him to buy the gun in the first place. Caroline, Crazy Legs's wife, knew he had the gun also. She hated guns, was terrified of the sound they made. The other dead Winslows, however, thought the oldest living Winslow was simply showing good prudence by carrying the weapon until this crisis with Little Eddie had been resolved.

Wild Bill was not so sure. He no longer knew what to think. He disliked the feel of the cold steel against his skin. And he knew from experience violence only begot more violence. He wanted to put the weapon away, remove the clip and lock the gun back in his dresser drawer. But at the same time it seemed wise to hang on to it, to keep it close by, just in case. He assured himself he would use the gun with extreme caution. *I'll only use it,* he thought, *if it becomes absolutely necessary; only if there's no other way out, no other course of action. Of course that's what they all say, that's what all the armed maniacs have been saying for a thousand years.*

He sighed again and looked out the window. And there they were, not thirty feet away, a whole flock, marching across the lawn and up onto the brick patio, pecking at the ground, searching for the fallen sunflower seeds Evangeline put out for the chickadees and the finches and the cardinals. Wild Bill could hardly believe his eyes. He felt the subtle, serene deliverance of déjà vu. They were right outside the window now. Had the window been open he could have reached out and grabbed their wings. But the window was closed, closed and locked up tighter than a bank vault. Closed and locked even on this hot and humid summer day because fear had overcome the sensibilities of those inside. Wild Bill took a head count. He counted nine hens and four cocks, thirteen birds in all, thirteen proud and defiant wild turkeys.

"I'm going to do it," he said out loud. "I'm going to knock down that turkey vulture at the end of the drive and replace it with a wild turkey, an American wild turkey. To hell with Crazy Legs and his turkey vulture. I've always hated that goddamn vulture."

Rosa came into the kitchen. "Who are you talking to, Grampa?"

The Wild One pointed out the window. "Look, Rosa, look what came to visit."

Rosa pressed her face against the glass. Her eyes grew wide. She had never seen anything like that before. "Wow! Grampa, what are they?"

"Those are turkeys, girl, wild turkeys, American wild turkeys."

"Turkeys. Like the stuff we eat on Thanksgiving?"

"That's right."

"Wow!" she said again. "I gotta get the others."

Soon they all congregated in the kitchen again, everyone but Madeline. She was up in her room, mad at the world. The kids flocked around the windows: Rosa and John and Paul and Katie and Constance. John and Paul had seen wild turkeys before, maybe even these same wild turkeys, but they didn't say anything about that. They acted like this was the first time for them too.

The turkeys moved away from the windows, across the patio,

and then back out onto the lawn. They walked slowly down past the swimming pool and around the fence on the far side of the tennis court.

"Where are they going?" asked Rosa.

"They're going home," said Evangeline.

"Wow!" said Rosa.

"Will they come back?" asked Constance.

"Sure, kid," said Wild Bill, "they'll be back. You just have to be patient is all."

Evangeline squeezed Billy Boy's shoulder.

They all watched the wild turkeys disappear into the underbrush.

A moment after the turkeys had gone the kids were ready to get back to the game Irene and Evangeline had promised they could play.

"Come on, Grampa," said Rosa, "you play too."

"Play what?"

"Hide-and-seek."

"Hide-and-seek?"

"House hide-and-seek," said Katie. "You can hide anywhere in the house you want."

Wild Bill watched out the window for Little Eddie. "I have no time for games."

"Oh come on, Grampa."

"Yeah, come on, Uncle Billy," said Paul. "You know all the best hiding places."

So the Wild One, after a few more minutes of hemming and hawing, agreed to play on two conditions. One: "Absolutely nobody leaves the house." And two: "I get to hide and not seek. I'm movin' too damn slow to be a seeker."

Paul and Katie volunteered to be the first seekers. All the others went off to hide. Irene, the new baby kicking up a storm, went with Constance. Rosa went with John. And Billy Boy went off with his sweet Evangeline.

"I have a third condition as well," he whispered to her as they made their way slowly up the front stairs.

"You're awfully demanding today."

He held on to her as he hobbled up the steps. "I have a special place I want to hide."

"And where's that?"

"A place I used to hide when I was a kid. You'll see."

They reached the landing at the top of the stairs and started down the hall, away from the master bedroom. At the end of the hall, just beyond the door to the third floor, was a large walk-in closet with shelves for blankets and pillows and towels and sheets. Billy Boy opened the door.

"In here?" asked Evangeline.

Billy Boy nodded. Evangeline went into the closet. The Wild One followed. He reached back and closed the door. It was pitch-black in the closet. He took her hand. "Come on," he said, "we're not quite there yet."

They made their way to the back of the closet. Billy Boy felt along the back wall for the latch. He unhooked the latch and pushed open a low, narrow door. Outside light flowed over them through a small round window.

"You'll have to crawl through on your knees," he said. "Watch your head."

Evangeline went down on her hands and knees and through the narrow opening. The Wild One followed. He had some trouble with his cast but finally managed to drag the thing into the crawl space. He closed the door.

"No one will ever find us in here," said Evangeline.

"Paul will eventually," said the Wild One. "He knows about this place."

"He does?"

Billy Boy nodded.

"I guess you guys have played hide-and-seek before."

"A few times."

"Never with me. Not in the house anyway. Out in the yard once or twice."

Billy Boy smiled. They were under the stairway to the third floor. The space was about six feet from front to back and maybe four feet wide. The round window looked out over the backyard. The Wild One positioned himself in front of the window.

"Is this why you wanted to hide here," Evangeline asked, "so you could keep an eye out for Edward?"

"Partly," he answered, "I guess."

He put his arm around her waist. They sat quietly for several minutes. It was warm and stuffy in the low, narrow crawl space. Billy Boy pushed open the window. He could see the front of the garage and the swimming pool and the tennis court and part of the burned-out shell of the cottage. But nothing moved, everything stood perfectly still. No breeze stirred the leaves or rippled the grass or disturbed the surface of the water.

More minutes passed. And then suddenly Evangeline began to cry very softly.

"What is it?" he asked. "What's the matter?"

"Nothing," she answered. "It's just that this is so crazy, so crazy and sad."

"Hiding up here in this cubbyhole?"

"No . . . I don't know . . . just everything."

He knew what she meant. "It's not exactly the reunion I'd planned when I asked you to call home the troops a few days ago."

"A few days? That seems like months ago."

He held her close.

She looked out the window at the lawn and the gardens. "There's so much to do," she said. "I'm so far behind. I've barely done anything since all this started."

"It doesn't matter. Everything looks beautiful."

"But the roses need pruning. The perennial beds need weeding. That sucker vine will take over if I give it half a chance. The annuals need water. They'll wilt and die in this heat without water. The azaleas and the rhododendrons need feeding. The mums need pinching. If I don't pinch them back they'll bloom in July and be all over by August." Evangeline spoke softly, monotonously. She seemed almost unaware that her mouth made sounds. She was just thinking out loud. "And the pool needs chlorine. It'll turn green in this humidity. And the tennis court needs brushing and rolling. And the grass needs cutting. And the—"

Billy Boy put his index finger gently over her lips. "We'll get to it all, sweetie, we'll get it all done . . . And if we don't, so what? You always say it's the doing, not the finishing . . ."

"But it's so sad," she whispered, and she looked out the window in the direction of the cottage, "it's just so sad."

Billy Boy followed her eyes. "We're going to rebuild it," he said. "We're going to replace everything, every last board, every last molding. We're going to make it exactly the same, only better."

"No," she said, "I don't care about that. It's not that. I know the walls can be replaced, rebuilt . . ." She started to cry again, not quite so softly this time.

Billy Boy held her even closer. He said nothing. She had taught him years before the special beauty of silence. He had long wished that he had learned the lesson as a much younger man.

Sometimes later, her face now wet with tears, she asked without wanting an answer, "What about the rocking chair?

What about that old rocker? Your grandfather sat in that chair... And what about the pillow my mama made me when I was a baby? And what about the picture of you and me that Paul drew at school last month? The one on the refrigerator. And what about John's bug collection? All those worms and flies and wasps and—" Her tears flowed freely now. The terrible fruits of the fire had finally reached her soul. Wild Bill knew it, and he had no idea what to do but some idea what to say.

"I love you," he said.

Evangeline tightened her grip on his hand. She sobbed like a little girl. Outside the summer hung still. The heat pressed down on the earth. Nothing that did not have to move moved. The storm clouds had stalled somewhere out to the west, beyond where they could see.

"Don't hate him," she said, her crying now almost under control. "Please, promise me. Promise me you won't hate him. It will do no good. You know it has never done anyone any good."

He promised her.

And then, after a moment, "It was meant to be. There is a reason for all of this. The fall. The fire. There must be a reason."

He nodded.

They heard someone open the outside closet door.

Evangeline wiped the tears from her cheeks. "In loss there is gain, Billy Boy. There is always gain. The Friends believe that beyond almost all else."

Billy Boy nodded again. He was the one who wanted to cry now.

"I love you too."

They heard someone lift the latch. The low, narrow door swung open. And there, in the beam of light, stood their son, Paul, a broad smile on his freckled face. "I found you!"

"That you did, boy, that you did," said Wild Bill. He grabbed his youngest son by the waist and pulled him into the crawl space. He tickled the boy in the ribs until the boy begged for mercy.

"I knew you'd be in here. I knew it, I knew it, I knew it."

"And you were right, boy, you were absolutely right. But now I want you to listen up. Here's what I want you to do. Later on, when Uncle Edward arrives, if Uncle Edward arrives, I want you to bring your brother and all your cousins up to this hiding place."

"But how will I know it's Uncle Edward? I've never seen Uncle Edward."

"Don't worry about that, you'll know."

"And when he comes will he be it, will he be the seeker?"

"That's right, Paul," said the Wild One, "Uncle Edward will be the seeker. And that's why I want you to lead your brother and your cousins up here."

"Doesn't Uncle Edward know about this place? Didn't he hide here when he was a kid?"

"He probably did," said Wild Bill, "but I'll bet he's forgotten all about it."

"Did you hide here as a kid?" Paul asked.

The Wild One thought back. "That was a long time ago, but yeah I think I did."

"So it'll be a good place to hide?"

The Wild One patted his boy on the back. "It'll be an excellent place."

They sat quietly for a few moments. The boy's mother and father wondered how much the boy knew, how much he understood. They hoped he knew very little. They hoped he understood next to nothing about all the chaos and confusion of the past twenty-four hours. They hoped his innocence had been spared by the flames and by the dark shadows of violence.

"Yo! What's going on? Where the hell is everybody?"

"Daddy?"

"Rosa?"

"Yo, W. B., where the hell are you?"

They heard the shouts of Joseph and Ginny and Emily. The search parties had returned home. They had crossed in front of the window and entered the house without the Wild One seeing them or hearing them. He shuddered ever so slightly.

"They're back," said Paul. He scrambled through the low doorway and out of the closet.

"I wonder if they found Edward?" Evangeline asked.

"I guess we best go and find out."

Evangeline crawled back through the narrow doorway. "I sure hope they found him."

"So do I," mumbled Billy Boy, too softly for her to hear, "so do I."

Chapter Thirty-six

———————————————— • ————————————————

At the top of the stairs Billy Boy stopped. He let go of Evangeline's hand. "You go on ahead," he said. "I'll be down in a minute."

She nodded. "Are you all right?"

"I'm fine. I just have to use the head."

Evangeline turned and started down the stairs. The Wild One hobbled along the hallway to the master bedroom. He pulled the pistol out of his pants. He stood there and stared at the handgun. He stared at it until it turned into a chalk-white dove and flew away. It flew across the room and out the window without even breaking a single pane of glass. "And I thought I was ready to be a Quaker," the Wild One said softly as he watched that dove rise into the afternoon sky, "thought I deserved to be a Friend. Here I am, packing a six-shooter against my own blood, and at the same time pretending like I've learned a thing or two about maybe being a decent human being."

He removed the clip from the gun and hid the clip on the top shelf of his closet, under a pile of sweaters. He then opened his dresser drawer and placed the gun inside. He locked the drawer and stuffed the key into the pocket of his khakis. *As soon as this is over,* he thought, *I'll bury the damn thing. I'll bury it up in the graveyard, have a little ceremony, just the gun and me.*

Virginia smiled.

Billy Boy left the bedroom and hobbled to the head of the stairs. But he did not start down, not yet. He continued along the hallway a bit farther, to the second bedroom on the left. He knocked softly on the door.

"Who is it?"

"It's your grandfather."

"What do you want?"

"I want to tell you something. Can I come in?"

After a moment, "It's open."

The Wild One pushed open the door and stepped into the room. Madeline lay on the bed, her eyes dry but red.

"I'm sorry, kid. I was out of line snapping at you like that, way out of line."

Her face softened.

He crossed the room and sat on the edge of the bed. "You were right, I am an old fart."

Her lip curled up just a little bit. "No you're not."

"Sure I am. I'm a grumpy old fart who thinks he knows everything and doesn't have to explain anything."

Madeline sat up, right beside her grandfather. "That's not true."

He smiled, leaned over, put his arms around her. She did not resist. He held her close. He held her for probably the first time in her life. He held her like he had never held the girl's mother. And he knew he never had and it made him want to cry but he held back the tears because he did not want to confuse and alienate another generation.

They went down the front stairs together, Madeline helping her grandfather negotiate the treads and risers, her arm around his waist, his arm around her shoulder. They entered the living room that way, a way no one had ever seen them before. Everyone in the room took a moment to stop and stare.

Wild Bill accepted the stares. He smiled at all those curious eyes. He could not see the dead but he could feel their presence. He knew they had come and he was pretty sure he knew why. "I don't see Edward," he said, after enough time had passed.

"Neither did we," said Ginny.

"No sign of him?"

"We found his food stash," answered Emily, "up in the woods behind the garage."

"So we know he's been out there?"

"We know someone's been out there," answered Ginny.

"But it must've been Edward?"

"Definitely," said Joseph. "I mean who the hell else could it be? From the looks of his camp he's been up there for at least a couple days."

*   *   *

The living room was overflowing with Winslows now, both dead and alive. And they were all Winslows, every last one of them except for the good doctor from way out west and of course sweet Evangeline. But before another year passed she would be one as well.

The living room was crowded, and growing more crowded all the time. More dead Winslows kept arriving. I won't list them all but you can be sure that just about every Winslow you've met during this narrative is either on the way or already occupying space in the living room of that big house in Far Hills. The word, you see, had gone out that a shooting, a potential shooting anyway, was in the making. And not just any run-of-the-mill shooting either. Not just some random, routine six-o'clock-news shooting. No, this was a one-of-a-kind, never before seen, totally unique and original to the New World Winslows type of shooting. And they all wanted to see it firsthand: Giles (scalped) and his wife Edith and their son Edmund (shot) and his wife Molly and their boy Freeman and his bride Eleanor and their oldest son Henry Lane and his wife Rebecca and their boy Jawbone (shot) and his wife Anna and their younger twin son Mad Dog and his wife Katherine and their boy Henry Lane III (shot) and his wife Lorelei and Lorelei's son William Giles and his bride Emily and their boy Barton (shot) and of course his young wife Dorothy who had mothered the already present master and builder of the Winslow Compound, John "Crazy Legs" Winslow. They were all there in the big house on the hill. Or else on their way. And why? Because it looked like for the very first time in their long and troubled history, one Winslow might actually take the life of another Winslow. So many of them had died violent deaths, lost their lives in New World wars and rebellions and revenge, but never had a single Winslow perished by the hand of his own blood. Three hundred years on the continent and that tragedy had not yet gone down.

"Okay, so it's him," said Ginny, "it's Edward. He's out there. Somewhere. So now what? Now what do we do?"

The Wild One had an answer for his daughter but first he wanted to hear what the others had to say.

"Like I've been saying all along," said Joseph, "we call the cops. We gotta call the cops. The guy's gone wacky on us."

"No," said Barton, "no cops."

"I think we should just keep looking," said Emily.

Mary shook her head. "There's too much space out there, too

much land. Even assuming he doesn't leave the property we could look for days and not find him."

"Especially if he doesn't want to be found," added Samantha.

"Fine," snapped Emily, "so what do you suggest?"

"I don't know," answered Mary. "I don't know. I just think wandering around in this heat is a waste of time and energy."

Emily started to respond but Henry, as Bobby still to most of those present, waved her off. "Mary's right. It is a waste of time. It's too damn hot out there. And like Samantha says, if he doesn't want us to find him we probably won't find him."

"Yeah," said Emily, "okay. Great. So everyone knows what we shouldn't do. But does anyone have any idea what we should do?"

Henry took a slow look around the room. He expected the old man to speak up but Wild Bill didn't say a word. "Yeah," said the oldest son, finally, "I know what we're gonna do."

"And what's that?" asked Emily.

"We're gonna wait."

Atta boy, roared the Wild One silently, *now you're thinking on your feet. That's exactly what we do. We just sit and wait. Let him come to us.*

"Wait?"

"That's right," said Henry, "we wait."

"And what if he doesn't come?"

"We'll wait some more."

"And what if he still doesn't come?"

"He'll come," said Samantha, very quietly. "Eventually he'll come."

"Okay, eventually he'll come," said Joseph. "So what do we do till then? Do we sit here in this house, in this sweatbox, with all the windows and doors closed and locked? Sit here and wait for him to come storming in here firearms a-blaz—"

"No," answered Henry, "we unlock the doors and we unlock the windows..."

Atta boy, the Wild One cheered to himself, *keep it up, boy, don't back down now.*

"We open the doors and we open the windows. We're not prisoners here. We're just here...because we...because we belong here."

No one said a word for quite a while, two or three minutes at least. It wasn't an uncomfortable silence; more of a reflective silence. Most of them were aware that the Wild One had said virtually nothing since entering the room. Most of them waited now for him to say something, anything. They expected him to take charge, to tell them what to do. That's the way it had always been, the way they assumed it would always be. But he didn't say a word. Instead, with the help of his granddaughter, he crossed the living room and settled down right in the middle of the long sofa; he sank down into one of the overstuffed, supersoft, goose-down cushions. He lifted his cast-covered leg and rested it on the glass coffee table in front of the sofa. "Ahh," he said, and smiled, "now that feels good, that feels wonderful. I might sit right here for the next ten years."

Most of those Winslows, both living and dead, turned and stared at the family patriarch once again. And they probably would have kept staring at him had not Evangeline said, "You all must be hungry from your long walk. Maybe it's time I fixed some lunch. John, Paul, why don't you come out into the kitchen and help me make some sandwiches?"

The two boys joined their mother.

"I'll give you a hand, Evangeline," said Irene. "Come on, Katie, Constance, you can help too."

The two girls joined their mother.

"Mama," asked Rosa, "can I help? I could make some icy tea."

"Sure," said Emily, "go ahead but not too much sugar."

"Okay." Rosa ran across the living room to catch up with the others.

The two dozen or so Winslows still in the living room listened to the sound of young Rosa's footsteps as she raced across the front foyer and through the dining room. After the footsteps faded they all took a moment to shift gears. Madeline sat down on the sofa beside her grandfather. Adam sat on the opposite side. Wild Bill put his arm around his grandson. "Pretty hot out there, hey, kid?" Adam nodded. Barton sat in the swivel chair where he had sat earlier listening to Bach. Joseph and Emily went around unlocking and opening the windows. Mary went into the front foyer and opened the front door. The Wild One considered telling her to keep the door closed and locked but instead he decided to keep his mouth closed. A very slight breeze eased its way through the open door and across the foyer. But by the time the breeze reached the living room it had all but dissipated. Henry sat down in the wing chair beside the sofa, the wing chair where the Wild One had always sat in the evenings, after dinner, reading his

newspaper and interrogating the kids on what they had learned in
school and what they had done after school to help their mother.
Ginny sat in the wing chair on the other side of the sofa, opposite
Henry, in front of the fireplace. Aaron leaned against the mantel-
piece, behind his wife, happy now just to be at rest, away from
that brutal sun. Samantha excused herself, said something about
going upstairs to wash her face and change her clothes. And the
dead, they just sort of hung around wherever they could find some
open space.

"So Daddy," said Ginny, after everyone had made a move,
settled down, done whatever they needed to do, "it seems like
ages ago but yesterday at the hospital you said you had some
things to tell us, some things you wanted to talk about. Maybe,
while we're waiting, this would be a good time."

The Wild One nodded. "Maybe it would."

"After all, we're all here. Most of us anyway."

The Wild One nodded again. "That's true," he said, and took a
look around the room, "we're almost all here. Really everyone but
Edward."

Ginny waited. "Well?"

Joseph stood opposite Aaron, on the other side of the mantel-
piece. Emily sat on the arm of the sofa, between Madeline and
Barton. Mary sat on the wide window seat which ran along the
front of the room beneath the large picture window. Every so
often she glanced out the window. She saw water spewing forth
from Lady Godiva's nipples. Someone had turned on the fountain. She saw the long expanse of lawn and the tall red maples
standing perfectly still under the summer sun. She could not yet
see the black storm clouds moving in from the west. She had the
impression the sun and the moon and the earth had stopped
moving, had ground to a cosmic halt. She thought she knew some
of what her father might say but certainly not all; she had lost some
of her faith in soothsaying.

"Well," said the Wild One, "I do have a few things I'd like to
say, if you all think you can bear with me for a few minutes."

Everyone in the room, with the possible exception of Crazy
Legs who feared a deluge of sentimental hogwash, seemed to
think they could.

William Bailey Richford needed some time to get started. He
had been waiting a long while for the opportunity to say his piece.
Now, with this Edward business hanging over the family's head,

he wasn't real sure what to say or where to begin. He finally decided to just roll on and try not to leave anything out. "I appreciate you all coming. It was no easy chore for most of you to get here." He paused for just a moment to remind himself not to hold back, not to hold anything in reserve. "When a man gets to be my age he thinks about things maybe more than he used to. This can be a good thing or a bad thing, I don't know. In my case I think it's a good thing. I wish I'd taken the time to think more as a younger man. But I was always too damn busy; never had any time to think things through. When you kids were little I spent most of my time thinking about money. I thought money was the most important thing in the world. I didn't think it was possible to have enough money, not with nine kids and a wife and dogs and cats and horses and goldfish all demanding food every day, every single day, seven days a week, three hundred and sixty-five days a year. For a long time, as some of you know better than others, we didn't have any money, no extra money anyway, that's for sure. We had this big beautiful house but barely enough cash to keep it going, to keep it painted and heated and stocked with chow. We came damn close to losing it many times in the late '40s and '50s and even the early '60s. Thank God I had no monthly mortgage payment to meet. We'd have been the first homeless family in Far Hills. But that didn't happen because old Crazy Legs had the financial sense to pay as he went. We own this place, and have from the beginning." The Wild One paused again. This time he took a moment to remember the old man down in Punta Gorda as he played out his final days under the guise of Gentleman Bart. And then he came back. "It may sound stupid now but I can remember the milkman delivering twelve quarts of milk every other day and still we never had enough; we always needed more; we always ran out before the milkman returned. You kids drank more damn milk than a whole herd of suckling calves. I used to think I'd be driven to the poorhouse by this family's unquenchable thirst for milk."

The Wild One shook his head but smiled. His kids hesitated, then smiled back. Most of them were still not sure whether the old man intended to throw down the gauntlet or wave the olive branch.

"I don't want to waste time boring you with the trials and tribulations of parenthood. It was our decision, mine and your mother's, to keep having kids. We could've stopped. We didn't owe any allegiance to the Pope. But I think now about having nine kids and I'm pretty sure we both must've been out of our minds."

Another smile from the Wild One brought a brief, cautious round of laughter from the gathered brood.

"Whether you care to believe me or not, I'm damn glad your mother and I kept copulating. I'm damn glad every single one of you came into the world. Maybe we haven't always seen eye to eye but . . . but so what? Look, I'm not here to try and make you see my side of things. I'm not interested in excuses or apologies. I did the best I could, the best I knew how. Nobody taught me how to raise kids. My old man was a drunk who hired someone else to do it. I just jumped in and started swimming. I was a lousy father sometimes, no doubt about that, I admit it. I was demanding and impatient, narrow-minded and selfish. Things were done my way or . . . or I guess they were done behind my back."

This time there was no hesitation. Everyone broke a smile. A few even laughed. The brothers and sisters exchanged glances. It looked like the old man was at least trying to light the pipe.

"Your mother and I fought all the time over you kids. I mean every single day. You might say we both had different agendas. We certainly had different expectations. She knew you all better than I did; knew you as people, not just as children. She believed in letting you find your own way, beat your own path, make your own mistakes. Me, I didn't have the ability or the sensitivity to see you as individuals; I saw you more as objects of manipulation. I wanted you to please me; I wanted you to do what would make me happy. I guess I figured that was your duty, your obligation."

No one laughed or smiled now. The white flag had been unfurled. Barton had tears in his eyes. So did some of the others, including more than just a few of the dead; the womenfolk mostly. No one, except maybe Evangeline, who was busy comforting Irene in the kitchen, had ever heard Wild Bill talk this way. Some of the deceased Winslows could not recall ever hearing any Winslow male speak this way. And the Wild One was not finished yet:

"Evangeline thinks I fell down the stairs on purpose. You might say she thinks God pushed me down the stairs. But since she believes God dwells inside of us and is a creator of our own making, then it follows that my fall was a consequence of my own desires. Meaning I fell and hurt myself so that all of you would feel obligated to come home. See, I didn't have the balls"—and the Wild One squeezed his granddaughter's hand—"excuse my French . . . the guts, I didn't have the guts, the courage, to simply ask all of you to come home for no other reason than because I wanted to see you, talk to you. Maybe five thousand times or more I've walked down those back stairs. I'd never fallen before, never even slipped. Why suddenly now?"

No one answered, at least not out loud.

Billy Boy paused, took his time, tried to decide how much or how little to say. He had said so little of consequence to his offspring over the years that he felt like he could easily turn into a rising river, a raging storm. . . . "I loved your mother," he said. "I hope you all know that, I hope you all believe that. Her death was the most difficult and terrifying experience of my life. Had I not been such an arrogant, selfish ass, your mother's death might have brought me closer to all of you. But it did just the opposite. Her death drove us further apart, aggravated the alienation we already suffered. I was too damn full of things like pride and ego and Winslow machismo to let any of you see me suffering, see me crying, see me afraid for the first time in my adult life. You all saw me with a stiff upper lip, giving orders, making demands, off to work, back to the job, carry on, carry on." The Wild One had to pause a long while before he mumbled, "Such bullshit." And then, "Anyway, these are some of the things I wanted to tell you. But, and I mean this, I'm not here to try to cover up the past. I'm not here to try to talk away forty years of neglect. I'd like to bury some hatchets but really I'm more interested in what's coming than what's been. I can't change what's already happened."

The others waited for more. Mary glanced out the window. She thought for a moment she saw Edward making his way down the drive beneath those tall red maples now swaying in the breeze; but it wasn't Edward, it was old Mad Dog, the last of the family dead to arrive. He had never been to the Compound before. He wondered what kind of skullduggery had earned his descendants the privilege of living in such highfalutin' lodgings. Out beyond the house, still a-ways off to the west, he could see those black clouds rising and hear the first faint echoes of thunder. But he knew he'd be safely inside before the storm struck.

"I can't change the past but I can at least try to do something about the future. I figure I've got a few good years left, maybe twenty if I'm lucky. Old Freeman Winslow lived to be damn close to a hundred. No reason I can't do the same. I'm going to keep working until the day I drop over dead, but I've promised Evangeline I'll start working less, start taking a little more time off. . . . Right, Evangeline. I guess you'd all like to know about that. Well, as I told you boys yesterday, I'm doing my damnedest to make that girl my wife." He paused while all those who had not already anticipated this announcement gasped. "If the destruction of the cottage did nothing else, I think it tore Bettina off my back. She'll demand a big chunk of the pie but believe me, whatever it takes, it'll be worth it." Again he paused, this time to stop himself from wasting even one more word on his hopefully soon-to-be-ex wife. "Sometime down the road, in the not too distant future, if she'll have me, and I think she will, even though I'm a gruff, ornery old fart"—and he winked at his granddaughter— "I'm going to marry that girl, make the whole thing legal, because as some of you have probably already noticed by the color of their eyes and the cut of their jaws, those two boys in the kitchen making sandwiches with their mama are products of our not-yet-sanctioned relationship. Those boys are your brothers, half-brothers anyway, full-blown Winslows, if not yet by name, definitely by birth."

The Wild One waited for this to take hold. He looked around the room at the faces of his sons and daughters.

"Are you shittin' me?" It was Joseph.

"Nope. Those are my boys. I hope to live long enough to see them reach manhood but if I don't, if I can't, for any reason, I expect each and every one of you to assist them in any way you can. I expect you to treat them like blood. They *are* blood."

While Wild Bill waited to see if anyone had anything to say, any charge to make, any stone to cast, young Rosa walked into the living room, stopped, took a long innocent look around, then crossed to her uncle from California. "No sandwiches ready yet," she said as she took the good doctor by the hand, "but Aunt Evangeline and Aunt Irene want me to bring Uncle Aaron into the kitchen."

"Why?" asked Ginny.

"I'm not supposed to tell you that," answered Rosa, as though Aunt Ginny should have known better than to even ask.

Aaron went without protest. He was happy to have a reason to leave the living room.

*　*　*

And in the kitchen, not thirty feet from where those Winslows packed the peace pipe, a woman, a Winslow by marriage, held the hand of her newfound friend, Evangeline, and took long, deep breaths to combat the terrific pains racing through her swollen belly.

The kiddie doctor from Bel Air walked into the kitchen clutching the hand of his niece and one look told him everything he needed to know.

"Let's get her upstairs," he said.

John and Paul and Katie and Constance stood to the side, their mouths hanging wide open, their hearts beating wildly.

"And let's just keep this quiet for the time being," continued the good doctor. "No need to get the others involved just yet. The important thing," and he took Irene's hand, partly to comfort her and partly to get a read on her pulse, "is to keep Mama calm."

Irene smiled, then grimaced as the new baby struck another blow for posterity.

Dr. Cohen, with Evangeline's help, brought Irene to her feet. "By the looks of these two beautiful girls," he said, looking at Katie and Constance, "I'd guess you'd been through this before."

Irene nodded. "You're really a doctor?"

"That's what they've been telling me now for. . . for almost eighteen years."

Irene smiled and cried and tried not to scream.

The kids, under strict orders not to say a word, followed Irene and Evangeline and Aaron through the dining room and into the front foyer. No one in the living room noticed the threesome as they started up the wide set of front stairs. The kids, all five of them, followed quietly close behind.

They settled Irene in the master bedroom. Evangeline turned on the air conditioner, set the fan as high as it would go. Katie and Constance and Rosa sat on the edge of the huge king-size bed. John and Paul stood by the door. Both mothers had already told the children they could stay as long as they wished, even while the new baby was being born. Katie had been there with her father when Constance was born. They could stay but they would have to be very quiet and do exactly what Uncle Aaron told them to do. Aaron was in the bathroom washing his hands and looking for clean white towels and trying to remember the things he used to know about delivering babies. His breathing was fast and shallow. He tried to relax. Maybe it'll be a false labor, he told the tired, sunburned face in the mirror, a false labor and then we can get her to a hospital.

Other things were happening as well. Other things too numerous to mention here; except possibly for one particular thing which no doubt needs a bit of updating. I'm talking, of course, about the whereabouts of wandering Edward. Too bad that police officer, who was far more concerned with Bill Winslow's continued financial support of his benevolent association than with Edward Winslow's somewhat dubious mental state, hadn't brought young Winslow down to the station for a more thorough questioning. Little Eddie was free, on his own, a satellite out of orbit. He was on his way back, on his way home, driving sensibly enough on the right side of the road, using his turn signals, watching his speed, yielding the right of way, obeying all but the most nonsensical traffic laws.

As Aaron left the master bath and entered the bedroom, Edward turned off Route 202 and started up into the hills. He drove slowly on the old switchback road. He drove very slowly, so slowly his speed barely registered on the car's speedometer.

"Anyway," said Billy Boy, "that's the way it is. John and Paul and Evangeline are part of this family. I don't want two separate families. I want one big family; preferably one big happy family. The way I see it, we're all in this together. We can go our separate ways, live our separate lives, live in the far corners of the world, pretend like the other people in this room do not even exist. But we know they do exist and the more we pretend they don't exist the more we'll struggle, the more we'll suffer. I've thought on this a long time, and I've probably changed my mind more times than I've changed my underwear, but I go along now with the old sages who said blood is our last, best hope. I think it always has been and always will be. Right now we think we've got this problem with Edward; we're worried about what he might do with that gun, what he might do with his anger and his frustration. But the problem is much bigger than Edward. There are a hell of a lot more dangerous people out there than your brother. He's not the one we need to worry about, not in the long run . . . I was going to say the world's turning to shit, what with all the violence and greed and graft, but I suppose the world's been turning to shit ever since the first caveman bashed the second caveman's brains out because the second caveman had something the first caveman wanted. But instead I'll just say that after living seventy years on the planet it's pretty clear to me you've got a very tough row to hoe if you go into the fields on your own, all by yourself, without any help from anyone. It's a tough row, and in the end, no matter how bountiful the harvest, a petty, self-serving row at best. You have to have help. And the best help, the most reliable help, if you ask me, is the help of blood. Blood is based on something magical, something maybe we can't completely understand. I guess that's why it's such a pain in the ass most of the time; that's why we're afraid of it, why we run away from it, why we kick it when it's down, turn our backs on it. But when it's right and it works and we see it clearly for what it is, it doesn't need definition or explanation . . ."

The Wild One trailed off. He feared he might be going too far, saying too much. He glanced around the room at the faces of his sons and daughters. There were six of them present. *Six out of nine*, thought the old man, *six out of nine ain't bad, ain't bad at all after all the bullshit we've been through . . .*

On the roof the first drops of rain splattered against the aging slate. They were huge drops, the size of marbles but very soft and warm and wet. They burst and ran off the slate, along the gutters, down the drains, into the earth . . . In the master bedroom it looked like Aaron's personal plea for a false labor would not be answered. Irene clutched at the bed sheets as she tried to relax, tried to calm her frantic breathing. Her water had broken. Her contractions ripped through her belly more frequently now, once every three to three and a half minutes. Aaron knew the contractions had reached the point of no return. *This baby*, he told himself, *is on its way.* The cervix had already started to visibly dilate. He had moved the children out into the sitting room, more for his own well-being than anything else. Evangeline stood close by at Irene's side. Aaron knew he would have to call Bobby soon. He kept constant track of the contractions on his solid-gold wristwatch.

"All this philosophical nonsense aside," continued Billy Boy, "I do have something in mind. I do have a specific reason why I wanted you all here." He paused, took a deep breath, wondered how it would sound saying it out loud after all the months and even years keeping it bottled up inside. Then something powerful hit him on the side of the head and he knew he had to press on, quickly, not waste a single moment more. "I think the time has come to circle the wagons, to make a stand. And I think this is the place to do it. Right here on this hilltop. . . ."

Edward had reached the hilltop. He'd reached the driveway. He slowed to a stop. A few drops of rain ran down his windshield. Little Eddie stuck his head out the window and stared at the sky. He did not see the two storms converging. He swung the car into the drive, right between the eagle and the turkey vulture. His right foot dancing lightly on the brake pedal, he rolled slowly toward the house...

Mary glanced out the picture window. She shuddered as she had a sudden premonition of her brother Edward closing in for the kill. But before his car pulled into view the sky drew her attention away. She saw for the first time the low black clouds now hanging directly over the house. They moved rapidly across the sky. The sun vanished. The day turned dark...

The contractions kept coming. But Irene had herself under control. She battled the pain as best she could... Edward kept coming as well. His face looked taut, gaunt, hollow. His eyes looked frightened, the eyes of a man with nowhere left to go, nowhere left to turn.

A cool, fresh breeze whipped through the front door. Everyone in the living room took a deep breath.

"We're dug in here, have been for a hundred years. We've got our sweat and our dead in this ground." The Wild One looked around the room again at his sons and daughters. He had their attention. "You all can tell me to go to grass if you want, but what I'm offering is the opportunity to come home, to come back to where I think you belong. Winslows have lived on this hilltop since Crazy Legs brought his family here in 1890. I'd like to see my great grandkids here in 2090. We've got the land, the space. There's plenty of room to spread out, enough room for every single one of you to stake a claim, plant some seeds, build a house. This is still a fine place to live, a safe place to live, an excellent place to raise a family."

The Wild One slowed, stopped, felt the pressure of the coming storm. Some of the others felt it also. A calm settled over the room. No one said a word, not out loud. None of them had expected this. This was much farther than any of them had expected old Wild Bill to go. They did not know what to say, how to respond.

Upstairs the air conditioner pushed cool air into the master bedroom. Irene was drenched in sweat. Evangeline held one hand, Aaron the other. She did not scream. She rested quietly waiting for the next explosion. Aaron glanced at his watch. He knew it was coming...

And then it did, all at once, without warning. Those black clouds dropped down and opened wide. Rain and wind and thunder and lightning came rushing out, pouring forth like an army bent on revenge, bent on beating into submission its archenemies: heat and humidity. In the house they heard the thunder and saw the flash of lightning at exactly the same moment. The storm could not have been any closer without actually occupying the living room. No one managed not to jump at least a little bit. None of them other than Mary had seen the storm coming. Upstairs they'd been too involved in the rising and falling of Irene's belly. And downstairs they'd all been mesmerized by the smell of smoke rising from the Wild One's ancient pipe.

Outside Edward felt pretty sure he'd been struck by lightning. He felt like the bolt had passed straight through his chest and gone out his back. His whole body shaking and quivering, he swung the car through the circle, past the flowing breasts of Lady Godiva, and up to the front entrance. He shut down the engine and stepped out. The pounding rain soaked him instantly from head to toe. He moved to the back of the car, a gaping hole in the middle of his torso, and opened the trunk. He reached into the trunk and filled his pockets with shells. Another burst of light and noise shook the earth. Little Eddie jumped. He slammed his head on the trunk lid. "Shit! Fuck!" He lifted out the Remington twelve-gauge. He shoved a shell into each of the two chambers. Sweating, trembling, soaking wet, his eyes as big as baseballs, he started up the marble stairs for the front door. . . .

Inside they had just recovered from the second blast. Barton and Emily and Joseph were on their feet, moving to close the open windows. The Wild One had more to say, at least he thought he did, but the storm had center stage now.

And then Edward was at the front door and through the front door and in the front hall and standing in the high, wide entrance to the living room. For a moment no one saw him. They were all too busy dealing with the wind and the rain. He just stood there shaking and dripping, the shotgun hanging at his side. And then the Wild One knew, without even looking, that the middle son had arrived, had finally ventured home. He waited for the thunder to retreat, and then said loudly and quite clearly, "Hello, Edward."

All eyes immediately raced from the father to the son. Most of the females in the room, both living and dead, gasped; a gasp far more pronounced than the one voiced earlier when Wild Bill had announced his intention to marry sweet Evangeline. This gasp carried a message of fear. It hung there in the air and then faded. No one moved. No one made a sound.

Upstairs Irene screamed. But downstairs no one heard. The steady rhythm of the air conditioner followed by another roar from the sky swallowed the scream and spit it out as a soft, smothered squeal.

And then down the front stairs came Samantha. She felt much better now. She had taken a cold shower. She had stood in front of the open window and felt the cool breeze on her damp skin. Her short wet hair was pulled back away from her face. She had on cool white shorts and a lightweight silk blouse. She reached the bottom step, turned toward the living room—"Edward!"

He swung around, raised the gun to his hip.

Samantha screamed.

In the master bedroom they did not hear the scream. But out in the sitting room the kids heard it loud and clear. They quickly made their way along the hallway to the top of the stairs.

"Edward!!!" shouted the Wild One.

Edward turned again, away from his wife. He had the gun up around his chest now, his index finger on the twin triggers. He pointed the twelve-gauge at his father.

The kids came bounding down the stairs, all five of them. Even with the thick carpet muffling their feet everyone in the living room heard them coming. Edward swung once again.

The kids came to a sudden halt right behind their Aunt Samantha.

"It's Uncle Edward!" shouted Rosa.

The sweat poured off Edward's face. His eyes twitched. His mouth searched for air.

"Goddamn you! Edward!!!" It was Wild Bill again, drawing his son's attention away from the children.

And again Edward turned.

As soon as he did the Wild One shouted, "Paul, go!" He could not see the kids from his position on the sofa but he knew the five of them stood there curious and confused. "Go where I told you to go! Take your brother and your cousins and go!"

The rain turned to hail, giant golf-ball-size chunks of hail.

They pounded the roof and crashed against the side of the house. One the size of a tennis ball hit the picture window over Mary's head. She screamed. The window cracked, a long splintery crack running from sash to sill.

"Go!" shouted Billy Boy, "Go! Now!"

"Come on," Paul shouted to the others, "follow me." The youngster turned and started up the stairs. John and Katie and Constance and Rosa followed without a word.

Edward heard them going and swung once again. But only his wife, shaking and pale as a ghost, remained in the hallway. The young man looked cornered, trapped, helpless, utterly hopeless. "No!" he shouted. "No! Stop!" He had the shotgun all the way up around his neck now.

"Motherfucking goddamn you Edward!!!" came the Wild One's loud, desperate voice.

It brought Edward back to the living room. But this time he raised the shotgun all the way up his face and pointed both barrels at his father's chest. Emily screamed. Ginny screamed. Madeline screamed. Mary screamed. The sky screamed, louder than ever before. Edward pulled one of the triggers, but the storm in the sky and the storm in his soul lifted the barrels high. By the time the shell detonated, the barrels stared straight up at the ceiling over the Wild One's head.

Upstairs they thought they heard the blast but decided it must've been the storm. Besides, Irene could not contain herself a moment longer. She let out a terrible scream as another contraction ripped through her abdomen.

"I think you best get Bobby," the good doctor told Evangeline. "This baby's not going to wait a whole lot longer."

The contraction passed. Irene grabbed Evangeline's hand and squeezed. "Wait, just wait! Don't go, not yet."

Downstairs a whole lot of Winslows found it impossible to make a move, to take even a shallow breath. The shotgun shell had sprayed the ceiling, sending chunks of plaster and bits of broken lath flying around the room. Several pellets from the shell had passed right through Gentleman Bart's stomach. "Jesus Christ," he shouted, "I thought I'd taken my last round at Gettysburg!"

Some of the dead laughed but of course the living heard not a word of this. Nor did they see Virginia crossing the room to her middle son's side. They could not see or hear her pleading in

Edward's ear, begging him: "Please put down the gun, please Edward, please please, for me, for your mother."

Edward looked totally bewildered, like he had no idea what he was doing or why. He turned the gun on his wife. "Don't stand there!" he screamed. "Not behind me! Not behind me!"

Samantha moved quickly past her husband into the living room. He shoved her with the barrel as she hurried by. She fell to the floor, bruised her hip, bloodied her knee. He ignored her cry of pain. He opened the shotgun, removed the spent cartridge, loaded another shell into the chamber. Both barrels were ready once again. "Nobody move!" He swung the barrels back and forth across the room. "Nobody! Nobody!"

Henry had seen enough. He moved out of the wing chair on the far side of the room. He stood and took a step forward.

"Sit down!" shouted Edward.

Henry took another step.

"Sit down!!!" Edward screamed at the top of his lungs.

Upstairs Irene screamed at the same moment. Several members of the family thought they heard the scream but none of them were sure who it was or where it came from.

Henry knew. He knew it was his wife. He took another step forward.

"Sit down! or I'll blow your ugly fucking head off!"

Henry kept coming. "Shut up, Edward!"

"No! You shut up!" Edward pointed the twelve-gauge at his brother's head. "Stop!"

Henry did not stop. He knew what he had to do.

His dead brother Bobby moved to Edward's side. He whispered in Eddie's ear, "Shoot the fucker, Eddie, shoot him down, shoot him dead."

While Virginia pleaded, "No, Edward, no. No more violence. Please, Edward, please! Please!"

"Shoot him, Edward, shoot him!"

"I'll kill you!" shouted Edward. "Take one more step and I'll kill you!"

"You're not going to kill anybody, Edward," Henry said calmly, and kept coming. "You're not going to kill me, you're not going to kill Wild Bill, you're not going to kill your wife, you're not—"

"Shut up," screamed Edward, "shut up!"

"No, brother, you shut up. Shut up and sit down."

"No!"

"Yes!"

This time they all heard the scream. It was a bloodcurdling scream that easily overwhelmed the thunder and the lightning and the hail that followed on its heels. It sent shivers down the spines of both the living and the dead.

But before anyone could respond the shotgun roared again. The shell exploded just over Henry's right shoulder. It slammed against the fireplace and sent slivers of splintered brick flying around the room.

The women, and this time most of the men, screamed.

Henry swallowed hard and kept coming. He walked right into the still-loaded barrel of that old Remington twelve-gauge. He stopped not more than an arm's length from his brother.

Edward's face looked ravaged. His hair was plastered to his scalp. His eyes had gone completely wild. Tears and sweat and spittle poured off his chin. A puddle of water flowed around his feet. The puddle looked ever so slightly tinged with yellow.

"That's my gun," said Henry. "If you wanted to use my gun you should've asked me. You had no right to just go into my truck and take it."

Edward had the barrel of the gun against his brother's chest. He had his finger on the trigger. He had pressure on the trigger. But every inch of his body and every ounce of his strength pleaded for mercy, pleaded for help...

No one moved. No one drew a breath. The storm took pause. The hail turned back to rain. Thunder rolled in the distance. Then came the sound of Wild Bill slamming his fist into his open palm. *Goddammit, Henry,* he almost said out loud, *it took you twenty years but I knew you could do it, boy, I knew it.*

And then, from the top of the stairs, sweet Evangeline shouted, "Bobby, you'd better come!"

"I'm on my way!" Henry reached out and took the shotgun from his brother. Edward did not resist. He had nothing left; no strength, no courage, no anger.

Henry charged up the stairs three at a time. At the top of the landing he found Constance and Katie and John and Paul and Rosa peering out of the hall closet.

"Go down and meet your Uncle Edward," he told them. "Go down and give him a hug." Then he turned and sprinted along the hallway to the master bedroom.

Edward dropped to his knees, covered his face with his hands, and began to weep. Still no one moved. The shock had not yet passed. . . . Finally Samantha stepped forward. She put her hand gently on his back. His body shuddered, then relaxed.

The kids came slowly down the stairs. Katie, the oldest, led the way. They made a tight circle and came across the front foyer.

Irene screamed. All of the women in the living room who had given birth recoiled.

"Hang on, kid," said Henry, now at her side, "hang on. It's almost over."

The kids stood close to their uncle. They could hear him crying. One by one they touched his back and whispered hello.

Irene squeezed her husband's arm and pushed.

Evangeline wiped her new friend's brow with a cool damp cloth.

Barton crossed to his brother. He put his hand on his brother's head. Emily followed close behind. She touched her brother's shoulder.

Wild Bill whispered first to Madeline, then to Adam, "Go on, go ahead. He won't hurt you."

They stood and went.

Irene squeezed and pushed and tried not to scream.

"Come on, kid," urged Henry, "come on, you can do this. You can do it. I know you can. I know it."

And sure enough she did. The baby dropped and less than half a minute later the newest Winslow slipped out of the birth canal into the waiting arms of Uncle Aaron. The good doctor examined the small wrinkled body, decided everything looked just fine, and announced, "It's a boy."

Edward still had his head buried in his hands. He continued to cry as his brothers and sisters made their way to his side, Mary and Joseph and Ginny. They touched him, stroked him, offered him a few quiet words of encouragement.

Henry could not believe his great good fortune. "Did you hear that, kid? Did you hear what he said? A boy, a little man."

Irene smiled and wept and quietly thanked the Lord.

Aaron wiped the baby clean with moist towels. He then placed the baby across Mama's belly and disappeared into the bathroom. He washed his hands and took his first decent breath in nearly half an hour.

"Check this out, kid," said Henry as he knelt down for a closer look at his son, "the little fella's already got himself a pecker. It's just about the size of my little toe."

Irene tried to smile. She shook her head. "My God! Think of the mischief he'll cause, the pain and heartache he'll spread across the countryside. What have I done? Send him back, send him back!"

Henry laughed, a loud booming laugh.

The laugh spread throughout the house. Downstairs they heard it loud and clear. It sounded to most of them like the wild, rowdy laugh of Wild Bill.

But Billy Boy had not yet moved off the sofa. He sat perfectly still, his face calm, maybe even serene. After another moment he stood and hobbled slowly across the living room. The younger Winslows made way. Wild Bill stood over his middle son. He put his hand on the back of his boy's neck. Edward had not felt that hand for more than fifteen years, not since before his mother's death, but he knew immediately the hand belonged to his father. He tried not to tremble.

"Welcome home, soldier. Welcome home."

The thunder and lightning had faded into the distance. The storm had passed. The house stood cool and quiet. Then the new baby began to cry. Everyone stopped to listen. Even Edward. It was a high, hopeful cry. It did not last long, just a few brief seconds.

The crying stopped as soon as Mama brought the baby to her breast. Immediately Little Bobby Winslow smiled and began to suckle . . .

Friday, June 21, 1991...
Summer Solstice

Epilogue

•

What a difference a year makes—weatherwise anyway. Last year on
the first day of summer all that heat and humidity and then that terrific
thunderstorm. This year a deep blue sky, high white fluffy clouds, a
gentle breeze, warm dry air, temperatures in the low seventies. An
absolutely perfect day for a wedding.

Let's go out the front door with the others, across the drive, and out
onto the front lawn. The chairs are set up there, maybe fifty of them,
plain folding chairs, facing away from the house. Most of the chairs are
occupied, just a few in the back remain empty. Take a seat if you wish,
or just stand; Quaker weddings don't last long, especially traditional
ones, and this one's about as traditional as they come in this final
decade of the twentieth century. There's no priest, no pastor, no
preacher of any kind; no choir, no crucifix or crosses. There's just the
couple who have decided to get married, and of course their guests whom
they've invited to witness their vows.

Evangeline asked for only one thing: to be married on the first day of
summer on the wide expanse of front lawn at the Winslow Compound.

She sits beside Billy Boy in the front row. They face front, away
from their guests. Directly behind them sit John and Paul. On either
side of the boys sit Katie and Constance. Rosa sits beside her mother.
Irene, holding Young Bobby, a year old today, sits beside her husband.
In the third row sit the Cohens, all four of them. They flew in yesterday
from Los Angeles. In the fourth row Samantha sits between Joseph and
Barton.

Everyone sits quietly, their hands folded, waiting. . .

Tragedy was averted a year ago on what the family now refers to as
Wild Thursday. No one died. No one was even wounded. The baby

*came and offered the promise of a happy ending. But alas . . . the dead
wait as well. Not too many have come today; not nearly the number
who turned out on the summer solstice 1990. Mostly the women buried
up on the hill have come: Virginia and Martha and Caroline and of
course Mary, the most recent relative to join the ranks of the deceased.
You may have read about her death in the newspapers:* AMERICAN
WOMAN RUN DOWN BY DOUBLE-DECKER. *Less than a fortnight
after Wild Thursday Mary flew back to London. She had every
intention of packing up her possessions, settling her affairs, and then
flying straight back to the States. But fate intervened. On the afternoon
she was to leave she made one last trip to Westminster Abbey. She
listened to the young boys sing the Evensong. But the hour grew late
and when the performance ended she had to hurry. She went out the
side entrance, crossed St. Margaret's, hurried across Parliament Square
in search of a cab, and* WHAM! *stepped right in front of that speeding
double-decker. Before she died she had only a moment to think of her
mother being run over by that runaway Rolls.*

*Wild Bill flew over to England to identify and claim the body. He
brought his daughter home for burial. For months afterward Mary
complained about being snatched away by the Grim Reaper long before
her time. The dead listened but didn't much sympathize, especially
Auntie Helen who believed her niece's death was long overdue.
Eventually, after enough time had passed up on the hill, Mary became
quite content with the slow, contemplative pace of death. She holds her
mother's hand now as they wait for the wedding to begin.*

*Billy Boy and sweet Evangeline stand, take a few steps forward
across the lush green grass, and turn around. They take a moment to
smile at their friends and family. Then they turn and face one another.*

"In the presence of God, and these our friends, I, William,
take thee, Evangeline, to be my wife, promising with Divine
assistance to be unto thee a loving and faithful husband so long as
we both shall live."

*So what about the Wild One's offer? Did any of the kids accept?
Mary was all set to accept. She planned to build a small house out on
the edge of the field beyond the graveyard. She wanted to collect all the
information she had gathered over the years and write a book about the*

Winslows; maybe not this book exactly but something along these lines. Too bad her plan didn't pan out.

Ginny of course went back to Bel Air with Aaron and Adam and Madeline. No way was Aaron about to pack up and move his practice to New Jersey. Besides, Ginny still had high hopes for that Big Break. She never got the part in that toothpaste commercial but she still goes to auditions whenever her agent gives her a nudge. She and Papa have made some progress. In the past year Wild Bill has been out to California twice, once with Evangeline and the kids and once alone. Both times he stayed in the Cohens' spare bedroom. And this is the third trip east for Ginny since Wild Thursday. She'd probably come even more often if the kids weren't still in school.

A couple days after Wild Thursday, Joseph flew back to Aspen. He had every intention of settling back into his trailside condo and resuming his reckless, bohemian life-style. Too bad the booze and the coke and maybe his cowardly conduct during the Edward affair finally caught up with him. He's been in and out of rehab for the last nine months. The condo's been sold and Winslow's West is on the balls of its ass. Nobody knows what's to become of brother Joseph.

Emily still lives in the apartment on Central Park (Bettina tried but couldn't quite squeeze that into the settlement) with Rosa. She, like her big sister, still goes to auditions but not too often and not with any great enthusiasm. Every Friday afternoon she and Rosa ride the train out to Far Hills to spend the weekend. Not too long ago she went out on a date with that crazy dude in the VW Cabriolet. He turned out not to be so crazy after all. He's the younger brother of one of Emily's old high school chums. For like ten years he's had a crush on her. Emily's seven and a half years older but she thinks she'll probably go out with him again anyway.

Barton celebrated when news of his van reached him in Far Hills a few days after Wild Thursday. He lives in the big house now, sleeps in his old bedroom. Most mornings he feels pretty good about things. He's studying architecture at Rutgers and has already designed a couple of passive solar houses. W. B. Winslow & Sons Construction plans on building one of his homes as soon as the New Jersey real estate market bounces back from its three-year lull. Barton spends as little time as possible by himself.

Edward, he's not doing too bad, considering. They thought he might be able to actually make the wedding but as the time grew near he just couldn't seem to get himself together. He still spends far too much time lying on his back staring at the ceiling.

Samantha and Ginny and Wild Bill drove him down to Carrier Clinic late in the afternoon on Wild Thursday. He checked himself into the mental-health facility voluntarily. He spent almost six months there receiving a wide variety of medication and therapy. For the last six months he has been a volunteer patient at the Friends Hospital in Philadelphia. The Quakers treat him with patience, kindness, and respect. The doctors say in time he will recover, will hopefully lead a normal life. In the meantime his family visits him. Someone drives down every few days. Sometimes Edward talks; sometimes he doesn't.

Samantha visits her husband every afternoon. She lives in Philadelphia now, has a job counseling drug addicts and alcoholics at Temple University Hospital. She's been trying to get Joseph to stop by for some counseling but so far he hasn't responded.

Bettina got the house in Bar Harbor and the house on Captiva. Wild Bill tried to hold on to the Florida house but in the end he went up to Virginia's grave, apologized, and then signed over the deed. I don't know the exact figures, but in addition to the real estate Bettina received some substantial cash: rumors suggest a one time seven-digit settlement. No one has seen or heard from her since the final papers were signed in early spring. Most of them suspect they never will.

As soon as those papers were signed Billy Boy moved out of the big house and into the brand-new cottage on the high ground behind the old hay barn. I call it a cottage because that's what he and Evangeline like to call it. But really it's more of a house. The downstairs looks pretty much like the old cottage Edward burned to the ground. There's a kitchen and a dining room and a living room where Billy Boy has an old rocker which looks a lot like the one lost in the fire. Where the bedrooms used to be there's now a large library where the family reads and where the Wild One occasionally works. The bedrooms are upstairs, just two of them at opposite ends of a short hallway. It's a simple, well-constructed house. Evangeline and Billy Boy designed it themselves. During the first weeks following Wild Thursday they thought they might forgo rebuilding the cottage, simply settle into the big house and make that their home. But neither of them was happy there. They needed a place they could call their own.

Which brings us to Henry, the present occupant of the big house, of that huge master bedroom conceived and built by old Crazy Legs. Henry jumped on the Wild One's offer, embraced it, took hold of it, held on and hasn't let go since. The Monday after Wild Thursday he went to work for Winslow Construction. I don't think he's taken a day off in the last year. He did drive back to Blue Mount with Irene and the kids for a few days last summer. They had to clean out their cabin and say good-bye to their friends and neighbors. Since then he's worked six days a week, fifteen hours a day. Some folks say he works harder than his old man did at that age.

He keeps telling Irene that the family is going to take a week and go up to the cabin for some rest and relaxation. But Irene's not holding her breath. She's not in any hurry to go back to the mountains anyway. She likes the Compound. She likes Evangeline and Emily and all the kids. She's trying to convince Bobby to have a couple more. Yup, she still thinks his name is Bobby. And so do most of the others. After Wild Thursday he never felt the need to tell anyone else. What difference does a name make anyway? Every once in a while the old man slips and calls him Henry, but both father and son ignore the slip and move on.

It's pretty clear now that if a Winslow had to die in the jungles of southeast Asia it had to be Bobby. Henry had to live, he had to survive. And he had to go through those twenty years of hell in order to have the courage and the insanity to walk straight into the barrel of that old Remington twelve-gauge. No one else in the family could have done it; not that day, not at that moment in history. None of the others, not even Wild Bill, could have faced Edward down on Wild Thursday. The young man was out of his mind, at the end of his rope. Bobby had to die so that Henry could live so that a terrible tragedy could be averted. Had Edward started killing he might have killed them all. Spilled blood often cannot be stopped until there is no more blood to spill.

Henry was the one destined from the very beginning to carry the Winslows into the twenty-first century. I doubt he will ever stray far from the Compound again. He'll stick there like glue, as tough and resilient as his old man ever was. He'll be equally possessive of that house and those rolling hills.

Three hundred and fifty years in the New World and it looks like the Winslows have found themselves another well-bred torchbearer. Maybe the old White Anglo-Saxon Protestant families of the New World are on the wane, out of favor, losing power, edging toward extinction, but barring any sudden, unexpected, natural, economic, or political calamities, it looks like this particular New World WASP family will see the light of another day, of another generation. In a couple hundred years when some fool writer like myself gets a notion to retell the story of the Winslows, old Henry Winslow of Far Hills, New Jersey, will make a pretty fair sideshow. The details of his life will surely have the readers flipping the pages, shaking their heads, wondering how he ever could *have strayed so far for all those many years. He'll be right up there with Freeman and Jawbone and Crazy Legs and Wild Bill. All he'll need is a good nickname. But I'll leave that up to the next joker who goes around. Right now it's time we got back to the wedding. Evangeline has a few final words she'd like to say.*

"In the presence of God, and these our friends, I, Evangeline, take thee, William, to be my husband, promising with Divine assistance to be unto thee a loving and faithful wife so long as we both shall live."

Amen!